LEFT
FOR DEAD

An absolutely addictive crime thriller with a huge twist

DEBORAH LUCY

DI Temple Book 3

Joffe Books, London
www.joffebooks.com

First published in Great Britain in 2022

This paperback edition was first published
in Great Britain in 2022

Cover art by Nebojša Zorić

ISBN: 978-1-80405-321-8

To my little brother, Johnny
1969-2021

PROLOGUE

The thick knot of the ligature thrust like a hard fist into the soft cartilage of his throat, slowly shutting off his airway. A raised purple bruise closed his left eye, obscuring the broken socket beneath and a deep vertical cut sliced through his bloodied lips. With his last breath trapped in a badly broken nose, his fight for life began to wane.

Lying on his back on the floor, a sudden bright light beckoned. A supreme sense of serenity replaced the pain of his broken body and when the whiteness of the light around him intensified, so did a sense of overwhelming peace and joy.

Younger, stronger and more agile, he beamed his ready smile. He felt warm, comforted and expectant as he moved forwards, his body floating effortlessly towards the promise of a wonderous place beyond. When vague figures came into view with hands outstretched urging him towards them, he continued blissfully on. Not until he was almost into their arms did he stop.

Suddenly, there they were; the faces so familiar to him, caught in the agony of their last moments before death, hope

1

crushed in their eyes. These were the faces that had haunted him almost all his life. He turned his head away, unable to look. They continued to beckon and as they moved towards him to draw him closer, he recoiled. He didn't want to be pulled into their arms or be among them. He wasn't ready to confront this horror. He stepped back and with every step away, the brightness of the light weakened until at last, the figures faded out of sight.

The bright light now gone, his body jolted at the return of the pain. Instinctively, his hand went to his throat and to the ligature. Eyes wide with fear, he knew he would die if he couldn't take a breath now. He desperately tugged at the knot, but it refused to yield. It was futile; he couldn't get any purchase on it and for the first time, he panicked. His other hand joined in the effort and guided by his mind's eye, his frail fingers frantically worked at the tightness. Time was running out.

He kept at it, trying to find a way to loosen the knot, but it wouldn't budge. Just as he'd resigned himself to his end, dying alone, gasping for breath on the floor, the tip of his index finger wormed its way through the tight folds. It created just enough of a gap for him to work some release from the stranglehold.

He opened his mouth to take in a precious gulp of air, but a steady trickle of blood had pooled at the back of his throat. Triggering his gag reflex, he suddenly coughed and gasped, his throat rattling in a last desperate fight for life. In the final seconds, he took in a precious gulp of air. His chest heaved through the agony; he could breathe.

Exhausted by his struggle, he lay still, his eyes open, blinking at the ceiling. In the quiet, he listened to the sound of his breathing, feeling pain at the rise and fall of his chest. After a while, he tried to lift himself up, but his bruised ribs had him straight back, this time landing his head on the edge of something sharp. To alleviate the discomfort, he moved his head to one side, bringing his eyes level with the floor.

It wasn't a familiar vantage point, but even without his glasses and the dim light he could see things weren't as they should be. He slowly scanned the room. Drawers had been pulled out and left overturned, their contents heaped on the carpet. The bone china his dead wife had lovingly collected, the little things that reminded him of her, now lay broken. Over in the corner, the TV screen was damaged and the sofa and his armchair had been upturned.

He cursed himself. In another time, he wouldn't have been put on the floor in the first place. He'd have taken on two men once; they wouldn't have got the better of his fitter, younger self. But even though he'd looked after himself, at ninety-seven, he had to concede he was no match for two young men. And they'd been too quick, too strong to stand up to. Besides which, he never expected to feel the force of another man's fist at his age nor such brutality in his own home, the one place he had every right to feel safe.

He only had himself to blame. When they found his money, his attackers thought there had to be more, so they kept at him. Finding his bank card, they wanted the PIN number, so they pulled him around by his tie taking him to one room after another. In their frustration, they punched him hard in the face, kicked at his body and legs until he went down, falling heavily on his hip. Then he'd felt the force of their boots as they kicked his back and ribs before finally, they used his tie like a rope. It chilled him thinking of them again now. He'd registered the subhuman look on their faces and it told him all he'd needed to know; they would stop at nothing. Not for the first time, he feared for his life.

He had to get help. If he could only get himself up, get to the phone, ring the police, ring his family, but there was no way he could get on his feet. From where he was lying in the lounge, he somehow had to make it to the hallway. He had to do it and yet right there and then it felt like a hopeless task.

He remained still, trying to gauge how long he'd been lying there. If he didn't move soon, it would be dark and nowadays, like it had when he was a small child, the dark tormented him. Usually awake long before dawn, he often lay staring into the blackness of the night where the long shadows took him to a time and horror he'd never forget; where he tried to make sense of it all, but the outcome never changed and still the dead stared back at him. Caught in those endlessly bleak hours when he should have been peacefully asleep, instead, night after night he relived the terror that had never let him go. And he knew if he went among the shadows tonight, alone and left for dead, it would at last break him. He trembled as he counselled himself.

'You've got to fight through the pain, Jackie. You've got to fight through the pain to survive. Come on, you've been through worse than this.'

Hearing himself speak gave him a small comfort. But he shivered, knowing he was going to have to draw on all his reserves. Again, he counselled himself.

'Come on, Jackie boy, you don't want them to find you like this, dead on the floor.'

This time he registered the quiver in his voice. He coughed, clearing his throat as if the gesture would gain his voice back its strength.

'You've got to be strong, Jackie, like the last time you had the stuffing knocked out of you. You came through then and you've got to do the same now.'

He went back in time, to that moment in 1944 when he'd been propped up against a low wall having been wounded by a bullet from a German sniper. He thought he was a goner then, too. So did a padre who, unable to stay with him, pressed a small Bible into his hands to give him solace in his last hours. Watching the padre walk away, he fingered the Bible's thin India paper, knowing exactly what it was good for.

He recalled his hand going inside his tunic and finding a small pouch. Tearing out the pages, he'd carefully pinched tobacco out onto the paper and rolled a cigarette. It had lit beautifully. When he exhaled, he'd said, 'Amen' and when that one finished, he tore out more pages to roll and light another. Now a tiny smile touched his lips as he remembered the sweet smell of burning tobacco as he drew on the end.

Using that little Bible to roll cigarettes had given him more comfort than any padre or prayer ever could. Besides which, the war had put a distance between him and God. He saw too much in 1940 for there to be any religion left in him. Like many men who survived those early days, he'd had to kill or be killed and he'd carried the burden and horror of his actions all his life. Lying still on the floor, he was there once again among the noise, the smoke, the gunfire and the chaos.

It had been every man for himself. Gun in hand with bayonet extended he fought for his life, pushing the steel blade into the yielding flesh of those who wanted to do the same to him. He would never forget the look in their eyes. That briefest of moments when the realisation of imminent death clouded their faces, that second before the light was snuffed out.

His eyes shut tight at the recollection. The horror of their deaths had remained locked inside his head ever since; he'd told no one of the lives he took. Over the years in the quiet of the night, he'd spoken to the memory of those men a thousand times, apologising and begging for forgiveness, telling them of his overwhelming regret that because of him, they hadn't returned home to their families as he had to his. Just as his face had been the last they'd seen before they died, he swore to them theirs would be the last he would see. He felt he owed them that at least.

Suddenly an overpowering desire to let go washed over him. Lying on his back alone he was a danger to himself. If he was to come through this, he'd have to fight again like he had before. He at least had to try. He shook himself.

'Come on, Jackie, you're not ready to give up just yet. You know what you have to do. The only thing you *can* do.'

Jack rolled onto his side and cried out with pain from his hip and ribs. To his despair, he was facing away from where he needed to be and he knew he'd have to move himself in the right direction before he could crawl across the floor to reach the hallway. Moving his foot slightly, he realised he only had one slipper on. This preoccupied him as slowly he turned himself and then rocked onto his front.

Leaning up on his elbows, broken bits of glass and china dug through into his skin. Then, using his arms and the better one of his legs, he started to inch across the carpet. It was going to take time, but he had to do it. He closed his eyes.

He was back in the tunnel; elbows in, head down, crawling along on his belly, pulling himself through. He could smell his own sweat again, taste the dust and feel the adrenalin. He'd escaped a terror then far worse than being beaten and robbed, but he'd been so young, so quick. Age and pain were against him now as he moved at a snail's pace across the floor around the overturned furniture.

'You can do this, Jackie boy, you can do this.'

He closed his eyes momentarily against the agony of his injured body and continued to move forward. He had to keep going. At last, feeling the hard wooden threshold of the hallway under his elbows, he lifted his head and opened his eyes. The cordless telephone sat on the table in a cradle; all he had to do was reach up in one last effort to get help. He rolled on to his side and stretched out his arm. He took hold of the cable and pulled it as hard as he could. The phone fell in front of him. He grabbed it and dialled, saving himself just enough puff to say his name and address. He rested on his back. Help was on its way.

He looked up at the ceiling. The boys had warned him not to keep money in the house, but he'd been saving it for his funeral. If he'd been less in pain he would have laughed; saving for his funeral had almost been the death of him. He should have listened to them.

'Bloody war hero they call you, Jackie. Bloody fool is what you really are. Bloody fool.'

He lay shivering with cold as the shock of the attack finally settled on him. For a second, he considered a violent death was probably no more than he deserved. He had blood on his hands and perhaps this was his punishment, although not a day had gone by when he hadn't said he was sorry for what he'd done. He couldn't imagine the men who'd

6

attacked him ever feeling sorry as he'd seen nothing human there.

Closing his eyes, one by one, the dead soldiers appeared to him again. This time, their faces were no longer set in the grimace of death; they were walking towards him with their arms outstretched, smiling.

CHAPTER 1

October 2019, Aswan, Egypt

The sweat-soaked bed sheet stuck like a second skin as the murdered woman's face pierced the deep unconsciousness of sleep. Fear snapped his eyes wide. Shocked awake, his head pressed back into the pillow. As his heart hammered against his chest, he closed his eyes again and saw her lying dead where he'd left her all those years ago. The bitch would haunt him until his last breath.

Lying in the darkness, he resurrected the past, going over and over it as he had done a thousand times before. He did it as a form of exorcism, only it never worked. Like now, she always returned and, alone in the depths of the night, there was no hiding from her or himself. Seeing her never ceased to remind him of his own failure.

He wished he'd never laid eyes on her. Nothing had been the same after that. Worse still, he'd discovered something about himself that he hadn't known until then. He discovered he wasn't the man he thought he was. Because ultimately, he'd been tested that day and he'd let people down. And knowledge of that and what happened had had the power to prick him ever since.

He should have completed the task that day. A sharp, short twist and snap to the neck. There would have been little resistance. It would have been quick, tidy. Instead, he'd panicked and lost control. He reckoned it would have taken about seven seconds; seven seconds against a lifetime's self-recrimination.

If he could have that time again, he'd do it without hesitation. He committed career suicide that day and anything would have been better than living the half-life he had since. Better than living with perpetual disappointment in himself, constantly wishing to go back to that exact moment again and do it differently. No amount of alcohol had taken the edge off that regret.

He shifted slowly, peeling away the damp sheet beneath him as he moved. Even in October it was warm still, but he couldn't blame the heat for his night sweats. He glanced at the neon digits of the clock beside his bed, 2.14 a.m. He swung round off the bed and went to the open window, looking out into the dark. It was quiet tonight and there was a cooling breeze from the direction of the Nile River.

He knew why she'd come to him tonight and his thoughts went to the day ahead, to the meeting. He pictured the scene; it would be like all the others that had occurred while he'd been in Aswan. Invited to the same hotel to a discreet table where Gibson, the summoner he'd met three times in the past fifteen years, would be waiting. At first, a cordial shake of hands after which Gibson's natural bonhomie would extend to a drink or five, along with an expensive lunch and civilised conversation. But the purpose for flying so many miles from London wasn't to check on his welfare; it was to let him know they would never let him go.

Because of what had happened, he'd spent his life looking over his shoulder. He'd failed all right, but he also knew things, things that couldn't be easily rubbed out. It was the world he moved in before his inaction had left him out in the cold, in the no man's land of mistrust. He wasn't *in*, but neither was he exactly out. His knowledge of events prevented that. So, he'd been watching the shadows ever since, always wary of a steel blade, or feeling the barrel of a silencer. Psychologically, it had taken its toll.

Early on, he'd tried hard to make up for it, get back on track. The irresistible pull distorted and corrupted him to the point he'd do anything to be part of it. To prove to them and to himself he'd later shown them that he could kill, but it was too late. Nothing he had done since had made up for that lapse, that one time that they'd needed him and he failed.

* * *

At 11.37 a.m., he looked out onto Abtal El Tahrir street from the back of an old black Lada as he was driven down towards the Old Cataract Hotel. He looked across the driver's shoulder, surveying the filthy, dented wreck so typical of taxis in Aswan. In front of the driver, on the dirty fur-covered dashboard rested a worn dog-eared copy of the Qur'an. Wooden beads and strings of plastic amulets swung down from the rear-view mirror. Pieces of cardboard and old matting covered rust holes in the floor and door panels. Tangled wires dangled beneath into the passenger footwell. It was a death trap.

The taxi lurched in and out of the traffic, passing slow donkey-drawn carts overladen with sugar cane and loping oxen, their bony backs beaten with long sticks to steer them down to the river's edge. Whipped up and speeding past them, the black horse-drawn tourist carriages added to the chaos, kicking up the dust and sand of the Nubian Desert that settled on the roads.

The driver stopped abruptly outside a small security station and barrier, signalling the entrance to the hotel. Guy Newland paid and stepped out onto the dusty road and into the heat. Moving forward, he saw two surly faced guards dressed in scruffy local military uniform standing either side of a red-and-white striped security barrier. With sub-machine guns hanging lazily from their shoulders, they maintained a lethargic stance even as they saw him approach.

As he drew closer, two more guards appeared from inside, making two more than usual. He quickly reasoned there was probably an important person staying; after all, the hotel attracted heads of state, high-ranking diplomats and the rich and famous. Seeing one of the guards slowly move a hand to his gun, Newland pulled himself up to his full height and addressed him in Arabic.

He knew the drill. The guard let him through the barrier and led him into a large, unfurnished room to the right where he was questioned further about the reason for his visit. Then, after a short wait, a meek-smiling black-suited assistant concierge appeared to escort him out of the room across a pristine garden courtyard and through an avenue of tall palm trees into the shade of the main hotel.

As he followed his escort inside, the luxurious serenity of the hotel turned the world into a sanctuary of quiet and order. The reassuringly opulent colonial glass and marble splendour of the foyer never failed to impress him. He walked through the highly decorative Moorish archways and across cool, polished marble floors, as fans spun discreetly overhead giving respite from the heat. Then he slowed deliberately, looking to his left towards a pair of open arched doors beautifully framing one of the best views of the Nile.

A vibrant green oasis of pristine landscaped gardens and elegant palm trees cascaded towards a bright turquoise pool and beyond, to the ancient beauty of Elephantine Island where the tops of the creamy billowing sails of feluccas were just visible on the ink blue river. Looking out onto the river and the island bathed in the golden light of the desert sun, the intensity and depth of colour lent a sense of glimpsing through a portal back into a biblical, other-worldly place in time.

He lingered, his eyes wide at the simplistic beauty of the scene. It never failed to touch his soul. The assistant concierge stopped and waited patiently, allowing him to take his fill. When he was ready, the concierge ushered him to a discreet dark-glassed corner, away from the sun and light,

11

where two club chairs were separated by a low table. On seeing them approach, a man in the shadows stood to greet him.

'Guy Newland?' the stranger asked.

Wait a minute, where was Gibson? Newland turned to speak to the concierge who had already disappeared. He hesitated, extending his hand as he answered.

'Yes?'

'Greene, Martin Greene.'

No sooner had Greene taken Newland's hand, he withdrew it, briefly brushing his palm on the side of his leg. Newland noted the gesture.

'Gibson usually comes . . .' Newland's voice faded as he eyed the man standing before him, quickly giving him a once-over.

Greene was slim and compact, probably mid-thirties, bright-eyed and fresh-faced, just like he himself had been once. The youth of the man irked him. Formally dressed in a sharply tailored navy suit and tie, Newland observed how Greene's white shirt puckered slightly at the buttons under the strain of his lean muscular chest. Untroubled by the heat and clinically clean and efficient-looking, Greene looked like he'd spent time in the elite forces. Newland prided himself on knowing a trained killer when he saw one.

Suddenly feeling the disadvantage of his shabby over-worn beige linen suit, white collarless cotton shirt and dusty sandals, Newland wished he'd taken more care with his appearance, got himself a haircut, at least shaved. Instead, he had dressed thinking he was meeting Gibson who he didn't have to impress. *Where the hell was Gibson?* Gibson was more his age. Gibson knew him, greeted him with the weary show of an old friend. With respect. Already, he didn't sense much in the way of respect coming from Martin Greene.

'Gibson's unwell.' Greene stiffened his posture as he spoke.

Both men sat down.

'Nothing serious, I hope,' said Newland sincerely, looking forward to seeing his old friend on his next visit.

'Unfortunately, it is. He won't be coming out again — not that there'd be any point.'

Newland frowned, ready to probe further, but his thoughts were upended by the quip Greene had finished with. What did he mean, *'not that there'd be any point?'* Greene gestured to a glass of water he'd already positioned on the low, heavy, smoked glass table in front of Newland. Gibson normally had a large whisky waiting for him.

Greene spoke slowly and quietly. 'Let's make this brief.'

He flicked a quick look at his watch.

'As you know, people were appreciative of your work out here during the Arab Spring and since. However, more recently things have changed.' Greene hesitated, reaching into the inside of his jacket. 'I've been sent here to tell you that there have been some unexpected developments of late. Some evidence has come to light concerning the past, it'll all become clear when you read this.' Greene passed Newland a folded press cutting.

Newland retrieved a pair of glasses from his top pocket. He unfolded the paper and peered at the article, his heart picking up pace as he read to the end. He kept his eyes on the paper even though he'd finished reading. In light of the visitation last night, he was shaken. He hadn't been expecting this. He was suddenly aware of a pulse in a vein to the left side of his head. He had to collect himself before looking at Greene.

Knowing that Newland had finished reading, Greene spoke.

'As you can see, it's generated some publicity.'

Newland shrugged in an effort to appear indifferent. 'So?'

Greene's eyes were hard. 'As we both know, the subject they are talking about is *you*.'

To his own surprise, Newland's mouth suddenly dried. 'How can you be sure?' His words caught in his throat. He reached for the glass on the table.

Greene was dismissive. 'It's you, Newland, and you know it.'

'Can't you . . . get it?' Newland tried not to sound desperate but failed.

Greene's response was curt. 'No.'

Newland's mind was reeling and the words came out before he could stop them.

'Why not? What's up with you lot, not up to the fucking job?' He turned again to the paper in his hands.

Martin Greene acknowledged the insult with a look of contempt. 'I know intervening has worked in this particular case in the past,' he said tightly, 'but that was then, this is now. Things move at a different pace these days.'

Newland looked back, incredulous. He went to speak, but Greene cut across him in a measured tone.

'I've read the file. Gone are the days when evidence bags were left under a desk, or in the corner of the room in a police station. They're all under lock and key now, it's all about integrity.'

'Fuck integrity.' Newland kept his voice low, the effort of which gave it an unintended edge. He leaned across the table between them. 'Get someone who knows what they're doing to go in and get it. No evidence, no case.'

'That's just not going to work,' Greene replied, keeping eye contact with Newland.

'Bullshit, I think we both know it can be done.'

'It's too late.' Greene nodded towards the press cutting still in Newland's hand. 'The sample is already in the system. There'd be no point in retrieving the original source. It's already yielded a result which is how we were able to check and which is why I'm here. Obviously, we haven't shared our knowledge . . . yet.'

'Then get into their system, delete the sample, or exchange it for another, don't tell me you can't.' The vein ticked in Newland's temple.

Greene gave a shrug. 'That's not possible.'

Newland sat back in his chair. 'Why are you refusing to help me?' He tried not to make it sound like the plea it was.

Greene spoke slowly. 'I think we've been helping you immeasurably over the years.' His face hardened. 'You see, this has come as much of a surprise to us as it has to you. We've had to make a plan. Best thing all round.'

'Oh?' Newland felt his throat tighten further so took another sip of water.

'You're coming back.'

'Oh no, no. *No*.' Newland shook his head. 'I *live* here.'

Greene ignored him, his voice dropping, barely audible. 'Not anymore. This changes things. You'll come back. We'll engineer your arrest. After all this time, you'll get ten years, no more. We'll arrange that, too. You'll be out in five, or less if you behave. On release you can do what you like — stay in England, come back here. New life. Fresh start. And your life as an asset will be spent; obviously that aspect will not come out.'

Newland processed what he was being told. Conscious of being in a public space, he struggled to keep his voice low.

'Now listen, you wait a minute. You said you'd read the file?'

'Of course.'

'Then you *know*.'

Greene remained calm, leaning towards him in his seat. 'Yes, I *know*. Which is why this is important.'

Newland tried to ignore the sweat trickling down the side of his face. 'I'm being set up.'

Greene scowled. 'No, Newland. This is down to you. And you know it. There is no "set up". DNA was left at the scene. Only you are responsible for that.'

'And if I refuse?'

'The matter can now be resolved once and for all, to everyone's satisfaction, including yours. If you do this our way, the case will be closed and you'll have your freedom after five years.'

'What if I don't want to spend the next five years in an English prison?'

'Cooperate and after five years you'll be a free man. Meetings like this cease.'

'I'm already a free man.'

'No, Newland, you're not. You know you're not. You haven't been for years and especially not now, with this development.' There was an edge to Greene's voice now. 'This puts a whole new light on things. This is why it's always so important to *clean up*, wouldn't you say? That's what you were supposed to do that day. In fact, you fucked up twice as I see it. Not only did you not clean up as instructed, but you left some of your own filth behind which lends a certain irony to it. As it is, we can all turn this to our collective advantage.'

As he watched Greene sitting in judgement, Newland considered reaching across the glass table and smashing his face on it. What had Greene ever done? But Newland knew everything he said was right. He should have done what he'd set out to do that day. He should have cleaned up thoroughly and in not doing so he had now trapped himself. But he objected to hearing it from someone like Greene. It would have been easier to take from Gibson.

Now he was wary; go back and go to prison? How could he take their word it would be five years? They could fix it, he knew that, but what if something went wrong? He didn't want to die in jail, he didn't deserve that. Despite the coolness of the room, he felt the sweat upon him. He wanted to try and maintain some control, but his body betrayed him.

'How can I trust what you say — that it will only be five?'

'Because you know we can make that happen.'

'It's not that easy. A five-year term . . .'

'We'll prepare you. It's being arranged as we speak.' Greene's voice was soft and low. 'You'll have a backstory which will cover the event and all the subsequent years. We have people in place to swear to it, who will give evidence to police if required. Records will be put in place.'

'My passport will tell a different story . . .'

'It won't by the time we've finished.'

'But how can I be sure it will only be five years?'

'You'll plead guilty immediately to negate the need for any protracted enquiries. Things have changed. Money's tight. Detective numbers have dwindled; there won't be the stomach to look much beyond your statement and plea. You will be contrite, speak of your deep remorse. It will be arranged for your sentence to reflect this. Like I said, ten years, out in five.'

Newland looked briefly skyward and then back down at his hands. The sweat was pouring out of him. He gave a half-hearted, defeated smile to Greene. He wasn't ready for prison, not now, not at his age. If this had to happen it should have been years ago, not when he was in his sixties. He felt sick at the prospect. He guessed it all came down to how much he still wanted to play the game. That was the undercurrent of the conversation. He held his head in his hands as he tried to think through the bombshell that had been dropped on him. He looked across to Greene.

'Look, you may as well know, I'm ill.' He knew it sounded pathetic, but he said it anyway. He wiped the sweat off his brow with his sleeve and nodded at it.

Greene was unmoved. 'In what way?'

'I'm waiting for a diagnosis. Things don't happen very quickly here. You could just leave me in Aswan. Who knows, I might not have five years anyway. I get to stay here and when I die, you can then reveal my DNA.'

'Whether you have five years or five months left, it won't make any difference. There's nothing on your file that says you're ill. You'll be fully assessed and afforded any medical attention you need once we get back. The plan's in place.'

'How do you know it will work? Look at me, what about my tan, you don't get this in England. You can't do anything about that.'

'In three months' time, you won't have a tan. It's cold and pretty inhospitable in the Welsh hills in the winter months. In three months' time, you'll be in a police cell looking pretty pale. We'll see to that.'

'And if I say no to all this?'

'From where I'm sitting, you have no choice.' Greene's words were left hanging in the air. 'You're booked on a flight to Cairo with me this afternoon. Then on to the UK where you'll be briefed and the process will begin.' Greene stopped. 'Look, Newland, you know why you have to do this. Time's up.' His tone was distinctly annoyed.

Newland stood. He didn't want to go back; not back to England, not back in time, certainly not to prison for five years. But there was clearly no reasoning with the man in front of him. Maybe it was still possible to get away. If he could just get out of there he could take his chances. He had contacts; there were Bedouin and Bishari he could pay to help him travel overland through the desert, where he could disappear. Anything was better than what was being suggested. Yes, that's what he'd do.

'All right. I'll do as you say. But I'll have to go back and get my passport.'

Greene reached inside his jacket. 'I have it here.' Greene produced Newland's passport. He held it out for him to take.

'We're going now, unless . . . ?'

Newland suddenly realised the meeting had been carefully choreographed. If he ran for it now, one of the extra guards he'd encountered on the way in was no doubt primed to kill him. It would be a 'security related shooting' requiring little by way of explanation to the authorities. The only alternative was to leave with Greene in a chauffeur-driven car to the airport, all the while under surveillance, to arrive back in the UK. They'd gone to a lot of trouble. There was no escape, only in death.

Somewhere deep in his subconscious he'd always known that this moment would come. The bitch appearing again in his sleep last night was testimony to that. It all came back to the fact he should have killed the boy. At least now he knew he'd been right to regret it ever since. Perhaps now her face would stop taunting him. And, if he did what Greene suggested he might even be able to forgive himself at last.

CHAPTER 2

February 2020, Wiltshire, England

'I, I can't . . .'

Vera Dart's voice broke in revulsion at what she'd seen that morning. Acid bile surged in her throat as another wave of sickness threatened. Fighting her body's intense need to retch, she closed her eyes and clenched her teeth hard. The sight of the dead man's face loomed large in her mind, and she struggled to shut it out. That and the dashboard covered in blood.

As she looked up at the uniformed police officer who stood in her lounge, without thinking she pushed her fingers through her short grey hair and held a fistful of it. It hadn't been a year since her husband had died suddenly and it had taken its toll. Now that was all flooding back, too. If only she hadn't gone out this morning, or if only she'd gone somewhere different.

From her place on the sofa, she suddenly rocked forward as her stomach lurched. Losing the fight to stop the powerful surge, she clamped her hand over her mouth. She ran from the room to a tiny downstairs toilet. At the commotion, a second female officer poked her head out of the kitchen.

'She all right?'

The male colleague grimaced. 'She's talking to the big porcelain telephone.'

'I'll bring this through.'

'It's all right, Mrs Dart,' the officer shouted out. 'Just you take your time.' He turned to his colleague and lowered his voice. 'She's hard work.'

He looked around. The furnishings were worn, stuck in a late eighties time warp. The newest thing in the room was a small flat-screen television.

Still on her knees bent over the toilet, Vera Dart reached up and pulled the flush handle. She couldn't get the picture of what she'd seen out of her head. She didn't want to deal with seeing someone dead again, it was too soon. She couldn't cope. She stood up and leaning on her hands on the wash basin for support, she caught sight of herself in a mirror on the wall.

Her seventy-one years sat heavily on her features following what she'd seen. Walking her husband's Jack Russell, Toby, twice a day since his death had kept her fit. She found it helped to brighten her mood, but this morning's walk to their usual place had left her shattered. It was normally such a peaceful spot, but she already knew she would never be able to go back there again. Now it was tainted with violence and death. As she washed her shaking hands, her eyes glistened with tears. She heard the officer call out.

'My colleague's making you a cup of tea. Let's see if that helps you to remember where you went.'

Vera Dart went back into the lounge, clutching a paper tissue. It was all so strange, so different from the day she had planned. She was supposed to be meeting friends later. Not now though. Somehow, she had to deal with this. She slumped down on the sofa next to a side table, peering up at the male police officer now standing by the door.

'My dog, you will find Toby, won't you? I couldn't see him in the fog. I don't want him up there on his own.'

The dog was her primary source of comfort, the little soul was all she had to get up for, all she had to live for. He was all that was left of her husband Frank who had chosen him. Now Toby was somewhere in the woods where they walked and she'd had to leave him there to ring the police. If only she'd remembered to charge her phone overnight, she could have stayed there until she'd found him.

'We'll look for him, I'm sure he'll turn up.'

The officer left the woman momentarily and walked from the lounge into a narrow hallway, talking low into his radio.

'191 Holiday, sarge. We're no further forward than what she said when she rang in. All we've been able to establish so far is that she went out this morning to walk her dog where she says she found a man dead in a vehicle. We don't know exactly where she went. There's no sign of the dog here. I think she's in shock. I've asked her to tell me where she went and all she says is "the woods".'

'Are there woods where you are?'

'There's a wooded area behind the house and also off the main drag and she's not said which it was she went to.'

'Has she described what she saw at all?'

'No, sarge, she's become more anxious since we arrived. She's also worried about her dog. It ran off and she hasn't seen it since.'

'According to the logs, she's also a vexatious complainer.'

Holiday moved from the hall to the kitchen where his colleague was to ensure Vera Dart didn't overhear the conversation.

'I can see fifteen previous calls in the last few months from her reporting neighbours, kids, parking, cat shit being thrown on her lawn. None of it substantiated. Look, go next door, see if you can find a neighbour; ask if they saw her go out this morning and saw what route she might have taken.'

'But why would she dial 999 if she'd seen nothing?'

'Attention seeking? Lonely? Who knows why they call in, but they do. This might be a load of shite.'

'I'm not sure, sarge. She looks pretty genuine to me, she's really shaken and she's just thrown up. She's as white as a sheet. If we could get a helicopter or a drone up it might help. Assuming what she says is true, it might locate the vehicle she says she's seen.'

'The fog's still too dense for a helicopter or drone to be any use,' came the answer. 'You can't see your hand in front of your face out there. Get all the information you can and take a statement off her. Then get back on patrol.'

'Roger.' PC Holiday confirmed his instructions as he followed his female colleague back into the lounge with a mug of tea.

'There you go, Mrs Dart,' the female officer coaxed. 'This will make you feel better. We're going to sit with you until you're able to tell us what happened this morning.'

She nodded weakly, taking the mug from the officer's hands.

'Can you tell me exactly what you saw, Mrs Dart, and the location?' The officers had seated themselves in armchairs facing her.

'I'll try.' She took the merest sip of tea but was grateful for it. It seemed to steady her. Her mind was in turmoil, but somehow she had to stop the jumble of thoughts, black out the image that prevented her from talking. She slowly took another sip and continued.

'I was walking my little Toby. We set off at seven fifteen this morning, as usual. As we drew nearer to the bottom of the lane to go up into the woods, he became more and more excited. The fog wasn't that thick when we left, but the further I went up the track, the thicker it became. He was pulling me hard this morning and the lead was cutting into my skin. As I unwound it, he pulled. It just ripped from my hand and Toby ran off up the track. I couldn't see where he was in the mist.'

She stopped again. Lifting the mug up to her lips, she now looked through the steam coming from it, at last being able to articulate what she had seen. She continued almost in a trance-like state.

'I shouted for Toby but he was gone, so I went after him. I walked up the track for a while, calling for him. I heard him bark a few times, so I kept calling. Then through the fog, towards the woods, I saw some headlights in the distance. So, I walked towards them, thinking someone might have seen Toby. It was a light-coloured vehicle, perhaps silver . . . it was then I came across the two men.'

The two officers exchanged a quick glance; PC Holiday mouthed, '*Two*?' at his colleague. There was silence as Vera Dart rested the mug of tea on a side table before continuing.

'I was going to ask them if they'd seen Toby . . .' She started to weep, dabbing at her eyes with tissues. 'As I approached the car, I saw one man at first. He was sitting in the passenger seat. It wasn't until I got closer that I saw . . .' Her voice trailed off.

'What did you see, Mrs Dart?'

'There was an ugly dark hole in the side of his head. He was dead. They both were.'

CHAPTER 3

'It's a real pea-souper out there with the latest from the Met office that it will be slow to clear. Leave extra time for your journey this morning and remember to avoid the M4 westbound where tailbacks go all the way back to junction thirteen. That's all for now, back in an hour with Ken Bruce . . .'

Temple eyed the clock. The journey could be a ball-ache at this time of the morning on any day of the week, but after nearly an hour of bumper-to-bumper stop-starting because of dense fog to get onto the slip road, he was at last grateful to see the nondescript building of the regional hub of the Major Crime Unit loom into sight.

As pleased as he was to be there, he already knew he didn't want too many journeys like that. He pulled into a parking space and before locking his car, he used his reflection in the door window to quickly straighten his tie. He looked back at himself; despite the journey and being late, he was buoyed up and optimistic. It was the chance he needed, a fresh start with a new team, new boss.

He walked towards the building and into reception to join a short queue. When his phone signalled an incoming text message, he quickly wrestled it from his jacket pocket and looked at the screen.

'Good luck, darling. New beginnings! See you tonight x.' He checked for any other messages and missed calls before putting the phone on silent.

'Yes, sir, how can I help?' A female receptionist spoke, forcing him to break his gaze from the phone.

'DI Temple to see Detective Superintendent Tina Shaw.'

'Can I see your ID please, sir, and if you could give me your car registration number?'

Temple obliged and was given a lanyard which enabled him to pass through a security door. Following directions given by the receptionist, he soon found himself in a dead-end corridor with only one office door. Looking briefly through a glass panel he saw a woman looking intently at her laptop screen. Without breaking her gaze, she answered to his light knock on the door.

'C'm in.'

Stepping inside, Temple walked into a wall of heat.

'DI Temple, ma'am. Apologies for being late. The traffic was bad, fog.'

He offered his best smile to her profile in readiness for her to look up, but she didn't move. In her brown trouser suit and navy polo neck, his new boss remained glued to her screen as he hesitated awkwardly by the door, keeping it open and letting some of the heat out. She looked up and with a flick of her eyes, she silently directed Temple to sit on the only other chair in the room.

Unsmiling, she frowned back to her laptop.

Sensing her lack of enthusiasm, he closed the door and sat down. He had attempted to find out about her before their meeting, but information was scant. All he'd managed to glean was that she had returned to her home force of Avon and Somerset two years ago, having transferred from Herefordshire. Facing her, Temple saw a small electric fan aimed at her feet as the source for the intense heat in the room, but Detective Superintendent Tina Shaw showed no sign of being adversely affected by it.

'Apologies again, ma'am, for being late.' He wasted another smile on her unmoving profile.

Avoiding eye contact, Tina Shaw maintained concentration on her screen. His lateness had annoyed her, but it was a notorious stretch of motorway and people were frequently caught up in some delay or other. What riled her far more was the fact he sat there at all.

'I haven't been able to see you before now,' she said at last, tight-lipped. 'I wanted to catch you on your first day.'

Under scrutiny with Temple now sitting in front of her, she at once became aware of her own appearance. Shifting slightly in her chair, she sat upright, conscious her five-foot-seven frame was overweight from lack of exercise and shit food on the run. For expediency that morning, she had pulled back her dirty blonde hair, brittled by years of cheap colouring, into a short ponytail, the overall look she knew was harsh.

* * *

Self-neglect over the years had been a trade-off she'd been willing to make for the sake of promotion as she worked hard to fight her way through the ranks. That had been fine when she was younger, but now it caught up with her and was something she regretted. These days, things changed faster than she could manage and the challenge of keeping pace with all that was going on kept her awake at night. Insomnia and long hours in the job had left her with bagged and hooded eyes, magnified under the thick lenses of the glasses she was forced to wear because of her increasing myopia and intolerance to contact lenses.

And now she had something else to keep her awake. Focusing on her screen, she scrolled through Temple's application form again. He'd been put through to first stage interviews a couple of months ago because he looked good on paper. His antecedents checked all the right boxes: surveillance; intelligence; burglary squad; years in CID; all standard fare for a career detective. Then his application said he'd been involved in a couple of recent high-profile murder investigations and he'd broken a county lines gang, all of which sounded impressive. But that wasn't all.

Now he was here she was able to size him up for the first time. Only after first round interviews had she been tipped off about his high-ranking connection and the associated story doing the rounds which made her determined to weed him out on the second interviews. On her return from annual leave, she found the panel had already sat without her — a mix-up with dates cited as the reason — by which time, Temple had been told he had the DI's job. Despite her protests and those of her boss, Detective Chief Superintendent Grant Lindford, who had been at the College of Policing at the time of the interviews, they were told there was nothing they could do about it. They had to abide by the panel's decision.

HR said she should be grateful. There weren't as many applicants for these roles nowadays; the police service was haemorrhaging detectives as sickness and stress levels were through the roof. At inspector rank there were no overtime payments, the workload on the MCU was high and the working hours long. She knew all that. But grateful that he'd applied? Not from what she'd heard.

She peered at him through her solid, black-rimmed glasses.

'So.' Her tone was clipped. 'You had a good second interview.'

The fan heater continued to pump out, circulating her floral perfume around the compact office. Temple said nothing.

She looked back at the screen. 'Detective Chief Superintendent Clive Harker fully endorsed your application, I see, although it's a bit short on detail. A man of few words it seems . . .'

He wasn't sure what she expected as an answer. 'Now Temporary Assistant Chief Constable Harker,' he offered, immediately reminded of Harker's recent and swift promotion by the also newly promoted Chief Constable Buller, having ousted his predecessor through disciplinary action.

A month on, the game of musical chairs had been completed when Buller slotted Detective Chief Superintendent Clive Harker into the role of temporary assistant chief constable. Temple knew what it felt like to be the subject of Buller's enthusiasm for suspension and disciplinary action, aided and abetted by Harker. But she wouldn't read about that on her screen. As far as he was concerned, Buller and Harker were two cheeks of the same arse.

'I couldn't comment, ma'am.'

'Is that right?' According to what she'd heard, he was very well placed to comment. She left silence in the air for a second or two as she continued to busy herself at her laptop. 'As you would expect, I like to find out about someone before they come onto the team, look beyond the application form. Read between the lines.'

She swivelled her seat and sitting back in her chair she studied him.

'Did I hear that you are related to ACC Harker?'

'I don't know, ma'am. I mean, I don't know what you've heard. We're not related. Not exactly.'

Lifting her chin, she looked at him, narrowing her eyes. 'What does "not exactly" mean?'

Temple spoke slowly, seemingly reluctantly. 'I had a relationship with his daughter, Gemma, many years ago, as a probationer. Only recently I found out there was a child, a daughter, Prayer, from that relationship. Gemma had her adopted as a baby. It all came as a bit of a surprise.'

Shaw raised her eyebrows. She already knew about him and Harker's wayward daughter Gemma since someone whispered in her ear. Apparently, everyone knew the story in his force.

'So, you *are* related to ACC Harker. You have his grandchild, that makes you related in my book.' As she suspected, jobs for the boys. 'You have friends in high places.'

She wanted him to know that she knew they weren't just related; from what she'd read they sounded like a double act.

'I wouldn't say we were friends—'

Not listening, she cut him off. 'And Gemma Harker — a sex worker, I believe — what contact do you have with her?'

'I've had little contact with Gemma since before Prayer was born. Just for the record, ma'am, she wasn't a sex worker when we were together all those years ago. She's given up that life and reconciled with her family. No doubt she'll put it behind her now. Second chances and all that . . .' He stopped talking.

Tina Shaw was unmoved. She pressed on, determined to get to the nub of the matter.

'You also worked with ACC Harker on a "special covert project".' She turned her head back to her screen. 'It says here it was "a complex undercover role" that identified ex Detective Sergeant Simon Sloper as corrupt.' She paused to look at him. 'A man who until that time also happened to be a good friend of ACC Harker's. Sounds to me like you have his confidence.'

Temple shifted slightly. He could see how it might look, but he couldn't tell her she was way off the mark. He wished he could tell her that in reality, because of his association with Gemma all those years ago, Harker held an intense dislike for him that bordered on neurosis. Truth was, Clive Harker wouldn't piss on him if he was on fire.

She leaned forward slightly. 'So, what happened to Sloper? He disappeared, didn't he?' She looked at him archly. 'Bit convenient, wasn't it, being ACC Harker's friend?'

Temple straightened in his seat, pricked by her inference.

'Sloper wasn't *my* friend, ma'am, far from it. Before his arrest, Sloper's actions led to the murder of a young girl and left me unconscious on a pavement.'

Every time he thought of it, he wished he'd turned to see Sloper about to put a brick in his head. If he'd have stopped him, it would have changed the course of so many things.

Temple continued. 'He's believed to be abroad, rumour has it Spain, perhaps South America, no one knows for certain despite an Interpol Red Notice. The way I see it, when Simon Sloper knocked me out that night, he prevented me from saving a girl he had already endangered. If it hadn't been for him, she'd be alive today. There's not just my blood on his hands and I won't forget that.'

The murder of fourteen-year-old China Lewis would stay with him always. He'd never forget the sight of her small, bruised and battered body as it was being uncovered from a shallow grave. He found the terror captured on her face still difficult to shake off. And Sloper had played just as much a part in her death as the man who killed her. Indirectly, Harker had too, by having a tin ear to the rumours about his friend's activities over the years.

Detective Superintendent Tina Shaw rocked back in her seat and through her solid lenses, locked Temple in her stare.

'Still, Sloper's escape from custody leaves a bad taste, wouldn't you say?'

'I agree, ma'am. Personally, I won't be happy until he's put before the court and he's sitting in prison under Rule 45. As far as I'm concerned, solitary's too good for him.'

'And yet no one seems to know where he is.' She employed a sarcastic tone. 'Amazing how someone can still disappear with all the technology and resources at our disposal.'

Her insinuation annoyed him, but he kept it in check.

'Ma'am, *I* haven't stopped looking for Sloper. I make regular bank and Interpol checks, but you're right, it's as if he's disappeared off the face of the earth.'

She was stony-faced and spoke slowly. 'As you might imagine, I expect the highest standards and integrity from my officers. And know this: I don't take risks. Everything is done by the book. I run a *very* tight ship here.'

'Of course, ma'am. I'd be disappointed if you didn't.'

She hardened her gaze, pausing for a second or two to emphasise her last words and choose her next.

'So, tell me about Operation Acre. I saw a piece in the *Telegraph* a few months ago, a bit of welcome publicity for the case. Although I'm not sure personal publicity is something to be welcomed as a DI on the MCU.'

Temple made an inward sigh.

She saw his hesitation. 'It's a fascinating story. I read that when you found your mother you were only seven years old, is that true?'

'That is true, ma'am,' he replied quietly.

She went on. 'It must be difficult for you, knowing that her killer has been out there for over thirty years and the crime remains unsolved?'

Temple eased his finger around his shirt collar.

'I've learned to live with it, ma'am,' he lied.

'They've found the killer's DNA now, haven't they, on a blue T-shirt you were wearing when he grabbed you? Every case needs a stroke of luck, even if it is more than thirty years on.'

'Like you say, ma'am, a welcome stroke of luck, although so far no one has managed to identify who the DNA belongs to. The killer remains as out of reach as ever. After all this time he could be dead, in fact, the more time passes he probably is.' He broke off abruptly.

'What I found interesting was the blue T-shirt turning up last year in the loft of Roy Filer, the original SIO on the case. Makes you wonder why a piece of crucial evidence would get separated and hidden away like that for so long.'

'I agree, ma'am. Much of the original file and exhibits went missing over the years with various changes in SIO and office moves as the case remained unsolved. Thankfully, after Filer's death, when he was clearing out the loft, his son realised he'd found an exhibit bag and handed it in. Why it was there is anyone's guess.'

'Intriguing. Tell me about the journalist who wrote the piece, what was her name?'

He hesitated. 'Sophie Twiner, ma'am.'

'She's the crime correspondent in a local rag, isn't she?' Tina Shaw had done her homework.

'Yes, ma'am.'

She looked back at him, expectantly. 'Well?'

'There's not much to tell. A few months ago, Sophie Twiner approached my uncle, Richard Temple, and convinced him she could help with the case. I'd already told her I didn't need that sort of help. Anyhow, he thought differently and the piece was syndicated to the broadsheets and red tops.'

'I'm not too keen on journalists, especially not local crime reporters with contacts to MCU DIs.'

'I'm not so keen myself, ma'am.'

'I don't want risks taken with investigations through leaks to the local press.'

'You've no worries on that score.'

'But you can't deny it had an effect, the force reactivated the investigation?'

'My uncle thinks it was all due to Sophie Twiner and the interest generated that they reopened the case. Yes, the article was sympathetic; it laid out the facts, some of which had been mis-reported over the years. She can do no wrong in his eyes, but I don't share his opinion. I didn't welcome the publicity. Sure, they've put a part-time enquiry team of two on it now, but as soon as the story wanes no doubt the enquiry will be quietly disbanded.'

'A bit cynical of you . . .' she said, knowing he was probably right.

'With respect, I think we both know how it goes, ma'am.'

She pinned him to the wall with a stare. 'With *respect*, DI Temple, for us going forward, don't assume to know how I think.'

He took the rebuke. 'Ma'am.'

She turned back to her screen. 'So, is it just the one child you have?'

'Sorry, ma'am?'

'Children? Just the one — Prayer — did you say?'

'No, Prayer who's adopted is the eldest, but I have another girl, Daisy, a boy, Ben, and a baby on the way. Due any day now.'

'Oh?' She paused, sitting back in her chair. 'The DI role is a big commitment. Are you sure this is the right move for you, *now*, I mean? You seem to have an awful lot going on and you say a new baby on the way?' She scribbled again.

Becoming irritated by the heat and her questioning, he wanted to remind her the interviews had finished, he'd already been given the job.

'Look, ma'am, it's a role I've wanted for a while. I'm here to give the job everything I have.'

'Glad to hear it.' She pressed on. 'Although I expect you'll be going off for a period of paternity leave . . .'

'I won't be taking paternity leave, ma'am. Everything's organised on that front. I just want to get on with the job.'

'Oh? I need someone who is fully committed, no distractions. Above all, someone who can cope with the pressure of the job. Are you sure with your baby on the way and everything else that you will be able to concentrate?' She feigned concern, but not enough to be convincing.

'Yes, ma'am, perfectly sure. I'm looking forward to meeting the MCU team. I just want to get started.'

She straightened in her chair, frowning at the sound of her mobile ringing. 'You'll have a new DCI soon; we're just waiting for the transfer to go through. As you know, you'll be responding to major crime to the south of the region across the two forces. At least the office in Marlborough is close to home and you shouldn't have to come out here often.' She wanted to emphasise that before picking up her mobile.

Temple took her cue for him to leave.

Tina Shaw lent only half her concentration to her call as she watched him close the door behind him. Nothing in their exchange had changed her mind about him. In fact, the meeting had reinforced her feelings. She felt his appointment had been foisted upon them and they'd been left to work it out.

The whole thing with him and Harker didn't pass the sniff test. And if the latest rumour about him was true, he was dangerous.

There was no place for a corrupt officer on the MCU; Temple had slid in under her radar. He had to go. The quickest route open to her was performance management. She'd write him off in the probationary period, backed up by Lindford. Three months tops, sooner if she could manage it. Then he'd be out.

CHAPTER 4

Wedging his car into a gap in the crowded car park at the rear of Marlborough police station, Temple grabbed his laptop and made for the back door where he let himself in and light-footed it straight up a narrow stairway to the first floor. Shaking off his meeting with Tina Shaw, he stepped into the corridor to see a familiar face walking towards him.

'Nice bit of parking, boss.' DS Charlie Eaton flashed a nervous grin and held out his hand. Tall and athletic, Eaton's tightly cropped, light-brown hair and fresh face belied his thirty-five years.

'I didn't know you were over here, Charlie. Good to see a friendly face.' He shook Eaton's hand. Sensing Eaton was a little hesitant, he had some banter.

'Like the waistcoat.'

Eaton gently tugged on the points of the garment to straighten it against his body.

'Trending in CID, boss, you need to get yourself one.'

'I'll leave that to you and the rest of the sharp suits.' They walked along the corridor to the main office. 'So, how long have you been here then?'

'Six months. I've been acting DI the last two months, waiting for them to appoint. I told the team I'd worked with you briefly before; they're looking forward to working with you.'

'That's good to know. Sorry to spoil your fun as acting DI.'

They stopped outside the main office.

'That's all right, it's been good experience and a welcome bit of extra.' Eaton held up his forefinger and thumb, rubbing them together. He kept him at the door. 'Boss, just before you arrived, we had a call from ma'am Shaw. She said you were on your way and to wait for you. Seems there's been a "niner" from a lady called Vera Dart down at Erlestoke who's saying she found two men dead in a car this morning while walking her dog.'

'Oh?'

'That's all we've got. They want us to be on standby as soon as the helicopter goes up. They're still waiting for the weather to clear.'

'I'll look in on the team, then we can go over there.'

'Trouble is, boss, control room have checked the system. Apparently, the lady's prone to making nuisance calls to police about problems with neighbours and children, which are unfounded. Going on her past performance, they're not sure whether this is rubbish or not. I haven't said anything to the team yet.'

'If there's nothing in it, we can do a handover over a cup of tea and a fried breakfast.' Temple couldn't think of a better way to christen his latest credit card. He tapped his pocket. 'My treat.'

On opening the door of the main office, Temple interrupted a man and woman having a heated exchange. Along with two other people in the room they turned to look at him.

He smiled. 'Morning, everyone.'

The people in the room were still.

'As you may or may not know, I'm DI Temple, good to meet you all.'

As he finished saying his name, he felt sure he saw a collective hardening on their faces. He checked himself, knowing he was prone to a healthy dose of paranoia honed through years of his dealings with Harker and time spent under investigation. He was more alert than most to a sideways look, a judgemental glance or people diverting their eyes as he approached. And because of that, he was trying not to read too much into how they were looking at him right now.

Although he didn't recognise anyone in front of him, he could tell by their faces there appeared to be recognition towards him. Silence hung in the air as his colleagues eyed him, their looks now set. He gave them the benefit of the doubt; maybe it was some kind of MCU initiation to see how the new boss reacted to being looked at like he was shit on their shoes. Eaton broke the awkward silence to make introductions.

'This is Clare Phillips, our civilian investigator and Holmes operative, DC Kelvin Stubbs, DC Ruby Smith and DC Tom Caine.'

Temple worked through reluctant handshakes, hoping their mood would soften with another smile and a bit of skin on skin. It didn't.

'We've got three off sick, all long-term, boss, one on mat leave and two on their jollies using up untaken leave,' Eaton went on to quickly explain, trying to cut through the increasingly tight atmosphere. 'There's another DC due to start in a couple of weeks and, of course, we've got a new DCI due too. That's why we're a bit thin.'

Despite the evident tension, Temple made a determined walk around the room. It was typical of any criminal investigation office; whiteboards on the walls were used as aide memoirs covered in various coloured inks detailing the progress of current investigations and relevant mobile phone numbers. Even though there was a lack of staff, desks were piled with overfilled cardboard boxes and columns of paper and files.

Watching Temple, Eaton filled the silence again. 'And we've been having a tidy up, too, boss, boxing up some old files and papers for archive.'

Temple continued to study the writing on the whiteboards and gravitated to one showing current cases. Skimming over it, he noted the various operational names before his eye was drawn to the bottom right-hand corner. There he saw a box with his name written inside, along with initials and numbers. He knew instantly what it was. Watching Temple, Charlie Eaton shot a glance at Ruby Smith who made a grimace. Turning back to them with a smile, Temple broke the silence.

'Well, I look forward to working with you all. Any problems or issues any of you have, just let me know and I'll do my best to sort them for you. I'll sit down with each of you over the coming days and go through your caseloads. It'll be a chance for us to break the . . . ice.'

The team shared glances as he left the room to find his new office. After the frosty reception, the bog-standard cubbyhole reserved for the DI became a welcome refuge. He shut the door and sat in a swivel chair. He leaned back and looked at the bare magnolia wall and as he grappled with the lever under the chair, Eaton poked his head around the door.

'Sorry about that, boss.'

'You lied to me, Charlie.' Temple pulled out the drawers of his desk.

'Boss?'

'You said they were looking forward to working with me. If that's what they're like when they're looking forward to working with someone, I wouldn't like to be the person they didn't.'

Eaton lowered his eyes to the floor.

'At least your name wasn't on the vote of no confidence on the whiteboard.'

Eaton hesitated. 'They run a book with everyone, boss, to see how long they'll last. I'll get the car ready. Do you want me to drive?'

'I'll do the driving, you can do the talking. Charlie, did the last DI work out of this office? I mean, there's nothing here, not even a paperclip.'

'She did, boss, but she was long gone before I arrived. Lasted six months, I believe, two months longer than the DI before her. Both went off with stress apparently. I worked out of the main office when I did the acting, didn't bother coming in here. See you downstairs.'

Temple shook his head. Three DIs inside a year, no wonder they were taking bets. Tina Shaw's grilling now made a bit more sense and explained his reception from the team. Picking up his laptop, he closed the door and headed down the stairs out to the backyard.

Charlie Eaton punched Vera Dart's address into a sat-nav and rested a police radio on the dashboard as Temple pulled out of the nick. The radio chattered in the background as they travelled. Temple took the quickest route and as he drove further south, the fog started to lift.

He looked across at Eaton. 'So, who's the new DCI then?'

'DCI Nadia Patel. By the sound of it, she's OK, I don't know what the delay is, but she should be with us in the next week or so. I hear she's transferring from Lancs.'

Temple nodded. It would be good to have the new DCI between him and Tina Shaw if their first meeting was going to be typical.

'What do I need to know about the team then, Charlie?'

Eaton kept his eyes to the front. 'Probably ought to make you aware, boss, if you don't know already, DC Kelvin Stubbs is the nephew of Detective Superintendent Mark Stubbs. You've heard that Mark's tipped to replace Clive Harker any day now?'

'Yes, I did hear that. I was in the same intake as Mark Stubbs, we did our probation together.'

Eaton was wary. 'Mark a mate of yours then, boss?'

'No, we never hit it off.' Temple had to hand it to Mark Stubbs; like some of his high-ranking peers, he'd chosen to put most of his effort into mastering the dark art of the promotion process instead of catching criminals. Through sustained grooming of senior officers, he'd made a rapid rise specialising in 'playing the game' instead of inventing ways to ensnare the criminal class. Cosying up to people he couldn't stand had been something Temple always found difficult to do. With his next appointment, all of Stubbs' arse licking would have paid off, he would be flying high.

'Kelvin anything like his uncle?'

Eaton's tone hardened. 'Could be his twin; they're close. Kelvin's very ambitious, nailed on for DS at the next round of promotions and being talked up for fast-tracking. According to "Uncle Mark", he'll be a super within three years, less. No hard grunt for him.'

'Three years? Not bad. He was having an argument with Ruby Smith when I walked in — do you know what that was about?'

Without turning his head, Eaton swiped his eyes to the right to catch Temple's profile. 'The team are under a bit of pressure at the moment.'

'Ruby got some time in?'

'Twelve years. She's from A and S, the MCU is a mix of both forces.'

'I wondered why I didn't know who she was.'

'Underneath all the make-up, she's a good worker, gets on with it. A bit like Clare Phillips, another grafter. Apart from that, it's the usual stuff anywhere you go.' Eaton eyed Temple again. 'You know how it is, boss, the same petty politics and little niggles teams have. But then we get a job in and they all come together and do what they need to do.'

'By the looks of them this morning, perhaps they would have preferred you to keep running things?'

Eaton looked out of the window. 'Not their decision to make.'

'Still, it can't be easy, another DI to get used to. They didn't seem that pleased, that's all.'

Eaton didn't turn. 'You know what it's like, boss, the place thrives on gossip and rumour.'

'Oh?' Temple glanced across at Eaton. 'So, what *is* the gossip and rumour?'

'Well, since you ask, if you really want to know . . .' Eaton stopped. Staring straight ahead, he cleared his throat and paused.

Temple looked at him. 'Go on.'

'You asked if there was anything you needed to know about the team . . .'

'And?'

Eaton took a deep breath. 'They think you let Sloper go.'

Temple blinked back at him. First ma'am Shaw, now Eaton, what the hell was going on? 'That's seriously doing the rounds?'

Seizing the moment, Eaton didn't hold back. 'Harker was running a covert op on Sloper, his best mate, which you were involved in. Sloper gets arrested, but then he escapes from custody. You can see how it looks . . .'

'How it looks?' Temple's grip increased on the steering wheel. 'Sloper escaping had nothing to do with *me*.'

Temple was quiet. Eaton was right; the place thrived on rumour. It took very little for that to be embellished and passed off as fact at the best of times. What had seemed like a good plan and had saved his job at the time, was now backfiring. He hadn't seen this coming; the difficulty he had was that the truth was locked in the pact he had brokered with Harker and that trapped him from telling anyone what really happened.

'What do you believe, Charlie?'

Eaton continued to stare ahead. 'You working with Harker was a bit of a surprise, boss, I have to say. Everyone knows you two don't get on, at least that's what we thought. Seems everyone was wrong.'

Temple shook his head.

Eaton pressed on. 'Anyway, it's not just that, is it?'

'What do you mean?'

Eaton turned to face him. 'They think you're here conducting another covert op . . .'

'What?'

'They think that's the real reason you're here. First Sloper, now someone on the team.'

Temple was stunned. 'Are you having a laugh?'

'Seriously, boss, they think you're UC, but they don't know who it is you're investigating or why. Since they found out you were appointed, they've all been looking at each other, wondering which one of them's bent. It's been really difficult.'

Now he understood why the team had treated him like they had. He was stony-faced. It was madness.

'Was this what Stubbs and Ruby were arguing about?'

'Probably; Kelvin told the team that Uncle Mark had confirmed there was no UC job running on the MCU from the Wilts side of things. If anyone would know, he would. So, it had to be from the Avon and Somerset side. As you can imagine, it's almost split the team.'

'Charlie, for the record, I'm not undercover or on any undercover op at MCU, for any force. I'm not looking at anyone, for fuck's sake.'

'Not being funny, boss, but if there was a covert op running and you are UC, you would say that, wouldn't you? If you didn't, your operation would be blown. The team are turning in on themselves.'

The thought of the team thinking he was there as part of a covert operation rocked him.

'Charlie, there is no covert operation . . .'

The thudding vibration of rotary blades cut through the air as the force helicopter flew low overhead. Temple leaned forward to see it going off into the distance. The tension had ramped up in the confines of the car; there was no point in having a go at Eaton, he at least had to try and keep him on side. He took a deep breath.

'So, tell me about the three who are sick.'

'Stress. One three months, the other four months now.'

'Job related?'

'One's seen one dead body too many. Not sure they'll be coming back. The other relates to divorce.'

'The third?'

'A two-week sick note for back pain.' Eaton looked out of the window.

Temple looked across to him. 'Real back pain? Or didn't want to work with the new DI?'

Temple caught Eaton's look. It was going from bad to worse; how long before more of the team followed suit? It was his first day and he wouldn't see the week out if they all downed tools.

'He's an old-timer, boss.'

'I don't care how much time he's got in, he has to come back. Who is he?'

'Les Ford.'

'Avon and Somerset?'

'Yes.'

'And the other one, divorce, did you say?'

'Yes, boss.'

'Look, it's tough, *I* should know, my ex, Leigh, posted everything on Facebook for all to read, but if everyone went off sick every time someone got a divorce . . . you've just got to tough it out.'

'I know, I know . . .' Eaton trailed off. 'I'll make some phone calls.'

It was quiet between them for a minute or so. Temple used the time to figure out how he was going to deal with things. It couldn't be a worse start. Somehow, he had to get the team on side. He'd need to spend the next few days talking with each of them; the least he had to do was reassure them he wasn't part of any covert operation, but quite how he could do that, he didn't know.

'Look, I'm glad you've raised it all, at least I know what's going on. Let's go and see what this is about and then I'll speak to them. I'll sort it. Clear the air. So, what do you know about ma'am Shaw, what's she like?'

Before he could answer, Eaton's mobile rang with a message from the control room.

'Boss, Bravo Echo have identified a possible site. There's a walled area at the top of a track into the Erlestoke Park

Wood. From the air, they think they can see a car parked. They're going to stay over it until we get there.'

At the small village of Erlestoke, Temple pulled into a spot on the side of the main road at the bottom of a narrow, roughly tarmacked track in between a row of houses. The helicopter sat above them in a sulky dull sky as Eaton and Temple got out of the car. Temple looked up and down the main road that ran through the centre of the village. There was no one about, but the low hovering sound of the helicopter would soon start to draw people out.

He nodded at the track. 'I don't want members of the public coming up until we know it's clear. Put a call in for the uniform patrol officer who's with the witness to stand there.' As they started to walk, Eaton relayed the message.

'He'll be here in two minutes.'

With the helicopter overhead marking the spot they needed to reach, they both moved slowly up the steep incline of the track. Although there was no sign of the fog that had been there earlier, the ground was damp and dewy. As the incline increased, they passed the end of the gardens of the houses on the main road, leaving the wood on their left and a copse area on the right.

Nearer the top of the incline, the tarmac finished and the earth began to plateau onto a small clearing in the wood. To the right of the clearing stood a high, red-brick wall. On the far corner of the wall, a silver Ford Ranger with its headlights dimmed was parked facing the wood. Just visible were two males sitting in the front seats, their heads bowed as if sleeping.

Eaton and Temple exchanged glances; Eaton was ready with his radio.

'Looks like Vera Dart might be right.'

CHAPTER 5

The noise from the helicopter continued overhead. As they walked towards the car, Eaton confirmed the situation to the control room.

'Can't get a vehicle check, there's a PNC outage at the moment . . .'

'We'll approach from here.' Temple indicated with a tilt of his head, seeing the offside car window open. They approached the Ranger cautiously, conscious they were trampling on a potential crime scene.

Reaching the window and bending down, Temple faced the profile of a man he guessed to be in his late twenties sitting in the passenger seat, his head slumped forward. A dark bloodied hole above his left ear was clearly visible on his close-shaven head. Putting his hand through the open window and touching the man's neck, Temple searched for his carotid artery.

Standing to the side of him and looking across to the driver's seat, Eaton indicated the futility of the gesture. 'They both look dead to me, boss.'

Next to the victim, the driver's head slumped slightly to the side towards the door. Looking through the open window, Temple could see he was covered in blood and brainy splatter. Bending down for a better view of the passenger's face, the earthy foul odour caught in his nostrils. He put his hand up to shield his nose.

'It looks like a butcher's in there. Hang on a minute, I know him.' Eaton looked across to the driver. 'It's Aaron Fortune. *Fuck*! And that's his brother, Liam.' Standing up, he arched backwards, trying to avoid the smell.

Temple moved slightly to try and get a better look at them both. Now Eaton said it, there was no mistaking the resemblance. 'Fuck,' he echoed.

'What's that, boss?'

Temple stayed silent, all the while increasing the pressure of his fingers on the victim's neck, noticing he now had blood on the sleeve of his jacket.

Eaton walked round to the other side of the vehicle.

'They're either sons of Elijah or Caleb Fortune. I'm not sure which. You had any dealings with the Fortunes, boss?'

Temple wished he hadn't. Thinking the day couldn't get any worse, it just had.

'Nicked Paul King a while back,' he said quietly, at the same time trying to process the victims' identities.

'That was you? I knew he was inside. Fucking hell.' Eaton bent down for a better view. He wrinkled his face. 'No firearms present which rules out some kind of suicide pact . . .'

From under his fingertips Temple felt a sudden trace of movement. He increased the pressure of his fingers.

'I think I've got a pulse. Quick, call for an ambulance . . .'

'*Shit*.' Eaton snatched up his radio for assistance. 'We need a paramedic and ambulance for two victims with gun-shot wounds to the head . . .' He listened to the response. 'There's a paramedic attending Vera Dart, boss. They're sending him over.'

'They'd better hurry up, the pulse is weak. Get hold of the helicopter, see if they can take him to hospital. Tell them to find somewhere to come down behind us, we don't want the rotor downdraft trashing the scene.'

Eaton walked into the clearing, all the time talking into the radio. Temple kept his fingers on Aaron Fortune's neck and as he waited, the flickering pulse faded further. At last, the paramedic walked briskly towards them, carrying a hold-all and a stretcher.

'Here! Gunshot wound to the head, he's barely breathing.' Temple stepped back as the paramedic set his bag on the ground and opened the car door to start his examination.

'His name's Aaron Fortune,' Temple offered.

'How long's he been here?' The paramedic lifted his patient's eyelids and shone a pen torch in his eyes.

'Don't know, anything from a few hours to possibly overnight.'

'What about this one?' The paramedic nodded towards his brother.

'He's gone.'

'This one won't be far behind.' The paramedic reached into his holdall to draw out the necessary equipment.

Temple stepped back to allow him to work and joined Eaton a few yards away in the clearing.

'Is he still alive?'

'Barely.'

Temple turned around. Surrounded by woods, the high red-bricked wall was part of a larger square structure, with a break in it for access through to the inside.

'What is this place?'

'I've just googled it, boss, it's an old walled garden, from an old manor house apparently. The manor house is long gone. It's now the home of the local cricket club.' Eaton turned, pointing out the various reference points. 'There's a makeshift parking area over there and they use the inside of the walled garden for their pitch, with the pavilion over there. The surrounding wood is owned by the MOD and is recreational. You can see all the different paths through the wood from this clearing, which takes you onto the ridge of Salisbury Plain.'

Temple took it in. 'You wouldn't know it was here from the main road.'

Inside the red-brick walled garden was a large, grassed area. Outside, beyond the clearing, the tall trees in the woods provided good cover.

'Better check out the pavilion.' Temple walked towards the wooden structure in the distance. To the front there was a slightly raised platform with a rail, with windows either side of a central door. When they reached it, Eaton covered his hand with his sleeve and tried the door handle.

'Locked.'

Temple peered in through the windows as Eaton went around the back, emerging from the other side.

'Nothing at the back, boss.'

'Windows are secure. Looks like it hasn't been disturbed.'

They walked back to the clearing.

Temple was already fighting to quell a sense of unease. 'One thing's for sure, it wasn't the cricket that brought them up here.'

'Not this or any other time of year.' Eaton pointed. 'Car engine off, lights on, they must have been waiting for someone. Then, bang, bang. There'll be people saying whoever did this has done society a favour. Outside the Fortune family, there won't be too many tears shed for them. Some might say it couldn't have happened to two more deserving people.'

He knew what Eaton said was right. He had to treat it like any other case, but already he was struggling to think past the fact it involved the Fortunes.

'Call the team over, Charlie. We passed a church on the bend, tell them to park in the grounds and walk up. We need this path sealed off, get the Forensics here and the tent up. Put a call in and map all local ANPR. We need house-to-house done on either side and opposite the track. We've lost time because of the fog, so let's get things moving; get someone to revisit Vera Dart. And if he makes it to hospital alive, make sure there's a guard put on Aaron.'

'Will do, boss, leave it to me.'

Temple checked on the paramedic who had been joined by a colleague from the helicopter. Still clinging to life, Aaron

Fortune had been carefully eased out of the car and, wearing an oxygen mask, had been strapped onto a stretcher. With the helicopter silent, Temple made the necessary call to the coroner, then Tina Shaw.

'Ma'am? Update from the 999 call this morning. We're at the scene of a murder at Erlestoke Park Wood. We have two victims in a car, each with a single gunshot wound to the head. The victims are brothers, Liam and Aaron Fortune, late twenties, early thirties. Liam Fortune is dead, Aaron's just about alive. Aaron and Liam are from a local organised crime family who operate in the south-west, thefts, aggravated and distraction burglaries and violence.'

'Describe the scene.'

'We're at a spot where the local cricket team play, not visible from the main drag through Erlestoke. Access is via a narrow single-track lane between a row of houses, on a steep incline. The top of the incline plateaus onto a clearing which is wooded on three sides and abuts the Plain. The land's owned by the military. They've parked up, headlights on, perhaps suggesting they're waiting for someone and they've both been shot in the head, above the ear. There's no sign of firearms in the car.'

'Sounds like an execution style shooting.'

'Could be.'

'On a military site, you say?'

'Yes.'

'They've obviously pissed someone off.'

'And at the moment Aaron is the only potential witness we have, ma'am.'

'What're his chances?'

'Doesn't look good.'

'How far away are they from home?'

'The Fortunes live between five and ten miles from here. They'll know the green roads so they may have come up here from another access point, other than the track from the main road. The other thing worth mentioning, ma'am, is nearby Erlestoke Prison.'

'Interesting. How far away's the prison from the scene?'

'About a mile. It holds Cat C males. I'll make it a line of enquiry.'

'Any drugs on the victims? That would be the obvious, they could have been supplying the prison or the military.'

'We've yet to do a thorough search of the vehicle and their clothes.'

'Better put a guard on Aaron when he gets to hospital.'

'Already being arranged, ma'am.'

'ANPR?'

'Charlie's on it. But there's opportunity for the killer to have fled through the wood.'

'OK.' She hesitated. 'Put the usual things in place. The prison and military have to be good lines of enquiry to start with. It can't be a coincidence them being there. And go around to the Fortunes and break the news. See what the reaction is. I'll inform the hierarchy. I'll ring you when I'm on my way.'

Her instruction prompted him. 'There's something I need to tell you, ma'am.'

'What is it?' she said impatiently.

'It might be better if I step away from this one.'

'Oh?'

'I've got history with the Fortunes. I arrested one of the cousins, Paul King, a few years ago, aggravated burglary. He got seven years and didn't thank me for it . . .'

'So?'

'They released him last year and he broke into my home. It earned him a recall to prison which angered the Fortunes, I don't think—'

Tina Shaw interrupted him. 'We'll talk about it when I get there, go and let the family know.'

'Not sure that's a good idea, ma'am . . .'

The line was already dead.

CHAPTER 6

Eaton finished a call. 'Intel have just confirmed that Liam and Aaron are both sons of Elijah Fortune.'

'They would be.' Temple fingered a growing pain in his neck.

'Do you want me to go, boss, might be a bit of a handful?'

Temple hesitated; he knew more than most what the Fortunes were like. Of course it would be better if Eaton went. It had been less than a year since he'd had a bad-tempered run-in with Elijah Fortune courtesy of Paul King. It was way too soon for him to see Elijah Fortune again.

'No, she asked me to go. I'll do it.'

'I'll get a patrol car to follow you over.'

'No need. I'll go alone, it'll be fine.'

'Better take this.' Eaton reached for a radio. 'Just in case.'

Temple used the drive over to think about what he was going into. He should have told ma'am Shaw about the fire. It might have swayed her. But he knew why he hadn't. That was best kept to himself.

More than once he felt like turning back, until it became too late and he pulled up outside the wrought-iron gates of the Fortunes' four-acre compound. He'd delivered enough death messages in his time to know it was the worst part of the job. Now he'd arrived, he wished he'd taken up Eaton's offer.

Inside the compound, a series of large, static mobile homes stood off a tarmac road with various trucks and vans randomly parked. Leaving his car, Temple walked through the open gates. Stepping over the threshold instantly triggered the savage barks of dogs from somewhere close he couldn't see. He stopped, but when the barks continued and the dogs didn't appear, he took a few steps inside. Suddenly, a couple of young lads in jeans and hoodies appeared. They couldn't have been more than twelve, but they already had the familiar Fortune swagger about them.

'What d'ya want?' one asked, head cocked to one side.

'I'm looking for Elijah Fortune, is he here?'

'Who are ya?' the second boy squinted at him.

'Police. I need to speak to Elijah and fast, it's really important. I need one of you to go and get him, please.'

'Nice manners,' one boy quipped as neither of them left his side. Instead, they circled him as the dogs continued to bark. Then, from nowhere, a familiar figure came bounding towards him.

'What do *you* want?'

Tall and thickset, with a dark number-one haircut, Georgie Munt strode towards him in camouflage combats and heavy boots. His mouth in a snarl, Munt's heavy shoulders were already straining under his shirt, ready for confrontation. Looking at him now, Temple could easily appreciate how he'd frightened his ex-wife Leigh a while back when he'd appeared outside their house threatening to burn it down.

Munt squared up within inches of him and spat on the ground near Temple's feet.

'Our Paul's still inside so you've got no business here. Go on, piss off.' Munt inched in closer.

Temple stood his ground. 'Calm down, Georgie, I need to see Elijah.'

Munt ignored him, narrowing his eyes. He spoke slowly, his voice dropping. 'You see, this is what we want to know;

how did you do it, eh, lawman? How did you get your gun back? Did you think we'd forgotten?'

Temple was stung. He knew exactly what Munt was referring to; the World War II pistol passed onto him by his grandfather had been the only thing resembling an heirloom he'd possessed. His neck felt rigid with tension but now was not the time to register the slightest discomfort.

Munt continued, taking a half step closer. 'See, I've done a bit of thinking.' Their faces were now inches apart. 'When our Paulie said he was going to "do" you on his release, you got yourself a gun, didn't ya?'

Temple could feel Munt's breath. He shouldn't have come. Munt was staring into the backs of his eyes, willing his face to betray him. Munt nodded and gave half a smile as he spoke.

'Makes sense. And you were waiting for him, waiting to use it. You were going to kill him, weren't ya? Now, my thinking is, you weren't meant to have that gun, were you? Not that sort of gun anyways, one that wasn't deactivated. It's against the rules.' He tutted, his smile widening. 'You must have proper shit yourself when our Paul found it and took it from your house the night he set it on fire. Paulie showed it to Elijah and told him exactly where he'd got it from. Of course, you knew all about it, because unlike the lies you told Elijah, the gun was yours.'

Temple had to hand it to them, they'd almost worked it out. And Munt was right; he'd armed himself with his grandfather's WWII handgun. After his mother's murder, there was no way he would stand by and see his family harmed again. With the evidence stacked against him and looking at a prison sentence, Paul King had vowed to exact revenge on Temple as they faced each other across an interview table.

King had been determined to hurt him, to make an example of him, to act as a deterrent to officers in the future so no one would make the mistake of arresting any of them again. They would become untouchable. Temple had been lucky he wasn't home the night King, not long after release, burgled his home and set it on fire, which had seen him recalled to prison. And now he couldn't afford to show Munt the slightest sign that he was on to something. The sooner he could get out of there the better.

'As I said to Elijah, Paul King may well have shown him a gun, but he didn't get it from my house. And as you seem to have forgotten, police recovered a gun near where King was staying at the time, no doubt where he'd hidden it. He may have had a gun, but it had nothing to do with me.'

Munt licked his lips. 'Paulie knew where he left the gun and it wasn't where the police found it. You're a fucking liar. *Jesus*, they probably gave it back to you.'

Their faces were so close there was almost no air between them. Behind him, the two boys had closed in like hyenas, hanging on Munt's every word.

'For the last time, I never had a gun and I don't have a gun.'

'You're a lying bastard.' Smiling, Munt stared into his eyes. 'And just who would you have got to do your dirty work for you?' He nodded. 'I've been thinking about that too. The fucking whore, Tara.'

He held on, not showing the slightest reaction at the mention of Tara's name, knowing it would seal her fate, but it was becoming hard. Caught in Munt's iron gaze, there was only so long he could match Munt's blinkless stare. For both their sakes, he had to move the conversation off the topic of the gun.

'I don't know what you're talking about and you're wasting my time. I've come here to see Elijah. Something bad's happened to Liam and Aaron.'

'Oh yeah, like what? Have you bastards taken them in?' Munt looked over Temple's shoulder and spoke rapidly to the two boys.

'No. I came here to tell Elijah they were found this morning, in their car. It's not good, Georgie, they've been shot. Liam's dead and Aaron's on his way to hospital. Aaron's in a bad way, he might not make it. We've started a murder enquiry.'

Suddenly, the two boys ran from behind Temple in the direction of the mobile homes. Caught off guard, Munt stepped back as if he'd taken a hit.

'*Jesus fucking Christ.* I saw them myself before they went out last night.' Munt's shoulders dropped. 'Why didn't you say?'

'I tried, but you wanted to rant on about an imaginary gun . . .'

'Fucking *shot*? Was it *your* lot? Was it the fucking police?' Now Munt was electrified and went to move on Temple, his arm drawn back, fist clenched. Temple stood firm.

'No, not by us, I don't know who shot them.'

'So, it could be your lot?'

'No, Georgie, it's not the police, if it had been the police I'd tell you.'

'But who else would shoot them? How can Liam be dead? Last night they were full of life. I've always looked out for them, we were like brothers . . .' He shook his head. 'No, no, *no* . . .' Munt cradled his head in his hands.

'Perhaps you know someone who might have done it, someone from your side?' he ventured.

Munt bridled at the suggestion; his face contorted. 'We sort our own shit out. You fuckers wouldn't even get to hear about it. This has nothing to do with anything that's going on with us. Remember, *you* had a gun, lawman. Paulie said so . . .'

'I never had a gun, Georgie. We've been through all that. Liam's been killed. I'm here investigating a crime.'

Munt rounded on him. 'If the police didn't shoot Liam and Aaron, then who the fuck did, eh?'

'We don't know. I need to know anything that can help us, until perhaps Aaron is able to tell us himself. We've got an enquiry going now . . .' He watched Munt spit again. 'And I have to tell Elijah and their mother so they can get to the hospital.'

'Where have they taken him?'

'Salisbury, they took him by helicopter. But he doesn't look good.'

'Fuck's sake! They were good boys . . .'

From the corner of his eye, Temple could see someone running towards him and a woman behind. Georgie Munt stepped towards them, again talking so rapidly Temple couldn't understand what was said. Elijah stopped.

'*You*?'

Temple faced him. 'Elijah.'

He'd put on more timber since Temple had last seen him. His heavy face set in a rage, his chest was heaving despite having only run a short way. A chunky gold chain hung across his open-necked shirt. Behind him the woman was wailing.

'Is it true? Is it true what these boys say?'

Elijah reached out and caught hold of Temple, holding a lapel of his jacket in a meaty fist. 'Is it true my boys are shot?' Elijah's face was too close for comfort.

'Liam's dead, Elijah. Aaron's been taken to hospital, you need to get there, fast.'

Behind Fortune the woman had sunk to the ground on her knees. 'My boys, my lovely boys . . . what have they done, what have they done to them?' Tears streamed down her face. 'Take me to my boys.'

At the sound of her shrieks, more children and women started to appear from other mobile homes. A couple of women crouched down beside her to see why she was crying.

With his wife's screams in his ears, Elijah Fortune lashed out; his hand still gripping Temple's lapel, he started to beat his fist into Temple's chest.

'They were good boys. Have you lot killed him? Eh, was it your lot?'

As Temple withstood Fortune's onslaught, Georgie Munt intervened. 'He says not, Elijah, it wasn't them.'

Munt moved and put his hand over Fortune's, in a bid to pull him away. The woman continued to cry out, her screams fading into a desperate high-pitched wail. Fortune turned to look at her, releasing Temple as he did.

'Woman, get up,' he instructed. 'Go and get yourself ready, we'll go to the hospital.'

Without questioning him, she stood and staggered back to her home. With her gone, the small crowd of onlookers walked towards Elijah and Munt. Barely able to contain himself, Elijah turned back to Temple. His voice dropped and turned menacing.

'What happened?'

'Liam and Aaron were found this morning by a lady walking her dog. They were sitting in their vehicle, each with a single gunshot wound. That's all I know until our enquiries get under way. My priority was seeing you.'

Elijah moved close again.

'Where?'

'Erlestoke. I'm sorry, Elijah.'

Fortune started to shout in his face. 'Get out. Go. *Go.*' He pushed Temple backwards towards the gate and Temple felt the sheer force of anger pumping through Elijah Fortune's body.

'We'll need to talk to you . . .'

'I said get out!' Fortune bellowed. 'Whoever's done this . . . whatever piece of fucking scum has done this, I will kill them.' Every sinew and vein in his tattooed neck strained with rage as the words spewed out of his mouth.

Temple stared at him, feeling the spray of spittle on his face, but he didn't turn his back. In this state, Elijah Fortune was beyond reason. Georgie Munt spoke up.

'Come on, Elijah, let's go and get Sharnie and go to Aaron.'

Elijah moved towards Munt. 'Whoever did this is going to die for it.' He held up his arms. 'I will kill them myself. With these hands.'

'We'll find the killer, Elijah,' said Temple as the man turned away from him.

'Just get out,' he snarled over his shoulder before walking away.

Following him, Munt suddenly stopped and turned. His eyes brimmed with tears.

'Where's Liam?'

'Salisbury.' Temple straightened his jacket. 'Someone will need to ID the body.'

Munt angrily jabbed his finger at him. 'We've got unfinished business. It isn't over. Don't think it is. We're coming for you, you lying bastard.'

Back in his car Temple leaned back into the headrest to relieve his banging head. All it had taken was for him to show up and he'd stirred a hornet's nest. He thought he'd got them off his back with regards to the gun. Worse still, Munt appeared to have figured out who'd helped him and they weren't going to let that go. He slammed his fist down onto the steering wheel. It had been stupid of him to come.

CHAPTER 7

'We'll also need a twenty-four-hour guard put on Aaron Fortune if you could factor that in, too, please.'

Detective Superintendent Tina Shaw finished outlining the detail to ACC Clive Harker. Professional courtesy dictated she inform him who was taking charge of the investigation but contacting Harker so soon after seeing Temple had her feeling as though she was being sucked into their orbit and she didn't like it.

'We can do that for you,' Harker confirmed lightly before his Glaswegian burr lowered to something more brooding. 'Jesus, Tina, the Elijah Fortune I know will not take this well.' He pressed his mobile to his ear as he swung in his chair in his new office. 'Take it from me, the Fortune family are trouble. These people don't play by the rules, not even criminal ones. Now they're victims, this will be unfamiliar territory for them. We need to get this right. *You* need to get this right, Tina.'

He paused just long enough for her to convey to him she was listening. Their paths had not crossed before, and she had yet to meet the man on the end of the phone.

'Tina, as SIO, you're going to have to go to the nth degree on this one. You're going to have to move fast if you're going to get a conviction. You need to keep on the front foot. Elijah Fortune will be like a wounded animal. I heard there was some delay getting the helicopter up?'

Tina Shaw paced around the confines of her small office, trying to keep her cool. 'The delay was due to the distress of the lady who found them. Then having to wait for the fog to clear before the helicopter could be deployed safely . . . sir.' Having to call him sir stuck in her craw and neither did she like the familiar tone he seemed intent on taking with her.

She didn't need him to tell her how to do her job, or that the investigation was going to be difficult.

Harker continued. 'If Aaron Fortune dies, they may start asking questions. If he lives, they'll wonder if Liam could have survived, too. It's going to make the investigation difficult if it wasn't already. These first few days are going to be make or break. This could make or break *you*, Tina.'

There was a pregnant pause. 'You'll need to justify it in future if there's a complaint.'

'Yes, I'm aware of that, sir.'

'You know how it is, Tina; this job with the Fortunes will follow you wherever you go, if you get it right, especially if you get it wrong. Elijah Fortune losing one, perhaps both of his sons if the other doesn't pull through, by God, he's going to be a man on a mission. I don't envy you this one, Tina.

'This sort of case tanks budgets and resources. The press will be onto it soon, too, doing their own investigations, speaking to witnesses, criticising the case in the news. In every murder investigation an SIO risks their reputation. You're only as good as your last enquiry. Of course, I'll let you have all the assistance I can.'

'Thank you, sir, we'll need to draw on some of your officers, no doubt, for local knowledge and intelligence particularly.'

'You only need to ask. We've been dealing with the victims of the Fortunes for years. The Fortunes are cunning and nasty. You'll have less than a fuck-all cat in hell's chance of finding out who did this unless you act quickly. It's going to be tough on you as SIO, Tina, good people get burned on cases like this, it could be a long and dirty job.'

She stopped pacing. The conversation was going nowhere. She was sick of listening to him.

'Thanks, sir, I need to get on.'

She finished the call and looked at her phone. A dirty job, he'd said; well, he'd know all about that. Still, she'd seen an opportunity and she wasn't going to waste it. She scrolled her phone for the number of her line manager, Grant Lindford.

* * *

At Erlestoke, Temple turned into the churchyard where Eaton had set up a base in the grounds. He parked and started to walk the hundred yards across the main road to where police tape blocked access to the path up to the woods.

Bothered by the exchange with Munt, he was deep in thought. Maybe he'd been naive to think he could just walk away from them last year, that there would be no comeback for getting the better of them. He thought he'd wrapped it all up; King recalled to prison, the gun picked up by the local plod and destroyed; he'd even ensured its discovery had been covered by Sophie Twiner in the local press, so why couldn't the Fortunes accept the gun was gone? But now he was right back in the middle of it again. And he only had himself to blame.

Grey clouds crowded the sky threatening icy rain, but it hadn't put off the locals who had gathered either side of the path entrance. As he approached, Temple did a sweep of the crowd and heard a man in his early twenties speaking into a phone. Catching a few words of the conversation, Temple stood at his elbow. The man stopped talking.

'You press?' snapped Temple.

The man turned. 'What if I am?'

'Who called you here?'

He frowned. 'A concerned resident. I'll have a quote off you if . . .'

Temple walked on, leaving the man talking to himself. He'd be lucky if it stayed out of the nationals. The locals murmured as he was nodded past the police guard. This time, with no helicopter, he walked slowly up the steep path to the wood in silence.

Approaching the clearing at the top, he was met with a subtle hum of activity under the descending canopy of threatening cloud. In his absence, the team of CSIs had moved into the clearing, a tent had been pitched over the car and another was on the opposite side of the path, from where four white-suited crime scene examiners went to and fro. Two light towers had been erected due to the lack of light coming through the trees despite it being mid-afternoon and a scenes-of-crime officer was placing foot plates on the ground. In front of him, Eaton stood talking with DC Ruby Smith. He interrupted them.

'How's it going, Charlie?'

'Fine, boss. Path turned up just as you left. As luck would have it, he was in the area when he took the call.'

'Who've we got?'

'Yardley. He's got photos and video. He's probably at Salisbury now.'

'Good, I've worked with Yardley.'

'Just being briefed by Ruby on house-to-house. She'll have a team ready by six p.m. this evening, hopefully catch those back from work today.'

Ruby wore a long black coat belted tightly against the cold. In the crook of her arm rested a hard A4 book in which she captured her notes. Her attractive face was framed by smooth, blonde, shoulder-length hair with a middle parting.

Temple noticed she'd touched up her make-up since he'd last seen her with fresh red lipstick. He also saw she was practically teetering in four-inch-high nude stiletto heels. Given their location, her footwear was totally impractical. He couldn't afford another member of staff absent if she snapped her ankle. She kept her head bent towards her book without looking up as he spoke to her.

'We're interested in any activity they might have heard last night or preceding nights. Especially any sound of gunshots last night.'

Ruby looked up unsmiling, still with the same wary look she had worn earlier that morning.

'I have done this before.'

Without waiting for him to respond she turned and walked away.

Eaton tried to smooth over the exchange.

'Look, boss, she knows what she's doing. If they can cover off the nearby houses tonight, we can use any new information in tomorrow morning's briefing.'

Temple was still watching her, ready to rush to her aid if she fell in her heels, but somehow, she easily navigated the uneven surface until she went out of sight.

'Ma'am turned up yet?'

'No show so far. How did you get on with the Fortunes?'

'As you would expect, Elijah lost it. Their mother, Sharnie, was in a state. They're on their way to the hospital. We'll need to take statements from them at some point.' He imagined how Munt would use the opportunity. 'Anything in the car or on the bodies?'

'Forensics have retrieved bullets; one from the footwell on the passenger side, the second from the door on the driver's side and a third, on the floor by the driver's door.'

'Three?'

'That's what they're telling me, so there may be another injury that's not obvious. And two cartridges have been found. Forensics have couriered them all off to national ballistics.'

'What about phones?'

'We've done a quick search of the car and their clothing and we haven't found any, boss.'

'They would have had phones, surely? Any drugs?'

'Nothing as yet. DC Caine's gone to the hospital with the path.' Eaton checked his watch. 'He'll start on Liam within the hour I'd have thought.'

'Let's start enquiries at the MOD and prison too . . .' Temple's mobile rang. He walked a couple of paces away from Eaton.

'Ma'am?'

'Temple, you're now SIO for the case.'

'Ma'am?'

'I've run it past Grant Lindford, he agrees. It comes with a temporary promotion to Acting DCI. *Temporary*, mind you. Congratulations, not bad for your first day.'

He registered the sarcasm in her voice. It was the last thing he wanted.

'Ma'am, I'm not sure that's a good idea. I told you I've had previous dealings with the family.'

'You said a cousin of theirs?'

'Yes, Paul King. King was released last year and then recalled to prison because he broke into my home.'

'Is King inside now?'

'Yes, ma'am.'

'And you delivered the death message to the family?'

'Yes.'

'How'd they take it?'

'To say I was unwelcome is an understatement.'

'All things considered, that's hardly surprising in the circumstances. As I see it, you investigated King years ago, he came out last year and now he's back inside, job done. He's out of the way.'

'Ma'am, I appreciate the promotion, but I still don't think it's appropriate for me to be SIO—'

'If it had been one of the Fortunes you'd put away that might be different, but a cousin, no, I'm satisfied. Besides, your knowledge of the family should give you a unique advantage which might be useful.'

'Ma'am, even so—'

Knowing she'd put him in a difficult position, she cut in. 'Look, we're short staffed until the new DCI turns up, which shouldn't be long now. I need you to step up.'

He was trapped. 'Ma'am.'

She continued. 'The enquiry will be known as Operation Mitre. Report any updates to me, day or night, text or ring. And Temple, regardless of any pre-cons that Liam and Aaron Fortune may have and the Fortune family's criminal past and lifestyle, their sons are now victims of crime. Put any prejudices regarding their past aside. I don't want to field any complaints where the family feel they haven't been treated with respect or enough resource hasn't been put in to find the killer.'

'Ma'am?'

'Look, I've got another incoming, I have to go. This is a good chance to get on side with the Fortunes. I expect you to reach out, build bridges. They need us, Temple. You might have put their cousin away, but now you can show them you can also catch their son's killer. Get into them and let's use this opportunity to change their perceptions.'

'Ma'am.'

'And I've also updated ACC Harker; he will be managing the community impact and will start with a Gold Group tomorrow, which as SIO you will be expected to attend. I'm sure you won't have a problem with that, will you?'

CHAPTER 8

Subdued, Temple turned back to Eaton.

'Looks like I'm Acting DCI and SIO.'

Eaton affected a smile. He'd heard a little of Temple's side of the conversation; the team had been on the verge of walking and if the job hadn't come in, they would have. They wanted Temple out and now he'd been promoted.

'You must have made a good first impression with ma'am Shaw, boss.'

Temple was downcast. 'I don't know about that. Whatever her reasons are for not coming over here, she's not sharing them with me. What are the rest of the team up to, Charlie?' He needed time to think.

'Stubbs is collating the pre-cons and background intel on Liam and Aaron. Too early for any word back from Tom at the hospital with the path. Clare's collating CCTV and looking for any ANPR. As you can see, Forensics are going all over the car and surrounds before it's removed to the lab for a more detailed search. They'll be undertaking a ground search for footprints, tyre marks, anything obvious. I'm also arranging for a fingertip search to take place in the morning after the car's been removed.'

Temple tried to concentrate. What Eaton hadn't mentioned was they would need to take statements from the family shortly and that point was getting nearer. Unfinished business, Munt said. Well, they had the opportunity to finish it now all right. As soon as news reached the Fortunes that he was SIO they would demand another, using their new 'victim' status to make up some cock and bull story about him being bent, offering them a gun for sale and given how the team felt, they'd be straight onto ma'am Shaw. He was on borrowed time. Only a quick arrest could change things.

'Killers always leave something behind, Charlie. We have to make sure we find it. Get the boots on the ground, as many as we can.'

A chill breeze shook the trees; under the thick canopy of branches the atmosphere felt strangely oppressive. Standing with Eaton watching the SOCOs working silently on the car, Temple drew his coat collar up.

'The local press are at the bottom of the track. They're as keen as we are to find out who did this.'

'I know, boss, but like us, they'll have to be patient. It will come.' Eaton thrust his hands deep into his mac pockets against the cold.

'Never mind being patient, we need to figure out what the fuck went on here last night, Charlie, and fast.'

'No doubt when Elijah Fortune sees his son on the slab, he'll come running to us to tell us who did it. They'll give us a name.'

'Don't hold your breath on that one. He gave no indication earlier he knew who it was and as soon as he does know who's responsible, he'll want to get to them first. He certainly won't be giving us the heads-up.' Temple started to move his neck side to side as it stiffened.

'Maybe.' Eaton nodded towards the car. 'So, what do you think, then, boss?'

Temple knew he had to form a hypothesis to frame the investigation around. 'We'll have to wait on Forensics to tell us about the bullets. If it was a single gun, then it was a single gunman. Whichever brother took the first bullet would have been witnessed by the other. In which case, who do you think was shot first, Liam or Aaron?'

Eaton took a step forward, pointing at the vehicle. 'Liam, because he's the driver and if you were the gunman, you wouldn't want him to drive away or at you. Then, the gunman walks round the front to come around to Aaron, all the time pointing the gun at him, making sure he stays in place.'

'But Aaron had his window down, so maybe he was shot first?'

'If Aaron was first, why didn't Liam drive away when Aaron was shot?'

'Why didn't either of them make a break for it?'

'Panicked, froze?'

'Or did Aaron wind his window down to talk to someone?'

Eaton spoke as he thought it through.

'In that case, maybe he was begging the killer not to shoot him. Something or someone bought them up here, a pre-arranged meet. The alternative is, it was completely random and they stumbled across someone, a stranger, who killed them.'

'And that someone would have been here with a gun doing what, if the Fortunes hadn't turned up?'

'Wrong place, wrong time? Mistaken identity?'

'Unlikely I'd say, but who knows, still possible in the realms of keeping an open mind.'

Surveying the scene, Eaton shook his head.

'Whoever's done this must have a death wish. You take one on, you take them all on. Let's face it, even cops think twice before dealing with them. I can't think of many who'd stand up to the Fortunes and think they'd get away with it, boss. Can you?'

* * *

Temple found a small gap in the shuttered window in a side room in ICU from which he could see Aaron Fortune. Elijah and Sharnie Fortune had been joined by brother Caleb Fortune and other male members of their extended family, young and old, who variously stood and sat around Aaron's bed. He watched as they exchanged worried glances, staring at Aaron and the host of different tubes and wires he was linked to that were helping to keep him alive.

'I've had to let them all in.' The constable on guard duty waved his notebook. 'The nurses wanted some of them out, but they wouldn't budge.'

'Don't worry, they're all family. At least with them in there, there's no chance of someone else going in there who's out to do him harm. You still need to stay. Do you have a replacement when you go off duty?'

'Yes, sir, it's all arranged. We'll be here until you tell us otherwise, or the situation changes.'

'Any idea when the doctors are coming back?'

'In about half an hour at six p.m.'

'Here's my mobile number, call me when they return.'

DC Tom Caine spotted Temple walking towards him as he balanced a Costa coffee and notebook in one hand with his phone pressed to his ear.

'All right, love, all right, look I have to go, not now, eh . . .'

Fifteen years in and Caine's second and younger wife was chewing his ear for a transfer. She was sick of picking up the slack at home with two under-fives and sick of the late nights and missed celebrations, as her husband worked on yet another tragedy for yet another family while he neglected his own. It was now 5.20 p.m. and she wanted to know if he was going to make his son's fifth birthday party.

'I'm not going to be there, something's come in, tell him happy birthday from me.'

Caine knew all he had to look forward to tonight was more shit when he put his key in the door and it was wearing him down. Still, he knew he would change the mood as soon as he told her he'd put in for a transfer off the team. She'd be over the moon. And the official reason he was going to give for the transfer now walked towards him, allowing him to save face with the big bosses. Better to say he wanted off because he didn't want to work with Temple, a bent officer, than because his wife was constantly nagging him. It would lend him some impressive kudos for his integrity which he could use on future application forms.

Caine silenced his phone and gestured to his coffee. 'Can I get you one, boss? Celebrate your new promotion?'

'News travels fast. No, I'm fine thanks, Tom. How's it going?'

'The path's done a quick summary report for us on Liam, he appreciates we want to advance the enquiry. He'll do a fuller version once he's tested all organs etc. He started to get a bit technical. From my notes it's pretty much like this . . .' He stooped to put his coffee cup on a low ledge so that he could flick through his notepad.

'He's confirmed that Liam's cause of death was by a single gunshot to the right side of his head, above the ear. There's one entry wound and one exit wound, cause of death was due to the peripheral damage caused by the bullet's kinetic energy as it travelled through to exit. Internally, the bullet's force fractured the skull and facial bones and caused what he termed as catastrophic injuries to the brain itself. There is evidence of glass residue in the wound, due to the close proximity of the firearm when fired. He says the gun was probably fired less than a foot away, through the door window. He'll do a kinetic energy versus velocity report, but he uses the term "high energy wound" due to the tissue damage of the bullet. However, he thinks that it's a medium velocity weapon, in his opinion, something akin to a handgun or automatic pistol, from his experience.'

'We'll have to wait to see what the national ballistics team say. Death instantaneous?'

'Yes. The bullet did the damage while travelling through the brain in a tumbling motion, hence it ending up in the offside footwell of the vehicle. The exit wound is lower than the entry wound, compatible with someone firing the gun from a standing position outside the car, causing the bullet to have a slight downward trajectory.'

'Anything else?'

'His last meal was about two hours before death. Time of death path says was approximately midnight. He's waiting for the toxicology reports to come through.'

'Find anything in his clothes? Phones?'

'No phones. There was a small bag of cocaine, enough for personal use, tucked in the front pocket of his jeans. A wad of cash in the back pocket in fifty-, twenty- and ten-pound notes, amounting to £750 plus some coins. No weapons on him. The clothes have been photographed by the CSI who came down here with me. They've bagged and sealed them as exhibits.'

'That's a bit of wedge to carry.'

'Probably small change to the likes of Liam Fortune.'

'You can finish up here now, Tom, I'll just look in on the path quickly. See you back for the evening briefing.'

Temple carried on to the mortuary in time to see Dr Tim Yardley pulling on a well-worn hacking jacket before he left for the evening.

'Good to see you again, Temple. I've spoken to your officer. Toxicology will obviously take time to come back, I have his email when they send the report through.'

'Thanks, Tim, he told me your thoughts about the travel of the bullet. Can I just confirm that there is only one entry and exit wound and nothing to indicate anything anywhere else on the body?'

'That's correct, only the head. There's more I need to do, but I concentrated on the head wound as I knew you'd want that information quick time. There's an area of "soot" around the entry wound above the right ear and glass fragments inside the wound. Your colleague said that the bullet had been fired through a car window, so that matches perfectly. The bullet has moved in a tumbling motion through the brain area in a slightly downward trajectory, exiting through the top of the jaw. This all has to do with the transfer of energy of the bullet as it is fired and how it travels through the barrel of the gun.'

'He mentioned kinetic energy?'

'Yes, I won't bore you with it at this time of day, it's complex, but should you get the case to court you may find it useful in terms of how the weapon was discharged and the proximity of the assailant to the victim. It will all be contained in my report. What I can tell you now is that the injuries sustained appear consistent with a close-range discharge of the firearm into the skull. My samples may also help should you need a match to the gun if you find it.'

'Time of death?'

'There are partially digested stomach contents — I know the remains of a burger and chips when I see it — which prove it was around midnight.'

'Thanks, Tim, that's really useful. How long before your report?'

'I need to check some velocity equations for accuracy and do a little research which will take about a week, perhaps less.'

Temple's mobile rang. The doctor was back on the ICU ward. Temple made sure to catch him as he came out of Aaron's room.

'I'm after a prognosis, Doctor, is that something you're now in a position to give?'

'We've conducted a brain scan and there's nothing we can do in terms of repairing the damage that's been done by the bullet. He's being kept technically alive due to the respirator next to him. There will come a time when we have to discuss with the family about turning the machine off. Always a tricky conversation. We'll be having a meeting later this evening with the care team to discuss when the family will be told at what stage the machine will be switched off.'

'I don't envy you that one, Doc. Just so that I understand, there's one bullet entry to the skull and no other wounds anywhere else on the body?'

'Yes, that's right, one entry and exit wound to the head, nothing elsewhere.'

'And you're sure there's no way back, that there's no chance of recovery?'

'Absolutely none. I hear his brother was shot dead beside him?'

'Yes.'

'I appreciate it's desperately sad for them, but there's nothing to be gained from keeping the machine on. There really is nothing more we can do due to the traumatic nature of his brain injuries. We have been encouraging his parents to contact as many family members as possible.'

'You might like to let us know when that conversation with them takes place, Doc.'

'Yes, of course. That will be the main topic of our meeting shortly. It will be sooner rather than later.'

'Days, weeks?'

'More in terms of hours, twenty-four or sooner.'

Temple looked into the room; Elijah and Sharnie Fortune sat either side of the bed, Sharnie's hand holding her son's. For the moment at least, they had the comfort of being able to hold him. Other family members were sitting on the end of the bed or else stood around him. He counted nine people in the tight space. All eyes were on Aaron, but from what the doctor had said, their vigil wouldn't be enough to save him.

Temple turned to the officer standing guard.

'I need more information on Liam and Aaron. As yet, none of the family are talking to us. If you hear anything from any of these people as they go in and out, make a note of it and pass it on either to me or the enquiry team.'

The officer nodded. Temple's mobile sounded an incoming text message. It was the press office with a statement attached for his sign-off. As Temple scrolled through it, the door of the room opened. He watched Sharnie Fortune step outside and close the door behind her.

She somehow looked smaller than she had done earlier. He guessed she was in her early fifties and tiny in comparison with Elijah's bulk. She looked shattered, her eyes raw from crying, her fingers fumbling with a tissue. With her head bent, her long black hair hung forward, shielding her face. As she moved away from the door, Temple seized the chance to speak to her while she was on her own. Seeing the strain of grief in her face, he spoke softly in the hope of appealing to her to help him.

'Mrs Fortune, Sharnie? I'm DI Temple, you saw me earlier. Can I ask you some questions, please?'

'I'm going to the ladies,' she said tearfully, walking off down the corridor and out through some double doors. He followed and waited for her to come out. On seeing him, she attempted to walk past.

'Sharnie, please. I want to catch Liam's killer and I need you to help me. I need to know what time Liam and Aaron left home yesterday, can you tell me that?'

She sniffed into a tissue. 'Can't remember.'

Temple walked beside her. 'Can you tell me the last time you did see them, then?'

'No. He's told me not to talk to you. We don't need the police. Elijah says he'll find who did this and make him pay.'

'Do you know who it is? Tell me if you know who it is. Sharnie, the only way to make the killer pay is to find him and put him through the courts. But I need your help. These early hours of an enquiry are really important. If you know who Liam and Aaron were meeting last night, or if they spoke of anyone, you need to tell me. We'd like to assign you a family liaison officer, someone who can help you and the family . . .'

She looked up sharply. 'No, we don't need anyone, no police, nothing.'

'It's standard practice.'

She looked at him for a moment. 'I don't care. We don't want it. When Elijah finds out who did this to my boys they're going to die.'

'That will mean you will lose Elijah too, you don't want that, do you, Sharnie? He'll go to prison if he harms anyone, you know that. If you help me, that won't happen and we'll find who killed Liam.'

She stopped walking.

'Please, Sharnie, we need to talk to both you and Elijah. Help us to find who did this. You must want that?'

'I want them back, that's all I want,' she said tearfully, her face hard. 'I want them back home. Can you do *that*?' Her voice strained as she tried to speak through her agony. 'My boy's lying down there in the mortuary. Can you bring my boy back from the dead?'

'I can't, but I *can* find the killer. To do that I need your help, Sharnie.'

She was shaking her head. 'No, no. You stop now. My boys went out yesterday morning and now I'm here. I want to take Liam and Aaron home. I don't want your questions. You can't help me. Leave me alone.'

'If you change your mind, Sharnie, you can ring me.' He pressed a piece of paper into her palm with his mobile number written on it. As she walked from him, her hand opened and he watched the paper slip to the floor.

CHAPTER 9

Guy Newland was freezing. He was discovering that Snowdonia was a bitter, unforgiving place during the winter. He'd spent the last three months holed up in the glacial, damp, god-forsaken stone cottage on a smallholding, with scrubby grass and a small piece of woodland. It was about as stark and remote as it was possible to be. The only source of heat in the cottage was a large fire in the living room hearth, which he had to constantly feed with logs.

It was minus six degrees and he had just come back inside from chopping more logs, leaving his fingers white and stiff from wielding a small hand axe. It was a chore that he took no pleasure in as he had to stand out in the freezing cold with the bitter wind running through him. The cold took so much energy from him. The fight to stay warm was a physical endurance. Softened by the Aswan sun, his body was now so stiff with cold he felt his bones would break. No matter what he seemed to wear, the arctic coldness pierced through every fibre.

There had been times when he was sure he'd die from cold in the night. No one was more surprised than he to wake up every morning, especially in January when the freezing temperature left ice on the insides of the bedroom windows.

The place chilled him to the bone. He had hated every moment since arriving there and sorely missed the intense lazy heat of Aswan. He hadn't appreciated quite how little effort it took to live there, unlike where he was now. Holed up in his miserable dank hovel, he dearly missed the warmth of the breeze from the Nile.

He could see why they had chosen this place; basic in terms of living comforts, it was designed to prepare him for the task ahead. Even the electricity was intermittent; he was constantly having to revert to candlelight when it failed and boiling any hot water required on the stove. After this, going to prison would seem like a five-star hotel. It also prepared him for the solitude. And from here, nestled in the landscape, they could easily keep an eye on him, using the natural dips and ledges of the surrounding hills from which he could be quietly and discreetly observed.

Well, almost. Once, when he'd looked out across the rocky hillside against a grey sky, he fancied he saw a glint of light when the sun peeked weakly through the clouds and glanced off the lens of a pair of binoculars. A brief shard of light in an unforgiving landscape that was otherwise wilderness, signalled that they were watching him. The special forces were widely known to train in the area and he imagined he'd been incorporated into some sort of surveillance training exercise. He suspected he was followed whenever he went on the ten-mile drive to the local pub and felt sure he recognised a man who followed him inside one evening, to be the same who tailed him in a vehicle another day.

So, for his own amusement, he had started to employ counter surveillance techniques on those journeys. He drove through a set of traffic lights too on one occasion. When he had to go outside, which was a frequent occurrence to cut the logs, he looked around, staring deliberately into the hills, letting them know if they were looking down on him, that he knew they were there.

But it was the cold that he still couldn't come to terms with. In January, it had been so bitter that he lay in bed for days, as to keep the fire going meant he had to go out in freezing temperatures. He could feel the cold weakening him, seeping into his marrow, sapping his will to live. He felt sure he wouldn't survive it, sure that he was on the verge of pneumonia. To ease things, he made sure he had a good supply of whisky. That seemed to be more effective at helping to keep out the cold than any amount of logs.

He spent much of his time alone, listening to the radio, stoking the fire and looking into the flames, preparing himself for a solitary existence in the months and years ahead. He had only a few days to wait to enact the brief he'd been given. The sooner he started his five-year stretch the sooner he'd be out. A few more days of freedom, of this rotten, half existence in the freezing cold. What had Greene said to him — something about paying for the consequences of his actions? Well, he felt he was atoning now, never mind what was to come. But before that, he'd arranged a parting gift for himself. A little something other than the fire and whisky to keep himself warm and while away the last few hours of freedom.

* * *

Temple scanned the room; a handful of uniform officers and a SOCO from the scene had joined the eight p.m. briefing at Marlborough police station. The presence of other people in the room diluted the atmosphere that had been apparent earlier, but perching on the edge of a desk, Temple sensed a smouldering resentment from the MCU team.

'OK, everyone. Thanks for your efforts today. Just a couple of housekeeping points before we start.' The room settled into silence. 'The enquiry will be known as Operation Mitre and for those who don't already know, I'm Acting DCI and SIO . . .'

The team took the news with knowing sideways nods and other non-verbal exchanges; like Tom Caine, they'd already heard it. By the looks on their faces, the news had landed like a lead balloon.

' . . . All overtime claims can be left on my desk in my office. Now that's out of the way, let's move on. As ever, the first twenty-four/forty-eight hours are crucial and everything we do in the first few days will help us progress as quickly as possible. Let's see if we can get an early resolution on this if we can, team.

'Motive will be key, so we have to consider everything. Given the location on MOD land and the proximity of the victims to the prison and with no named suspects yet, these will be lines of enquiry at this stage.

'A press release has gone out with basic information. It's really important that information and intelligence on the case stays out of the press, as the Fortunes read newspapers as a source of their own intelligence gathering. If anyone is contacted by the media, either put them on to me or the force press office. Clare, can you please monitor social media for comments now the press release has been put out . . .'

Clare Phillips looked back at him ready to mount a challenge. Temple anticipated the question she was about to ask.

'Yes, I know the press office are supposed to do that, but it wouldn't do any harm to keep an eye on it ourselves. Besides, I want any information in our time and not theirs.'

'Boss.' Clare Phillips briefly looked at Eaton who nodded in confirmation before turning to her laptop and Googling the local press outlets.

'The Fortune family have given no indication or suggestion so far of anyone they suspect of being involved. Currently, they are refusing a FLO and refusing to engage with the enquiry. I'm going to go back to the hospital tomorrow morning to try again to see if they'll talk to us. However, from my earlier dealings with them, Elijah Fortune is saying that he will kill whoever's responsible.

'I appreciate that can be seen as quite a normal reaction for a parent in the circumstances, but I think in this case, there's every possibility that he will try and carry out that threat. As we know and from my own experience with a cousin of theirs, Paul King, who's currently in Horfield

Prison, they think nothing of using extreme violence in their day-to-day activities. King terrified a number of elderly people during a spate of burglaries and fraud which is typically how they operate. Which is why it's going to be really important to keep the names of any suspects within these walls.'

Temple continued. 'So, please be aware of what you are saying and doing around the family — and the press — who may pass information, intelligence, or off-the-cuff remarks back to them. Everything that is said in these briefings and in our dealings with each other is not for public consumption.

'Once we know the result of the ballistics tests, we will be in a better position to prioritise and target our enquiries and we'll need to handle this information carefully. Any news on when the results are likely to be, Charlie?'

Eaton referred to a notebook. 'The bullets and recovered cartridge cases have been couriered to NABIS and will be fast-tracked, as much as they can be with their current caseload. From my conversations with them over the phone, they tell me they could be back with us within forty-eight hours. To any of you who don't know, unique marks are left on a bullet that are equivalent to DNA or a fingerprint in terms of determining the gun it was fired from. If we find the gun, the bullet will match it through the way it passed down the shaft when it was fired.'

'Thanks, Charlie. So, before we go around the room, be mindful of everything I've said. I know I'm stating the obvious and if that offends some of you, I'm sorry, but I think in this case, it's worth doing.' Temple looked around. 'If you can update us on what you've been doing so far — if we can start with you, Kelvin, please?'

Kelvin Stubbs turned the pages of his notebook and avoiding eye contact with Temple, looked up and addressed the room.

'According to PNC and local intel, there's a fair bit of old information on Elijah and Caleb Fortune and Georgie Munt, who is related as offspring from a sister of Elijah and Caleb. The mother, Sharnie Fortune, was previously Sharnie King, her widowed sister is the mother of Paul King. Liam and Aaron are two of five children of Elijah and Sharnie, most with precons, who, along with the six offspring of Caleb Fortune, interchange their identities when stopped by police, as well as using aliases. We're in the process of mapping the interconnecting relationships. As we know, they are an established crime family, mainly aggravated burglary, assault, theft, receiving stolen goods and money laundering. They are very active.

'To concentrate on the victims, Liam Fortune has three previous convictions for theft in the county and Aaron Fortune also has precons for aggravated burglary here too, but these go back ten years. Nothing since.'

Eaton cut in. 'The lack of convictions means they're good at what they do. Or at least, they were.'

Stubbs nodded. 'And checking with colleagues from surrounding counties, in Hampshire and Gloucestershire, they suspect the Fortune brothers were active there. The cases are reported but the evidence is inconsistent. The victims are usually elderly and make unreliable witnesses. This has helped the Fortunes evade capture for quite some time. They will have criminal associates which is being worked on and mapped as we speak.'

Temple took advantage of a slight pause. 'Thanks, Kelvin. Have we spoken to Intel regarding tasking any of their sources?'

Stubbs responded. 'All done. As soon as I get anything I'll report back.'

'Anything else? Any girlfriends?'

'No girlfriends identified at this stage and no phones were found on the victims. It's likely the killer took the phones; it's also likely they were pay-as-you-go. As yet we have no established phone numbers for the Fortunes.'

'Can you explore our options for cell site analysis from local masts?'

'I've got the experts on it.'

'Have we got a family liaison officer in yet?' asked Tom Caine.

'No. I asked but as I said earlier they've refused an FLO. They don't want to speak to us, but I'm still hopeful that may change in the next twenty-four hours.' Temple nodded towards Ruby, who turned to the room.

'Uniforms are finalising the house-to-house. It's a relatively small catchment given the rural nature and location of the scene, so I'll chase and collate these before leaving tonight. Should be ready to give you anything significant tomorrow morning.'

Eaton cut in. 'Can we make sure we ask about any CCTV cameras or Ring doorbells householders might have, anything at the church etc.'

'That's happening but nothing so far. There is a camera on one of the nearby properties but it's only a dummy. I've also managed to speak to Vera Dart, the lady who found the Fortune brothers. She's on mild medication following a doctor's visit. Everything she's told us in her statement appears to check out with the local doctor and neighbours. She's been widowed in the last year and is still a bit frail.'

'Too frail to have shot the Fortune brothers?' asked Temple.

'There's no way she's capable of that. She's clearly in shock at the discovery and she keeps asking for her dog which has still not returned. If anyone comes across her Jack Russell roaming in the woods, his name is Toby, and it would be good to get him back to her as soon as possible.'

Temple nodded. 'Scene-of-crime?'

Alison Rickman spoke to the room. 'The car has been taken off to the lab for analysis which will take a few days. The scene is being mapped in terms of entrance and exits and we've taken some ground prints of tyre tracks and footprints. We'd appreciate it if both yourself, boss, and DS Eaton could give us your shoes for imprints in the morning so that we can eliminate yours from any others we find at the scene. As soon as we have anything back from the NABIS team, we'll let you know.'

'Thanks, Alison, you and your colleagues are at the centre of this case, so it's really important that we get updates as soon as possible. Time of death has been calculated by the undigested burger and chips that Liam Fortune had eaten before going to Erlestoke Woods. There will be CCTV somewhere with the Fortunes on it from around nine p.m. that evening. Can someone take an action please to scan a five-to-ten-mile radius from the Fortunes' address for the local McDonald's, Burger King and other such outlets.'

As he finished, Clare looked up from her laptop.

'The local online newspapers are reporting the case on their front pages. A double shooting is always going to be big news. Some of them have also got it on their Facebook pages, both inviting comments from members of the public. Bearing in mind this only went out about an hour ago, there are ninety-eight comments already.' She read some of them out. '"*Whoever's done it deserves a medal, not time . . . About time . . . A taste of their own medicine . . . LOL . . . Liam Fortune's going to hell where he belongs . . .*" is the comment under that and this one, "*Don't help the police, whoever did this has performed a public service. They shouldn't be convicted.*" There's not a lot of sympathy.'

Low murmurs and nods came from those in the room.

'What site is that?'

'*Wiltshire Daily Record* website, boss, and on their Facebook page.'

He nodded. It was the rag that Sophie Twiner worked for.

'Keep monitoring, Clare, flag any you think we need to look at and we'll think about putting out another public appeal for information. Before you go, everyone, let's keep focused. The Fortunes will never win any popularity contests, but that doesn't take away the fact we need to deal with this murder in the same way as we would for any other family. If privately our thoughts echo those that Clare read out, let's keep it that way, we've got a job to do. Let's find Liam Fortune's killer. There'll be a further briefing with actions in the morning.'

The team made moves to disperse.

Eaton rolled his shirt sleeves up. 'Boss, I'm happy to take the overnight call. We've covered all the immediate actions;

we're waiting on Forensics, I'll get onto the MOD tomorrow and Kelvin has started making inroads with the prison. The scene's guarded, I've done a weather check, there's no rain due until late tomorrow afternoon so it gives us time to make some progress when we get the search teams together.'

'We need something, Charlie, anything. We need to put some urgency behind it.' Temple was convinced if they could make a quick arrest, it would take the sting out of the Fortunes.

'I understand, boss. And there's still time for them to tell us who it was. Why don't you get yourself home, I'll wrap up here?'

'I'm going to stay and have a word with the team. I need to sort this out. We can't go on like this.'

'Leave it with me, I'll speak to them in a minute.'

'It's me they've got an issue with, Charlie; it'd be better if I did it.'

Eaton held up his phone. 'Look, boss, we're part of a WhatsApp group. There are messages flying all over the place at the moment. Your promotion has got them fired up, they're really pissy. They want to see me when you've gone. I'll text you.'

CHAPTER 10

Temple eased himself on to a bar stool at the White Bear pub in Trowbridge and looked around. More shabby than the soulless chic it was trying hard to be, it looked like the locals had voted with their feet. He pulled his phone out to check for any message from Eaton. There was nothing. Perhaps he should have insisted on speaking to the team; he couldn't work without them behind him and in just one day, he faced a mutiny. All the years he'd wanted to join the MCU and it was fast turning into a nightmare.

'What can I get you?' The man behind the counter was straight-faced.

'A glass of water please.'

'Tap or bottle?'

'Tap will do.'

He turned and filled a glass, positioning a bar mat in front of Temple before setting it down.

Temple stated the obvious. 'Not many in.'

A couple sat at a table in the corner and two barflies were perched further along. He remembered a time when customers had to fight to get to the bar.

'They don't come out 'til late,' the barman replied, clearly with no interest in keeping the conversation going.

Temple took a sip of water. 'I was looking for Tara, Tara Leyton. She in tonight?'

'No.'

'Do you know when she's next in?'

'She don't work here anymore.'

'Oh?' said Temple, hoping the man would be more forthcoming. As he went to turn away, Temple tried again. 'Do you know where she's gone, did she go to another pub or . . . ?'

The man stopped. 'No.'

'Do you know why she left?'

'She wasn't well, so she packed it in.'

'Is she all right?'

The man suddenly showed irritation. 'Look, mate, she hasn't worked here for months, six months, longer.' He tapped the side of his head with his finger. 'She wasn't right up here.'

'Oh?'

'She changed, went a bit weird, crazy. Then she stopped coming in. Left her boyfriend too, apparently.'

'Zac? Does she still live locally?'

'No idea. Not interested.' He turned and walked away.

Temple left the water on the bar and walked out. If the guy was right and Tara had at last seen sense and split from Zac Finch, she wouldn't be at the flat they'd shared. It might also account for her not answering the number he had for her. But what was all that about her being ill?

He'd last seen her when she had visited Finch in hospital. Since then, he'd kept a wide berth because of all the grief with the gun. She'd helped him out of a very tight spot with the Fortunes and he owed her for what she'd done for him. He'd seen what happened to her ex, Finch, when he'd fallen foul of the Fortunes, so he knew Munt wouldn't think twice of hospitalising Tara. After all she'd done for Temple, he couldn't let that happen. He had to find her before Munt did.

* * *

As Temple lifted the latch and pushed open the door of the thatched cottage, he was greeted by the cosy warmth of the open fire. Stepping over the threshold he quietly shut the door and felt the old walls close around him like a hug. He could hear the gentle crack of the flames through the half open door to the lounge and the air held the aroma of something good waiting for him in the oven. He closed the door softly behind him.

It was always like this when she was here. She'd turned the awkward, confined space of the place he had come to hate into something resembling a home. He stood in the doorway of the cramped lounge where two women sat next to each other on the sofa. Callie St George was the first to see him and leaped up to greet him.

'Darling! So how was the first day?' She slipped her arms behind his neck, holding her hands at the back of his head, before kissing him on the lips.

'That's the nicest thing that's happened so far today.' Temple held her body close to him as her dark auburn hair brushed against his face. She made him feel like the luckiest man alive.

Their attraction to one another had been instant but the longer the relationship went on, he remained under no illusion; she was way out of his league and it was unlikely to last. It was easy for him; he adored her golden auburn hair and creamy white skin. But with her cut-glass accent, privately educated background and her father in the House of Lords, he had no idea what she saw in him when she moved in the circles she did. Maybe he was a bit of rough, or maybe it was the job; whatever the attraction was, all he knew was she was doing him good. He hadn't touched a sleeping pill in weeks.

In the few months they had been together, her nurturing personality had brought some much needed calm into his life. She loved Daisy and Ben, his children, and they returned that love in spades. She'd even managed to forge a friendship with Leigh, which following their divorce, was more than he'd managed to do. With eight years separating them, where most people his age had baggage, his was more like luggage; he regularly told himself there was sure to come a day when she would tire of that and him. She would walk one day and he already knew that when that day came, the thought of her with someone else was going to hurt. But until then, he'd make the most of things.

Callie put her head back to study his face close-up and their eyes locked. Her fingers were gently entwined in his hair.

'Well?'

'Busy,' he replied, preferring to kiss her again rather than answer questions. She felt like a prize he'd won every time he saw her. She had a wisdom and confidence that belied her lovely face. Now his hands were around her small waist; in her skinny jeans and her oversized cashmere jumper, she felt soft and comforting.

She looked into his face, frowning slightly. 'You look a little tense?'

'You look gorgeous,' he replied, as he touched her hair with his fingers, wanting to bury his face in it, but suddenly remembering Ana, the au pair, was in the room.

Callie smiled. 'A glass of wine, I think, so you can relax.'

'After the day I've had, that would go down really well.'

'Have you not had a good day?' Ana said.

Temple responded to her soft Portuguese accent which he found as endearing as her nature.

'Let's say it's been eventful.'

Callie put her hand in his. 'Ben's in bed, so come and have supper while you tell us about it.' She led him into the kitchen as Ana followed, both wanting more information.

'Has anyone heard from Leigh today?' Temple asked. 'I kept my phone on, with the volume up just in case.'

'I have,' Callie said over her shoulder. 'They've checked her dates again, she's overdue. She's got an appointment at the hospital, they're going to induce her soon. Leigh's come round to your suggestion for Daisy to stay with us while she gets herself ready and she'll drop her off tomorrow.'

'OK, any day now then. Let me know as soon as anything happens.'

'Of course, just keep your phone switched on.'

He watched as Callie busied herself at the chopping board. She looked out of place under the low-beamed ceiling of the tiny space but that was because he knew she was usually in a kitchen four times its size at the home she shared with her father which was much better suited to her culinary skills.

He undid his tie and took off his jacket. 'I'm sorry it's so late. I've picked up my first job, so this might be typical for the next few weeks. What smells so good?'

'Coq au vin,' Callie said brightly.

'We thought we'd cook something that won't spoil,' Ana replied, as she set down a table mat and knife and fork in front of him, scooping up a tendril of her dark hair behind her ears.

He watched Callie carefully dish the meal onto a plate, then snip some fresh chives over the top before delivering it to him at the table. As well as other things, she had made some welcome changes to his cuisine since she came into his life. It wasn't that Ana was a bad cook, more that Callie was Cordon Bleu trained. He wasn't even sure what it meant, but he knew that whatever he tasted was far from ordinary. His cupboards were now full of condiments, spices and foodstuffs he'd never previously heard of. He feasted his eyes on the dish in front of him with the two women sitting across the table, eager for him to speak.

'You've both eaten?' he asked.

'Yes, yes. Now, spill. Tell us about your day.' Callie was ready to interrogate, her eyes were wide in anticipation.

'Not much to tell, really.' Temple forked some chicken into his mouth. He deliberately delayed telling them what they wanted to hear, in part because he was still trying to make sense of the day himself. He also wanted to buy himself some time to work out how much he should tell them. 'This is delicious.'

Callie sat with her elbows on the table, her hands fixed under her chin.

'Come on, don't tease! Tell us about your new boss, what's she like, I want to picture her?' She was interested to learn all about the woman who oversaw a team of detectives.

'My boss? Oh, she's something else . . .'

'Really?' Callie looked at Ana wide-eyed. 'Who would you say she looks like?'

'I'm joking. We had an interesting exchange first thing this morning, I think I've got some work to do there, she didn't seem overly keen.'

'That's fine,' Callie said. 'I don't want her to be keen on you.' She reached across the table and touched his arm.

'Then, this afternoon, she promoted me to Acting DCI and I'm SIO on a murder that came in this morning.'

Callie slapped her hand on the table. 'But that's great! Promotion on day one doesn't sound like someone who's not keen on you.' Callie turned to Ana. 'That sounds more like someone I need to keep an eye on,' she joked.

Ana shook her head. 'I think you're safe, Callie.'

Temple swallowed. 'Totally safe. It sounds good, but I don't think it was meant in that way. It doesn't matter. In any case, it's only temporary.'

Callie beamed. 'What about your team?'

'They're OK,' he lied, deciding not to confide about them. He still hadn't got over them thinking he was working undercover. The whole day had turned into a baptism of fire and he was still smarting from it.

'And the murder?' Callie asked quietly. 'I don't want to know specifics — but how bad is it?' She had become fascinated by his work in the four months she'd known him. 'Unless there are children involved, in which case, don't tell me any more.'

'No, no children involved, well, not young ones any-way.' He continued to eat.

'Thank goodness.' She renewed her interest. 'So, what's happened?'

'You wouldn't sleep if I told you.' He winked at Ana. 'I'll leave you to read about it in tomorrow's rag. In fact, you can read it now, it's already online.'

Callie and Ana huddled round an iPad at the table and in a few quick clicks they were on the *Wiltshire Daily Record* website.

'My God,' said Ana, looking up at him. 'You've seen these two men today . . .'

'The poor family,' said Callie gravely, her hand at her throat. 'It doesn't bear thinking about.'

'Then don't, shut the lid down.' They ignored him, both riveted to the screen, with Callie reading out the content this time.

' . . . Two men were found at Erlestoke in a silver Ford Ranger with gunshot wounds to the head, leaving one dead . . .'

Temple stopped eating. 'Does it say that?'

'Yes. It says they are from a crime family . . .'

Callie finished reading it all out loud, as Ana re-read it on screen.

'Do you know who did this?' Ana asked without looking up.

He continued eating. 'Not yet. I think I'll have quite a few more late nights before we do.'

Breaking her gaze from the screen, Callie looked at him over the iPad. 'We have the fundraiser tomorrow night, do you think you'll make it?'

'No, you'll have to count me out. Sorry.'

'That's a pity.'

Temple finished eating and went into the small lounge, leaving Ana to make her nightly pilgrimage to her boyfriend at the Red Lion pub and Callie to pack the dishwasher. He poked at the dying embers of the open fire and checked his phone for any message from Eaton, before sitting on the sofa and opening his iPad, going straight to the *Wiltshire Daily Record* site to read the front-page article.

The piece Callie had read out contained details he was sure he hadn't mentioned in his press statement. He deliberately hadn't disclosed where on their bodies Liam and Aaron had been shot, neither had he revealed the colour and make of the vehicle and yet reading the article now he could see both pieces of information.

He scrolled up to the beginning of the article to see the author's name, '*Sophie Twiner, senior crime correspondent*'. Someone on the team clearly had a line into her. They'd ignored all he'd said about confidentiality. They were challenging his authority, or more likely, making it clear that as far as they were concerned, he didn't have any.

He had to speak to them, if only for the sake of the enquiry. If he couldn't get them behind him, if they didn't trust him and wouldn't work for him, it made his position impossible. What he couldn't understand was how he'd ended up in exactly the situation he'd helped Harker avoid when he'd bartered with him to keep his job. Given the well gossiped bad blood between them, he hadn't figured people would align him so closely to Harker, who had typically taken all the credit for catching Sloper, avoiding being tarred with the same brush. The irony of it all choked him; the idea that Harker had run a covert operation on Sloper, had been all his. What had seemed a perfectly good way to save his own neck at the time, now threatened his job with the MCU. And he only had himself to blame.

CHAPTER 11

Newland sat in a quiet nook of the small remote pub, gazing into the honied hues of a glass of Glenfiddich. Away from the main bar area and a small smattering of locals, thick granite walls enclosed him on three sides. The small space was almost dark and there was only enough room for one tiny table and one chair, which meant he had it to himself.

Looking into the liquid, he reflected on the previous evening, reliving his liaison with a blonde woman whose name he couldn't now recall. What *was* her name? How was it that he could recall every inch of her body, but he couldn't remember her name? After a while he gave up trying. He'd fucked her which was all that mattered.

After tonight, he wouldn't feel a naked woman against him for a long time. She'd been younger than he expected, but not too young. There was no pleasure for him in that. No, she'd been just right. Not too slim, kind of pretty in a plain way and happy to do exactly what he wanted. He'd unleashed all his pent-up appetites and he'd fucked her like there was no tomorrow.

All he had to do now was make sure he remembered every detail of the nearly three and a half hours they were together so that he could relive it in the coming years.

Something to keep his mind on in the future, something to recall whenever he needed, to keep him warm. Looking into his glass, he was now a voyeur, watching as he turned her in different positions and pumped himself inside her; in another blink of an eye, he gazed at her body as she sat astride, writhing on him.

There was plenty to keep him occupied and he'd need it, especially in the next forty-eight hours. He couldn't remember her name and in a short time he'd forget her face, but he wouldn't easily forget all the things they'd done together. She'd taken instruction quite well and he made sure he'd got his money's worth and then some, oh yes.

He downed the whisky and went up for another, keeping his head bowed as he stood at the bar. He decided to buy one for her, whatever her name was, drink it for her too. It was only right, after all. Ordering two doubles, he slyly eyed the only three other customers scattered at tables nearby. Who was in here watching him tonight? The customers looked like locals as much as he might be able to tell from his previous visits; it couldn't be anyone in the bar. It didn't matter, not yet. He still had the drinks to devour. He carried the two glasses back to his table in the nook, tripping slightly on the way as the sole of one of his shoes caught the unevenness of the flagstones.

He looked at the liquid levelling in the two glasses. Right then it felt as precious as gold. This was another thing he'd miss badly.

'Absent friends,' he murmured, as he emptied one of the doubles into his mouth and held it there. Making a bowl with his tongue, he savoured it, along with another recollection of whatever her name was. Then he swirled it around his cheeks, rinsing it through his teeth before swallowing.

Picking up and draining the next, he then placed one glass inside the other and sat for a few seconds more.

Suddenly, he made his move. Scraping his chair back, he pulled on his coat and walked across the flagstone floor, lifting the heavy latch on the black painted door for the last time. He walked into the dark, the cold night air hitting him as he crossed the car park, into his car. He sat there for a few minutes, watching and listening to see if anyone followed him outside. He was surprised when no one did. *They'd said it would be tonight.*

He felt sure they'd be watching him in the pub and watching him now. But after ten minutes, no one had come after him. Perhaps they could see him and were waiting for him to drive off. He put his seat belt on and started the car. Everything he did, every small act felt significant, magnified somehow. He switched on the headlights, keeping the car static. He turned on the wipers, clearing some night mist. Looking through the clear screen he gripped the steering wheel. *Why was he doing this?* Why didn't he just drive off in the opposite direction, out of Wales? Better still, get out of the car and walk off? Disappear into the black of the night. But he knew he couldn't. Because wherever he went, they would find him.

He pulled slowly out of the car park and onto the road and the five-and-a-half-mile journey back to the smallholding, through unlit dark and narrow country lanes. As he drove on, he checked the rear-view mirror constantly for signs that he was being followed. Then, three miles into his journey, in the distance behind him, headlights appeared. He drove a little further on, the headlights were still there. *Was this it?* Further still, the headlights drew closer. He was nearly home for Christ's sake. He put his foot on the accelerator. May as well make it interesting. It was then he saw it. The unmistakeable blue of a police strobe light behind him. The headlights flashed. *This was it.* There'd be no going back.

He slowed down, coming to a stop. He kept the car running as he sat. His heart was beating fiercely and his mouth was dry. He wound down the window. The police patrol car pulled up behind him. With the blue light pulsing on the roof, the officer got out of the passenger door, leaving the driver inside. He approached the driver's side.

'Evening sir. Could you tell me your name, please?'

'Guy Newland.' Newland studied the face of the person peering down at him through the open window. *Was he for real?* He looked at the uniform — it looked genuine enough, but then it would, wouldn't it?

'Could you switch off the engine, please. We've had a report that you are driving under the influence of alcohol. I have a breathalyser machine here which I would like you to blow into.' The officer produced a handheld device, showed Newland the current neutral reading and explained how it would work.

Still seated in his car, Newland did as instructed and put his lips to a plastic nozzle, pushing a long breath into it until told to stop. The officer withdrew it and they both waited.

'The breathalyser has shown a positive result, sir, which means you are over the required alcohol limit for driving. I am arresting you on suspicion of being in charge of a vehicle while over the legal limit. Can you get out of the car please, sir?'

Newland knew he was well over the limit, but he didn't feel the least bit worse for wear. Now everything happened in slow motion. He released his seat belt and got out of the car. Closing the door, he breathed in through his nostrils. He was expected to go quietly, but now, feeling the cold air on him again, other possibilities rushed into his head.

Just as it had back in Aswan, in the hotel, it crossed his mind to run. He was still in the open, until he got into the police car, the opportunity was there. He quickly weighed the situation; they didn't carry guns here, they wouldn't gun him down, not like at the hotel. Or was this particular officer carrying a firearm in case he did just that? How far would he get? It was pitch black, he could dart over a hedge, even at his age. He watched his feet move, step by step towards the officer and the waiting police car. No, it was no use. He had to take them at their word. Five years they said. God willing, he could do it.

The forty-five-minute journey to the police station at Caernarfon passed in silence. For most of the time, he looked out of the window into the darkness. On arrival, he was led to the custody suite. Now everything happened fast. He was booked in, processed. They wanted his belt, shoes. Fingerprints. Then, the all-important DNA sample. His mouth dried again at this point.

He was put into a cell. For a moment, the walls seemed to close in on him. It was how they said it would be, what they'd prepared him for. Even so, his stomach churned with the realisation he was now incarcerated. He should have made a run for it. Taken his chance while he could. Now it was too late.

He sat on the hard plastic bench and looked around him. Better get used to this, he told himself. Did he *really* deserve to be here? The last few months had been difficult. It was as far away from his life in Aswan as it could be. He missed the place. Missed his old life. Missed the heat. Now he was set to miss more than that — his freedom. For five years.

He sat back and covered his face with his hands. Suddenly, he remembered. *Melanie.* Her name was Melanie, he was sure of it. Yes! The image of her last night came back to him. He lay down and closed his eyes. He could while away the hours until daylight watching her bouncing on his balls.

Even now, Newland wondered if by some miracle or even some mistake, he might still walk free in the morning. There was always hope.

CHAPTER 12

'Stacey-Ann Millward, at fifty-four The High Street, that's the house next door but one to the house immediately to the left of the path, thinks she heard three gunshots, or something sounding like gunshots on the Sunday evening. Says she heard them as clear as anything.'

Ruby Smith had the attention of the room as she gave her early-morning update on the house-to-house enquiries to her colleagues in the MCU main office. Her immaculately applied make-up was finished with a generous layer of dark pink lipstick. Her blonde hair was fixed behind her head and she was wearing a high-necked cream blouse and check trousers. Her heels were as high as they were the day before, but taupe. It was a carefully curated look.

'Three gunshots?' Stubbs asked.

'That's what she says.' Ruby continued. 'From the house immediately to the right of the path, the occupants, Jason Freely and Ty Harris, say they didn't hear anything.'

'They didn't hear the gunshots that Stacey-Ann Millward did?'

'No.'

'And they live closer?'

'Yes. According to the officer who saw them, they said even if they knew who did it, they wouldn't tell the police. They'd seen the comments on the news websites and said whoever did it is a hero.'

'OK, anything else of significance from the house-to-house, Ruby?' Temple asked, rubbing his eyes with his finger and thumb. He'd been awake until the early hours thinking about the murder and trying to second-guess what the Fortunes would do next. It made him oblivious to the clipped tone Ruby directed towards him.

'Mrs Amelia Fernandez at The Old Bakery, High Street, says that a neighbour, Harry Staunton, has a firearm and she sees him frequently walking up the path into the woods to shoot rabbits. She mentioned it because she said it frightened her children to see him walking with a bunch of dead rabbits and a gun over his shoulder. They moved in from London six months ago. Still getting used to the rural ways.'

'It's the way of the countryside,' Eaton remarked. 'People keep guns and go shooting.'

'Tap on his door,' Temple instructed. 'Let's make an enquiry with Firearms Licensing, just to see how many in the immediate vicinity are on the register. We need to establish if he was out that night. Anything else, Ruby?'

'There was one house with no reply, the house directly opposite the entrance to the path, so we'll go back again today. We need statements taken from all those identified in the house-to-house.'

Tom Caine raised his hand. 'I'll take those actions.'

'So where are we with the MOD and Erlestoke Prison? Kelvin?' Temple looked across the room; the atmosphere was buzzing with the new information and had seemed to dilute the tension between him and the team.

Stubbs finished scribbling a note. 'Early days yet, but I've had a phone call already this morning. Apparently, due to an internal security matter, visiting orders were cancelled for the weekend before the shootings and there's no intel on the Fortunes being involved in drug dealing. The MOD were on exercise on Salisbury Plain at the weekend, towards Larkhill. I've spoken to the RMP; they've got an AWOL they're looking for at the moment. A private, five years in, been missing before. They're going to pass me all the details once they've run it past the higher-ups.'

Temple nodded. 'Any firearms missing?'

'They haven't said at this stage.'

'Check with them, Kelvin. Let's have the detail for tonight's briefing. Clare, anything to report?'

'More of the same online. The comments on the murder have increased across the website of the *Daily Record* and their Facebook page as Ruby mentioned. I've looked at some of them on Facebook and followed some back to a "communities" page where there are a number of postings about the Fortunes in general now.'

Temple nodded. 'I saw some of them last night.'

'There's not much in the way of sympathy. General consensus seems to be they got what was coming to them.'

'OK, continue to monitor it.' Temple checked his watch. 'I'm conscious that we have a search team arriving at the scene soon and I want to go out there to see them. Can we have forensics next please, where's Alison?'

Her head popped over a laptop. 'I'm here, boss. As you know the bullets have been sent off, there's no update on those yet. We'll keep pressing. We have taken a number of impressions from the ground which luckily was semi-soft . . .'

'Had it rained on the night of the shooting?'

'No, it had rained the day before and along with the dense fog kept the added moisture in the air which kept the ground soft.'

'You still want shoe prints from me and Charlie?'

'Yes, please. We've also asked for those of the paramedics who attended. We have taken some impressions of footwear, but we need to eliminate those who were initially at the scene so that we can see what we have. I think the footprints of our murderer have ultimately been overtrodden by the activity to save Aaron Fortune, that couldn't be helped. The car remains at the lab where we are continuing to test and analyse for gunshot residue and contact marks, map blood splatter etc. Likewise, the clothes and footwear of the victims are undergoing the same analysis, as are their belongings and the money found in one of the victim's possession. It's a little early for anything more at this point, I'm afraid.'

'The information from the bullets will be key, but we'll just have to wait, it seems. Can you put all the pressure you can on NABIS to get it back to us ASAP?'

'Will do, boss.'

Temple looked around the room. 'Before any of you go, I have to reiterate what I said about not speaking to the press. There were a few details that didn't go out in the press statement that still found their way into the *Wiltshire Daily Record.*'

Temple scanned the faces in the room and was met with blank stares.

'There's every likelihood that the nationals will soon pick up on the story, so I'll say it again, all press enquiries are to go through the press department. This is due to the sensitive nature of the family we're dealing with. If anyone here speaks to the press, they'll be off the enquiry. Can I make it any plainer than that?'

There was shaking of heads, along with a collective low mumble as they started to move.

'Finally, just to make you aware; the doctor will be speaking to the Fortunes this morning to tell them they will be turning off Aaron's ventilator later this evening. It's expected that Aaron will die either later tonight or tomorrow morning, at which time, this obviously becomes a double murder enquiry. Let's see everyone back here at nineteen hundred this evening, please.'

They left him talking to their backs.

* * *

The search coordinators were poring over a map to decide the parameters of the fingertip search when Temple and Eaton joined them in the mobile unit.

The sergeant peered from under a peaked cap. 'There's rain predicted for later this morning, so we want to get on with it.'

'That's not what it said in yesterday's forecast.' Eaton reached for his mobile to interrogate the internet.

Temple pointed to the scene on the map. 'This is where the car was. The obvious entry and exit point to the site is via the path, which is wide enough for one car. The path opens up at the top to a clearing in the woods, right by the old walled garden.

'Our victims will have been familiar with green roads. Whichever way they have come onto the site, they have parked at the clearing. We can start by conducting a thorough search where the car was found and then assessing what paths to take as they go into the woods.'

'I understand, boss. I'll get the men up there and get on with it. We'll want to get as much done as we can before the rain comes.'

Temple and Eaton followed the search team to the site, walking a short distance behind.

'How did your talk with the team go last night?'

Eaton looked down and watched his feet as they walked up the path. 'They want to speak to ma'am Shaw, boss; they're angry that you're here, angry at your promotion, they're angry full stop.'

It was a blow. And he wouldn't be able to count on Shaw if they approached her.

'If what they thought was true, Charlie, I could understand it, but it's not. They're putting two and two together and coming up with ten. I caught a corrupt officer in the act; it would earn some people a pat on the back. I had nothing to do with what happened afterwards when Sloper was taken into custody. And I'm not on any covert operation for anyone. I'll speak to them myself later, before ma'am Shaw gets involved. We need them to focus on this enquiry, not on their imaginary grievances.'

'They don't see it as imaginary, boss. They think they'll be tainted by association if they continue working with you. If that wasn't enough it also bothers them that whoever it is on the team you're looking at, whether that's an individual or collectively, they think they're being set up.'

'Yes, I get it, Charlie, I understand what they're thinking, but they're wrong. And their grievances *are* imaginary because none of what they're thinking actually exists. I'm not looking at anyone. They've been listening to rumours, rumours on fucking steroids.'

It was starting to spiral out of control. With all this on their minds, they wouldn't be focusing on the enquiry, and getting the Fortunes off his back with a quick arrest had to be the priority.

They'd reached the clearing and watched as the search team formed a line and started the examination of the scene. Temple and Eaton entered the walled garden.

'We'll have to cover this area off as well.' Eaton gestured the expanse with his arms. 'If the search team move quickly, boss, what other route shall we ask them to take before the rain sets in?'

Temple looked out onto four distinct paths leading in different directions. 'The killer could have gone anywhere, although if it was me, I'd have trampled across the undergrowth, to hide traces of where I'd been.

'Ask them to scope two of the paths and the adjacent undergrowth.'

Temple's mobile alerted him to a text.

He grimaced. 'That's all I need, an invite to the Gold Group meeting. That's a couple of hours that I'll never get back.'

'Rather you than me, boss . . . with Mr Harker.' Eaton whipped a quick look at him. 'I'll look after things here.'

'Keep at them, Charlie, we need something to get our teeth into. We have to come out of today with something, anything . . .'

'We'll keep grafting . . .'

Temple tried to keep a lid on his frustration. 'I'm going back to the hospital to get the latest before the meeting. Keep the search team out there for as long as possible. Ring me with anything that'll get me out of that bloody meeting.'

Eaton watched him go.

When Temple arrived at the ICU, he found that Aaron had been moved to a room in a side ward. Temple approached the PC on scene guard duty.

'The doctors have had the conversation with them then?'

'Yes, sir. He was moved earlier. The relatives have come to say their goodbyes. I understand the doctor said the ventilator will be switched off around seven p.m. tonight. The nurses say it could take him up to a further twenty-four hours to die.'

'There's a lot of people here.' Temple looked at a queue waiting to go inside. The scene guard was next to useless in the face of all the people saying their goodbyes.

'Even more have been in and gone, sir, and there are more in Costa's, waiting for those in the room to come out. I haven't been able to stop them.'

'Where's Elijah and Sharnie Fortune?'

'They're with the doctor and nurses in a room over there.' The PC indicated towards a closed door.

Temple knocked gently. Without waiting, he turned the handle. It risked stoking more bad feeling with Elijah and the Fortune family, but it could be the last chance he'd have to speak to them. Perhaps, in the company of others, they might be more forthcoming.

Elijah and Sharnie Fortune sat at a round table with a nurse and the same doctor that Temple had spoken to the evening before. Sharnie Fortune cried noisily into a tissue as Elijah tried to comfort her. They all looked up as he stood in the doorway.

Elijah didn't disguise his anger. 'Have you come to tell me you know who did this?'

'No, and I'm sorry about the intrusion but I need your help. Can I ask you both what time Liam and Aaron left home the evening before last and what they intended to do?'

Sharnie Fortune cried even louder at the question, Elijah stood up, scraping the chair across the floor.

'You're supposed to be helping us, you bastard. If you can't tell us who did this, you better fuck off. You're fucking useless. We're not answering to you or any other of your officers, so leave us alone. Leave this woman alone too.' He indicated to Sharnie. 'She told me you spoke to her. Leave her be, do you hear me? My boy's life is draining away in there . . .' His voice broke.

'All we want to do, Elijah, is progress the investigation. We really do need your help, we want to find out who did this as much as you. Liam had a lot of money on him when he died, do you know why?'

The doctor looked expectantly at Elijah.

'No, and I'll want it back. All of it. Now, no more. Not with any of us, we won't be talking. Just fuck off and leave us alone. I've told you, we'll deal with it. We don't need you.'

'Let Aaron die in peace,' Sharnie sobbed.

The doctor and nurse looked again at Temple. Now he had to speak over Sharnie Fortune's ever louder sobs.

'I want to find the killer, Elijah, all I'm asking is for some cooperation so that I can do that. We have the resources—'

Elijah Fortune cut in. 'You're not the only one with resources. Don't think I'm going to let this go.'

'Don't take the law into your own hands, Elijah, leave it to us, work with me, help us.'

'Help *you*? Why would I help *you*? I swear before these witnesses, I will find who did this.' He turned to the doctor, pointing at Temple. 'I want my family left alone. Get rid of that bluebottle standing outside my boy's room. No more police. Especially *him*. I want this man banned from coming anywhere near my boy.'

CHAPTER 13

People started to gather around an oblong wooden table for the Gold Group meeting. Temple sat near to a woman he didn't know with a laptop ready to take minutes. The door opened and he watched Clive Harker enter, proudly shouldering his new ACC insignia. Temple had gone to the MCU in a bid to keep away from Harker and here they were, in the same room. He decided he'd keep it brief and get out.

Harker looked stockier in uniform, the cloth less forgiving than his expensively tailored suits. Standing at his place at the head of the table, Temple could see that he had already relaxed into his new role; he was smiling at the people around the table, even having a short laugh with one of the senior officers present.

Harker skimmed the room, noting who was there before finally sitting down and getting the meeting underway. After introductions, he looked down at a notebook he'd placed in front of him and spoke to that rather than look up.

'Would you give us a situation report please, DI Temple?' Harker said his name slowly, typically ignoring the acting rank bestowed on him. Temple noted he was on his best behaviour; the rough Glaswegian accent normally reserved for shredding him, now manifested as a soft burr. The room fell silent as Temple spoke, all eyes fixed on him and what he was saying. He gave them the bare bones.

'The enquiry is at an early stage, however, we have conducted house-to-house enquiries, a fingertip search of the scene is being undertaken as we speak and forensic analysis is underway. Bullets have been retrieved from the scene and have been fast-tracked to NABIS, National Ballistics Intelligence Service, for analysis. I've officers working on the information from the house-to-house enquiries and we are conducting intelligence enquiries with neighbouring forces.'

Playing to his audience, Harker listened patiently.

'Do you have any suspects at the moment?' he purred, assuming the role of chief inquisitor.

Temple turned to him. 'Not as yet, sir, no. We hope to make a breakthrough in the next forty-eight hours from the results from the ballistics team.'

'Are the family engaging with an FLO?'

'No, and there's not a chance of that happening.'

Harker nodded. 'Thank you, DI Temple. Does anyone have any questions?'

'Yes.' The man from the council spoke up. 'Do we think that the rest of the Fortune family are safe? Could it be that they have been targeted?'

Temple responded. 'I asked a relative of theirs whether the shooting could be connected to any recent activity on their part, but was assured that wasn't the case. We won't know for sure until our enquiries progress. I'll be sharing my ideas with my immediate line management.'

'Do we want to increase patrols in the area, to provide public reassurance?' The man from the council looked at the ops commander, who in turn looked at Harker. He nodded.

Harker leaned forward, looking at the ops commander. 'Increase the patrols in the area where the Fortune family live, let them know we're there, as an added protection.' He then turned to Temple. 'Is there anything else you need?'

'I'm drawing on local resources due to long-term sickness and maternity leave, so long as I'm able to continue to do that, the enquiry can be resourced properly.'

The meeting was going better than anticipated. The group, including Harker, started to talk among themselves. The press officer had a question.

'Are you yet in a position to make any public appeals?'

'We asked for more information in our initial statement. At the moment there is some reaction to the shootings from the public via the local newspaper website and Facebook page, which we are monitoring.'

Harker's ears pricked up. 'And what is the local reaction?'

'There are largely negative comments, which will be down to the nature of the Fortunes' criminal lifestyle. Collectively, they are a well-known family in the community.'

Harker sat up in his seat. 'We need to make sure the comments are not inciting any action against the Fortune family, Temple. Do I have to send officers round to these people?'

'No, sir, they're just expressing how they feel to an article in a newspaper. Let's not forget the Fortunes' criminal activity, the public are reacting to that. We might not like their thoughts, but the last time I looked, people can still engage in freedom of expression, just about.'

Harker frowned. 'Make sure we monitor any website and Facebook comments for anything of an abusive nature.' He was displaying his newly formed inclusivity and woke credentials for all to see.

'We're on it, sir.'

'I can't stress enough, Temple, the Fortunes are victims here. People have to learn they can't just say anything they like on social media and there not be a consequence. We have to see the bigger picture.'

The man from the council nodded gravely.

Temple spoke. 'We'll continue to monitor the online comments, for intelligence purposes. We simply haven't got the resources to start recording all the negative comments, if that's what's required and with respect, that's not what we're here to do.'

'We could keep an eye on the online comments, sir,' the press representative spoke up.

'That would be helpful.' Harker nodded.

Temple's phone bleeped with an incoming text message.

'If we're all done, I am needed back at the enquiry.' Temple looked briefly at Harker.

'I'm not in favour of meetings for the sake of meetings,' Harker said, 'I think we've covered all we can at this stage. I suggest we reconvene in forty-eight hours.'

The people in the room started to ready themselves to leave. As Temple stood and gathered up his notebook from the table, Harker approached.

'Before you go, I'd like a word.'

They both watched the room clear and the door closed behind the last to leave. Only then did Harker speak further, the gruff offhand manner he reserved for Temple returning as soon as he was out of earshot of others.

'We have a domestic issue to deal with, Temple.'

Temple frowned. 'We do?'

'Concerning my granddaughter, Prayer.'

Temple flashed him a look; it was typical of Harker to claim her as his own.

'You see, we need to make some decisions, decisions that I'm more than happy to make, be in no doubt about that.' Harker paused, looking down. 'But my wife and daughter seem to think that you should be included.'

'What sort of decisions?'

'How we progress the current situation with Prayer.'

'And what is the current situation?'

'She wants more access to us, with a view to living with us.'

'No doubt her adoptive parents would also be interested in whatever decisions *you* think need to be made about *their* daughter.'

'Don't get smart with me.' His voice dropped to the familiar low menacing growl. 'Let me be clear, I don't give jack shit for what you think.' Harker tried to temper his ire, but always found that difficult whenever he saw Temple.

'As far as I'm concerned, you're the lowest denominator in all this. I never understood what Gemma saw in you all those years ago and don't think now, because of Prayer, that's going to change. You may well be her father, but that means diddly fuck as far as I'm concerned. But Gemma and her mother Rita are insisting that they won't talk about things unless you are there too. They want you to come to the house, so that we can get a few things sorted out.'

Harker knew he had to be careful where Gemma was concerned. The balance of power had changed since Prayer had come into their lives and for the first time in a long time, he had to prioritise Gemma's demands for fear of her taking off again and taking Prayer with her.

Suddenly the door opened and people began to enter for the next meeting. Harker turned and held up his hand.

'Out!' he barked.

The response was immediate; the people at the door quickly looked between Harker and Temple and retreated.

'Let's discuss this later. Can you come around tonight?'

'No.'

'Tomorrow then?'

'I'm not sure I've got time for it, with the enquiry.'

Harker's eyes widened. 'We'll have to discuss it sooner or later, and I'd rather it be sooner.'

Wanting to get away, Temple caved. 'I'll be there.'

CHAPTER 14

Stood down, the search team milled around outside the mobile incident van. The grey clouds above threatened rain, but it was still dry. Pulling into the church car park Temple was annoyed to find them not still searching the woods and went into the incident unit to speak to the two search coordinators.

'I thought you were staying out until it rained?'

'It's going to piss down any minute now, boss.'

Looking out of the open door, Temple saw the first of heavy drops of rain. 'You're in the wrong job.'

'When you've been doing this for as long as we have, you can smell it travelling in the air.'

'So, what did you find?'

'We have a few things for you.' The officer nodded across to a colleague.

A search coordinator held up a plastic bag containing several smaller plastic bags with various objects.

'There's nothing in that bag there,' Temple remarked, looking at them. He'd been hoping for more and it didn't seem much for all the effort.

'There's something in all the bags, boss, you just can't see it from where you are.'

'Then talk me through it.'

'We've found three cigarette butts, a hair grip, an expired credit card in the name of someone called Teresa Arnold, a used condom, a small glass bead is in the bag you said had nothing in it and the remnants of a paper tissue.'

Temple took a closer look. 'And what search parameter did all that come from?' He referred them back to the map which was laid out.

'This area here.' A red line marked a small patch on the map. 'We didn't have time to take it any further before the prospect of rain.'

'So, you'll be back tomorrow to take these pathways through the woods?'

'Yes, boss. Unfortunately, this takes time.'

'We'll get that little lot off to Forensics.'

As the search coordinators filed out, Charlie Eaton stepped through the door.

'Boss, news from scene-of-crime. They did some tyre impressions from the track leading up to the clearing. It looks as though the victims' car came up the track from the main road and therefore not via a green road. A tyre impression taken from a path near the clearing and leading into the woods was that from a motorbike, another was from a pushbike.'

'Feed that into Clare so that she can put it on Holmes, Charlie. Look, we need to give them our shoe prints, so let's go back up to the forensic tent. I want to see where they found all the tyre tracks for myself.'

They walked back to the scene and Temple pulled up the collar on his jacket against the rain. He was irritable.

'They're turning Aaron's machine off at seven tonight. A double murder, the family are hostile and we've got no fucking idea what's going on.'

Eaton turned to him. 'Meeting not go too well then, boss?'

'The meeting was fine. Time's ticking away, Charlie, and we're no further forward.'

'What if the Fortunes already know who the killer is?'

'I saw Elijah earlier. I'm pretty sure they've no idea.'

They walked on silently, up the track to the top. The forensic tent was still in situ, with two white-suited scene-of-crime officers continuing to work on the scene. Once foot-wear impressions were taken, they put on white shoe covers before going back outside and using the metal stepping plates, they walked into the clearing.

'There's a motorbike tyre mark going off into the woods along that track,' Eaton pointed. The track was the width for a single walker.

Temple nodded at their overshoes. 'Before it gets too wet, let's go and see how far it goes.'

Temple and Eaton walked carefully either side of the track, treading on the sprouting spring grass and leaf debris. The tyre impression was clear in the soft ground as they walked deeper into the woods, when suddenly the tyre mark veered off the track to the right.

'If this is our killer, it would have been dark at the time of the shootings, so he wouldn't have been able to look behind him and see the tyre tracks,' Eaton remarked.

'But he knew that he'd be leaving a trail behind him and that would be broken by coming off the path. From here, the bike could have gone in any direction. I'll go through the wood to see if I can track it, you follow the path down, just in case the tyre track appears again.'

Temple walked into the woods, sheltered from most of the rain by the mass of overlaying branches. He stopped to check the shoe protectors, ensuring they were still in place before walking further, looking for any signs of the route the motorbike would have taken. There were clumps of bushes and in some parts the undergrowth came up to calf level. As he looked into the distance to find the route the bike had taken, his foot trod on something, causing him to look down.

He stepped back. Underneath his foot was a red strap of some description. He bent down to pick it up, then noticed that it was longer than he'd thought and as he traced it with his eyes, it led into a patch of ferns. As he moved forward, tracking the red line, he saw it. Lying in the undergrowth was the torso of a small dog.

Crouching down, he saw the features in its small scull were no longer distinguishable. Something heavy had been used to crush the dog's head. The lead was attached to the red collar still around its neck. He could see a silver name disc, so reached down using a stick to lift it. It was inscribed 'Toby'.

Suddenly, Temple felt he wasn't alone. As rain dripped off branches onto the leaves on the ground, he heard the crack of branches. He stood up, looking around. There was no one there. He looked back down to the dog.

'You all right, boss?'

Temple jumped. 'Where the fuck did you come from, Eaton?'

Eaton grinned. 'I could see *you*, boss, then you disappeared.'

'Down there.' Temple nodded towards the ground.

Eaton looked. 'The dog.' He moved closer, moving some blades of grass with his foot. He looked back at Temple. 'You said you wanted a lead, boss.'

Temple ignored his attempt at humour. 'Charlie, get onto the helicopter and get them up here with some heat-seeking equipment.'

'Boss?'

'You know what this means? The killer was here after the murder when Vera Dart was walking her dog.'

CHAPTER 15

'Keep the element of surprise at all times. That's the way to deal with people. Some of them can be a bit lively and want to fight back.'

Georgie Munt's face was set in a hard mask. The kids needed some distraction from their cousins' shooting. And there was a way for them to channel their feelings right now which they might put to good use in the future.

'Go in hard and fast. Frighten them.' Munt undid his shirt and exposing his body, he pointed. 'You punch them hard, right here. This is the solar plexus. It'll do for them every time, you'll get no trouble after that. It'll take the wind out of them.'

Two young boys not yet in their teens approached him. 'Right there?'

He took their fists in his hands and positioned them on his body. 'In there. And besides, when they're old they've got brittle bones, they break easily. Remember, they're like babies, really soft.'

'Same with a woman?'

'Women are even easier. You slap them. Hard. Right in their face.' He indicated with his hand.

'That works?'

'The harder the better. Catches them off guard. Once you've done that, grab their hair and pull it back, yank their head down. It's all you need to show them you're in control. Then they'll do anything.'

'What if it doesn't work?'

'It will. They care about their face and hair, so that's what you attack. If she fights back, punch her in there.' He indicated to his abdomen, his face twisting. 'It'll finish her.'

The two boys looked at one another and sniggered.

'Any trouble, push them to the ground. Guaranteed to break a hip or leg, they'll be in so much pain they'll be whimpering like a dog. Then you can kick the bastards. Just don't stamp on them, because that'll leave a mark. That'll get you ten years if they find your shoes. Always get rid of your shoes.'

'Have you ever been inside, Georgie?' asked one of them, his face animated from his lesson.

He took a moment before replying. 'I have and believe me, it's not somewhere you want to go. You can't get out until you've done your time, you're trapped. Like Paulie. It's to be avoided at all costs, d'you hear me, all costs. Don't let them catch you.'

One of the boys looked down at his feet before cocking his head to the side. 'What about Liam and Aaron?' he said quietly.

'Leave that to me.'

'But whoever's shot them has got away with it . . .'

Munt lowered his voice. 'No one's got away with anything. And no one *will* get away with it.'

'What will you do to him when you find him, Georgie?'

'Oh, we've got something really special lined up for that.'

* * *

Eaton stood writing on a whiteboard as Temple was about to start when ma'am Shaw breezed through the door for the evening briefing. The room was full of a mix of the MCU, forensic and uniform officers all in individual huddles of conversation.

'Hello, team. I just thought I'd come over and see how we're all getting on.' She smiled.

Temple quickly glanced at Eaton before she made a beeline for him. Gazing at him through her thick lenses, he found the distortion of her magnified eyes disconcerting.

'How's it going?'

'I was going to ring and update you with a few developments after this evening's briefing, ma'am.' He hadn't factored she would turn up. He was going to speak to the team before they went home tonight in an effort to head them off taking their grievances to her. Perhaps they'd already been in touch with her, maybe that was why she was here. But there was no indication by her smiles she was here for a showdown.

'Well, now you don't have to. I hadn't heard anything from you, so I thought I'd stop by on the way home. Thought you and the team might want some . . . moral support.' She looked round the room. He tried to take the measure of her words, but she wasn't giving anything away.

'We're just about to start if you want to take a seat, ma'am.'

Keen to get underway, Temple raised his voice.

'OK, if we're ready, please.' The room fell silent. 'If I can start by informing everyone that I have just had a text from the PC at the hospital to say that a few minutes ago, Aaron Fortune died, the machine keeping him alive having been turned off. This is now a double murder investigation.'

Tina Shaw looked up at him sharply as he paused briefly to let the information sink into the room.

'If it wasn't already enough of a challenge, Elijah Fortune made it clear to me today that the family will not be engaging with anyone from the enquiry. This is obviously a sensitive time for them, so I still hope they'll change their minds in the following days and weeks.'

Sitting alongside him, Tina Shaw turned. 'Did you speak to Elijah Fortune personally?'

'I did, ma'am.'

'Did you offer an FLO?'

'I did, they refused.'

'We'll speak after the briefing.' She turned to the team. 'We need to continue to try and engage with the family for a number of reasons, not least of which to give them confidence in our investigation and to get their help. Perhaps we might try a different approach.' She turned her attention back to Temple. 'Perhaps a female officer might reach out to his wife, see if we can get her on side?'

'They are pretty adamant, ma'am. Sharnie Fortune does as Elijah tells her, but if you think it's worth a try, we'll look at it. From what Elijah said to me at the hospital, they seem to think they can take this on themselves. We mustn't lose sight of the fact that this is a hardened crime family we're dealing with.'

Tina Shaw snapped back. 'Let's also not lose sight of the fact this is a grieving family. Perhaps there are other barriers we need to negotiate and break down. Perhaps with the death of Aaron, they might open up to cooperating.'

Temple couldn't help himself. 'We're not dealing with the Von Trapps here, ma'am. This isn't about a failure on our part to engage. The Fortunes are never going to let an FLO have access to the inner workings of their lives.'

Eaton spoke up. 'We'll think of a way we can make an approach, ma'am, perhaps send Ruby in to speak to them.' He nodded across to Ruby.

Temple continued. 'Moving on. Today, we discovered Vera Dart's dog. It was found in the woods, with its head crushed. Needless to say, Mrs Dart was heartbroken when she was given the news.'

The team quickly exchanged views before Temple continued.

'This could be significant. It's possible the same person who shot Liam and Aaron also killed the dog. The killer may have remained hidden, keeping a watch from the woods after the murder, or left the scene and returned in the morning.

Vera Dart was an early riser and she took her dog for a walk before eight a.m. I think the dog ran into the wood and located the killer. Vera Dart said in her statement that she heard the dog bark. I think the killer silenced the dog to stop her going to find it. If Vera Dart had followed the dog into the woods, she might have been killed too. She had a lucky escape. The dog lead and collar has been given to Forensics. It gives us another dynamic to consider; why the killer returned to the scene or why they stayed to keep watch.'

The room remained silent. Tina Shaw was listening intently. 'It's an interesting theory.'

'We know some killers return to the scene.'

'Perhaps we need to get some offender profiling . . .'

'It's a bit hit-and-miss, ma'am, in the early stages, the profile tends to end up so wide it could fit any one of us . . .'

'Even so, I'll get on to the NCA, see if they can help. We can't take the risk of not using it should our offender turn out to fit the profile.'

Temple remained unconvinced but he acquiesced. 'Ma'am. Can we now have an update from Tom, please.'

Caine was ready. 'I took a statement from Stacey-Ann Millward this morning following her comments to the house-to-house team. There's not much more than she told them. She said she was in her back bedroom with the window open when she heard three shots. She says she heard them about eleven thirty p.m., which puts it in the realms of the time of death of Liam Fortune.

'She says they followed each other with a slight gap between. She likened it to an exhaust firing, which is what she thought it was. She says she can be certain of the time as she remembers looking at her watch. I asked her if she had seen or heard anyone going to and from the path, but she says all she heard that evening was what she now knows to be the gunshots.'

'Thanks, Tom. The timings are consistent with the time of death given by the path. Right, Kelvin, what have you got for us?'

'In answer to your earlier query there are no firearms missing from the MOD. I've tasked more sources to see if we can find some intelligence on the Fortunes and any reason for Liam and Aaron being at Erlestoke Woods that night. It might turn something up in time for tomorrow night's briefing, boss.'

'Quick as you can, Kelvin, we need to find out what the word is. Is there anything else tonight, people? Right, don't forget what I said about the press, there are to be no briefings. DS Eaton will be giving out actions, that's all for tonight, team, thanks for your efforts.'

Everyone stirred. Temple was keen to speak to them before they left, but with ma'am Shaw there, he'd have to wait. He turned to reassure her.

'It's still early days, ma'am, we're not quite forty-eight hours in. And without any cooperation from the family, we need time for evidence and intel to starting filtering through. We have a meeting with the forensic team in the morning so I'm hopeful that that will give us the leads we need to start making inroads.'

To his relief, Tina Shaw put on her coat. 'Glad to hear you giving people a warning about speaking to the press.'

'A couple of things appeared in the local rag that I didn't authorise.'

'Oh?'

'Nothing drastic, just two details but information is getting out.'

'I don't have to remind you about our conversation already, do I?'

'No, you don't, ma'am. But someone in the room's got a line to the local press and I've made it quite clear that if it happens again, they're out.'

She arched a single eyebrow at his comment. 'I updated ACC Harker earlier, he told me about the Gold Group meeting. Said they were going to put on extra patrols where the Fortunes live.'

'For community reassurance and just in case they are being targeted. Elijah Fortune says he will kill whoever has shot his sons. At least increased patrols might make him think twice, but I doubt it. He seemed pretty convincing to me.'

'An eye for an eye isn't going to help the situation. Pity you haven't been able to get them to cooperate and get a FLO in there. As SIO, you need to try a bit harder with them. We don't want to lose them at this stage.'

'Not engaging with the police and taking matters into their own hands is in their DNA. The best way to take the sting out of the Fortunes is to find the killer.'

'We still have to do all we can to continue to try and engage with them. They've lost two sons, they won't be thinking straight. We really need them onside.'

'I hear you, ma'am. We'll keep trying.'

She paused while she looked in her handbag for her car keys. 'I also don't have to remind you that resources are finite, budgets need to be controlled.'

'No, ma'am, I am aware.'

'For this case there's more if you need it.' She adjusted her bag on her shoulder. 'I'm chasing the new DCI's appointment. I'm hoping DCI Patel can be here by next week. As soon as she starts, she can take over as SIO. Perhaps she'll have more luck with the Fortunes.'

Temple stared at her back as she walked out of the office door.

'Thanks for the vote of confidence, ma'am.'

Ready to tackle the team, he looked around. The only people left in the office were a few of the uniform and forensic officers. The MCU had left.

CHAPTER 16

He'd badly needed to speak to the team before they went to Tina Shaw but getting them on their own was proving difficult. Their grievance towards him distracted them, wasting time and energy they could use to focus on the enquiry. He wouldn't be able to stay on the MCU if they had no confidence in him and that's what they would tell her if they got to her before he spoke to them. If he could speak to them and they could get a quick arrest, it would change everything.

He brooded on ma'am Shaw's comments about not losing the Fortunes as he drove home. Like a red rag to a bull, he'd lost the Fortunes the moment they saw him, before he'd managed to say a word. At least all the time the Fortunes refused to speak to anyone else they couldn't drop him in the shit. It gave him more time. But not much. They were bound to want to talk soon if there was no progress. He hated to admit it, but things were closing in and fast moving out of his control. There was also something else he had to do.

Enquiries in and around Trowbridge to find Tara had drawn a blank, but he knew it would only be a matter of time before Munt would seek her out. The sooner he found her the better.

Temple lifted the latch on the cottage. He hadn't seen Daisy for a few days and he wanted to make sure she was all right, especially with Leigh's new baby due any day, but by the time he arrived home he'd left it too late to catch her before Ana put her to sleep in his bed. With him now home, Ana went to the pub.

Having checked both the children were sleeping soundly, Temple poured himself a glass of red wine and sat on the sofa next to the duvet and pillow that Ana had put out for him. With Callie at a charity event, the place wasn't the same. With nothing to stay up for, he arranged the pillow and shook out the duvet, kicking off his shoes and getting himself ready for his makeshift bed. He gulped his wine and turning off the lamp to his side, he took off his shirt and trousers before covering himself with the duvet.

* * *

'Daddy! Daddy, wake up. Daddy!' Daisy pulled at Temple's arm to stir him on the sofa. Despite the awkwardness of his position with his legs dangling off the end, he was in a deep sleep.

'Daddy, please!' Daisy was desperate and landed a punch to his chest. He woke with a start.

'What is it, Dais?' He tried to prise his eyes apart, but it was as though they were glued together. Gradually through half open eyes he saw her by the side of him in her pink flamingo pyjamas.

'Someone's trying to get in.'

He sat up. '*What? Where?*'

He could see her eyes were like saucers. 'In the kitchen. I could hear someone outside. I came down the stairs and the door handle was moving. Someone was trying to get in.'

He leaped up in his boxer shorts and taking Daisy by the arms he sat her on the sofa.

'Stay here.'

In the dark, he went into the kitchen. It was silent. He looked across to the clock: 4.37 a.m. He tried the handle of the back door. Still locked. He took the key from a nearby drawer, unlocked it and went outside. Barefoot, he stepped out onto slabbed patio. It was pitch black and freezing. He looked around, his eyes adjusting to the darkness in the garden. There was no one there.

Temple went back inside and locked the door. He went back to Daisy and pulled his shirt on.

'There's no one there, Dais. Tell me again, what happened?'

'I heard someone outside,' she insisted.

'What did you hear exactly?'

'Like someone trying to come in the door.'

'I didn't hear anything.'

'I was in bed and I heard it,' she insisted. 'I came down and went in the kitchen and the door handle was moving up and down.' He followed her as she started out to the kitchen to show him.

'Are you sure?'

'Yes.' Daisy pointed at the door.

'You actually saw it?'

'Yes.'

He pulled out a kitchen chair and sat on it as Daisy stood in front of him. 'Are you sure you weren't dreaming?'

'No, Daddy, I saw it moving. It was going up and down and I saw someone outside.' She was adamant. 'I saw someone trying to get in through the kitchen door. Then I ran and got you.'

'What did they look like?'

'I couldn't see in the dark.'

He drew her to him and hugged her. Had she heard someone, he would have heard it too, surely?

'You nearly gave me a bloody heart attack, Dais. There's no one there, no one at all. But you should have come and got me first before going to the door. If you ever hear something like that again promise me you will come and get me first?'

'Yes, Daddy.'

'Are you all right?'

'Yes,' she said quietly and snuggled into him.

'Anyway, what were you doing awake, Dais?'

'The noise from outside woke me.'

In an effort not to worry her he made light of the situation.

'You'd have probably flattened them if they'd come in anyway. Now, show me the best defence move that you've been learning.' She leaped up and playfully demonstrated what she'd learned in Taekwondo.

'That's good, they'd have had no chance with you, Dais.' He kissed her head. 'You haven't got anything to worry about, you know that, don't you?'

She looked down at the floor. 'Mummy's going into hospital . . .'

'And she'll be fine. Then you'll have a new brother or sister.' He looked into her face as he said it and the realisation of what it would mean hit home. Leigh had said it enough and she meant it; she and Daisy would move away, a long way away. Alone together for the first time in a long while, Temple and his daughter suddenly shared that knowledge without speaking and the pain of that departure. Daisy flung herself into his arms and they hugged one another tightly.

'You'd better go back to bed, Dais. Come on, I'll take you up.' He walked with her up the stairs and tucked her back into bed.

'I want to stay here with you, you and Callie and Ben,' she said quietly.

'I want you to stay too, sweetheart.' He kissed her. 'We'll work it out, Dais, I promise.'

She smiled at him and turned onto her side.

Before going back downstairs, he carefully lifted the latch on Ben's room and put his head round the door; he was sleeping. He stood outside Ana's room and could also hear her sleeping.

Making himself a cup of tea, he waited by the kitchen door, looking out into the darkness of the garden while the kettle boiled. Had Daisy really seen someone trying to get in? If she'd seen the door handle moving, why hadn't she screamed? He would have heard her and been able to run outside and catch whoever was there.

Perhaps she hadn't seen anyone at all. Perhaps with the baby on the way, she just wanted him to know she was there. He'd ask Eaton to cover the weekend for him; at least he could make sure he spent time with his daughter.

CHAPTER 17

Eaton put his head round the door of Temple's office.

'Boss, SOCOs are here. We're in the main room. They've got some news.'

Two female crime scene investigators sat at a table talking through papers in front of them when Temple and Eaton joined them.

'We have the ballistics information,' one said, putting on her glasses.

Temple was eager to hear. 'Let's have it. I can't speak for you, Charlie, but please explain in Janet-and-John language for me because it's important I understand this and get it right.'

'Of course. We'll take each of the victims in turn and start with Liam Fortune. He was found in the driver's seat with a bullet wound to the right side of the head, above the ear. From his position, we know he was approached from outside the car. The window was wound up and a gun was fired through the window. We have confirmed this from conchoidal fractures in the side window glass from the hole caused by the bullet . . .'

'Wait a minute,' Temple was writing. 'What did you say?'

'Conchoidal.'

'And by that you mean the spidery cracks that you get when a window is impacted?'

'Yes, that's right.'

'OK, carry on.'

'The bullet appears to have entered the victim and exited into the footwell on the passenger side where it was retrieved. We'll call this bullet A. The shell casing was found underneath the car, behind the front right wheel, near to where we think the suspect was standing when they fired the shot and we've also recovered another shell casing. We haven't found a third.

'In relation to the passenger, Aaron Fortune, he was shot in similar circumstances with a single bullet to the left side of his head. The window of the car was wound down in his case. However, two bullets were retrieved from the footwell in the driver's side and we're calling these bullet B and bullet C. Again, there was only one wound, but two bullets were fired. Bullet B is different from bullet C inasmuch as it's fairly intact as it hasn't gone through the body and has only come into contact with the inside of the vehicle. What ballistics have been able to tell us is the striation marks on all the bullets are the same.'

'Which means?'

'That all the bullets were fired from the same gun. As you probably know, the striation marks made in the barrel of the gun during manufacture when it is rifled, imprint on the bullet as it travels through. Each barrel will have its own unique markings when it's rifled, so any bullet fired can be uniquely traced back to a particular gun.'

Temple and Eaton exchanged glances. 'Can you get fingerprints from the bullets?' asked Eaton.

'There's some new technology and we've submitted the bullets and cartridge cases for DART testing.'

'DART?'

'Direct Ammunition Recovery Technique — in basic terms it will look for a DNA profile. Before DART, a fingerprint or DNA such as sweat wouldn't survive the intense heat of the firing process. Once fired a bullet can lose its shape as it comes into contact with the blunt object it's fired at. It can mean there is little left to examine. It's new technology so we'll see what comes of it.'

'And the gun? Can you tell us what gun it was fired from?'

'The message is they are just waiting for one of their team to come back from leave tomorrow to confirm. They think they're sure but don't want to say until they can be a hundred percent.'

'So did they say what they thought it might be?'

'No.'

'OK. Is there anything more?'

'We're in the process of documenting all this for when you bring your suspect to court. We're still examining the clothing and matching blood spatter to the wounds of both men, as well as that on the inside of the vehicle. But in basic terms, it's all as we've just outlined. If you recover the gun, we'll be able to match it to the bullets and, of course, harvest more forensic information from the gun itself. As soon as they let us know, we'll ring you tomorrow and tell you exactly what gun you're looking for.'

'And the cigarette butts found at the scene?'

'We're on to those, they might be waiting for us when we get back to the office.'

With the forensic team gone, the main office door opened and Clare Phillips came in, holding her laptop.

'I just wanted to wait until the forensic team left, there's something you need to see.'

'What is it?' Eaton asked.

'The *Wiltshire Daily Record* have the story on their front page again today.' She put her laptop in front of them. The online banner headline read '*Cops Search Wood*'. The byline under that was '*Dead dog discovered in search*'.

Temple was instantly annoyed. 'Unless Vera Dart is speaking to the press, which is highly unlikely, how would they know about the dog? We only discussed that in last night's briefing. Despite everything I've said to them, someone on the team is briefing the press.'

Eaton attempted to calm him. 'If there were any press bods there yesterday, they could have picked it up from one of the onlookers or neighbours.'

'I hope you're right, Charlie, and it's not one of ours.'

Clare interrupted them. 'But that's not what I was showing you.' She scrolled down to the comment sections. 'Word on the street is the Fortunes have put out a bounty on the killer.'

CHAPTER 18

They hunched around the screen to read the online comments section and the message that Clare was pointing to. Interspersed among the other threads, two people were having a conversation:

Caj: Fortune's offering £50k.
Mdog: for information?
Caj: DOA. COD.

Eaton looked at Temple. 'Genuine?'

'I hope it isn't, but it's there in black and white. Through these two jokers, Elijah Fortune's putting out a public appeal for information.'

'It might be all talk. Something someone's just put out there.'

'It could be. But you didn't see Elijah when I told him Liam was dead. We can't ignore it. Speak to Stubbs, see if he knows about it and if not, see if he can find someone who does. If this is what the Fortunes meant by them dealing with it, we'll have to pay them a visit.'

Temple started dialling his mobile.

'Good work, Clare, well done for picking that thread out among all the rest. I'll ring the *Record* and see if we can find out who "Caj" and "Mdog" are. Keep monitoring it.'

Clare listened intently. 'Will do.'

Sophie Twiner would drop most things for a call to meet with Temple and within half an hour he was letting her into the main entrance and into a small side room.

'So, what's it about?' Twiner scanned his face. As she sat down, she put her shoulder bag by the side of her chair before looking up at him.

'Are we talking Op Mitre — that is the operational name for the double shooting, isn't it?'

'You seem to be well informed, as ever.'

'Or is it Op Acre you want to see me about?' She took a notebook out of her bag. 'Do I have to use this, or can I record you?' She held up her phone.

'Notes, if you don't mind.'

Temple could see she had clearly made an effort that morning, wearing an expensive-looking bodycon dress which flattered her lean gym-toned frame. She looked across at Temple who was now sitting opposite her and after slipping her coat off her shoulders, she swept her long blonde hair to one side, before resting her elbows on the table.

'I want to talk about Op Mitre. This won't take long,' Temple told her.

'I'd heard you've been promoted, lucky you.'

He frowned. 'The promotion's only temporary, it serves an admin purpose, nothing more. And who told you anyway?'

'Oh, you know, a *source*,' she said coyly. 'So, how can I help you?'

'There's a few things actually. Firstly, I need to know who's feeding you or your editor, Rob Carroll, the headlines regarding Op Mitre.'

'Now that would be very bad manners. Just because *you* do your best not to speak to me, thankfully others don't feel the same way.'

'Is it a police officer? Just tell me that.'

She feigned horror at the suggestion. 'No, I won't.'

'Please, Sophie?' She was different than when he'd first met her. She'd been self-assured enough then all right, but now she was flying. She was still in her mid-twenties but lately seemed to have assumed an air beyond her years and experience.

'I might be persuaded in the right circumstances,' she said softly, holding his gaze.

She was irritating him. 'This isn't a game. It's serious, someone could be put in danger.'

She looked as if she was giving it some thought, as if she was about to cave. He watched her. It was going to be easier than he thought. She pulled back.

'No, I can't. Look, what I can tell you is, it's not me they're talking to. It's Rob. Take it up with him, but I tell you now, the response will be the same. You know how it works.'

He couldn't tell if she was lying. 'Sophie, I just wanted help from either you or Rob before the paper ends up making an already bad situation even worse.'

Her smile disappeared and she set down her pad and pen on the table in front of her.

'You can't stop people giving us information. Rob won't be party to that.'

He noted the easy and authoritative way she spoke on behalf of her boss.

'Just think about what you're doing before you publish.'

'Anything else you'd like me to do?'

'Yes, there is. Can you tell me if the paper is able to identify the readers who leave comments?'

'Everyone has to register but they give fake details nine times out of ten. They hide behind the anonymity their online identities give them. What's the problem?'

'Someone has left a comment on the article.'

She sat back in the chair defensively. 'Oh? So you're joining the rest of the thought police now, are you? The chief's going to join the rest of the idiots in extending police powers to what people are allowed to say?'

'Just hang on a minute. It's not about that. Most of the comments are from the public giving their views on the

Fortunes, I haven't got a problem with that, they're entitled to their opinions. That's not what I'm on about.'

'So?'

'A comment's been posted that suggested the Fortunes have put out a fifty-grand bounty for the killer, dead or alive, cash on delivery.'

Her eyes widened. 'You don't think it's true, do you?'

'Off the record, there might be something in it.'

'We're not responsible for what people post online . . .'

'Look, because of the people we're dealing with, this situation has the potential to escalate.'

'So, what do you want?'

'I'd like you to remove the comments about the fifty grand pronto and provide the details of who posted them.'

'I'll have to speak to our bods in IT. And so I end up doing you yet another favour.' She looked at him with a wry smile.

'Sophie, we're professionals, aren't we?'

'When it suits you, it seems.' She hesitated for a second, dropping her voice. 'For one night we were lovers, or had you forgotten? No, of course you haven't. How many people know *that*? You were very keen that night, drunk but keen.' She leaned forward, biting her bottom lip. She hadn't given up on a repeat performance, even though he'd been very cool towards her since, despite her help with Op Acre. 'As I remember, you particularly liked the way I . . .'

'Sophie . . . please?' It had been a mistake to appeal to her, he should have gone to Rob Carroll instead. Now it was time she went.

'We all work on favours, not just you . . .' she started.

'If we're talking favours, I think we're more than even on that score. I could accuse you of cynically targeting my uncle Richard to get the story on Op Acre to increase your currency and enhance your career. I hear there's talk of a media award for you?'

The smile was back. 'There is and promotion. I don't think Richard Temple has any complaints. He's very happy.

The pieces I wrote had influence, got your investigation reopened. Yes, I benefited from it too, so as I see it that's a win-win all round.'

'Like I said, I think we're even. It's up to you, Sophie. I'll be recording that I've made a formal approach to you and the newspaper and asked you to be responsible in your reporting and to remove the comments I told you about.'

She leaned to the side to retrieve her bag and stood up. 'I don't think we need any lectures on responsible reporting. I'll pass on what you've said to Rob.' She put her coat on. 'It's always nice to see you. I'll contact Callie next week, see when she's free for a coffee.' She knew that would annoy him. 'She doesn't know about us, does she?'

He tensed slightly. 'There was and is no "us", Sophie, so there's nothing to tell.'

'Thought not.' She smiled at him. Her friendship with Callie had been born out of the contact and article she had written about Op Acre, even so, it wouldn't stop her taking an opportunity with Temple as and when it came her way again — and it would. Persistence had paid off before. 'You need to lighten up,' she said brightly. 'See you soon.'

Winking at him, she brushed past and out of the station.

Upstairs in the main office alone, Eaton greeted him with a lukewarm cup of coffee.

'We've just found CCTV of Liam and Aaron at McDonald's in Trowbridge almost two hours before they were shot. I've looked at it, boss. They were alone in the car and got the burgers at the drive-through. Then, they parked up in the car park, ate the burgers, dumped the rubbish in the bin and sat in the car a bit longer before driving off. No one followed them. At least we know what location they came from prior to Erlestoke Woods and what time they left.'

'Did they pay cash?'

'By the looks of it. I'm getting the other ANPR sites in the vicinity checked now. We've also organised a further search of the woods, starting in about an hour. How did you get on?'

'Waste of time. I was hoping she might tell me who was giving her information on the case, as well as take down the reference to the fifty grand online. She was having none of it.'

'You must be losing your touch, boss.'

'I'm losing something, Charlie, mainly my patience.'

'Let's do as ma'am Shaw suggests, boss. Let's put Ruby to the Fortunes, see if she can get into them.'

It was unlikely to succeed but Temple had to show willing. He couldn't ignore Tina Shaw's request as much as he wanted to. Trouble was, if Sharnie Fortune or Munt did speak, Ruby would come back with far more than she bargained for.

'Suppose it's worth a try. She might get Sharnie Fortune to come across. For all we know, while we're scrabbling around trying to work this out, Elijah might have a good idea who it is he's looking for. Especially if his attempts at offering money for information are successful.'

Temple's mobile sounded.

'Just to let you know, we drove the exhibits from the line search over to the lab. One of the cigarettes is a match for Aaron Fortune, for the other two no matches on the DNA database.'

Temple relayed the information to Eaton.

'That was the reason Aaron's window was wound down, he was having a fag and when he was finished, he flicked it out. The search team indicated they found it within the vicinity of the car, on the passenger side.'

Temple's phone rang again.

'Tom Caine, boss. I've got something for you.'

Temple could hear the excitement in his voice. He put his mobile on the desk on loudspeaker.

'Let's have it, Tom.'

'I've just stepped outside from speaking with Harry Staunton, the old boy who lives in the village, who one of the neighbours saw with rabbits over his shoulder and his gun. He lives here alone, his wife died a few years ago. He's seventy-four. We had a chat and he let me have a look at where he keeps his guns. According to Firearms Licensing, he has a shotgun which he says is for shooting clays and the like and a.22 air rifle.'

'So far, so normal?'

'That's what I thought, but listen to this. We're talking about his guns and he suddenly says there was another gun, but he's lost it.'

Temple looked across to Eaton. 'Go on.'

'He then went on to tell me that his grandson, Matthew, was in the army. When he left the army in 2014, Matthew started to visit him regularly and when Staunton's wife died, they became close. One day, Matthew showed him a gun. Said it was a war trophy, that he'd brought it back from Afghanistan as it saved his life. Harry Staunton said his grandson gave it to him to keep at the house, so Staunton wrapped it in a scarf and hid it away. Then he says he went to find it one day and it was gone. He looked around for it but hasn't seen it since.'

'Did the grandson take it back?'

'He says no.'

'How can he be so sure?'

'The grandson's dead. He committed suicide, hanged himself nearly two years ago. Staunton said he suffered for years from some kind of PTSD from his service in Afghanistan.'

'What was the gun?'

'He said Matthew told him it was US army issue. Says he'd know it if he was shown a picture of it.'

'US — United States?'

'Yes.'

'Was the grandson American then?'

'No, he served with the British army. He told his grandfather that he was out on a joint operation with US, Canadian and other forces in Lashkar Gar in Afghanistan when he found himself running down a muddy goat track. He said he got into some trouble and then got cut off from his unit. He said he was saved from certain death by a Special

Forces US marine who shot a Taliban sniper aiming for him. In the aftermath, the marine tossed the gun over to him so that he could see the weapon that saved his life, only for the marine to get shot in the head by another sniper. He said his grandson escaped, taking the gun so that he didn't leave it behind for the Taliban. As it saved his life and cost the life of the man who saved him, he kept it and smuggled it back.'

'And when did Staunton last see it?'

'He doesn't remember. But a few months ago, he says he blocked his kitchen sink and couldn't fix it himself and had to call in a plumber. He'd hidden the gun under the sink so knew he had to move it before the plumber arrived. When he went to find it, it was gone.'

'Could he have put it somewhere else?'

'He says no.'

'And he never reported it missing when he couldn't find it?'

'No. He said he hadn't given too much thought to it since his grandson hanged himself. He said that was the reason he tucked it away because of the lad's state of mind. It was only when he had trouble with the sink that he remembered it and it wasn't there.'

'But couldn't the grandson still have retrieved it before he died without Staunton knowing? Perhaps he knew where it was kept?'

'Staunton's adamant that he didn't tell the grandson where he kept it, because he was worried that he'd use it. That's not all. Listen to this. Staunton was able to identify Liam and Aaron Fortune from their photo in the local paper.'

'He recognised them?'

'Yes. I told him we were doing house-to-house for a murder enquiry and Staunton said he'd seen them both in the woods.'

'What were they doing when he saw them in the woods?'

'He says that he came across them late one evening, during the summer last year, in the walled garden. He says they were up there with other people with dogs.'

'What, lamping?'

'No. Dog fighting at the far end inside the wall.'

'Liam and Aaron were dog fighting?'

'That's what he says.'

'There were dogs barking when I went to see the Fortunes. And?'

'He heard all the commotion on his way back home through the woods one evening when he was coming back from rabbiting. He said there were too many of them there for him to intervene. But he clearly remembers Liam and Aaron Fortune as being the ringleaders. He said that the dogs were baited and that one dog killed the other. He described watching as one of them ripped the ears off the other and clamped its jaws on its neck. Said it sickened him.'

'Sickened him enough to do something about it?'

'Who knows, boss.'

'What feel do you get from him, Tom?'

'I don't know. He's definitely been living on his own for too long. He's unkempt, a little bit unsteady and forgetful, the house is a tip, the inside's virtually yellow from nicotine staining. He rambles a bit, but he got really fired up about the dog fighting.'

'When was the last time he was up at the woods?'

'Saturday, he says, so about twenty-four hours before the shootings. He showed me some rabbit skins out by the back door. To be honest, they could have been there any length of time in the last week or so.'

'And where does he say he was on the night of the shooting?'

'Says he stayed indoors.'

'Any alibi?'

'No. He lives alone, he's a widower. I've run him through PNC and there's nothing. I've asked him back to the station for a statement and he's happy to come.'

'Seize his other guns and take him to Trowbridge, I'll meet you there. I want to get a look at him.'

Temple terminated the call.

Eaton spoke. 'He knows the Fortunes by sight and says he was in the woods the day before they were shot. Then he gives a load of bollocks about a lost gun.'

Temple nodded. 'From what Tom's said, it sounds like Staunton stopped just short of an admission. Perhaps that's what he's building up to, admission by increments.'

Eaton reached for his phone. 'We might have him, boss. I'll get Stubbsy onto the dog fighting.'

At that moment, Clare entered the office. 'Just to let you know, the online comment about the fifty-grand bounty has been deleted.'

Buoyed by the prospect of a suspect, Temple searched for his car keys. 'I got through to Sophie Twiner after all.'

CHAPTER 19

'Well, what do you think?' Caine sat across from Temple in the canteen, stirring a cup of coffee.

'If he's lying to us, he's good at it. He didn't so much as twitch when you were talking to him. He wasn't bothered by your questions at all. You can't rehearse that. He kept eye contact all the time. He was so calm.'

'He was that all right. He had no idea he was being observed. He wasn't the least bit fazed about where he was, or his statement being taken. He wants to help, he said, even offered up his DNA. Why would he do that? Because he's confident he's covered his tracks.'

'But why speak out and put yourself there if that's the case?'

'Classic case of wanting to be seen to help. Ian Huntley did it.'

'I remember.' Temple took a sip of coffee. 'It does feel as if we're close to something, I just don't know what. What's it they say about telling a lie, put elements of truth in to make it more convincing to tell. But he didn't flinch in there.'

'And the story the grandson gave him about the gun, boss?'

'We've only got Harry Staunton's word for it. Contact the parents of the grandson, Tom, let's see if his story tallies with them, see if the grandson is dead like he says. See if they saw or heard of the US army gun, find out what sort of relationship they have with Harry Staunton and what they say about their son's relationship with his grandfather. Check his military career. Stubbs is on to the intel about the Fortunes and dog baiting, but it's the gun side of it that we need to work on. Grief does strange things to people. He said his grandson died nearly two years ago; perhaps he's not over it.'

Temple went back to the office.

Eaton was eager. 'How was he?'

'He was fully cooperative. He denied shooting Liam and Aaron. He displayed none of the signs of being someone who was nervous or concerned about where he was.'

'Maybe he's the coolest killer you've ever met.'

'If he did it, he would be. I need it to be him, Charlie. But we need some forensics to put him there.'

'DNA, swabs?'

'He's offered up his DNA. Same with the swabs from his hands and nails for gunshot residue, in fact, he couldn't have been more helpful. How often do killers do that? Forensics will have the results in the morning. Tom's making some enquiries with his family. Should be able to brief later.'

'Look, boss, maybe Staunton's a good bluffer. If the swabs come back positive . . .'

Temple finished his sentence. 'If the swabs come back positive, he's nicked.'

'Where is he now?'

'Tom's taking him home, we haven't got enough to keep him. We need something to link him forensically. If he *is* the killer, Charlie, why say he saw the Fortunes? Why put himself there? Why tell us about a missing gun?'

'Perhaps he was just waiting for the knock on the door. Maybe he thinks we know more than we do. Perhaps he thinks we're on to him and he's trying to think clever, cover his bases. Or maybe this is his way of starting to unload about it.'

'Let's hope so.'

'I've got a good feeling about this, boss.'

'Mark him as a person of interest in the policy book, pending results from Forensics.'

'I've googled the US army firearms. There's a list including a Beretta, Colt and Glock, to name a few.'

'We'll have to wait for Forensics on the bullets.'

Temple was suddenly optimistic. It was a ray of hope. This time tomorrow, Harry Staunton could be in the custody suite at Swindon station charged with two counts of murder. It would be a quick result after all. He could distance himself from the Fortunes. It was a good note to end the day on.

He looked at his watch. 'I need a favour, Charlie. I have to be somewhere else and I need to go now, can you take this evening's briefing?'

''Course.'

'Thanks. I'll keep my phone on. See you first thing in the morning.'

* * *

Parking a couple of streets away, Temple made his way to a flat above a defunct shop in Maristow Street, Westbury. Some discreet enquiries with the DWP had suggested this address would be good. After pressing on the doorbell a few times there was no response. He stepped out of the small recess of the front door and looked up at the window to where a greying net curtain hung. There was no sign of anyone being in. He checked his phone for the time; he had to go back to the cottage to pick Callie up before going onto Harker's. They'd be late if he didn't make a move soon.

He pressed the doorbell once more and stepped back to look up at the window. Nothing. He'd have to come back tomorrow. He walked back to his car and as he neared the end of the street, a woman walking with her head down turned in off the main drag.

'Tara.'

At the sound of her name, she looked up in surprise. Seeing Temple, she was like a rabbit caught in headlights.

'No, no, no,' she said quietly, shaking her head as the two of them stood facing each other.

Although she had always been slim, she now looked gaunt.

'Tara, what's wrong?'

Nervously, she started to back away from him. 'Whatever it is, I can't help you.'

'It's OK, it's OK.' He stood still, not wanting her to bolt. He continued to look her over as he spoke to reassure her. 'I just wanted to speak to you, nothing more.' He reached out to touch her arm, but she stepped back again.

'I can't help you. Not this time.'

'Tara, it's OK, I don't want your help. I just want to talk to you. Could we go back to yours instead of standing here on the street?'

She stared at him for a moment. Then her eyes started to dart for an escape.

'Tara, please?'

She gave in and moved towards him and, now in step beside her, they walked to her address where she opened the door, letting him inside. He followed her up a flight of narrow stairs onto a small landing at the top where she opened another door. Entering, she walked over to the far corner of the room to where there was a tiny kitchenette. Without filling it, she switched the kettle on.

Temple stepped inside and glanced around; it was a tiny bedsit with an old brown chest of drawers on one side and an unmade single bed that doubled as a makeshift sofa on the other. A cheap brown carpet covered the floor. It was dank and he could see his breath in the air; he looked around for a heat source but couldn't see one.

He looked across to her. 'So, what's with this nice new flat then?'

She remained still, with her back to him, her head bent down. He continued to look around.

'How come you moved? What happened, Tara?' She still didn't respond. 'Tara?'

She turned and he could see she had started to cry.

He went to her. 'Hey, come on. I didn't mean to upset you.' He put his arm around her and as he did, she turned into him, burying her face in his shoulder. As he held her, her body was suddenly wracked with deep heavy sobs. It was all he could do to keep her on her feet. He steered her towards the bed and sat down next to her. She produced a paper tissue from her sleeve and continue to cry into it.

'What's all this about, Tara? You can tell me, you know you can.' He waited for her to calm and finally the tears stopped. He left her on the bed to finish making the tea and taking the mug over to her, he sat down on the bed beside her.

'You've lost a lot of weight, Tara, you're skin and bone, what's going on? All this crying isn't like the old Tara I know.'

She looked at him, her face red and eyes swollen. 'The old Tara?' She sniffed, her voice hard. 'She's gone.'

'What do you mean?' he asked gently.

'I kept telling myself that I'd be all right, that I'd cope and then suddenly, I lost it. It all caught up with me. I was a wreck. And I've been like this ever since.' Again, her head dropped.

He coaxed her. 'Tell me what happened.'

She turned her face to his. Once more, her voice was hard. 'I had to have an abortion.' She looked at her lap.

He didn't know what he'd expected her to say but it wasn't that.

'I see.'

'I couldn't have it growing inside me. I had to get it out.'

He put his hand on hers. 'I heard you and Zac had split up.'

She shook her head. 'It wasn't Zac's.'

'Not Zac's? Did he find out, is that why you split up?'

'No, he didn't have a clue. He didn't know anything about it. Still doesn't.'

'Then what happened? Didn't you want to keep it?'

'God no. I had to get the fucking thing out of me.'

145

She started to cry again. He'd never seen her like this. She'd always been strong and ballsy.

'Then whose was it, Tara?' he coaxed.

She looked up at him.

'Paul King. It was King's baby.'

He blinked back at her. 'King? But he scared you shitless.'

'Still does.' She looked back into her lap.

Suddenly his mind raced back to when he last saw her.

'Tara, when was this?' He put his mug of tea down on the floor. 'You didn't tell me everything that happened that night, did you? I asked you if they had sexually assaulted you and you told me they hadn't.'

She looked at him, big tears brimming in her eyes, and shook her head.

'It wasn't the night when they put me in the inspection pit in the garage.' She let out a hard sarcastic laugh. 'Even *that* night, when they put me in there, when all those men stood around me, looking down on me and undid their trousers, when I didn't know what was going to happen next, even *that* wasn't what tipped me over. When they stood there with their cocks out and all of them pissed on me, even when they got their rabid dogs in and scared the shit out of me, threatening to put the dogs in there with me, even all *that* didn't tip me over.' She stopped.

'Tara?'

'It should have done, but it didn't. I came through that all right.'

She was trembling.

He touched her hand. 'I want to help.'

She looked away from him now, then spoke quietly. 'King caught me one day at the flat.' She stopped. 'He'd been watching porn all day with Zac and when Zac went to the toilet, King came into the kitchen. I was at the sink when suddenly he was up behind me, telling me not to move. I froze as soon as I felt his hands on me. He turned me round, pulled my jeans down and helped himself, just like that. It

146

was the worst five minutes of my life. Five minutes doesn't sound like much, does it, but it felt like five hours. I know it was five minutes because I watched the clock on the wall the whole time.'

He took in what she said. 'When?'

'The day you came for the gun. After he did it, he just carried on as normal. I had to stay in the flat and go to the pub that evening with them like nothing had happened.'

He tried to suppress his anger. 'Why didn't you tell me? I could have arrested him for it.'

Her voice was tearful. 'I've thought about that since. I'd have been crucified in court. They would all have found out I was your informant and had been for years. They'd have killed me for *that*, let alone helping you get the gun back. It would all have come out.'

Temple closed his eyes. 'I've not told anyone you give me information. I'm so sorry. This is my fault, I shouldn't have asked you to help me . . .'

Her voice was hard. 'I had to help you. I wanted him put away. Zac was letting him stay at the flat. All they did was watch fucking porn all day, *all day*. He was always going to do it. Besides, do you really think King would have let me report him for rape? *Do you*? It would never have got to court, he'd have seen to that, him and the others.'

Temple nodded. As much as he hated to admit it, she was right. King and the Fortunes would have run her into the ground. No one in their right mind would take them on and not expect trouble, Eaton had said that. King was still trying to exact revenge on him for his prison sentence and probably wouldn't give up until he had his pound of flesh. As Munt had reminded him, they had unfinished business. Tara wouldn't have stood a chance.

'What bothered me more than all of what happened in the kitchen with King, and more than all that happened at the garage, was when I found out I was pregnant. That's what tipped me over the edge, that's what sent me off my head.'

'I'm so sorry, Tara . . .'

She continued. 'I just wanted it out of me because all the time it was inside me, it really fucked my head up. The thought of having something living inside me put there by that piece of scum, that piece of shit, I just wanted it gone. All the time I was pregnant I knew I was giving oxygen to something evil. I was allowing it to grow.'

He was next to her with his arm around her. 'Did you tell Finch?'

She shook her head. 'He wouldn't have believed me. Zac was part of the problem. He gravitated towards them all once he had the garage; the Fortunes, Georgie Munt, they used him, he was their useful idiot. He let King stay with us when he got out of prison, he let that fucking psychopath stay with us in the flat. And if they asked him if he could live there again when he comes out, Zac would say yes, regardless of anything I said.'

'I'm so sorry, Tara, I feel useless.' Temple held her hands in his.

'It's not your fault. You always said I should leave Zac, get myself a better life. I should have listened sooner. Then I wouldn't have ended up like this.'

'Maybe if I hadn't have put you in that position, we could have done something . . .'

'I've thought about it a lot. Perhaps it needed to happen to make me see. I was playing a dangerous game, you told me enough times to get out, but I stayed. It was me who came to you all those years ago, remember, because I didn't like what I was seeing and hearing. I was glad to help you.'

'You were scared and I shouldn't have asked for your help.'

'I was scared of King and I was annoyed at myself for feeling that way. Why should they go around like they do, frightening and hurting people, taking things that don't belong to them just because they can? At least in helping you, it got him recalled to prison.'

A silence settled between them.

'So how come you're here?'

'I left Zac and got this place as a stop gap. It was all I could find at short notice without a big deposit. I know it's depressing, the place sums up how I feel. I had the abortion, but I kept thinking that it might still be inside me, I was terrified that it wasn't all out. It took over, I couldn't think of anything else. Acute anxiety with depression they call it. I'm better than I was. All the time I can see my stomach's flat, I know it's not in there. It's mad, I know. I'm getting counselling for it now. Trouble is, I don't like going out and I have to go out to get my counselling.' She attempted to smile. 'I've just been to pick up some more happy pills, I ran out . . .'

'Is there anyone who can help you? Your mum . . . ?'

She looked up sharply. 'No. I'll deal with this on my own. I just need more time.'

'Then you'll have to accept my help. I don't know if you've heard but Liam and Aaron Fortune have been murdered . . .'

She was startled and momentarily taken out of her own problems. 'Someone's killed Liam and Aaron? *Fuck*.'

'And I'm investigating. I had to go and see the Fortunes and bumped into Munt. Thing is, Tara, Georgie Munt's been thinking things over too and he's worked out that you helped me get the gun back.' Her eyes widened, he had her full attention. 'So I've got to get you away from here before he finds you . . .'

She stared past him with a faraway look. 'They were there that night too with their dogs, when they put me in the inspection pit . . .'

'Who were? Liam and Aaron?'

She nodded. 'They pissed on me too.'

'Tara, give me twenty-four hours to think of something, somewhere you can go, and I'll be back. Stay put until then, don't answer the door to anyone. Don't go out. You've got my number, ring me at any time.'

She started to cry again and he put his arms around her.

'Just do as I say. Lock the door after I'm gone. I'll get you away. I promise.'

CHAPTER 20

'When was the last time you saw Gemma?'

From his profile, Callie could see Temple's jaw was tense. He was staring straight ahead, his grip tight around the steering wheel. She was glad she'd insisted on going with him. Her curiosity regarding Gemma and the Harker's had got the better of her and she wanted finally to be able to put faces to the names. But she hadn't seen Temple like this before. He'd hardly said two words since he'd finished work. She edged her voice.

'Darling?'

'Sorry, I was elsewhere. What did you say?'

'Heavy day?' she asked, concerned. 'Or aren't you looking forward to meeting Harker?'

He looked across to her. 'It's not that, although I could do without it. I have to deal with something else and I'm not sure what to do.'

'Sounds mysterious. It's clearly bothering you. You look like you have the weight of the world on you, let's hurry up and get this over with and you can tell me about it. Maybe I can help.'

He reached out and held her hand.

'Like you say, let's get this over with.' He returned his hand to the wheel.

'So, when was the last time you saw Gemma?'

He sighed.

'I haven't seen her since I took a statement from her for the abduction. She texted me before Christmas to say she was living back with Harker and she was introducing them to Prayer, but nothing since.'

'What's she like?' Callie asked quietly.

'When she came to me for help that night, I hardly recognised her. She wasn't the person I once knew.'

Callie looked across at him. 'You were attracted to her once.'

'Yes, I know. But that was before the drugs and prostitution.'

'Does Prayer look like her mother?'

'No, I think she looks a lot like *my* mother. Prayer's dark blonde, whereas Gemma . . . she had your colouring when we were together.'

'You didn't say. So you have a "thing" for redheads, do you?'

'I do have a bit of a weakness you could say . . .' He smiled. She was pleased to see him lighten up for the first time that evening.

'You're full of surprises. So where did you get your dark hair from?' she asked.

'My father, I guess.'

'And you've really no idea who he was?'

'Nope. My mother never told me, never told anyone, not even Richard. It never came up. I was only seven when she died, so I suppose I would have asked as I got older, but then she wasn't there.'

'What about your birth certificate?'

'She didn't register my birth when I was born, which was only discovered when my grandfather and Richard went to order it. It didn't exist. They had to register me; seems

Gabriella wasn't too hot on the finer details of administration at the time.'

'How odd. And Clive Harker, what's he like?'

'You can see for yourself, we're here.' Temple parked at the bottom of Harker's drive in Wanborough in front of his Mercedes.

They both walked up the incline and as they approached the house, an outside light came on. Typical of Harker, the house was large, detached and set up from the road, higher than those around it. The front door was opened by Rita Harker before they reached it. She greeted Temple with a warm smile.

Standing aside to let them in from the cold, she touched Temple's arm and looked into his eyes. She spoke in a low voice.

'I haven't had a chance to say thank you until now. From what Gemma's told me I know we've got you to thank for rescuing Prayer from those drug dealers. When you did that, you rescued Gemma too. I'm not going to go over the past, but I'd given up hope of ever being close to Gemma again, never mind any thoughts of having a grandchild. She went to you for help and you didn't turn your back on her and I'll always be grateful to you for that.'

'That's kind of you, Rita.'

'I mean it. Having Gemma back has transformed us. And of course, Prayer's part of you too, so I have another thing to be grateful to you for.'

Conscious of Callie standing by, Temple turned. 'This is Callie St George, my partner.'

'Oh? Nice to meet you, Callie. St George is an unusual name, our MP used to be called that.'

'Theo St George is my father.'

Temple felt a strange sense of pride hearing her say it, knowing that tonight in Harker's house, it might lend some weight behind him.

Rita Harker looked surprised and impressed at once. 'I knew your father, he's a nice man and a good MP.'

'Thank you.' Callie beamed. 'He's in the House of Lords now so he's still accessible.'

'We could do with more like him.'

Temple explained. 'I've told Callie all about Gemma and Prayer.'

Rita nodded and ushered them inside into the lounge where Clive Harker and Gemma waited. It was the first time in many years that Temple had been invited over the threshold of the Harker household. For a second, he couldn't help but compare it to the miserable bedsit he'd been in earlier and his thoughts went immediately to Tara sitting alone there.

They went into a large lounge of beige and creams, with comfortable furniture arranged around a centrepiece fireplace against the wall. It was a different property to where all the drama had unfolded on the night Harker had been arrested for assaulting his daughter. The Harkers had moved away from that home and the memory of it. Even Gemma wouldn't have known this house until recently.

Rita introduced Callie to Harker and Gemma, mentioning Callie's father Theo and, as Temple had hoped, for a few seconds it caught Harker off guard. As for Gemma, Temple could see she had transformed in the last five months since he'd last seen her.

She'd put on weight which suited her and cut and coloured her hair. She looked softer somehow and refreshed. She was wearing faded jeans and a cream-coloured jumper. The biggest transformation came when she smiled. She revealed a youthful set of gleaming white teeth. Her days spent on drugs and on the streets as a sex worker in Swindon looked to be far behind her. Being back in the family fold appeared to be working out well.

'You're looking much better than the last time I saw you, Gem,' Temple told her, as he watched her sink into an armchair.

She smiled. 'I feel much better. Mum's been taking care of me, spoiling me. Feeding me up.' She quickly eyed her father, as her mother left to fetch tea and coffee. 'And of course, there's Prayer for me to think about now. I need to be here.'

Temple knew what she meant. If Prayer was to be in Gemma's life, she needed to keep her safe in the confines of a secure and happy family unit, and here, she could access the respectability and stability Prayer was used to. He had to concede, it was an astute move on her part even if it meant cosying back up to her father, a man she had for years determinedly embarrassed with her drug taking and sex work. She obviously now thought it was a trade-off worth making. And, knowing Clive Harker as he did, if having Prayer in his life meant forgiving Gemma for all the pain she'd caused him, so be it.

Sitting in her company again, Temple still didn't feel quite as forgiving towards Gemma as her father clearly did. They were playing happy families now, but it had been him Gemma had turned to for help, rather than her father, when Prayer had been abducted from her flat for a drug debt, involving Simon Sloper. He knew how close they'd come to losing Prayer and the fact they hadn't was due to the upbringing and resilience instilled in Prayer by her adoptive parents, of that he was sure.

Gemma continued. 'I've got a lot to be grateful for. And Mum and Dad absolutely adore Prayer. She so well-mannered and sweet natured—'

'And clever,' Harker interjected, 'she's a chip off the old block, all right. Really smart.'

Gemma nodded. 'That's a lot down to Patrick and Fiona. They really looked after my baby.'

'Their baby,' Temple reminded her.

Harker shot him a look. The familiar growl was back. 'It's down to her genes, you can't get around that. It's obvious.'

Temple watched Harker standing by his fireplace. His anger was barely being kept in check and the situation was becoming intensely awkward for all concerned. Thing was, they hadn't all been in the same room together since the night it had all kicked off, when Harker had found the then nineteen-year-old Gemma with her head buried in Temple's groin on the sofa. The night the punches flew and Harker had mistakenly broken Gemma's jaw in a punch meant for Temple, the night of Harker's arrest and detention in a cell. That night had a lot to answer for. Suddenly, it was as if the nearly seventeen years since that night fell away as if they hadn't passed at all.

Harker started the conversation afresh. 'I'd like to talk about Prayer and her future with us.' He stopped to look around, to check everyone was listening before carrying on. 'Of course, we've got the court case for the abduction to deal with in the summer, but after that, I'd like to propose a more permanent arrangement. Next month she'll be seventeen. That's nearly seventeen years without knowing she existed and now we do, I want her in our lives.'

'And what does Prayer think? Have we asked her?' Temple asked without looking at him. The sooner they got to the point the better. He'd rather spend his time trying to find a solution for Tara.

'She's keen for that too.' As Harker spoke, Gemma sat silent, fixing her gaze on the coffee table. 'She clearly wants to get to know us, get to know Gemma. She even said we were her family. This is what she wants.'

'And so why am I here?' asked Temple irritably. 'Seems like you've got it all worked out. Never mind Patrick and Fiona Taylor, who've been her family since she was born, two people we have a lot to thank for, in fact, we are all indebted to.'

Gemma looked at Temple. 'I agree with you, as does Mum. We have to do this carefully. I don't want the Taylors upset.'

'I just think enough time's been wasted.' Harker ventured, his voice a low growl. 'Prayer wants to get to know her birth family, so I think it's only right that we make that happen, with something more permanent. And fast.'

Temple looked at Harker. 'And what about the Taylors? The people who have brought her up? What do you say to them? Do they know *you* want something more permanent?'

Harker sighed. 'Look, let's remember Prayer approached Gemma in the first place because she wanted to know about her birth mother. Now she wants to know about us too. That's only natural. I think we ought to help Prayer and approach the Taylors.'

Temple shot him a look. 'That's not a good idea. You can't go barging in on them, trampling over a family's hopes and dreams. Prayer is their daughter too, whether you like it or not. She has plans to go to university. When I spoke to her, she told me how the Taylors have set money aside for her to go and study law. We shouldn't interrupt that. I think we should be encouraging Prayer to continue with those plans—'

Harker interrupted. 'She can still go to university. I'll pay,' he started to pace.

Temple was finding it difficult to keep his temper, conscious that he was in Harker's house. 'The money and who pays is not an issue. The Taylors have already invested themselves in Prayer and her future, just like you want to now.'

Harker bridled. 'She's a bright girl with a good brain. I've met her, she tells me she's interested in law. Her parents are architects and she can't have the discussions with them that she's had with me. She's hungry for information and direction. She's got talent, I can see her through her degree, I have the contacts to get her into chambers. The Taylors won't be able to do *that*. Prayer's got the ability to go all the way. I know it. And I've got the means to match anything the Taylors have. There are no limits where Prayer's concerned.'

It was obvious to Temple that Harker was reflecting the life he should have had with Gemma onto Prayer. Through Prayer, Harker would have the chance to turn the clock back to the life he should have had nurturing Gemma through her medical studies, before she branded herself as a sex worker and drug user.

'At the end of the day, it's what Prayer wants that's important,' Harker declared.

'It *is*, Dad, but we need to be fair to the Taylors. I can't have Prayer turning her back on them.' Gemma looked at her mother who had returned with a tray of teas and coffees which she set down on the table.

'I agree.' Rita Harker looked at her daughter. 'We've talked about this; Gemma had to give up her baby and let's make no bones about it, Prayer would not have been the same girl if Gemma had kept her, given her lifestyle at the time. We all agree on that.' She stopped for a moment to put her arm briefly around Gemma's shoulder. 'The Taylors must be lovely people and we have to take their feelings into consideration.'

Gemma spoke again. 'Prayer's excited. She's excited by the fact her granddad's a police officer and so is her father.' She looked at Temple. 'She can't wait to meet you again. She keeps asking me for your mobile number and address. She wants to study law and thinks that this is where she fits now. Since she visited, she says she feels she needs to be closer to us. It seems the whole abduction business didn't put her off, she says it reinforced her wanting to be with us. She says she loves Patrick and Fiona, but now she wants to be with the people she says she feels a strong connection with.'

'If she'd have stayed with the Taylors, she'd never have come within a hair's breadth of being abducted or needing rescuing,' Temple pointed out. He was angry. It was a mess. Of course, he wanted to see his daughter, but he felt a huge debt of gratitude to Patrick and Fiona Taylor. Prayer had been lovingly bought up by a couple who clearly cherished her. They had the Taylors to thank for the girl they had today.

The atmosphere in the room was strained to breaking point. Temple wanted out. He could see why Gemma and Rita had wanted him to be part of the conversation, but he couldn't see Harker backing down. When he thought about the Taylors, he felt guilty about Prayer wanting to see him. Patrick Taylor had been her father, *was* her father. Of course, Temple was proud of her, proud of her achievements, of what she wanted to do. But that had all been instilled and nurtured in her by the Taylors. He had no right to claim any part of it and Prayer needed to acknowledge that. The thought of suddenly usurping Patrick Taylor in Prayer's affections didn't sit well.

Callie had been listening to the conversation. 'I think you can all achieve what you want and carefully considering the feelings of the Taylors will pay off.' She spoke softly but her cut-glass accent added authority. The room was quiet. 'It will show Prayer she needs to be considerate too. I should imagine they'd be devastated if she turned her back on them. Handled carefully, it might be possible for everyone to have a hand in parenting Prayer in the future. She'd have all of you to turn to without having to make a choice as to which family she prefers spending time with.'

'That's it.' Gemma nodded towards Callie in agreement. 'I don't want her to have to make a choice, let her have all of us. I don't want her to choose.' She looked across at Harker. Silence settled again for a few moments.

'Did you want to talk about the trial too?' asked Temple, breaking the silence and wanting to move things on so they could leave. He checked his phone for any messages as he spoke. 'Has Prayer told the Taylors about it yet?'

Gemma responded. 'The Taylors still know nothing about the abduction. Prayer doesn't want them to know, says that they would stop her visits — obviously.' She looked down as she finished, her guilt regarding the situation on show for all to see.

'How has she managed that?' Temple asked.

'She's given the CPS this address to send her letters to,' Gemma informed him.

'And how will she explain her absence from school to attend the trial?' Temple was becoming increasingly angry.

'The trial is set for August — in the school holidays. She will ask to spend time with me. I, we—' Gemma looked across at her father — 'will take her to court. Once she has given her evidence, it'll be over.'

Harker nodded in agreement.

Temple looked at Harker and Gemma. 'You seem to have it all worked out. If I could speak to Prayer myself now,

I would tell her if only she would be patient, she could have everything she wants.'

'He's right,' exclaimed Gemma.

'Of course he is,' affirmed Rita Harker. 'When Prayer's eighteen, we can't stop her making her own decisions about where she bases herself. Until that time, another year, we tell her — we *all* tell her, you too, Clive — that she is to remain living at the Taylors' house and that she can visit us in the holidays.'

* * *

Temple pulled the car up outside the lychgate at the church at Avebury and turned off the car engine. The drive back had taken place largely in silence due to him mentally trying to resolve the more pressing matter of Tara. He sat clutching the steering wheel.

Callie undid her seat belt. 'I don't know about you, but I could do with a glass of wine after that.'

'Thanks for coming.' He undid his own seat belt but made no move to get out of the car.

'I wouldn't have missed it for the world. Clive Harker was everything I imagined him to be. Gemma and her mother weren't though. How do they put up with it?'

He took hold of the steering wheel again and looked out of the windscreen, back to the past. 'Gemma didn't, she took off. For years she made sure he couldn't control her, but she damaged herself in the process.'

'You really didn't know she was pregnant when you parted?'

'Not an inkling. Neither did she at first. She said she found out at three months. By that time, she was on heroin and selling herself to get it.'

Callie spoke softly. 'You know as a baby, Prayer was probably addicted when she was born. She would have needed to be weaned off.'

'I know, the thought has crossed my mind. I should have gone after Gemma all those years ago and not listened to Harker's threats to keep away from her or he'd see me run out of the force. But I didn't. I wanted to keep my job. I was going to find my mother's killer. So I caved, I let her go. We don't deserve to have Prayer in our lives. We both deserted her.' He released his grip of the steering wheel. 'That's why I feel so strongly for the Taylors. They did the job we should have, and luckily for all of us, Prayer's been in the best of hands.'

Callie reached out and lightly stroked his face. 'Come on, let's go in.'

Daisy was sitting with Ana by the fire, waiting for them to come back before going to bed. When she saw them coming through the door, she leaped up joyfully.

'Am I in Ben's room tonight, Daddy?'

Callie responded, stroking the little girl's hair. 'Yes, if you don't mind, Daisy, then I can stay over tonight.'

'That'll be nice.' Temple kissed Callie's cheek.

'I don't mind,' Daisy said, bouncing up to Callie.

'Make sure you're quiet, we don't want to wake Ben. Come on, I'll take you up.' Temple followed Daisy up the stairs while Callie went into the kitchen to get them some wine.

'You too?' She turned to Ana, holding a third glass in her hand.

'No, I'll go to the pub now you're back. See you in the morning.'

'OK, darling. Take care in the dark.'

Temple and Daisy crept into the tiny bedroom where his son slept. They had squeezed in a single pump-up mattress where the low eaves under the slope of the thatched roof dropped to the floor. It was far from ideal, but Daisy considered it a small price to pay when Callie slept over. It was much more fun when she was around.

'Shhh, he's fast asleep. Come here.' Temple kissed her forehead before she lay down.

He looked at her as she snuggled under a duvet. 'Don't bang your head in the morning,' he whispered.

'I won't.'

He put his fingers to his lips and crept out of the room. Hearing Callie in the kitchen, he went into the lounge and, opening his iPad, went to the website of the *Wiltshire Daily Record*. He clicked on the piece about the Fortunes and down to the comments section. Checking the thread concerning the bounty was no longer there, as Clare had said, he scrolled through the growing number of remarks left by the public: *Fucking scumbags got what they deserve. Whoever shot them deserves a medal.* He thought about Tara and what she'd told him again. The sooner he could get her out the better.

Callie came in with two glasses of wine.

'So, what's the problem that you've been preoccupied with all night?'

She sat on the sofa with him and watched as he took a deep mouthful from the glass.

'I have to help someone, help them get away to keep them safe and I'm trying to figure out the best way to do it.'

'Like a police protection scheme?'

'Yes and no. This is a mess of my own making, so it's down to me to sort it out. Unofficially.'

'Now you've really got me intrigued.'

Temple relayed how he had arrested Paul King for aggravated burglary and his threats to harm him, Daisy and Leigh on his release from prison. He told her about sleeping with the gun under his pillow and how King had broken in one night looking for him and had instead found and taken the gun and set the house on fire. He told her about Tara and how she'd helped him retrieve the gun.

'Munt's worked it out. Tara's in a bad way. She's in no fit state to stand up to him if he finds her. She'll tell him she helped me, even if she doesn't mean to, even without saying the words, he'll know. I have to get her out of the way before he gets to her because he'll kill her.'

Callie listened, enthralled. 'You're right. She needs to go somewhere no one can find her until all this blows over.'

'I'm not sure it will ever blow over. The Fortunes just won't let things go.'

Callie was thinking. 'Tara also needs rest by the sounds of it. Her flat sounds pretty awful.'

'You should have seen it. No wonder it didn't require a deposit.'

She looked at him. 'You like Tara, don't you?'

'I do and I can't turn my back on her. She's helped me over the years with information, she's never taken any money for it and she really saved my neck with the gun. I owe her big time.'

Callie sat for a moment, locked in thought. Then she put her arm in his.

'I think I can help. Don't dismiss this out of hand — think about what I'm going to suggest because I think it could be the perfect solution.' She took his hand as she spoke slowly. 'We have a house, well, Father does, it came through my mother's family. He probably would have given it up years ago after my mother's death, but it's too heavenly. It's sitting empty at this time of the year except for a gardener and a cleaner. Tara could go there. It's warming up and I think she'll find it restful. Look, I have a picture of it here . . .'

As she reached for her phone, he'd already made up his mind to refuse. He had no ready solution himself and it was very generous of her, but it was too much. She scrolled through her photos and finding what she was looking for handed the phone to him.

He could see a substantial stone property in among hills, with a large pool set among tree-lined terraces. 'Where is it?'

'Corfu.'

'Callie, that's a bit more than a house, it's an estate.'

'It came to us through my mother when she married my father. Do you think Tara would like it?'

'Tara would think it was wonderful from where she is now. But I'm not dragging you or Theo into this. It's my problem, I just thought you might be able to help me figure it out. I shouldn't have told you.'

'And I can help, so let me. You're not dragging me into anything. It's the perfect solution. No one will find her there.

You get peace of mind that she's out of harm's way, Tara gets a chance to recuperate from what she's been through. Everyone's happy.'

'No. Besides, we could be talking months, three, four.'

She wasn't fazed. 'That's all right. There are two tiny cottages in the grounds, so really, it wouldn't matter if it was longer. Let's at least give it a try. Does she have a passport?'

'Not sure.' He frowned. 'It's lovely of you, it really is. But I can't do it. I'm not getting you involved. And what you're suggesting will cost money I just don't have.'

'Darling, listen. There are permanent staff over there, a cleaner, gardener and a cook. They are retained, paid for whether we're there or not. With Tara going out there, at least it will give them all something to do.'

'I'm not sure. It feels like I'm taking advantage . . . it's just too generous an offer.' He stopped, while he took hold of her hand. 'Seriously, Callie, I'll never be able to repay you, ever.'

'I don't need repaying, besides what's brought this on?'

'Seeing the photo you've just shown me, you telling me about a beautiful house in Corfu, that came through the family. It reminds me where you come from, shows me where I don't come from and more to the point, what I can't give you.'

She pressed his hand. 'Don't let it get in the way of "us". I want to share what I have with you. We're a team now and I want to help where I can. Let's use "where I come from", as you put it, as a force for good where we can. And as I see it, there's a perfectly good house sitting in Corfu offering a perfectly good solution to a serious problem.'

He kissed her hand. The whole thing didn't sit comfortably with him, but neither did Munt turning up on Tara's doorstep. He knew without a doubt Munt would either kill her or seriously harm her. He'd made Tara a solemn promise to get her out and yet he was trapped by his own lack of resources. But he owed it to Tara to keep her safe.

In paying his debt of gratitude to Tara, he would be eternally indebted to Callie. Could it work? It would solve a problem, one he otherwise didn't have an answer to. Besides, it was one thing for him and Callie to sit and sort out something for Tara, it was another for Tara to agree to it. There was still room for the plan to stall.

'It all depends on whether Tara agrees to go.'

'If she does, give her my mobile number, tell her I'll ring her first thing in the morning to arrange everything. It's a few hours away on the plane. She could be in Corfu watching the sun set tomorrow evening.' She smiled away his scepticism.

He leaned in to kiss her. 'Are you sure about all this? What about Theo?'

'He'll be only too pleased to be able to help someone in trouble. Now, why don't you get in touch with Tara while I make a few phone calls?'

Temple scooped up his phone. 'I'll ring her now.'

CHAPTER 21

With everyone in the MCU office keen to make an early start, Temple was buoyed by a buzz about the place when he stepped over the threshold in the main office.

'Morning, everyone.'

He thought they might have turned a corner, but as his presence quickly filtered through the room, the familiar strained atmosphere switched back on. He ignored it, making for Tom Caine who was in a huddle in the corner with Eaton.

'How did you get on, Tom?'

'Didn't finish 'til late last night, boss, I managed to speak to Harry Staunton's son and checked out the story about the grandson.'

'I'm just getting up to speed with it . . .' Eaton said. 'Tina Shaw's here, boss, she's just gone to the ladies.'

'Does she know about Harry Staunton?'

'I said we had a suspect that Tom was working on.' Eaton looked over Temple's shoulder. 'And she's back in the room.'

'Well, let's get the briefing underway and Tom can tell us all.'

Eaton called to the room. 'OK, everyone, we've got lots to do today. We'll hear from Tom first regarding Harry Staunton.'

Tina Shaw sidled up next to Temple, where he could sense her bristling.

'Everything all right, ma'am?'

Her voice was low. 'You tell me, Temple. We need to speak after the briefing.' The smiles from yesterday were gone and her mouth had its usual tightness. 'Have you acted on my suggestion yet to get the Fortunes on board?'

'Not yet, ma'am, but I will. There's been a couple of developments. Things have moved on.'

'Oh?'

He nodded towards Caine who was about to speak.

'Just to bring everyone up to speed on the lead that came from house-to-house enquiries. I met with Mr Harry Staunton yesterday who agreed to give a statement at the station. When I asked him if he could show me his gun cabinet to check his guns against his licence, he told me about a gun he'd lost that his grandson, Matthew Staunton, had given to him.

'Matthew was ex-British army and kept the gun as a trophy from his army days, illegally obviously. Mr Staunton thinks it was US army issue and said that his grandson showed it to him, saying that it had saved his life. When Matthew had psychiatric problems as a result of PTSD, Harry Staunton took it off him and hid it. It didn't stop Matthew subsequently committing suicide by hanging. Harry says he went to look for the gun one day about three months ago and it was missing. He didn't report it to police.

'He gave me the telephone number for his son, David Staunton. I made contact and he verified everything Harry said about his grandson being in the army, having problems with PTSD and hanging himself. His father found him. However, David Staunton said he didn't know anything about the firearm, neither Matthew having it nor his father hiding it. He said his father has become increasingly forgetful over the last few years and Matthew's death was a particular blow to him as they were very close. David Staunton went so far as to doubt there even was a gun and said not to put too much store in what his father said on that score. David Staunton is keen for his father to move into care accommodation.'

The room was silent.

'In summary, Harry Staunton says the last time he was in the woods was on Saturday, the day prior to the shooting, and he says he was in bed on the night of the shooting. He said he could identify Liam and Aaron Fortune from their photo in the news, as he saw them at a dog fight that he witnessed at Erlestoke Woods. He says from what he can recall, that was late August last year, so about six months ago. He says there were between ten and fifteen cars and vans parked up, where cars normally park for the cricket. There were two dogs present that he saw, which he thinks were pit bulls, with more in vans. Pit bulls are illegal under the Dangerous Dogs Act, as are dog fights. One of the dogs he seemed to think belonged to the Fortune brothers, both of whom he identified as being present. He describes the scene in the walled garden as having some kind of temporary structure within which the dogs were fighting with men around the outside, cheering the dogs on.

'He described watching through a gap in the wall, so he could see the dogs as they fought. It was just the one occasion that he says he saw them there with the dogs, but it left a lasting impression on him. While I was with him, I also saw some night vision goggles at his house and a camouflage jacket he says he wears when he goes out. He handed over his camouflage jacket, the clothes he said he was wearing on Sunday and they have been sent to Forensics.'

Before anyone could speak, the door opened and Alison Rickman entered. As everyone turned to look, she spoke.

'Apologies — I've got the information from ballistics about the gun that I knew you would want urgently. You need to look for a Glock.'

Both Eaton and Tom Caine looked at Temple. All eyes were now on Alison.

'You're sure?' Temple asked.

'Yes, it's definitely a Glock. For those who aren't familiar, Glocks are popular self-loading, semi-automatic, sidearm pistols, typically used by the police and military around the world. They are light, compact, easy to carry and easy to hide. We know a Glock was used because it has an elliptical firing pin impression and a rectangular outline around it from the firing pin tunnel. That's exactly what we have on the two cartridge cases recovered from the scene.'

'You mentioned military?' Temple asked.

'Yes. Glocks are standard military issue in many countries around the world.'

'Someone take an action to check if that includes US military prior to 2014.'

The CSI continued. 'I also have the results of the swabs taken from Harry Staunton yesterday.' She paused. Eaton broke the silence.

'Go on.'

'There were no traces of gunshot residue found on Mr Staunton's hands or in his fingernails. This does tend to suggest that it wasn't him who pulled the trigger.'

'How can you be so sure?' Eaton asked.

'At the ranges that both victims were shot, it's inconceivable that tiny traces of gunshot residue would not have been left from firing. Even if the man had scrubbed his hands, we still would have found something in the nail scrapings. More so in Mr Staunton's case as his nails are uncut and as it happens, the man isn't overly hygienic, shall we say. There were traces of other things under his nails that was quite compacted and, if he had fired a Glock pistol, that would have included gunshot residue. There was nothing there.'

Temple pressed on. 'But what if he'd been wearing gloves?'

'There still would have been transfer as he took the gloves off and this would have been on his hands and in the nail scrapings. We found some soft "bacterial matter", shall we say, under his nails and any GSR would have been in that. We've also swabbed the camouflage jacket that DC Caine told us he'd been wearing. Again, gunshot residue would have found its way into the threads and fibres of the garment, indistinguishable to the naked eye. There was nothing. When I say nothing, there was other matter, so the garment hadn't been cleaned.'

The silence in the room broke as everyone started to talk to each other.

Tina Shaw faced Temple. 'Well, this is all very interesting. Was this the development that you mentioned?'

'Yes and no. What we haven't got to yet is that the Fortunes may have issued a £50,000 bounty for the killer. It was suggested in a comment we picked up online. I have to take it seriously.'

They walked towards the back of the office away from the others as they continued their conversation.

Tina Shaw wasn't convinced. 'In the world they live in, it might be just them showing a bit of bravado and bluster.'

Temple shook his head. 'Ma'am, I was there when Elijah Fortune vowed to kill whoever killed his sons. That wasn't bravado or bluster. I don't doubt Elijah's intent for a second.'

'Elijah Fortune doesn't have the resources we have to find whoever did this.'

'We can't discount that Elijah Fortune already has an inkling of who he's after. Dead or alive, the message said, cash on delivery.'

She frowned, suddenly becoming impatient. 'And you think it's this Harry Staunton?'

'You heard it, ma'am. He says he's "lost" a gun. He lives near to the scene and puts himself in the woods twenty-four hours prior to the killing and says he knows both Fortune brothers by sight which makes him a person of interest, if not a suspect.'

'True, but the lack of gun residue is a bit of a problem.'

'Maybe he's covered his tracks. Perhaps he's smarter than he appears and he's considered gunshot residue and how to ensure it doesn't appear forensically. But if it is him, we'll need to move fast to get him into custody before Elijah Fortune finds him.'

She peered at him, keeping her voice low, ensuring he had to move close to hear her. 'How come you think you know so much about what Elijah Fortune will do?'

He had to be careful. 'Just the feeling I got when I went to tell him—'

She cut him off. 'Just a feeling? Would that be a "gut" feeling? There's no room for gut feelings or gut instincts. Feelings and instincts don't detect crime; facts and evidence do. You need to direct your focus on finding the killer, instead of second-guessing what Elijah Fortune may or may not do.' She drew herself up. 'Are you having trouble focusing on this investigation, Temple?'

'No, ma'am. I'll discuss the lack of gunshot residue with Charlie and work a way forward.'

She pierced him with a look before turning to face the room where Tom was speaking. Her voice remained low. 'I have a request for a transfer on my desk for your man Caine there.' She nodded.

'Oh?'

'And he's not the only one who's unhappy. Seems you haven't made the right impression with the team, Temple, which is putting it mildly. They all think you're part of a covert operation . . .'

'I know, ma'am, which is not true.'

'Is that right? If you're part of some covert op and this involves people higher up the food chain, you need to tell me *now*.'

'Ma'am, I'm not. There's no covert op—'

'If you're lying to me, Temple, there will be no way back. The new DCI will be here in the next few days, so you need to sort this out before they *all* vote with their feet and this turns into a shit show. I'm all that stands between you and the whole team walking out and guess what, if I have to choose, it will be them.' She walked away, picked up her coat and made for the door.

Watching her go, Eaton slowly approached. 'You all right, boss?'

170

'Yes, just got another love bite from ma'am Shaw.'

'Thought so. She didn't look too happy.'

'Neither am I. Did you know about Caine putting in for a transfer?'

'I know he was thinking about it. I didn't know he'd actually done it.'

'He has and she seems to think it's down to me.'

'Caine's missus has been on at him for a while now.'

'They have to focus on the enquiry, Charlie, we could be close to an arrest. As soon as we have someone in custody, I'll sit down with them all, but we can't allow this to be a distraction.'

Eaton nodded. 'While you and Tina were locking horns, we've checked on the gun. US Special Forces army issue before and post 2014 was a nine millimetre Glock 19. Now they're standard issue to all US army. If Staunton's story is right, that's what his grandson brought back from Afghanistan and that's the weapon we need to find. Looks like Staunton's our man.'

Temple stood up and put his jacket on. 'Tom's had a go at him, now I'm going to see him.'

* * *

Callie re-checked the flight times on her iPad and keyed in all the information required to make the purchase with a credit card and set up the e-ticket.

'All done.' She smiled.

Tara sat down beside her. 'Just like that,' she said flatly.

'Just like that.' Callie touched her hand. With nowhere else to sit, they were side by side on Tara's bed. 'All you have to do is make sure you have everything.'

Tara looked at her case open on the floor and pulled on the sleeves of her cardigan, stretching them over her hands. 'I just want to get out of here.'

'Good, because it's time we went. You have a plane to catch. I can tell you all about the house and Corfu on the way. I'm sure you'll like it.'

Tara looked bemused. 'I'm sure I will, it's just all happened so quickly.' Since Temple had talked it through with her last night, she hadn't known quite what to think. She was slow to move, as if suddenly she wasn't sure she should be going.

'Are you sure it'll be OK? I can't pay . . .'

'Tara, darling, it's all taken care of. You're expected now, the people at the house are looking forward to seeing you, looking forward to taking care of you. You'll have your own room overlooking the sea and your meals cooked for you. Just accept the hospitality for what it is and enjoy it. You've had a tough time, now you can take time to recover properly.'

Tara allowed herself a slight smile. A few hours ago, she knew nothing of Callie St George, let alone be going to stay in a house she'd arranged in Corfu. What was it they said, the kindness of strangers? When Temple said he could help, she had never envisaged anything like this. It had been a long time since anyone had shown any kindness or willingness to help and she was finding it difficult to accept it now it was being offered.

Callie turned and hugged her. 'Come on, it's time we made a move.'

Kneeling on the floor, Tara ran through a quick checklist before zipping her case. Suddenly, tears pricked her eyes.

'I'm still not sure . . .'

'If you don't like it when you're there, you can always come back.'

Tara moved with Callie towards the door and took a last look behind her. The drab room lost its grip on her.

'Let's go.'

CHAPTER 22

The handcuffs caught Guy Newland's wrist as he was escorted to a waiting unmarked police car. He was put into the back seat where he had his seat belt put on for him. He'd been told that the driver and passenger were detectives from Operation Acre who were transferring him to Swindon custody unit for questioning. The journey was going to be long, well over four hours, traffic permitting, so they told him to make himself as comfortable as possible.

Newland welcomed being outside a cell again. His short stint in the custody suite at Caernarfon had been a foretaste of things to come and he didn't like it. An hour into the drive to Swindon, he sat looking out of the darkened tinted window thinking about ways to break free.

The driver and passenger in the front had a whiff of suppressed excitement about them. Not that he'd gained that from anything they'd said as they hadn't engaged him in any banter since they'd left. Instead, the journey was conducted mostly in silence, save for a few unintelligible murmurs between the two men in the front. However, he'd picked up enough from that and their NVCs to feel their anticipation of their arrival at Swindon.

Eventually they passed over the Prince of Wales bridge on the M4 and Newland looked out onto the expanse of the River Severn either side. With the prospect of jail looming, he mused, even though he was handcuffed, he'd take his chance if the opportunity presented. His back started to ache having been sitting for so long and he broke the silence as they reached the other side of the bridge.

'Any chance of a comfort break?'

The front passenger turned.

'Can you wait?'

'Not really. I need a shit.'

'There's services in about five miles, we can stop then. And I'll be coming in with you.'

Newland settled his back into the seat. Now he thought of it, he'd been a fool. He should have made a run for it back at the Old Cataract Hotel. He could have run to any one of the exits to the Nile instead of trying to get out the same way he'd gone in. He should have jumped in the river; one of the many passing feluccas would have picked him up and he would have had a chance of escape. He'd let slip another chance at the pub. He could have just walked out into the night. He hadn't known for sure that he was under surveillance that night. Even when he'd been stopped by police, he could have at least tried to make a run for it. Now he was in the last chance saloon. He *had* to do it now. Perhaps the fact that he hadn't tried before would make it appear less likely that he would make an escape attempt now, although the cop in the passenger seat had said he would follow him into the toilet.

Newland could see the service station looming and readied himself. If he could get away, he could lose himself in the crowds. The police car drove on past.

'You said we could stop . . .'

'You'll have to hold it, we'll be in the nick in half an hour.'

Finally, the car swept into Gable Cross police station and round to the rear entrance, where they pulled in. The driver and his colleague got out, and the driver opened the rear door.

'Can you come with me, please? Mind your head.'

Newland was directed into another custody suite where a desk sergeant booked him in. Becoming familiar with this procedure now and flanked by his two travelling companions, Newland didn't have to wait long before they were joined by a third and fourth officer. As they stood a little away from him, he couldn't overhear their conversation, but it was obvious to Newland that they had turned up just to look at him. Once processed, Newland was shown to a room and told to wait to be examined by the force duty medical officer who would determine his level of fitness for interview. It was another form-filling exercise with the doctor swiftly declaring he was medically fit before turning him over to the waiting officers outside.

'If you would come with us, please, the duty solicitor will see you.'

Newland was shown into an empty room. A few minutes later, a woman in a tight grey skirt suit joined him and introduced herself. He studied her as she spoke.

'Mr Guy Newland? I'm Kate Clarey from Parson Harding solicitors. I'm here to represent you. I've had a quick look at the charge sheet. You do understand you have been arrested on suspicion of murder?'

She looked far too young for him to take seriously. 'I'm guilty of manslaughter. I just want to answer the questions and get it over with.'

'Are you sure you know what you're doing? Are you sure you want to continue to state that? Have you been told to say that?'

He stared at her. 'Listen to me. If you want to be useful, give me a pen and paper.'

She obliged, handing him a fountain pen and writing pad. He scribbled on it.

He pushed the pad back to her. 'You can make contact with these people.'

She looked back at him. 'Who or what is this?'

'They are people at a charity who will help me. Ring the number, tell them my name. Tell them I've pleaded guilty.'

'You do realise the consequences of what you're saying? You're looking at a long prison sentence.'

He hesitated for a moment. 'I've lived with this for a long time. This is me unburdening my conscience. Something I have to do.'

'I'll come into the interview with you before I call this number. Just let me know at any time if you change your mind during the interview and we'll get it stopped and reconvene. I just hope you know what you're doing. I'm sure there are mitigating circumstances we could look into. My advice is not to plead guilty.'

'Just put the call into that number.'

Kate Clarey moved towards the door and they both went outside where she indicated to two waiting officers they were ready. They walked a short distance to an interview room where one of Newland's travelling companions sat, along with a female detective. There was an energy in the room. The male detective looked away as Newland entered, referring to a notebook, ready to start his line of questioning. The female next to him looked across at Newland, clearly eager for the proceedings to start.

Newland quickly assessed his interrogators. Jesus Christ, after Martin Greene and the solicitor sitting next to him and now these two, it was the final insult. They were all kids. The female, a detective sergeant, was wearing her most serious face, the one reserved for people such as him. She was young but tired looking. Her male counterpart was possibly the same age but with more agile, angular features and hawk-like eyes. The pair couldn't be more than thirty. He thought of himself at their age, what he'd seen, what he'd done. Perhaps they were the B or C team, which might bode well. After the preliminaries, the interview commenced.

The female officer started. 'So, Mr Newland, you admitted to our colleagues yesterday that in an area known as Fyfield Down, Avebury, in the county of Wiltshire on 25 June 1984, you murdered Gabriella Temple, aged 29, is that correct?'

Newland swallowed before answering. 'I admitted to her killing, yes. But I didn't murder her.'

'And can you describe for us, please, how you killed Miss Temple?'

The image of her lying on a makeshift bed came instantly into Newland's mind. Despite the passage of time, she was so vivid she may as well have been in the room.

'I strangled her.'

'Thank you, Mr Newland. We will, however, need more detail. If you can tell us please what led up to that?' She held a pen in her hand ready to take notes.

Kate Clarey shot a sideways look at Newland as he continued.

'Look, I've told you — your colleagues in Wales — I strangled her, you've got my DNA.'

'Yes, I know we've got your DNA. For the benefit of the tape, Mr Newland's DNA has been matched with a sample on the DNA database which was taken from a blue T-shirt worn by the victim's son. What we're interested in, Mr Newland, are the events that led up to the murder of Miss Temple and how your DNA ended up on the boy's T-shirt.'

'I don't know. I must have touched him.'

Her eyes were piercing. 'You touched him?'

'Yes. I must have done, mustn't I? Otherwise, how else would it be there?'

'In what way did you touch him, Mr Newland?'

'I don't know, sort of . . . shoved him.'

'So, are you saying that you physically touched the boy?'

'Yes, I did, I pushed him. I grabbed his T-shirt and I shoved him out of my way.'

'Shoved? Grabbed? Pushed? What was it?' She was poised with her pen to write down what he said.

'Does it matter?'

'Yes. Did you want to harm him?'

'No.' The stupid bitch was getting to him. 'Not harm him, no.'

'Are you sure about that?'

'Yes.'

'Were you going to kill him too, was that your intention?'

Newland bridled. 'No, no of course not. If I was going to kill him, I'd have done it.' He heard his words. If only he had.

'Let's go back. Talk me up to that point.'

'Look, I'd been to the summer solstice event at the stones, in Avebury. A couple of days later, I was wandering through a small copse and I came across a caravan. The door was open, so I went in with the intention of helping myself to any food. When I went in, there was a woman, half dressed, sitting at a work top with loads of pills. I startled her and she started shouting. We got into an argument. She was shouting at me. I wanted to keep her quiet and I reached out and grabbed her throat. We ended up having a bit of a . . . tussle . . . and then before I know it, I'm holding her down on a bed and she's dead. It was as quick as that.'

'Her top was torn, Mr Newland.'

'Was it? Then that happened during the tussle.'

'No, it was torn from her. Was your attack sexually motivated, Mr Newland?'

Newland started up. 'No, no. It was nothing like that. I know what you're trying to do. You can get me more time by adding sex as a motive. Listen to me, it was a spur of the moment thing, she started shouting, screaming at me loudly. All I wanted to do was shut her up, stop her from shouting. I didn't want to hit her, so I grabbed her throat. Then she started fighting back at me. Instinctively, I started to defend myself and that's how it ended up. I didn't want sex for God's sake. I didn't want to kill her. I just wanted some food.'

'You saw her with the pills, did you want them, was that what this was about, the drugs?'

'No, I did not want the drugs.'

'Did you take the drugs there?'

'No, I didn't. I didn't have any drugs, she was sat in front of them when I went inside, I didn't want her drugs.'

'Did you know her?'

'No.'

'Had you seen her before?'

'No.'

'Not down at the stones, at Avebury?'

'I said *no*.'

'She was very attractive.'

'Was she?'

'Yes, didn't you think so?'

'I didn't think about it.'

'She was an attractive young woman and you found her on her own, in a caravan in the middle of nowhere. You thought you'd take your opportunity, didn't you?'

'No.'

'Are you sure about that?'

'Yes, I'm sure.'

'Did you know she had a son?'

'No, how could I?'

'So, what were you going to do with the boy?'

'What do you mean, what was I going to do with the boy? I wasn't going to do anything with him.'

'You grabbed him. You see, I have his statement here.' The officer read from an iPad. 'He says you grabbed him and pushed him. Were you going to kill him too, Guy? Or did you have other ideas? Perhaps you were disturbed by something outside and made your escape instead? Is that what happened?'

'No. No.'

Kate Clarey looked at Newland but remained silent.

The officer persisted. 'Then why lay hands on him?'

'I hid from him. I could hear him approaching the caravan. He was singing. So, I stepped back away from the open door, hoping he wouldn't see me. I wanted to get out more than anything. He was in my way, stood looking at his mother. I had to shove him out of the way to get out of the door.'

'Is that right?'

'Yes, it is. That's exactly what happened. I fought with his mother, strangling her in the process, and shoved him out of the way to make my escape. I wanted food, I didn't want sex with her and I didn't want to kill the boy.' He looked again at the solicitor.

'So, you *did* want to kill Miss Temple?'

'No, I didn't. I wish I'd never set eyes on her. I only wanted some food and we ended up in a ridiculous fight and I ended up strangling her. Look, yes, I killed her. It wasn't intentional, it wasn't something I woke up to do that day. If anything, it was an accident. She flared up and I reacted. When the boy came back, I only wanted to get out, so I shoved him out of the way. If he's saying there was anything more than that, then he's lying.'

'So this was completely opportunistic?'

'Yes, it was.'

'Then let's just go over it again.'

'No, no, I'm not going over it again. I've told you what happened. That's it.'

'But that's not it, Guy, is it? There were pills scattered all over the bed . . .'

'The pills were flying all over the place.'

'There were pills in her mouth, rammed down her throat.'

Newland flinched. 'I don't know about that.'

'Contaminated pills. Did you take them to her?'

'No, I've told you, I didn't have any pills.'

'So how did that happen?'

Newland sat in silence, looking back at the detective. 'I've got no more to say.'

'You've had a long time to think about it, haven't you, Mr Newland? A long time to come up with something, with this story. And now you can't bring yourself to tell us the truth about what happened.'

Newland didn't take the bait. The solicitor spoke. 'My client wishes to terminate the interview. He won't be answering any more questions.'

Newland nodded in agreement. 'I'm not saying any more, you have all I'm going to say. I did it, but it was unintentional. That's all you need to know.'

The detectives looked at one another and concluded the interview. Newland was shown back to a cell. The solicitor asked if he wanted to change his plea. After the questioning it was tempting, but he declined. He had to stick to his brief although it had been difficult when they suggested it was a sexually motivated attack.

Sitting back in the cell he put his head in his hands. He allowed himself a small, desperate laugh. The suggestion that he had wanted to kill the boy was ironic. If only he *had* killed him, he wouldn't be here now. The terrible irony was, he'd been trapped by his own conscience. And now he was paying for it.

CHAPTER 23

While Harry Staunton turned his back to fill the kettle at the sink, Temple took the opportunity to look around the small kitchen. A yellowed net curtain hung halfway across the window clouded with dirt and grease from cooking. Dark finger-marks covered the once beige cupboards and the lino on the floor was marked and filthy. The work surfaces were cluttered; there was a stack of pill box organisers by a toaster. A flowered curtain which also looked as if it doubled as a handwipe hung at the glass in the back door to the garden. A trapped odour of some kind of fish dish from days ago clung around the room. The place was a homage to the neglect of living alone.

The small wooden table where Temple sat was pushed against the wall and had the remnants of Harry Staunton's toast-and-butter breakfast scattered on it. The knife black-ened by burned crumbs rested in softened butter left out in a dish with no cover. Alongside it sat a half-filled ashtray. Now he could see the state that Harry Staunton lived in, Temple had misgivings about accepting the cup of tea that Harry had insisted on making him. The old man opened the fridge to get the milk.

'Don't worry about that smell.' Harry Staunton half-turned as he spoke in his thick West Country burr. 'That's just a ripe bit of Stilton.' He left the fridge door open as he pottered to where the cups were by the kettle. The smell coming from the fridge was vile. Temple wasn't altogether sure it was only the cheese. He held his breath. The odour was particularly nasty and there was nowhere in the confines of the small kitchen to avoid it.

'Makes some people jump a bit when they smells it.'

Finally, Harry Staunton closed the fridge door.

'What people would they be then, Harry?'

'Oh, just me son, David and his wife who turn up every now and then.' Balancing a roll-up between his fingers, he delivered two mugs of tea to the table, putting Temple's in front of him. Temple looked at the milky brew and noted the dark stained chip on the rim. The mug had been rinsed under the tap, but Temple could still see the old drips down the side of it from when the last user drank from it, along with a dirty thumb mark on the handle. He remembered what the CSI had said about what was under Staunton's fingernails.

'When was the last time your son visited?' Temple looked at the man sitting across from him. His face had all the lines and crags one would expect for someone of seventy-four, but his eyes were clear enough and sharp. Under an old peak cap, strands of grey hair poked out. His bushy grey beard covered his face, curling around his mouth. As he lifted the mug to his lips it left his moustache wet which he was ready to lick. He set his mug down on the table and took a draw from the roll-up.

'A few months ago. They want me to move out. They say it's too much for me here now, to keep up, without the wife and all. But I said to them, where would I go? I'm not going into no care home, they can bugger that. Stuck inside. I like it here, it's my home. It's not like I've lost my faculties or my mobility. I can still get about all right.' He tapped the side of his head. 'There's nothing wrong up here.'

'I expect they just want to make sure you're taking care of yourself.'

'I'm all right here. I'll clean up in a while. My wife used to do that, see. Not my area of expertise. I'm more of an outdoors person, in the garden, in the woods.' There was silence for a few seconds, before Harry Staunton continued. 'So, I've had your man out here and I've been to the police station, now, what is it that *you* want? I've told them what I know. They've even taken my guns — temporarily, they said . . .' The man's voice trailed off.

'It's like this, Harry. I don't know how much you read in the papers about what happens—'

Before he could finish, Staunton interrupted him.

'I keep up with things, don't you worry.' He nodded to a pile of newspapers on a worktop. 'I know what happens in your murder investigations. I see it on the news and on the telly.'

'What happens then, Harry? You tell me.'

'When someone gets murdered, you're looking to see who done it. Them two men were shot up near the cricket club and now, because I've got guns and I goes up there, you're asking me to help with your enquiries. You think I did it.'

Temple looked at him. 'Did you do it, Harry? Did you shoot them?'

Staunton was incredulous. 'Of course I didn't. Why would I do that? Just because I have a couple of guns and go shooting.'

'These days, people don't need much reason to do anything.'

'I kill rabbits, not people.' Harry Staunton held Temple's gaze. 'That'd be a different kettle of fish altogether.'

'It would.' Temple studied him as he spoke. 'Did you know the Fortune brothers?'

'No. But I'd seen them though, up there before, like I told your detective. There was a dog fight. That's how I knew who they were in the paper. It was bloody nasty, two animals going at one another like that and them standing there, goading them on, laughing. It was barbaric.'

'You see, Harry, I'm intrigued about the gun you say you lost. Did you give it to anyone?'

'No, I lost it because it's not here.'

'You're sure of that?'

'If it was here, I'd hand it over to you now, but it's not.'

'What sort of gun was it?'

'I can't remember the name of it.'

'Harry, you're interested in guns, you use guns, how can you forget the name of it?'

'I don't know. Look, if it helps, I'll draw a picture of it for you. There's an envelope from my electricity bill and a pencil over there.'

Temple went to where Staunton indicated and found a used white envelope and a short stub of pencil. Harry Staunton brushed some crumbs from the table onto the floor and turning the envelope over, he took the pencil. His roll-up abandoned in the ashtray, he started to draw. As he did, Temple watched him. He would have been a tall man once, but now he had a stoop and there was no weight on his bony frame.

'So, you got a good look at the gun that your grandson Matthew showed you?'

Staunton looked up. 'Oh yes. Saved his life, see. So I was grateful to it. Still am. It brought him back safe to us, I had time with him before he . . .'

Temple watched as Harry Staunton finished drawing.

'Can you sign and date it for me, Harry, please, and put the time on it.'

''Course. There, that's the gun, as I remember it.' Staunton pushed the drawing across the table and rescued his cigarette from the ashtray.

Temple studied the drawing.

'Are you sure that's it?'

'Yes, that's it, that's what Matthew gave me to look after.' The roll-up had almost vanished between his fingers, but he still managed to put it to his lips and draw from it.

'You sure you haven't got this gun here, Harry?'

'I told your detective. I had it hidden. Then, when I went to look for it, it was gone.'

'Where did you hide it?'

'I'll show you.'

Staunton squashed the remnants of the roll-up into the ashtray with his fingertip before standing up and walking to the sink. Slowly, he bent down on all fours and pushed at the kick board under the kitchen sink. 'I hid it in there.' He indicated that he'd pushed it to the back. 'You'd have to know it was there.'

Temple got up. 'You got a torch, Harry?'

'By the door there.'

Temple fetched the torch and joined Harry on the floor. He bent down, putting his head on the dirty linoleum. Staunton slid out of the way, still on his knees, allowing Temple to pull the kick board right out and shine the torch into the void. Temple could see to the back to the outside wall and along under the cupboards. It was empty.

'Is there any chance that you've put it somewhere else and forgot?'

'No, that's where I put it. I thought it was safe under there. I pushed it right back against the wall. Even taking this off, you couldn't see it unless you looked. You'd have to know it was there and I was the only one who did.'

'Then how can you account for it not being there?'

'I can't. It doesn't make sense.'

'You're right, it doesn't. Have you had any break-ins?'

'No. Who would break in here?'

'See, Harry, I've only got your word for it that this gun exists. The only other person who might have known about it was your grandson, Matthew.'

'I was the only one who knew where it was.'

'Do you think Matthew knew where it was and moved it before he killed himself?'

'I didn't tell him where it was.' He stood up, holding onto the sink to help him. 'I'm in trouble for not reporting it missing, aren't I?'

'Harry, you knew at the time that it was illegal to have it, for Matthew to have it. It's a serious offence. You could go to prison. Why didn't you hand it in or report it when Matthew gave it to you? Or at least say something when you couldn't find it?'

'I meant to when Matthew died. He had such a good turnout at his funeral.' Staunton was quiet for a moment. 'You know how it is, one day goes into another and before you know it, other things take priority. Then you forget.' He reached for some cigarette papers and a lighter on the windowsill and sat back down at the table.

'And after Matthew died you didn't see it again?'

'No, I had this trouble with the sink and suddenly remembered it. I knew I had to get it out of the way in case the plumber got under there. That's when I couldn't find it.'

'And the plumber definitely came after you looked for it?'

'Yes, I mean, it would be easy enough for me to say it disappeared after he came, but it didn't. Look, there's his card.' Staunton went over to a frame on the wall where the card had been poked into. He retrieved it and gave it to Temple.

'How did you feel when you couldn't find the gun, Harry?'

'Well, a bit worried like. Sick.'

'Did you look elsewhere for it?'

'Looked everywhere, started to doubt myself as to where I left it, but I know, *I know* that's where I put it. Made me guts wrench when I couldn't find it.'

Temple sympathised with the old man. He knew exactly how that felt.

'Did you ever use it, Harry?'

'No, not my type. I didn't show any interest in it deliberately. I persuaded Matthew to give it to me and I wrapped it up in one of the wife's old scarves and hid it from him. He would get himself into a bit of a state sometimes, see. I worried that he'd just pick it up one day and use it on himself.'

'Was it loaded?'

'No, but he kept the ammo for it. Another reason for me to hide it. He told me he was able to source the ammo via the

187

internet with his computer. He was really pleased about that. He did shoot with it see, before I took it.'

'Have his parents still got his computer?'

'No. They seemed to think it didn't help him. He kept looking stuff up on it which didn't help his moods. They destroyed it after he died. He couldn't cope when he came back. Couldn't cope with what he'd seen, what he'd been through. He was disturbed by it, Mr Temple.' Staunton now had a faraway look. 'We tried to get him help and it seemed to work at first, but it wasn't enough. He would worry a lot. He used to tell me little bits. The mates he'd lost. It was the IEDs. They'd terrified him. He said they'd disguise them in the roads, put them in logs, in the walls, even on donkeys and dogs. Then they'd just blow them up when the soldiers were near. Terrible. He was very jumpy at times. He didn't like going out much when he came back.'

'He sounds very brave, Harry. Your son David, does he visit you often?' Temple watched as Harry deftly started to roll himself another cigarette.

'Now and then, they've had it rough, they had a lot to put up with. But I'm all right here on my own.'

Temple nodded towards a daily dispensing package for medication on the worktop.

'What are the tablets for?'

'A bit of angina, type two diabetes. Heart's a bit weak, they say. I get a bit breathless now and then, that's all.' He licked the edge of the Rizla paper and finished rolling.

They briefly sat looking at one another in silence as Harry lit up.

'Do you mind if I have a look around, Harry?'

'Please yourself. You haven't drunk your tea yet.'

'I'm sorry, I meant to tell you, I only drink coffee.' Temple left the table and walked through to a lounge area. He could appreciate why Harry's son wanted him to move out. The same stale fish smell in the kitchen permeated through to the lounge. The shade from a tree outside the window kept the room dark. It was devoid of any homely comforts, with more yellowing newspapers stacked by the side of a worn settee and the place looked as if it hadn't seen a hoover in a long while. A pile of mail sat on top of an ancient television set and dingy nets hung at the window. A shabby armchair was drawn up near an old, tiled fireplace. On the mantle was a framed photo of Matthew in his army uniform somewhere hot.

Harry Staunton remained in the kitchen as Temple carried on looking through the house. After looking in a downstairs loo and in an understairs cupboard, Temple made his way upstairs. The main bedroom where Harry slept was like the rest of the house. The spare bedroom was the tidiest room in the place. Without his wife, Harry had slowly turned his home into a man cave. Temple looked in a wardrobe, some drawers. Going back downstairs to the kitchen, he noticed a door. It led to a pantry-type space, where a metal gun cabinet stood. The gun cabinet was open and empty.

'Do you mind if I have a nosey outside, Harry?'

'Carry on, fill your boots, that's what the young'un's say today, isn't it, fill your boots.'

As he went outside, Temple surmised that Staunton wasn't the least bit concerned by the intrusion. To the side of the house was open access to the garden from the road. There was a hard standing with an old Nissan saloon parked on it. In the garden near the back door was a long table with some rabbit skins on it, above which was a row of hooks. At the end of the garden was a large shed that Temple made his way to. The door was open; inside, there was a small work bench and various garden tools, hung up in rows. It was tidier than the house.

Back inside, Temple joined Harry Staunton in the kitchen. He opened his notebook and wrote inside.

'Can you please read what it says here, Harry, and sign if you agree with it?'

Harry Staunton carefully read what Temple had written and signed.

'Harry, I need to eliminate you from my enquiries and the only way I can do that is to find the gun.'

'I don't know where it is, Mr Temple, you can search the place if you want to.'

'I'd like to do that, Harry. I'll ask some officers to come and look for it in case you've mislaid it if that's all right. Will you come back to the station just to answer a few more questions? You're not under arrest and you'll be free to go. Just helping us with our enquiries. I'll get someone to come and pick you up.'

Staunton looked up at him as he held another roll-up to his lips and flicked the lighter.

'All right, Mr Temple. But I'll tell you now, I did not shoot those boys. And I don't know who did.'

CHAPTER 24

'The place is a shit hole like Tom said.'

Temple gladly took a mug of tea from Eaton. 'He showed me where he says he hid the gun, but he could just as easily have put it somewhere else and forgotten or deliberately hidden it. The place is full of wooden floorboards and there's a loft hatch. I want a thorough search done to see if we can locate it.'

'The search team will probably end up tidying the place up for him by the sounds of it.'

'Look at this.' Temple gave Eaton the envelope with Staunton's drawing on it.

Sitting down at his desk, Eaton turned to his laptop. 'He's drawn a Glock 19, boss.' He tapped on the keyboard and pointed to the screen. 'He's even drawn the seven bars on the slide. When are we arresting him?'

'Let's see if the gun turns up in the search. All the time there's no forensics I want us to tread carefully with Staunton. He's got angina and other health issues, I don't want him dying on us. How quickly can we get the search arranged?'

Eaton picked up the internal phone and dialled. 'I'll see if they can get on it this afternoon. Where's Staunton now?'

'I had Tom pick him up and drive him over to Trowbridge nick to make an additional statement. Told him to take his time.'

Eaton continued his update while he waited for the phone to be answered. 'The path sent the report on Aaron. It was much the same as Liam's.'

'Why have we got three bullets when Aaron and Liam each have a single wound?'

'Perhaps Harry Staunton missed his first shot?'

'Maybe. But if he had, would the Fortunes have just sat there? They're not the Chuckle Brothers, they were a pair of nasty bastards, just like their cousin Paul King.'

'Maybe Staunton can come over all Dirty Harry with the right gun?'

'It's still two against one. He's an old thin bloke, no match for Liam and Aaron.'

'Boss, the killer had a Glock in his hand, I mean, you're going to take a bit of notice of that, even if it *is* Harry Staunton standing with it.'

'True, but if one brother's got a gun to his head, the other one wouldn't be just sitting and watching, would he? The Fortunes prey on old people, gun or no gun, I still don't think they'd sit and take it.'

'I'm not . . .' Eaton broke off when his call was answered. As he spoke to the search team, he looked at his screen, scanning his emails. He ended the call.

'We've got the team going into Staunton's this afternoon. And, you know you just said you had no forensics on Harry, well they've just emailed to say they've got a positive DNA result for Harry Staunton on one of the fag butts from the woods.'

Temple recalled all the cigarettes he'd seen Staunton light in the time he'd been with him.

'Staunton's a chain smoker, his house is bloody yellow from it. And we know he put himself in the wood on the Saturday.'

'So he says. It could as easily have been Sunday.'

'It could,' Temple conceded. 'But the amount Staunton smokes, the woods will be littered with his fag butts so it wouldn't be unusual to find one.'

'Boss, it looks to me as if Staunton is trying too hard, like he's trying to keep one step ahead of us, trying to cover all the angles. He's been carrying the Glock when he goes out shooting. Then, he comes across the Fortunes one night and decides he'll use it on them. He's told us he was in the woods twenty-four hours before the shooting because he knows we'll find a fag butt. He's told us some cock and bull story about losing the gun because he's trying to distance himself from it and knows when we find it, we'll trace it back to him.' Eaton sat back in his chair.

'What about the lack of gunshot residue? He would have fired the gun three times.'

'He's been careful; he wore gloves and disposed of all the clothing he was wearing.'

'You're missing one other thing, Charlie.'

'Boss?'

'Motive. Why would he do it?'

'I don't know, he's an animal lover. He saw them that night and they said something to him. I don't know. Boss, we need to nick him.'

Temple was quiet for a moment. Eaton was right; they could build a circumstantial case against Staunton. They could wrap the case up as he'd wanted. But now he wasn't sure. Having spent time with him, Temple believed Harry Staunton when he said he'd lost the gun. It chimed with his own loss of a gun, especially as both circumstances involved the Fortunes. And as badly as he wanted the case wrapped up, he believed Staunton when he said he hadn't shot them.

Eaton looked back him expectantly. 'Boss?'

'What time's the search?'

'They're going into Staunton's at one p.m.'

'Let's see if they find the gun. I'll get an update from Tom and make a decision then.'

CHAPTER 25

Detective Superintendent Mark Stubbs hotfooted it down the back stairs to the office of ACC Clive Harker. He could have phoned, but for what he had to impart he thought it was better to see the ACC in person. His fingers straightened the knot of his expensive woven silk tie before he tapped on the door. Without waiting, he half opened it and put his head around.

'Have you got five minutes, sir?'

Harker was sitting behind his desk, looking intently at his laptop screen. Seeing Stubbs, he broke into a smile.

'Come in, Mark.' He waited until he'd shut the door. 'If this is about your promotion, it's a done deal. Best man for the job. Congratulations!' Harker stood up and went to shake Stubbs' hand. He lowered his voice slightly as if to reinforce the message. 'Keep it quiet until you hear officially from HR.'

Stubbs couldn't suppress a wide smile, although he would have been surprised if the job hadn't gone his way. 'Thanks, sir, that's good news.'

'It wasn't really in any doubt.' Harker tempered his accent, conscious that the more excited he became the less intelligible his words were to some ears. After all the years he'd spent south of the border, his voice had never softened. 'You were the standout candidate, Mark. Sit down.'

They chewed over the new promotion for a while before Stubbs could contain himself no longer and admitted it hadn't been the reason for his visit.

'I actually came to see you about something else, sir. The other night, I took a call from North Wales Police.'

'Oh? What do they want? Mutual aid or something?'

Stubbs knew the importance of his message but remained calm. 'No, in fact, they've just done us a favour.'

'That makes a change. What is it?'

'It seems the other night, they made an arrest, drink driving. When they get the bloke back to Caernarfon police station, they do the usual, take his DNA and shut him in the cell overnight until he sobers up. On running him through the DNA database, it came back with a match.' Stubbs paused.

Harker was unimpressed. 'And?'

'It matches the DNA profile we have for Operation Acre.'

Harker's jaw slackened. 'Are they sure?'

'Absolutely. There's no doubt; it's a match with the DNA found on the blue T-shirt.'

Harker threw himself back in his chair. '*Jesus Christ.* That's been unsolved for over thirty years.'

Stubbs leaned forward, eager to impart his information. 'Thirty-three or thereabouts. When they rang me, I sent the two officers from Op Acre to bring the suspect back. I instructed the Acre team to treat the whole thing as highly confidential. They were interviewing him yesterday.'

'Who is he?'

'His name is Guy Newland, sixty-four years old and a reclusive character. What we know is he's been living on a smallholding in the Welsh mountains for the last ten years or so. Prior to that he moved around the Herefordshire area. He's been going about his business, living under the radar until he got nicked for drink driving and was kept in the cells to sober up. The next day they go in and tell him that he's come up on the DNA database against a cold case murder enquiry and they arrest him on suspicion of the murder of Gabriella Temple. With that, he says, yes, I did it. It's made some detective constable's day down there. Made ours.'

'Herefordshire?'

'Apparently. Nice and rural, plenty of scope for keeping a low profile.'

'So, where is he?'

'We've got him at Swindon. He's holding his hands up for the murder, so it should be pretty straightforward. I've started speaking to CPS and they've been contacted by a defence barrister acting on Newland's behalf. He's been instructed from some legal charity or other that Newland put his solicitor onto. Newland's hoping for a reduced sentence for manslaughter. All parties are putting things in motion. I wish all cases went this quickly, the barrister seems to know what levers to pull. He'll be before the court in the morning. He could be in Crown Court for sentencing in days.'

'What a capture!' Harker was up on his feet. 'I'll have to go along and tell the chief. This will be good publicity, Mark.'

'I'll alert the comms department.'

'That's a good first job in the new role for you, Mark. Solving a cold case murder enquiry with the help of our Welsh colleagues.'

'Just one thing. When should we inform Temple?'

In his enthusiasm to hear the details, Harker hadn't considered Temple. Now he did, his thoughts suddenly turned to Prayer too. None of this had been mentioned to her, yet. After all, biologically, it was her grandmother who had been murdered. His voice was quieter now.

'We need to think it through. Temple's on the MCU. He's dealing with the shooting of the Fortune brothers at the moment, at Erlestoke.'

Stubbs saw Harker's demeanour change as he paced around the room.

'My nephew Kelvin's on the MCU with him. I could contact him and ask him where Temple is?'

'No, don't do that. There's not just Temple, there's his uncle we need to be mindful of.'

'As I said, I've managed to keep it "q" so far.'

'Not sure how Temple and his uncle are going to deal with the news. We need to get on the front foot.'

'Sir?'

'I want us to claim success for this, Mark. DNA testing the blue T-shirt, reopening Op Acre, putting a team on it, working with colleagues in North Wales. All of it. Temple and his uncle worked for years on it and got nowhere. We'll invite that gobby journalist Twiner they have working for them to cover it, we need to make sure she gets a good news story from our angle. Let's get things in place.'

'And Temple, sir?'

'I'll speak to Temple within twenty-four hours. Keep me updated with any developments. Wait a minute, you said Newland would be in court in the morning?'

'Yes, sir, apparently the defence barrister wants it "in camera". From what you've said, that suits us. This is a massive achievement, Clive. No more resources going into it. Case closed.'

Mark Stubbs left Harker sitting at his desk mulling over how he would break the news to Temple. It was an extraordinary turn of events. His thoughts inevitably turned to Prayer; one day, he would be able to explain to her how he, her maternal grandfather, had helped to find the killer of her paternal grandmother. In her eyes, he'd be a hero, he'd make sure of it.

CHAPTER 26

Eaton ended a call on his mobile.

'Negative, boss. A team of five search officers have been there for three and a half hours, going through every cranny of Staunton's house. They haven't found the gun.'

'Can they be sure it's not there?'

'They've looked everywhere. They've gone over the place with handheld metal detectors too, all furnishings, all beds. They tell me that no part of the carpets haven't been lifted and they've been in the loft. It's not hidden on the premises. So, he's left it somewhere else.'

'Or it's as he says, it's been taken.'

'He could have buried it in the garden or left it in the woods, boss, it could be anywhere.'

Before they could discuss it any further, the main office door opened and Alison Rickman burst through.

'Just thought I'd bring this news in person.'

Eaton swivelled round in his chair. 'What have you got, Allie?'

'There's a partial DNA profile from your man, Harry Staunton, on the dog collar.'

Eaton turned to Temple. 'It's him, boss. We haven't got the gun, but we've got this.'

'Wait.' Temple was conscious of both Eaton and Alison looking at him. 'I'm going out.' He pulled on his jacket and made for the door.

'Boss . . . ?'

Temple cut Eaton off. 'I said *wait*. Contact Tom and see how he's getting on. Tell him about the fag butt but not about the dog collar. Not yet. In the meantime, get hold of Ruby, tell her to get herself ready to go and visit the Fortunes this evening.'

* * *

Leigh Temple walked slowly through the lychgate and into the churchyard at Avebury, towards the cottage. She watched Daisy run ahead, her padded coat over her red gingham school dress flapping behind her where she had left it undone. She hated to admit it, but it made sense for Daisy to spend the rest of the week at the cottage. It was one of her ex-husband's better ideas, but she'd never tell him that; she would have to go into hospital at some point soon, so at least she wouldn't have to worry about Daisy if something happened fast. Even so, she would still pick her up from school.

The baby was moving less now which she was thankful for; a sign that the end was in sight. She was days overdue now and sick of being pregnant. She wanted it over. She was tired with it all; tired in herself and tired with the upheaval it had all brought, not least of which had been to her body and mind. She'd seen her medical notes and like anyone over thirty-five and pregnant, she'd been referred to as a 'geriatric mother' and that had hurt. Neither had she been prepared for the sheer range of emotions she could feel at any given time, as her hormones gave her a rollercoaster ride. And she wanted the cumbersome bump gone. She put her arm across her stomach and patted it as she walked.

'Come on, Lily,' she muttered quietly. 'Hurry up and come out now, love.'

She'd kept the sex of the baby to herself. It had been the one little bit of control she could have over everything and everyone around her. She hadn't even confided in Daisy. It wasn't fair to ask her to keep it a secret, so she had decided not to tell her. She knew Daisy would be thrilled to have a sister, although secretly, Leigh had wished for a boy; she fancied it would have cut Temple that little bit more.

Still, not long now and they'd all know soon enough. She could barely wait; it meant she'd be able to get on with her life, her new life, away from here, away from Temple and his new girlfriend. As she got nearer to the cottage, Leigh saw Daisy disappear inside and heard her calling out.

'Callie, Callie . . .'

Saint bloody Callie. She knew she shouldn't think of Callie like that, but it depended on her hormones as to whether she liked her or resented her. Trouble was, as it had turned out, Callie St George had been a great help to her. As much as she'd expected or wanted to initially, Leigh had difficulty disliking her, even though she'd tried. She deeply resented the way Temple had quickly moved into another relationship and there was a lot to resent in his new choice of partner too. The woman she referred to as 'Posh Spice' when gossiping to her friends was sickeningly pretty and younger than she was. She had youth, looks and money, none of which Leigh felt she had much of while being pregnant.

But as soon as Callie confided that she would never know the joy of having her own child due to rigorous treatment for a childhood cancer, disarmed by her openness, Leigh couldn't help but take to her. Since the divorce, she'd had to think through a lot of things, like the prospect of Temple maybe marrying again one day. She figured at least if it was Callie, there would be no 'second family' for Daisy to have to deal with and that would never change.

So, within a few weeks of meeting her ex-husband's new girlfriend, she was drawn in and they were both discussing her maternity notes and all her antenatal woes. She had found a new friend and for her part, Callie had listened and helped out with childcare, shopping and had even attended an antenatal class with her. Leigh didn't quite know how this pretty woman with her cut-glass accent had managed to have such a calming and positive effect on them all, but she had, which left Leigh feeling mean-spirited when she tried to dislike her.

The first time Callie had taken Daisy back to her home, which they all now easily referred to as 'the big house' as if they'd known it and her all their lives, it was days before Daisy had stopped talking about it. It had been 'Callie this' and 'Callie that'. And then it was 'Callie and Daddy this' and 'Callie and Daddy that'. And it hit Leigh hard. Although she'd been the instigator of their divorce, she hadn't figured on seeing Temple so happy so soon afterwards, especially not with someone like Callie St George. Hearing Daisy referring to them as a couple so freely and easily was another thing that cut deep.

She quickly discovered all the time she saw Callie on her own that she could feel friendly towards her, but she found it too difficult to watch her playing happy families with Temple. It pierced her to see them share a happiness she and Temple couldn't seem to find when they were married. And she took her frustrations and spite out on him. She couldn't help herself. She just couldn't forgive him which was why she wanted to carry on with her plan to leave.

Inside the cottage, she kicked off her shoes in the small hall area.

'How are you, Leigh?' Ana called from the kitchen. 'It won't be long now.'

Before joining Ana in the kitchen, Leigh popped her head around the door of the lounge to see Daisy and Ben together. She called out to him and he turned and smiled at her. She could see how much he looked like his dad and it reinforced her plan for moving away. It was ridiculous to resent the three-year-old boy, but she did and she hated herself for it. But every time she saw him, like now, he was a constant reminder to the conversation that had upended her life. A reminder of the day Temple had told her of Ben's existence, of him being in social care, living with foster parents because his mother had died of a vicious cancer, leaving him alone in the world. Except, he wasn't alone, he had a father. And that's when he broke the news that the boy was his, the product of a fling, a one- or two-night stand.

And, having given him the choice, Temple had chosen Ben over her and their new baby and Daisy. He'd given up all of them for him. She understood why he'd done it; the alternative was to leave the boy in care and she knew he wouldn't do that. But neither could she have the little boy as part of their family, a constant reminder to her of Temple's infidelity. She'd have had to betray herself to keep them together as a family and she couldn't wake up to that every day, as much as he begged her to try. As soon as her baby was born, she would move away from the situation and move on with her life.

Going into the kitchen, she eased herself down into a chair by the kitchen table.

'My feet are killing me.'

'They look swollen.' Ana put a cup of tea in her hand.

'The baby's stopped moving quite so much so hopefully it's getting ready to come out.'

'This time next week, the baby will be in your arms.' Ana beamed. 'Are you all ready now?'

'Nearly. I've packed a case, ready to grab. There's just a few small bits to get.'

'We can't wait!'

'No Callie today?' asked Leigh, looking around.

'She'll be here later. They went over to see Clive Harker last night.'

'What for?'

'I don't know, something to do with Prayer, I think.' Ana looked at her apologetically.

Leigh let out a disapproving sigh. And there was another reminder of why her divorce had been a good idea.

'I'll be here with Daisy and Ben, so you don't have to worry about her.'

'Thanks, Ana. In that case, I'll have my tea and get on my way, before the traffic gets too bad.' And before there was any prospect of Temple coming through the door.

'I'll tell them you called in. Will you bring Daisy from school tomorrow?'

'Yes, I miss her otherwise. Picking her up gets me out of the house too. I have to say it is nice being able to lie in and not get up early in the morning to get her ready. I'm making the most of it while I can.'

Leigh drank her tea and said her goodbyes to Daisy and Ben before making to leave. She forced her feet back in her shoes, wishing she hadn't taken them off. For once, she wished she wasn't going off to be at home alone. But Ana was right, it wouldn't be like this for much longer. She pulled her coat back on and walked slowly back out to the car.

CHAPTER 27

Vera Dart stepped forward with a cup of tea that Temple had no trouble in accepting. Sitting in her living room was a world away from Harry Staunton's kitchen.

'I'm really sorry we've had to come back to you again, but I wonder if you can help me?'

'If I can.' She looked up at him wearily, pulling a shawl tightly across her shoulders. 'You're not going to show me anything are you, regarding Toby?'

'No, I'm not going to show you anything, don't worry, Mrs Dart. The reason I need to speak to you *is* about Toby though.'

'Oh?'

'When you walked Toby, did you used to see anyone on your walks?'

Vera Dart sat in thought. 'We would see anyone who's local and who would be up and about in the morning, or at teatime when we went for his second walk of the day.'

'And that would be neighbours?'

'Yes.'

'Any in particular?'

'There's not many of the old ones left around here, lot of new people have moved in . . .' Her voice trailed off.

'Mrs Dart?'

'But there are a couple who've been here for years, like us. Harry's one of them, Millie's another . . .'

'Harry? Harry Staunton?'

'Yes,' she said, suddenly bright. 'I knew his wife. When she was alive, we'd see them in the pub sometimes, have a natter, you know.' She shook her head as her tone changed. 'Not anymore though.'

'So, you know Harry Staunton to stop and talk to?'

She shrugged. 'Of course.'

'Might you see him on your walks?'

'Yes. Harry's another early riser, like me.' She tugged at her shawl again.

'When was the last time you saw Harry Staunton when walking Toby?'

'Just the other morning.'

'When?'

Her eyes clouded. 'The day before . . .'

'The day before you discovered the victims?'

'Yes.'

'Are you sure?'

'Yes.'

'And how did Harry seem to you?'

She shrugged. 'Same as always. We see him often enough, he greets the dog as much as me.'

'And how would Toby typically react to Harry Staunton?'

'They were great friends. He'd always make a fuss of Toby when he saw him.'

'He'd touch the dog?'

'Oh yes.'

'Can you describe what he'd do when he saw Toby?'

'He'd ruffle the top of his head, stroke his ears, his neck.' She suddenly realised the oddness of the question and frowned. 'Why do you ask if he'd touched Toby? What's this got to do with Harry?'

'We're conducting a few lines of enquiry, nothing specific. Look, this might seem an odd thing to ask, Mrs Dart, but what usually happened when you brought Toby back? I mean, when you came back from your walks, did you wash him, hose him down at all, get the mud off him?'

'No, Toby didn't like the hose being turned on him. I'd keep a towel by the back door and towel him dry to get any mud off.'

Back in his car, Temple relayed the conversation to Eaton.

'So let me get this right, according to Vera Dart, if she met Harry Staunton out walking, he would make a fuss of the dog, so you're saying it could be argued that the DNA emanates from one of those meetings?'

'Yes, she saw Staunton only the day before.'

'It could also mean that as the dog knew Staunton, that's why it ran into the wood. If Staunton was the killer and he was watching in the wood that morning, he'd have had to silence the dog because if Vera Dart followed the noise of its barking, she would have discovered him.'

'I know, I thought of that too.'

Eaton persisted. 'It might also account for the fact that the Fortunes still had their money intact. Staunton wasn't interested in it.'

'I know, but what *would* have been his motivation? Look, I'm coming back, we'll discuss the arrest.'

Temple knew everything Eaton had said was possible. Through his own admission, Staunton had put himself right in the line of sight as a prime suspect. Perhaps Staunton *was* trying to play it clever; perhaps he thought that without the gun he was safe. But it still didn't feel right. Both he and Staunton had lost guns and both instances involved the Fortunes in some way; yes, the circumstances were different, but it couldn't be a coincidence, could it?

Temple made his way back to Marlborough. It was rush hour and temporary lights for roadworks along the A4 had him stuck in a long line of static traffic. He turned the ignition off. His mobile sounded an incoming text. It was Callie.

Just to let you know I saw Tara onto the plane, watched it go and now I'm almost home. See you later darling xxx.

He quickly replied, *XXXX*.

With the line of cars still not moving, he checked his messages for any news of Leigh, before straying into his emails. At that moment, he answered another incoming call.

Eaton sounded urgent. 'Boss, are you near?'

'Fairly, just stuck in traffic. What's the problem?'

'Just got word that Elijah Fortune has been taken into hospital with a heart attack.'

CHAPTER 28

There was a slight buzz in the office when Temple arrived back.

'Any more news?'

Eaton looked up from his screen. 'Not at the moment.'

'So, what happened?'

'One of the patrols saw an ambulance going to the Fortunes and radioed in to find out what the shout was. Elijah Fortune has had a suspected heart attack. They've taken him to the Great Western at Swindon. There won't be much point in Ruby going over there tonight, boss, Sharnie Fortune will be at the hospital.'

'You're right. We've missed an opportunity.' Temple sat down, surveying the whiteboard. 'Elijah looked as strong as an ox the last time I saw him. A bit breathless but still full of swagger. Perhaps everything just came on top.'

'It might help if we arrest Staunton. At least it'll show them we've got the killer. Might bring Elijah's blood pressure down a few notches.'

'What's the latest from Tom?'

'When Tom told Staunton that we'd found a fag butt of his near the scene, he said, "but I go in the woods with my fags". I told you, boss, he's figured it out. He knows we'll find stuff and he's worked out an answer for it.'

Temple sensed Eaton's frustration. Impetus was gaining around the imminent arrest of Staunton and he felt he was the only one who wasn't being swept up in it. As Eaton became distracted by a phone call, Temple slipped out of the main office into his own and closed the door. With everyone looking to him for an arrest strategy he needed to think.

The only rationale he had for not wanting to arrest Staunton was his belief he was telling the truth when he said he knew nothing about the shootings. And a nagging feeling that somehow this was all mixed up with the Fortunes and their quest for a gun, but it was hardly a rationale he could share. His hand reached up to his neck. He'd badly wanted a suspect and now he had one. He had to admit, on the face of it, everything pointed to Harry Staunton.

* * *

Tina Shaw tried to ignore her mobile ringing. Annoyed at its persistence, she snatched it up.

'Is that DS Tina Shaw?'

Her tone was brusque. 'Yes?'

'This is Commander Tony Rushall from the SCO35 at the Met. I've been given your number by ACC Harker. Can we go to landline through the main operator, I'd like to talk to you about a developing situation?'

'Of course.' Tina Shaw gave the landline and her extension number and ten seconds later her desk phone was ringing.

Rushall continued his conversation. 'We're in a fast-moving, long-term, covert operation. I don't want to reveal too much, simply because we have to be careful to protect four years of covert investigation.'

He grabbed her attention with mention of a covert op. 'So why are you calling?'

'To inform you that we have surveillance officers gathering information on an organised crime group in the London area. We have intelligence that suggests some members of the group are travelling to members of an organised crime group in your area.'

'And which OCG would that be?'

'The Fortunes.'

'Oh? We have a double murder investigation involving the Fortunes — I'm sorry, who did you say you were again?'

'Detective Chief Superintendent Tony Rushall, Covert Intelligence Command Met Police. ACC Harker said you would be interested. Tina, I haven't got much time right now to talk, I'm happy to come down tomorrow . . .'

'You wait a minute. You're going to need to be a bit more forthcoming with your "intelligence". Are you saying your OCG is involved in my case?'

'No, Tina. Our intelligence suggests they are visiting the family. We've heard the Fortunes being referred to as relatives. It seems Elijah Fortune has asked for help.'

'What sort of help?'

'That's all we've got now.'

'And what source has this come from?'

'We've got a lump on the car they're travelling in.'

'And where are they now?'

'Coming up to junction 15 M4, at Swindon.'

'I understand. And you have surveillance operatives on them, you say?'

'Yes.' Rushall suppressed a sigh.

'Who's got the ground command?'

'DS Zoe Cartwright.'

'I'd appreciate it if DS Cartwright could meet with me and the SIO in my murder case at Marlborough police station in an hour.'

Tina Shaw grabbed her mobile and called Grant Lindford.

CHAPTER 29

Trapped in his office with Tina Shaw impatiently drumming her fingers on the other side of his desk, Temple reached across from his chair and pulled at the door handle. It hit the metal stop on the floor with more force than he intended and Tina Shaw looked up.

'Just a bit warm in here, ma'am.' In the confined space, the strength of her floral perfume threatened to choke him.

'Really?' She was feeling the cold. Still, she needed to be there. She wanted to see DS Cartwright for herself. Following her conversation with Temple and him denying being involved in any internal covert op, the out-of-the-blue call from the Met regarding covert obs on some characters linked to the Fortunes, raised her suspicions. If Temple was involved in an internal covert operation, he would of course lie to her about its existence; any undercover officer worth their salt would lie when challenged to save their operation. And, as she and Grant Lindford had discussed, it would make sense that as SIO in Op Mitre, his attention was being diverted by running parallel investigations. That was good enough reason as any for bringing in extra resources for the covert op.

'I'll close it when DS Cartwright arrives.'

'She'll be sitting on my bloody lap.' Tina Shaw tried to make some space; the room was cramped already and there was hardly any space for the third chair Temple had brought in.

'You can sit here if you want, ma'am.'

'Stay where you are, it won't take long. Where the bloody hell is she? So, talk to me about your arrest strategy.' Temple noted her clipped tone.

'I'm not sure there's enough to arrest, ma'am . . .'

As he spoke, a slim female figure in a baseball cap, washed denim jeans and a hoody appeared in the doorway.

'I'm looking for Detective Superintendent Tina Shaw?'

'You've found her.' Temple nodded towards Tina Shaw, grateful for the timely intrusion. 'Come in, take a seat. Can I get you a coffee?'

Zoe Cartwright was unsmiling, her jaw tense from the unwelcome pit stop.

'No, I'm all right, I really haven't got long.'

Temple recognised the hard-wired look on her make-up free face; she was feeling the pressure and she probably ate, slept and breathed the job like there was nothing else in the world.

She stepped into the cramped office and sat on the edge of the chair. Temple leaned across, pushing the door to a close. Sceptical, Tina Shaw gave her a cursory glance. Cartwright's nondescript, androgynous look was typical; even so, she looked ridiculously young to take ground command for an out-of-area surveillance op. She was in at the deep end.

'I won't keep you here any longer than necessary.'

Temple briefly outlined the Op Mitre investigation. 'The "help" your subjects are being asked to provide is likely to be referring to Elijah Fortune finding his sons' killers. There's a suggestion online that the Fortunes have issued a bounty of £50k.'

Zoe Cartwright raised her eyebrows. 'Interesting.'

Tina Shaw spoke, watching Temple and Cartwright intently. 'So we would very much appreciate it if you could keep us in the loop for any intel you get from the car that relates to our crime family.'

'Can't see why not.' Cartwright shrugged. 'As you now know, our target is in a car with three other males. Thanks to the lump on the car, on the journey we've heard Fortune being referred to as a "cousin", although this is the first time the Fortunes have featured in our enquiry in four years.'

Temple swallowed before speaking, trying hard to mask his concern regarding the conversations in the car being monitored.

'Thing is, we can't discount that the Fortunes already know who the killer is. We haven't been able to get near them in terms of family liaison or telephony. That's where you have an advantage on us, Zoe. Any name or names that come out, we'd be grateful if you can let us know.'

Tina Shaw cut in. 'We have a suspect who will be arrested very shortly.' She gave Temple a long look. 'We'll let you know when that happens. In the meantime, if you can give us anything that helps with our investigation . . .'

Cartwright turned to Temple. 'As I say, I don't think there's a problem with that. I'll be the point of contact. I'll let you know if anything comes up and likewise, if there's anything you think we ought to know.' Temple and Cartwright swapped mobile numbers.

'What do your OCG members look like? It would be good to know in case we come across them,' Temple asked.

Cartwright straightened. 'I can't tell you that. The investigation is sensitive. No names or descriptions. You know what it's like, officers move to different forces, you don't know who knows who. We have to guard against corruption. I'd also appreciate it if you didn't mention our meeting or our involvement to your wider MCU team.'

'Fair enough.'

'This is ridiculous,' Tina Shaw snorted, instantly alert at the refusal to share names and descriptions. She eyed them, looking for any giveaways of familiarity between them. There was a distinct possibility the car could be full of Met officers, not OCGs from London and that Cartwright and her crew were part of the covert op calvary, Op Mitre being conveniently used as cover. What had Cartwright said? She didn't want the existence of the Met team mentioned to the wider MCU? What the fuck was really going on here?

Temple continued. 'But there are four in the car?'

'Yes. Now, if that's all?' Cartwright sprang up, clearly desperate to get out of the station and back to her team.

Temple opened the door. 'Thanks for your time, Zoe, I'll be in touch.'

'Likewise.'

Cartwright left the room and Temple closed the door behind her. He was preoccupied; there were four in the car and a Met team listening in. They only had to mention his name. He needed space to think and he couldn't with Tina Shaw still in the room.

She watched him. 'Typical arrogance from the Met. No respect for rank . . .'

He tried to concentrate. 'She was just trying to protect her investigation, ma'am.'

'Is that right? So tell me, why exactly isn't Staunton in the cells? I thought he was the main suspect? You seemed particularly enthused about him before.'

'Ma'am, there's not enough . . . yet.'

'*Really*?'

'Really. If there was, I wouldn't hesitate, he'd be in the cells, as you say.'

'And while you dither, Elijah Fortune is turning to his relatives to ask them for help. If you arrest Staunton, Fortune wouldn't need any help and that London crew would bugger off back where they came from.' She glared at him. 'Temple, get CPS advice on the evidence so far. Do it first thing. Then we can get Staunton in the cells.'

He escaped the room and after speaking briefly to Eaton, left the station. Sitting in his car, Temple considered the exchange with DS Cartwright. The Met investigation ramped up the pressure. The Fortunes not engaging with the enquiry had played to his advantage so far. But now, with a listening device on the car, if his name was mentioned and the Fortunes said he had had a gun, Cartwright would have him arrested for corruption. He hadn't seen this coming.

Staunton's arrest would put an end to it all, and as ma'am Shaw said, the OCGs from London would return. It would be job done and he'd be safe. But he couldn't arrest someone with a heart condition he felt sure wasn't responsible for the murder.

But one word in that car would see him in a Met cell. His gut knotted. It could all be over for him in hours.

CHAPTER 30

'You look worn out.' Callie had waited up.

'It's been a long day.'

'Yes, we've had one of those here too. Are you hungry?'

'I am, but not enough to eat at this time of night. Any news? Leigh? Tara?'

'Leigh's still waiting, all's fine and yes, I had a call an hour ago from Tara to say thank you, she loves the place.'

'She's safe. At least that's one thing less to think about . . . thanks to *you*.' He leaned in and kissed her. 'From the photo you showed me I'm not surprised she loves it. I just hope she doesn't get homesick.'

'We can both ring her regularly to check on her. I'll get you a cup of coffee. So, how's your day been?'

He slumped into a chair in the kitchen and took off his tie as Callie put the kettle on.

'It's been a strange one. We could be on the verge of making an arrest, but I'm not as convinced as everyone else he's our man.'

She turned. 'So how is it that he'll be arrested?'

'His DNA is on two exhibits found in the wood. He also told us he knows both the deceased men by sight and says he

216

lost a gun that looks very much like the one that was used to kill our victims.'

'And you don't think it's him *because*?'

'I spent some time with him this morning. He denies shooting them and seemed completely genuine.'

'How do you know that just from talking to him?'

'The way he reacts. He keeps eye contact, he's not at all nervous, he doesn't do any of the things that guilty people usually do when they're trying to convince you they're not.' He put his head back and looked at the ceiling.

She joined him at the table, fascinated by their conversation. 'How can you be sure?'

He sat forward, resting his elbows on the table. 'I just don't see it in him. I wish I did, I could certainly do with an arrest.'

'What will you do?'

'Find the killer. In the meantime, I've got to manage a team — and my boss — all of whom are convinced we already have our man.'

She put a cup of coffee on the table. 'You can forget about it now for a few hours. Do you want to hear about my day?'

'Love to.'

'Father had a small drama and had to call the plumber out. The kitchen sink was blocked with grease and fat. Have you ever tried calling a plumber?'

'No.' Temple stirred himself while Callie carried on talking. He'd thrown his jacket over another chair and went to get it. He searched in the pocket, retrieving the card that Harry Staunton had given him of the plumber he'd called when his sink had been blocked.

'I've got details of one here . . .'

'I've done it now, but goodness me, they don't make it easy . . .'

He turned the card over in his hand. 'That's funny. It says Caxton Electricals. I'm sure Harry Staunton said he'd called the number to unblock his sink.'

* * *

Sitting on the bench in his cell in Swindon custody unit, the only thing Guy Newland had to entertain himself was reliving his time with the lovely Melanie. Closing his eyes, he watched as he traced the length of her spine with his finger. Her back had been so soft. He could see his hands on her hips steadying her as he moved faster, back and forth inside her before his hand went to her shoulder pulling her in to him tighter. Then he'd grabbed her hair, a good fistful of it, pulling her head back. It had been like riding a pony.

Suddenly, he looked up as the hatch on the door was opened and closed, then the door was unlocked.

'Can you come with me, please, Mr Newland.'

Newland shuffled over to the police officer and was escorted down the corridor of other doors to the main custody centre desk. The place was quiet. There were only three people present apart from himself. Newland looked around and saw a clock on the wall; it said eleven fifteen, but was that day or night? He'd lost track.

He'd taken to sleeping at any given time between interviews and there was no indication from the windowless custody centre whether it was morning or evening.

From behind the desk stood one of his interviewers. Another officer next to him was seated, tapping on a keyboard. The only other officer his side of the desk was still standing behind him.

'Mr Guy Newland. You are charged that on the 25 June 1984, you did wilfully murder Miss Gabriella Mary Temple, aged twenty-nine, in the vicinity of Fyfield Down, near Avebury in the county of Wiltshire.'

Newland blinked back at them, banishing an image of her face as it flashed before his eyes. There, it was done. Perhaps now the bitch would leave him alone.

CHAPTER 31

Temple turned the card over in his hand as he held his mobile to his ear. It went to voicemail. He terminated the call. It was just after six thirty a.m., perhaps he was calling too early. He tapped Caxton Electricals into Google and headed off to the address in Melksham.

Slowing in the road outside the house number on the card, Temple saw a white van with signage parked on the driveway. He parked up, blocking its exit onto the road and walked up to the front door. Pressing a doorbell, he waited a few seconds before pressing again. An internal door opened and a tall male in his late thirties in a white T-shirt and blue cargo shorts appeared, standing bare-footed on the threshold. His dark hair was wet as if he'd run from the shower.

'Can I help you?' The man spoke to Temple through the porch without opening the outer door.

'I'm looking for the owner of the van.'

'Yes, that's me, Dean Caxton.'

Temple held out his warrant card. 'Can I have a word, Dean?' Watching Caxton, Temple felt sure he saw the briefest flicker of apprehension pass across his face before he replied.

''Course, come in.'

Remaining on the threshold and holding onto the door frame, Caxton stretched across the porch and opened the outer door. Temple noted the initials 'CB' tattooed on Caxton's forearm. Once inside, the man continued to stand in the door opening. The space was snug as the two men faced each other.

'I just want to see if you can clear something up for me, if you could.'

'Oh? What's that then?' Caxton asked, unsmiling.

'I was making some enquiries and someone said that they'd had some trouble with a blocked sink and called a plumber and gave me this card. Only, I see you're electricals so would that be right?' Temple held the card out.

'That's one of the old cards,' Caxton commented. 'We've got new ones now.'

'We?'

'Me and my cousin.'

'So, do you do plumbing as well?'

Caxton hesitated. 'I do electricals and my cousin does plumbing.'

'So, someone can ring this number and get you both?'

'Yes, the new cards have plumbing on them too.'

Temple nodded. 'So perhaps it's your cousin I need to speak to then? Is he here?'

'No, he doesn't live here.'

'Do you have a name and address for him?'

'Ryan.'

'Ryan?'

'Ryan Hobbs.'

'Ryan Hobbs,' Temple deliberately repeated as he tapped the name into his phone.

'Why do you want to speak to him?' Caxton asked.

'I just want to ask him a couple of questions about a visit he made to unblock a sink.'

'When was that?'

'That's what I want to find out, I've been told it was a couple of months ago.'

Caxton sounded disinterested. 'Oh right.'

'So, I'll need his address and mobile number too.'

'Yeah, right. I'll need to get my phone.' Caxton left Temple in the porch and went into the kitchen, returning with his mobile. He gave Temple the details he wanted.

'Look, I'm seeing him later, perhaps I could ask him whatever it is you want to know?'

'No thanks, I need to see him myself. But while I'm here, have you ever done any work for anyone at Erlestoke?'

There was a slight hesitation before Caxton answered. 'I'd have to look . . .'

'OK, well, perhaps I'll come back to you on that. Thanks for your help.'

Temple went back to his car. He dialled Ryan Hobbs' number. It was engaged. Then his phone indicated an incoming text. *Gold Group meeting this afternoon at 2 p.m., Headquarters.*

Temple rang Ryan Hobbs' number again. This time, it rang out. He knew the address that Caxton had given him was just a few streets away, so he headed there. He pulled up at the semi-detached property and knocked on the door, but there was no answer. Returning to Caxton's property, he saw that the van had gone from the drive.

Back at Marlborough police station, Temple put his head round the main office which was deserted apart from Eaton.

'Morning, boss, I've arranged the meeting with a bod from CPS.'

'I've got a 2 p.m. with Harker if we can avoid that time.'

'He'll be here at noon.'

Temple's phone started to ring and looking down at the screen his heart started thumping. He went into his own office to take the call.

'What is it, Zoe?'

'The crew we're on split up in the early hours, leaving the car with the lump on parked up. They took off in the Fortunes' cars, so we had to make a choice on who to keep eyes on. The ones we stayed with took us on an early-morning ride to Horfield Prison in Bristol. They picked up another one of the tribe. Just thought you'd like to know, Paul King was released this morning.'

CHAPTER 32

'They've let him out for compassionate reasons for the deaths of his cousins and the fact his uncle is now in hospital.'

'What a fucking joke . . .'

'Apparently it doesn't look too good for the guy in hospital from what they were saying in the car yesterday.'

'So where are they all now?'

'They're all back at the Fortunes at the moment.'

'Thanks, Zoe, appreciate it.'

A thatched cottage was a firelighter's dream and made them all vulnerable to one of King's nocturnal visits now he was out of the confines of the prison. Temple picked up his phone.

'I hate to ask, Callie, I really do, but I need another favour and fast.'

She obviously sensed the urgency in his voice. 'Anything, you know that.'

'They've released Paul King, the man I've told you about. I might be overreacting, but I wonder if you could take the kids and Ana to your place for a few days? I know it's a big ask but you'll all be safe over there.'

'Of course. There's plenty of room, I can pack them up now. But what about you?'

'I can stay at the cottage, someone has to look after the place.'

'And what if King turns up?'

'Then he'll find me and we can finish this once and for all.'

'I don't like the sound of that.'

'So long as you can all get away, I can take care of things.'

'Darling, what if things get nasty?'

'If I have to get an armed response group out it will be much easier without a house full of people and kids. I don't want them, you or Ana frightened.'

'Of course. Leave it to me. I'll let Leigh know.'

'Just tell Leigh there's been a flood or something and you're moving out, otherwise she'll freak and take Daisy back. I'll ring you later.'

It was a short-term solution, but even a few days would give him enough time to think about how to manage with King being back on the streets and deal with it if he turned up.

On the arrival of the CPS case manager, they gathered in the main office as Eaton talked through the evidence against Staunton. Sipping a coffee as he waited for Eaton to finish, he finally gave his opinion.

'With both the DNA evidence from the cigarette butt and the dog collar it could be argued that it puts Staunton at the scene, there's no denying that, however—'

Eaton interrupted. 'And the dog collar would put him at the scene *after* the crime was committed, so he's there before and after. As he lives nearby, he's a matter of ten minutes' walk away if that.'

The case manager patiently waited for Eaton to finish. '*However*, Staunton knows the dog and owner and by the owner's admission, had encountered the dog only days before.'

'The day before the murder,' Temple corrected.

Taking another quick sip of coffee, he nodded in acknowledgement. 'The day before the murder. The DNA is on the dog collar, not the lead, which could be from petting the dog when Staunton saw him with his owner. He also frequents the woods on a regular basis and will naturally have left behind cigarette butts because of his rampant smoking habit; Staunton clearly states he was there on the Saturday preceding the crime, you can see where I'm going with this. The admission of having lost a gun which you say is *similar* to the one used by the killer is a factor in your favour . . .'

'I'm confident we'll find it,' Eaton said, looking at Temple.

'But until you do, it's very circumstantial. There's something to build on here, but finding the gun is crucial to the case. As it stands there's not enough. I'd hold off your arrest. You'll need more or you'll waste your time.'

He picked up his phone and left the office. As soon as the door closed, deflated, Eaton swung round in his chair.

'Do you want to inform ma'am Shaw, boss? She's not going to be happy.'

'You don't seem to be too happy either, but you heard the man, we need more.'

'It's Staunton. I know it is.' Eaton beat his fist on the desk in front of him. 'It's like he knows we'll find evidence of him in the woods, so he tells us he's been there the day before, he tells us he's conveniently lost a gun which happens to be exactly like the one we're looking for, but oh no, he didn't shoot the Fortunes, who incidentally, he also tells us he knows by sight. He's running rings around us, boss.'

'Maybe. Ring ma'am Shaw, Charlie, it'll be better coming from you. At least now it's CPS saying we need more and not just me. We'll have to think about something else too. I want CCTV and an alarm put in Staunton's home address. Someone here is leaking information and if the Fortunes get a sniff that he's been questioned, they'll be in there. We need to make sure he's protected. If they can't do it this morning, then we'll have to rehouse Staunton until they do.'

'I'll ring tech support.'

Temple could see Eaton was downcast. 'You all right, Charlie?'

'Look, boss, I thought you wanted a quick resolution on this one and Harry Staunton's put himself into the eye of the investigation. You've seen other cases where murderers do that; they volunteer to help, thinking they're being clever, that they'll never be suspected because they've put themselves forward and then it turns out they did it.'

'You're right, and if it is him, as CPS have just said, we haven't got enough. All I know is we need to find the gun.'

Eaton fired up again. 'The gun being lost is a load of bullshit. Don't be fooled by him, boss. He knows where the gun is because he's used it and he's hidden it.'

'Look, Staunton's an old man. He's taking a load of pills. If he suddenly turns his toes up on us, we'll never know, so we need to go careful with him. If he's playing with us, we'll need to be patient.'

He caught the way Eaton looked at him; he was becoming frustrated with him, and Temple couldn't blame him. Staunton had as good as gifted himself to the investigation. Arresting him would take the pressure off in so many ways. But sitting in among the filth of Staunton's kitchen and listening to his story about losing the gun chimed with Temple's own experience. It couldn't be a coincidence. He knew the lengths the Fortunes were prepared to go to get a gun, he just couldn't work out how they'd ended up on the wrong end of one.

CHAPTER 33

'Ryan Hobbs?'

The voice paused. 'Yes?'

'DI Temple, I'm making some enquiries on a local investigation and I wonder if I can come and see you?'

Again there was a pause.

'Hello?'

'I'm a bit busy. If you tell me what it is, I might be able to help you over the phone.'

'I'd rather come and see you if that's OK?'

There was a momentary silence.

'I'm working.'

Temple persisted. 'I can come to you.'

'I'm at a client's . . .'

'This really won't take long.'

'I'm really busy, why don't you tell me what it is—'

'Ryan, I need to see you. Can you tell me where I can find you, preferably today?'

'I'm doing some work in a pub, the Three Tuns, Sandy Lane, it's closed for refurbishment . . .'

'I'll see you in twenty.'

Hobbs was sitting in his white van when Temple pulled up. As he walked toward it, Hobbs slowly got out of the driver's side.

Temple held out his warrant card as he approached.

'Appreciate you're busy, I won't keep you; I just want to ask you a few questions in relation to a job you went to at Erlestoke. I wonder if you can remember?'

Temple eyed him. Ryan Hobbs was in his late twenties and the family resemblance to his older cousin was clear, albeit Hobbs was leaner and unlike Caxton's close-cropped hair, Hobbs' dark hair was tied back at the nape of his neck. He was in work gear, a thick padded check shirt against the cold and knee pads tied around his legs.

Hobbs squinted as a shard of sunlight broke through light grey cloud.

'Um, yeah, maybe. I think so, it would have been a while back.'

'Who called you out, can you remember?'

Hobbs shook his head, looking down out of the sun. 'I think it was an old boy . . .'

'Did you know him?'

'No.'

'And what did he want?'

'I think it was a blocked sink.' Hobbs continued to break his gaze from Temple.

'And can you describe what you had to do?'

'I said, I had to unblock his sink.'

'And what did that entail then, Ryan?'

'Looking at the pipework.'

'And?'

'There was probably some gunge in the U bend.'

'While you were there, did you need to take the kick board out?'

Hobbs shook his head. 'Not that I can remember.'

'And when you were under the sink, in the cupboard, did you see anything that might have been out of place there?'

Hobbs swallowed and shook his head again. 'No.'

'Do you have a record of your visit?'

'Expect so.'

'Could you tell me what day it was?'

227

'I'd have to have a look.'

'Is that something you can do now?'

'No, I'll look when I get home.'

'It would be really useful if you can provide me with the date for that job. I'll call round later this evening, if that's OK? I know where you live.'

Hobbs looked uncomfortable at the prospect. 'Don't know what time I'll finish here. I can ring you with it.'

'Yes OK, you do that. That would be helpful.'

Back in his car, Temple watched Hobbs sit back inside his van as he ran both him and his cousin Caxton through the system. When they came back negative, he made his way to head office.

CHAPTER 34

As he was about to go into the meeting room at Headquarters to join the Gold Group, Temple's mobile signalled a call from DC Paul Wright, an old friend from his police probation days. Before Wright had a chance to speak, Temple cut in.

'Call you back, mate, just going into a meeting.'

As Temple opened the door, Clive Harker looked up from his mobile from his position at the far end of the large oblong conference table.

'Come in, sit down.'

The room was empty apart from Harker. 'I thought the meeting started at two p.m.?'

Harker set his phone down. 'We've postponed it until three p.m.'

'No one told me. I'll go back . . .' Temple's phone rang again; it was Paul Wright and Temple terminated the call, this time without speaking.

'Take a seat. I postponed the meeting to talk to *you*.' Harker leaned forward and rested his elbows on the table.

'Oh?' In his experience, Harker generally wore his mood on his face, giving a useful second or two's advantage to what was coming, only now Temple was finding his expression hard to read. He remained standing.

'You need to sit down, Temple. I've got something to tell you. Something important.'

Harker paused momentarily as Temple took a seat half-way down the table, ensuring distance between them.

Harker could contain himself no longer. 'We've . . . found your mother's killer.'

'What?'

Harker nodded. 'It's true. We've found your mother's killer. He's in custody.'

Temple reeled; he had never expected to hear anyone say those words. He suddenly felt lightheaded as he stared at Harker, who was animated by their exchange.

'What? *Really?*' The news had rendered him almost speechless. Was it true?

'Really.'

'But *how*? Where?'

'The DNA from the blue T-shirt, *your* blue T-shirt, was matched to a man who was taken into custody RSA . . . drink driving . . .'

'I know what RSA is . . .' Temple said impatiently, not quite able to believe what was coming out of Harker's mouth. The whole exchange was starting to feel surreal.

Harker went on. 'And when they processed him and took his DNA it came up as a match.'

'Not a partial or . . .'

'A complete match. We've got him.'

As his words sunk in, Temple was suddenly hungry for detail.

'Who the fuck is he? And where was this?'

Harker spoke slowly. 'His name is Guy Newland. He's sixty-four years old . . .'

After all these years, all the searching, looking at endless statements, a *name*. Like a sudden shot of adrenalin, Temple was up on his feet, pacing the room.

'Guy? Guy Newland?' he repeated. 'I've not heard that name before . . .'

'Well, there. It's him. That's who it is.'

Temple was thinking fast. 'So, he was about twenty-nine when he killed her . . .'

Harker continued. 'And he was picked up in Wales.'

Temple stopped pacing and turned back to look at Harker.

'Where the fuck's he been all this time?'

'In the Brecon Beacons, keeping a low profile living on a remote smallholding. He's been there for years apparently.'

'And then he was picked up for being over the limit?'

Harker continued to watch him. 'He's probably been driving over the limit for years. This time, the local plod got lucky. And so did we.'

Temple was having difficulty processing the information. It was what he'd wanted to hear for so long and yet now, it was such an anti-climax. He'd always imagined having a great sense of euphoria when he finally discovered the identity of his mother's killer, but now he felt nothing like that. *Why?* He paced about the room again.

'It's unbelievable.'

'Believe it. The Op Acre team brought him back here and have been questioning him. He's coughed it. Says he's guilty, so there'll be no trial. He's been charged with your mother's murder. They'll also add another charge today, actual bodily harm to *you*.'

Temple was back there. He remembered how he'd found his mother and pulled at her arm trying to wake her. He saw her face, lifeless, like he'd never seen it before. She had always been so animated, so beautiful, so full of life. Then he saw the hand coming towards him, grabbing his T-shirt and pushing him backwards. He felt his jaw snap down on his tongue when his head had hit the small oven and the warm blood in his mouth again. He recalled it all, the flies, the maggots, the smell. The fear. The sense of loss. It was all a mad kaleidoscope of thoughts.

'Have you told Richard, my uncle?'

'No, we wanted to tell you first. I'll go out and see him myself if you can remind me of his address.'

'I'll tell him.'

'I would like to tell him myself.'

Temple insisted. 'No, *I'll* go. It'll be better from me. It'll be a shock.'

'Suit yourself.' Harker's voice had resumed its hard edge.

'I want to see him.' Temple heard his own voice. 'I want to see this Guy Newland.'

Harker looked at him. 'I don't think that's wise.'

'Wise or not, Clive, I want to see the man I've been hunting nearly my whole life. In fact, it's very wise, for *me*.'

'Let's get this clear right now. He's in custody at Swindon, you can find that out for yourself anyway. And now I'm telling you to stay away. You are not to go and just in case you misunderstand, that's an *order*, remember those? Stay. Away. There's a photo of him in the system, look at that if you want to see him. Psychiatric reports are underway; his barrister is apparently very insistent we get on with it, get him in front of the judge, get the sentencing done. He's pulling out all the stops. You can see him then, with everyone else, when he's in court.'

'I want to see him before that. I want to look at the bastard.'

Harker stood. 'That won't be happening. I've spoken to Tina Shaw; she's happy for you to take a back seat on Op Mitre. Take some leave. She's sent Eaton over for the Gold Group meeting at three, we thought you'd want to be with your family.'

Temple imagined Harker and Tina Shaw in conversation about how to handle him without any of his own input. No doubt they wanted him tucked out of the way, sitting at home. That would suit everyone. He wouldn't be able to reach Newland from there.

'I just need a few hours this afternoon to go and tell Richard and everyone else. I don't need to take a "back seat". Op Mitre's my enquiry and I need to finish it. So, I won't be taking leave. I'll be back at Marlborough later today.'

CHAPTER 35

After all these years he had a name — and that name had a face. He'd looked on the system before leaving, taking a photo of it on his mobile. Richard would want to see it. Now that face was burned in his eyes. It was all he could do to concentrate as he drove down to Hindon.

Fifteen minutes into his journey he had an incoming call.

'Have you heard?' asked DC Paul Wright.

'Hello, Paul, yes, Harker's just told me.'

'I did try to ring, I wanted to get to you before that bastard, it would have to be him to be the one to tell you. I heard this morning, in Swindon. I had to check it out before contacting you . . . I couldn't believe it at first.'

'Me neither. What do you know? Harker's just told me the basics.'

'He's been in custody for days, but they've been keeping it under wraps. It's all very tight, but I spoke to one of the officers on Op Acre.'

'Is it true they caught him through drink driving?'

'Yes. I asked what he'd said about the murder. Apparently, it was opportunistic, he's saying that he was simply passing by and saw the caravan door open and went inside looking for food. He saw Gabriella and they got into an argument. She started screaming and he put his hands around her throat . . .' Wright stopped suddenly. 'Sorry, mate. How are you?'

'I'm all right, a bit dazed, I suppose, just coming out of the blue like that. I always thought it would be left to us to find the killer, you, me and Richard. We all pored over the case enough. I always imagined if the killer was found, it would be because of something that we did, a name or evidence we uncovered. There was no interest for so long and now this.'

'I know what you mean. It's been a long time coming. And Newland was never a name that featured. He's come out of the blue, like you said.'

'It's taken me completely by surprise. I'm on my way to tell Richard, so I'll have any information I can get as he'll be asking questions too. The more I can tell him the better. Harker didn't mention any of this.'

Wright continued. 'Apparently Newland didn't want to talk about the pills being in her throat. He clammed up. So, they don't believe all of his account . . .'

The signal started to drop out as Temple neared Salisbury Plain.

'I can't hear you now, mate. I'll catch you later, Paul, we'll have a beer . . .'

* * *

Richard Temple sat in his chair by the inglenook fireplace of his old cottage nursing a glass of brandy in his hands. He'd listened to what Temple had to tell him and now the two of them sat opposite each other in disbelief. Richard lifted the glass to his lips, his hands trembling.

'I'm shaking. I think it's with quiet rage.' He stopped for a moment. 'Have you still got the gun old Dad gave you?'

'What? Why do you ask?'

'I feel as if I could shoot the bastard. I mean, I really do. If he was here now, I'd shoot him.'

'No, I haven't, Rich, and even if I did, I wouldn't give it to you for that. He's not worth it.'

Temple stabbed at the newly lit fire with an iron poker. 'It's strange. It's something we've wanted for so long and yet now we know . . .'

Richard nodded at a log basket on the stone hearth next to Temple. He shivered in his thick jumper. 'I can't quite believe it . . .'

Temple took a log from the basket and put it on the fire and they both watched as the flames engulfed it.

Richard looked at him. 'I think it's because we didn't have the satisfaction of finding him ourselves. I'm not sure from what you've told me that we would ever have found him though. Of all the names we had, his wasn't one of them among all the drug dealers, Hells Angels and the like. We can't even say it was all the publicity from the article last year that helped either.'

'I know. All those years wasted looking in the wrong direction. We lost focus, *I* lost focus. From what Harker said earlier, it was all meaningless.'

Richard looked into the fire and shook his head. 'If she'd only left for Glastonbury earlier with everyone else, she wouldn't have been there and he wouldn't have come across her. She was in the wrong place at the wrong time. Why couldn't the bastard just have walked by, or had the argument with her and left? Why did he have to kill her?'

'I've often wondered if I'd have been there instead of down at the stones if he'd have stopped by at all. The sight of a kid there might have put him off and he would have kept walking. If I'd have been there that day, it might all have been so different.'

'Thank God you weren't there when it happened. He'd have probably killed you too.'

'But he was still there when I returned so why didn't he, Rich? Why didn't he kill me as well?'

'I don't know. And I hate to say it, but I have to be grateful to him that he didn't.'

'We shouldn't feel grateful to him for anything. Anyway, we've only got his version of events.'

'You're right. Old Dad went to his grave never knowing who killed his Ella. He used to call her Ella, he rarely called her Gabriella, do you know why?'

'No.' Temple indulged him. Richard had told him many times before, but it might bring him comfort to recount the story again now.

'Because he loved the music of Ella Fitzgerald and when she was in her early teens, he used to play it and she'd sing along with him and dance around the room. My two Ella's, he used to say. My God he loved her.'

'Then why did she move away?'

Richard didn't look up from the mesmerising flames. 'She was super bright, your mother, cleverer than me. Old Dad sent us both off to university, me with my archaeology and Gabs with her art history. She was going to be a teacher. She came home all the time she was at uni, but when she left, she never looked back. Dad had high hopes for her. She told him she had a job in a museum in London at one time. He liked the thought of that. And that's what we thought she was doing, living in London, getting on with her life. Then she bought the caravan and took herself off, left it all behind.

'She'd ring and write us postcards now and then, they're here somewhere, Dad kept them, but we didn't see her much. Dad worried about her when she told us she was pregnant. He pressed her to tell him who your father was, but all she would say was that it was complicated, which could mean a myriad of things and we took it at the time to mean he was married. It's only since that we wished we'd asked more questions.

'There was certainly more to Gabby than met the eye. All that stuff in the papers about her being a hippy and drug taker, it just didn't fit. I never saw her take drugs in all the time I knew her, but you saw a different side. After she died the way she did, having you here was what kept us going, I think.'

Temple leaned forward and tapped Richard gently on the knee.

'If you hadn't both taken me in, they'd have put me in care.'

'The social workers were circling so we had to claim you for our own as soon as we could. It was an awful time. And now finally, we know who did it.'

'I want to see him, Rich. I want to look him in the eye and find out what really happened. I want to know how he's lived with himself.'

'There will be questions we both have that we'll probably never get the answers to.'

Temple stood. 'Rich, I'm going to have to go. I'd have brought Callie with me only she's looking after the children. I've got to get back and tell her what's happened.'

'Bring her back as soon as you can. I enjoy our chats, she's a keeper that one.'

Temple smiled for the first time since he walked through the door. 'I will. Daisy and Ben love her.'

'You too?'

'Yes, I think so. There's no tension between us like there was with me and Leigh, but then Leigh had a lot to put up with.'

'She certainly did, it can't have been easy having all this hanging over the both of you. How is she?'

'She's due any day now. She's still not really talking to me, she communicates through Callie. They've struck up a friendship, don't ask me how she's done it. Callie could work as a peace envoy for the United Nations.'

'You'll be moving in very different circles now then, what with her father in the House of Lords and all that heavy politicking nonsense.'

'And that might be the sticking point. We're from very different backgrounds, we'll have to see . . .'

'Love conquers all, or so I'm told. So, what about Prayer, when can I meet her?'

'As soon as she wants to, I'll bring her down. She looks like Mum.' He was by the door now. 'I'll keep you posted on developments with Newland. We'll go to court to see him sentenced.'

'You bet we will.' Richard took Temple's arm. 'Listen to me. Don't be hard on yourself about searching all those years. Ultimately, you know you did find your mother's killer, but in a different way. You were at the scene and he grabbed you. That's what caught the bastard. Without you and your little blue T-shirt, we still wouldn't know.'

CHAPTER 36

'It's extraordinary.'

Callie leaned back in her armchair in Theo St George's comfortable sitting room in Huish, staring straight ahead, her eyes round. Opposite her, Leigh tried hard to hold back but suddenly burst into tears.

'When I think of all the years you spent looking for this . . . *bastard* . . . and now you say you would never have found him. Years wasted, just wasted . . .'

Temple glanced at Callie before going to Leigh and putting his arm around her shoulder.

'All I can say is that I'm sorry.'

Leigh shrugged away Temple's arm and talked bitterly through her tears. 'Finding him was all that mattered to you. This hung over us all our married life, all Daisy's life, and it was all for nothing because it wasn't you who found him.'

Callie went to her, taking her hand. 'You've taken the brunt of this, Leigh, but don't upset yourself, darling. I know it's easy for me to say because I've come in on the end of it, but this cloud has been lifted for all of you, for Daisy, for Ben, for the little one waiting to be born.' She took Temple's hand. 'And for you, of course. You've all been through a terrible time.'

Callie coaxed Leigh into the kitchen to make her some tea, leaving Temple by himself. Leigh was right; he'd spent decades trying to find the killer, years looking back at the past rather than living in the here and now. And for what? For someone else to find him. She had every right to feel bitter. Callie returned with a cup of tea.

'I'm sorry . . .' He started.

'Don't apologise. I'll look after her. Ana's with Ben and Daisy playing in their rooms. You must feel shattered, poor darling.'

'I don't know how I feel. The more I tell it to myself, the more real it's beginning to seem. I left Richard sinking a bottle of brandy.'

'Perhaps you should have stayed with him and helped him with that.'

'I can't, I've got the enquiry.'

'When the enquiry's over, we're having a holiday. You need and deserve it.'

'We can't, Callie. I just can't afford it at the moment.'

She kissed him. 'We'll see.'

'Are you sure your father doesn't mind everyone being here?'

'He's in London and staying there over the weekend. Besides, he wouldn't mind a bit even if he was here. I just can't believe it about Op Acre. I'll ring Sophie Twiner, we have to let her know.'

Temple grimaced. He could imagine Sophie Twiner's reaction. She'd probably be knocking at their door within the hour. He was determined she wouldn't find him there.

'I'll finish my tea and get back to work. I'll be at the cottage tonight, but I'll ring you.'

'I can't say I'm happy about you staying there. Promise me you'll take care.'

'I'll be fine, go back to Leigh. I'll just drink this and come and say goodbye.'

Callie kissed him on the forehead and went back to the kitchen. Temple sank his weight back into the comfort of plump feather-filled cushions on the sofa and looked up at the ceiling. *Guy Newland*. He couldn't help but repeat his name again and again. None of them had ever heard his name when they woke that morning. Now they'd never forget it.

* * *

The room hushed when Temple walked into the main office at Marlborough police station. Eaton approached him.

'Hello, boss. We've heard the news about Op Acre . . .'

Temple nodded in acknowledgement but didn't want to talk about it. He was subdued and suddenly tired. He was trying not to let the thoughts of Newland eat him up; he needed the distraction of the case as much for his own sake as anything else. He had to carry on as normal, delay thinking of Newland until later. He went into his office and Eaton followed.

'Thanks for sitting on that Gold Group. Was Harker OK?'

'Yes, he was all right, no dramas.'

'Any more resignations I need to know about?'

Eaton frowned. 'None that I'm aware of.'

'I have to go out in a minute to see Ryan Hobbs, the guy I went to see earlier today. He's going to give me the exact date he went over to mend Staunton's sink.'

Eaton shook his head. 'You've had a day of it, boss, why don't you just phone him? Or let me do it. You look knackered.'

Temple ignored him. The afternoon felt as if it was dragging and he may as well be at Ryan Hobbs' place as anywhere. 'We need to get the date,' he insisted. 'Then we can put it to Staunton. Besides, I just felt this Hobbs bloke was a bit "off" and I want him to make the effort.'

Eaton continued to study him. 'Perhaps he's on PNC.'

'He's not, neither is his cousin, Dean Caxton.'

'Maybe it's like people say, as soon as a cop speaks to you, you feel guilty even though you haven't done anything. It's a complex some people have.'

'Maybe.'

'Look, do you want me to come with you?'

'No, it's nothing I can't handle.'

'Seriously, why don't you go home, boss? I'll see this Hobbs bloke.'

'I need to keep busy, Charlie. How's Staunton holding up?'

'He's all right, he's back home.'

'CCTV and alarm installed at his house?'

'All done.'

'Right, I'll see you in the morning.'

* * *

Temple pulled up outside Ryan Hobbs' house. The day's events had finally caught up with him and he felt shattered. As soon as the enquiry with Hobbs was over, he promised himself he'd get back to the cottage. Until then, he would push Newland to the back of his mind. He knew his whole evening would be taken up thinking about the bastard and that would be best done with a full glass in his hand.

Looking at the house, he couldn't see any sign of Hobbs' van, so he knocked on the front door. It was answered by a pregnant woman.

'You look as if you haven't got long to go.' Temple forced a smile.

She smiled back, her hand instantly touching her stomach. 'Due any day now, thank goodness.'

'Your first?'

'Yes, we can hardly wait now.'

Perhaps he shouldn't have come after all. He was finding it an effort to make the necessary small talk. He pressed on. 'Exciting times. I've come to see Ryan Hobbs, is he in?'

'He's not come home yet. He might be with his cousin, Dean.'

'I saw them both earlier.' Temple held out his warrant card. 'Are you Ryan's wife?'

'Not quite.' She held up her hand showing a solitaire diamond ring. 'Perhaps after this one's born.' She frowned. 'He's not in any trouble, is he?'

'No. He was helping me with an enquiry I had. Do you mind if I ask your name?'

'Sam, Sam Mason.'

'He said he'd be back about now but said to wait for him if he was late,' he lied.

'I suppose you'd better come in then.' She opened the door wider for Temple to enter. 'He shouldn't be long.'

He continued talking as he followed her into the kitchen. 'Do you know what you're having?'

'A boy.'

'Picked a name yet?'

'Jack.'

'Good name.'

'Yes, he'll be named after Ryan and Dean's great-grandfather, Jack Bartlett. If I can hang on another week, Jack Bartlett Dean Hobbs might be born on his birthday.'

'That's nice. Make a great photo, the newest generation with the oldest.'

'It would have. Jack died just under five months ago. Ryan always said if he had a boy, he would call him Jack. Jack was a war hero. Do you want a cup of tea?'

'Black, no sugar, please.'

'That's nice and easy.' She turned away to put the kettle on. 'So, what's Ryan helping you with?'

'He did a job for someone, unblocked the sink and he's going to let me know what date that was. You were saying about Jack, Ryan's great-grandfather?'

'Oh yes, baby brain! That's what they tell you. You forget things when you're pregnant. And the hormones, don't get me started. Shall we go into the living room?'

Temple followed Sam Mason and sat on a grey sofa as she closed the curtains against the darkening afternoon, before easing herself into an armchair. Temple looked around; the place was fresh and bright, a flat-screen TV was hung above a mantelpiece and a modern wooden shelving unit was in a recess. He put his cup of tea on a wooden coffee table in front of him.

'I've been cleaning like a demon, getting everything ready. They call it nesting. I just want it to hurry up now. It's so uncomfortable. I don't want to wait another week, even it is for old Jack's birthday. It's all right for men, they're not carrying this weight around.'

He thought of Leigh. 'I can imagine it gets really uncomfortable. You were saying about Jack Bartlett being a war hero?'

'Oh yes. Jack was a real gentleman, a gentle man too, if you know what I mean. And he was such a smart man, he always wore a suit and tie. I knew him for three years before he died. There he is, up there, the one on the left.'

She indicated to two framed photos on the wall, divided by a smaller, box display frame.

'Dean and Ryan used to sit with him and ask him to tell them stories of things he did during the war. He was a gunner at the siege of Calais and was taken prisoner by the Germans in 1940. He escaped in 1942 and then went back for D-Day when he was wounded. I only know all this because they talk about it so often, it's ingrained in me.' She smiled.

Temple gazed up at a black-and-white photo of a man in army uniform. He'd seen similar of his own grandfather and had listened to the stories he'd told him.

'He used to get invited to memorial days. Dean and Ryan took him back to Calais once. He would go on the Remembrance Day parade, with his two medals . . .' Her voice faded.

He let Sam Mason's chatter wash over him.

'They don't make them like that anymore.' He picked his tea up and resolved to leave as soon as he finished it. He'd come back tomorrow.

'They don't. So, we'll have another Jack soon because old Jack's father who is in the frame next to him, was also named Jack. Father and son; one in the First World War and one in the Second. We put him alongside his two First World War medals.'

'Perhaps they'll inspire him to follow them into the army.'

'They inspired Dean. He joined up. It wasn't for Ryan though, not after hearing some of the things Dean told him. I'm not sure I'd want my son joining either.' She laid her hand across her stomach.

'Oh? I met Dean earlier.' He drained his cup.

'Ryan's really proud of him, he looks up to him, Dean being that bit older. They're like brothers more than cousins. They work well together.'

'They been working together long?'

'About eighteen months, a bit longer maybe. They've both had their trades for years, just come together lately . . .'

At that moment they heard a key in the door. At last.

'Here he is.' Sam Mason pulled herself up out the chair. Just as she stood up, Ryan Hobbs appeared in the doorway. Temple looked up, in time to see the surprise register in Ryan's face when he saw him.

'*You*! What are you doing here?' Hobbs clenched his jaw.

'Hello again, Ryan. You did say you'd find out that date for me.'

Hobbs flicked a look at Sam before he turned back to Temple. 'Wait there.'

Hobbs walked off and Sam followed him. Temple went to get a better look of the photo of Jack Bartlett on the wall. In between the two photos was a box frame containing the two First World War medals Sam spoke of, to the left of which was a photo of the father, another Jack Bartlett. It was a nice tribute to two men who'd fought for their country. Temple went over to the shelving unit where he'd seen another photo. He picked it up for a better look. He recognised a slightly younger Dean Caxton dressed in army desert camouflage standing somewhere hot and dusty.

Looking sullen, Hobbs appeared at the door as Temple set the photo frame down.

'25 November I was there, at Erlestoke.'

'Three months ago. I see, thanks. Had you been there before?'

'No.'

'I'll be off then.' Temple made towards the door and then stopped, pointing to the photo of Caxton. 'Do you know where that was taken?'

Before he could say, Sam looked over Hobbs' shoulder and provided the answer.

'Afghanistan.'

CHAPTER 37

Temple parked outside the lychgate at Avebury churchyard. He could see by the clock in his car that it was eight thirty p.m. and with the prospect of an empty house waiting for him, he sat for a moment. Throughout the journey home, he'd relived his earlier meeting with Harker and the moment he told him about Newland. He had so many questions still and now he was alone he could give in to the rush of emotion that had threatened to overwhelm him all afternoon.

Where had the bastard been all these years? Why hadn't he come across his name before? How far off the mark had they been? Right off it, by the sounds of it. An 'opportunist' Wright had said, Newland had been a passer-by who happened to stop and kill. And that's just how it happened sometimes, Temple knew that. Richard was right; his mother had simply been in the wrong place at the wrong time.

Richard was right about another thing; he'd so wanted to find the killer himself that in a way he now felt cheated. He always thought he would be the one to find him, to piece together the puzzle after all the years of police apathy towards the case, but in the end, it had come down to another officer and a routine stop. He suddenly realised he didn't know the officer's name; he had to see him and thank him for bringing the whole miserable quest to an end. For the first time in his life, he could really let go. There was nothing more to do. It was truly over.

Temple stepped out of the car into the darkness and walked in the opposite direction to the lychgate. He wasn't sure what good it would do, but right there and then, he felt the need to make a short pilgrimage. The night was cold but dry and he could find himself there on foot in thirty minutes.

He walked up to the junction of the main road. Crossing over, he headed up Green Street, past the few houses and chapel until the road narrowed into an ancient stony track. The moon was large, giving a good light as he continued uphill, climbing towards Fyfield Down. Flanked by low banks and fields either side, he continued, the path now deeply carved by tractor ruts. He wasn't wearing the shoes for it, but oddly, that seemed to make it even more the right thing to do. He walked on until he saw a small circular plantation of tall trees in the distance. Turning off the path and across a grassy field, he continued uphill. Turning, he briefly looked back towards Avebury, down across the fields he had run across as a boy, before continuing on. Finally, at the summit of the hill, he reached the trees so familiar to him.

Standing in the moonlight, the circle of beech trees lent an eerie presence. He hadn't been here in ages. He walked around the perimeter and found the spot where all those years ago he had run to the caravan only to find his mother dead. Now he went inside the copse, under the knitted canopy of dry leaves that clung onto the branches. He stood still and looked around at the shadows on the trees. A strong breeze ruffled the branches over his head.

'We found him, Mum,' he whispered. 'It took a bit of time, but we've got him. No thanks to me. But at least you can rest now. We all can.'

He stayed at the spot for a while, deep in thought, before heading back downhill, out over the field and back down the path, down to the church and the cottage. He needed the drink he'd been promising himself. Inside, it

248

was empty, cold and unwelcoming without the fire lit. It wouldn't be worth the trouble of lighting one before he went to bed, so he put a side lamp on in the living room and went to the kitchen.

Pouring himself a glass of red wine from a bottle left on the side, he sat down in the living room. It was so quiet he realised it was the first time he'd been in the tiny cottage alone. Without Callie, Ana and the children and a fire in the hearth, the place was miserable. He'd never felt at home here in fact, he realised he'd never felt at home anywhere but at the house he had with Leigh. He let out a deep sigh.

News of Newland's capture had affected him more than he wanted to admit. In one afternoon, his life had turned on its head. Seeing Leigh's reaction earlier made him realise the effect his constant quest had had on his life and those close to him. If he'd been the one to find the killer it might have been justified, in fact it *would* have been justified, but not now.

His absurd notion that only he could find the killer had changed their lives in so many ways. And it wasn't just Leigh. He'd even let Harker warn him off Gemma all those years ago because he wanted to keep his job to find the killer. If he hadn't, her life undoubtedly would have been different and in turn, Prayer's too. They were all collateral damage, thanks to Newland's actions and his own failure to find him.

Perhaps if the original enquiry team had tried harder at the start and found Newland in the vicinity at the time, that would have made a difference. And what about the original SIO? He would never know what influence his mother's lifestyle had had on Roy Filer and on his decision making. He felt sure Filer had written her off as just another hippy, another crustie as they were referred to back then. And what had Filer been thinking when he tucked the blue T-shirt away in his loft all those years ago? Had he already lost control of exhibits and had taken the blue T-shirt to protect it, or had he deliberately hidden the evidence? What had turned out to be a stellar piece of evidence could so easily have ended up in a rubbish bin when Filer's son had found it.

And after Filer, it had always been a half-hearted effort by subsequent SIOs as they'd picked up where each had left off, scratching around for evidence, exhibits lost and fighting a general apathy among their colleagues. He imagined it must have been hard to generate any enthusiasm; it had been treated as one of those unsolvable cases that would forever remain a mystery. Until now.

He drained his wine glass. It was no use looking back, but he couldn't help it and his thoughts ran like a roller coaster. Now it was over, he was forced to re-examine his life. The reality was hard to take; Leigh was right, his quest had all been for nothing. He shouldn't have let it shape things in the way it had. He could and should have behaved differently.

Leigh had finally refused to put up with him. He'd asked too much of her. The endless distraction of trying to find his mother's killer, the demands of the job, not to mention the other women, which she'd once likened to some Oedipus/Freudian search for his mother, with some survivor syndrome guilt thrown in. Maybe she was right and if she was, they really hadn't stood a chance. She was also right to be angry with him. He was angry with himself. And in the middle of it had been Daisy. He had a lot of making up to do.

Then there was Newland. When would they move him from Swindon? Harker had said psychiatric reports were already being prepared; he'd like to see those at some point, to see inside the mind of this killer. He wanted to find out all he could about the man he'd been pursuing all these years. There were so many questions he wanted answers to.

Suddenly, he heard the sound of something being knocked over outside the front door. He grabbed an iron poker from the fire. If it was Paul King, he'd picked the right night to come calling. He turned off the lamp and with the poker gripped in his hand, he opened the door.

'Sophie? What are you doing here?'

'I heard the news and had to come by.'

'It's a bit late,' Temple protested. He set the poker down against the wall before turning on the light. 'I was just going to bed.'

She smiled at him. 'Is that an invitation?' She stepped forward across the threshold and into the small hallway. 'It's a bit dark in here, but I like the dark . . .'

Temple closed the door. She turned to him, reaching out and resting her hand on his chest. Because they'd once spent the night together, she appeared to feel an entitlement to touch him.

'I rang Callie, she said she was at the house and that you were here alone.' She moved closer to him. 'I just wanted to see how you are, it's been quite a day for you by all accounts.' She shook her hair back from her face.

'It's all still sinking in and it's a bit late, Sophie, we can do this another time.'

She kept talking. 'How's Richard? When can we sit down and do an interview?' There was an excitement in her voice. 'It must have been such a shock. I mean, really, after all these years . . .'

'It was, but let's not do this now.'

'. . . to suddenly find out like that . . .'

'Like I said, it's still sinking in . . .'

'And you didn't know him?'

'No idea . . .'

She cut him off. 'Look,' she said, her voice low. She moved her body in closer to him. 'I understand if you don't want to talk.' Her face was now inches from his.

'Sophie . . .'

'Talk's the last thing you need in this sort of circumstance. This must have been such a hard day for you.' Her hands travelled to the open neck of his shirt and she fingered a button. 'We could take up where we left the last time. It's exactly what you need now. We could both go upstairs. You know what I can do to relax you, don't you, just think about it . . .'

His hand covered hers. 'Let me stop you there. All I want to do is sleep — on my own.'

She tried to appeal to him with her eyes, but he opened the front door.

'We'll catch up another time.'

She was clearly put out but tried not to show it. 'Well, if you're sure. I'll hold you to that.' Reluctantly she moved towards the door, turning to face him. 'Rob Carroll got in touch earlier. I'm to see Harker tomorrow morning for a piece on Acre—'

'You do what you have to do, Sophie.' He thought of Tina Shaw and her words of warning about bringing press attention to himself. An article with Sophie Twiner certainly wouldn't help that relationship. 'Beside which, I don't want the publicity.'

Her voice suddenly hardened. 'I was hoping I could go to Rob Carroll with *your* story, rather than write Harker's tomorrow. The last piece for the *Telegraph* really pissed Harker off.'

'I can imagine.'

'You're not listening to me, are you? Don't say I didn't offer. I really thought we could help each other.'

It was with relief he watched her finally step back over the threshold of the door.

'We can help each other, Sophie, just not in the way you expected.'

He closed the door.

CHAPTER 38

'You all right, boss, you look a bit rough?' Eaton caught Temple as soon as he stepped into the main office. 'I have to say I didn't expect you this morning, I was just going to start the briefing . . .'

'This is my enquiry, Charlie, why wouldn't I be here?' Temple was irritable, having spent most of the night lying awake.

Eaton sensed his mood. 'Of course.' His voice dropped to almost a whisper. 'Boss, there's been a development. You need to hear this.' Eaton waved his hand towards Kelvin Stubbs to join them as he walked Temple away out of the earshot of others.

Stubbs weaved his way around his desk to reach their huddle. 'I have something.' Stubbs was visibly excited. 'Word on the street is that Georgie Munt is looking for a woman.'

Stubbs had his full attention. 'Tell me more.'

'We tasked one of the CHIS about the bounty and they say that Munt is looking for Tara Leyton. He's asking about for people to tell him where she is.'

The news caught Temple off guard. 'Hang on, let me get this right. The CHIS says this?'

'Yes.'

'They mentioned her name in relation to the bounty?'

'No, not exactly. But Munt's looking for her. It could be that he thinks she's linked to the murders. It could be a woman we're looking for.'

Temple processed what he was saying at the same time as giving Stubbs a response. 'That's a bit of a leap, Kelvin. Let's not start guessing the inner workings of Munt's mind.'

'Boss?' Stubbs frowned. Temple surmised he had been expecting a much more enthusiastic response.

Temple tried to gauge if Stubbs knew more than he was letting on. 'Let's not forget who we're dealing with; Munt could be up to all sorts of things under the cover of the Fortunes' murders. He could be looking for this woman for any number of reasons. Let's not draw the wrong conclusions. Who else knows about this?'

Eaton spoke. 'Us three and the CHIS.'

'Let's just take the briefing and we'll talk after. Say nothing to the team. This information is highly confidential. There's a leak in the room so we keep it tight.'

Temple stepped outside to the yard briefly, he had to get some air. Hearing Tara's name had taken him by surprise; hearing Stubbs say he thought she was connected to the murders had taken his breath away. For a second, his mind veered. Should he consider Tara as a suspect? Was she capable of shooting the Fortune brothers? Had he missed a trick? Had she played him? If she had, he'd just helped her out of the country.

No, he was sure. He'd seen the state of her and believed her story. She'd always been straight with him in the past. It just wasn't in her. Besides, if she'd have shot anyone, it would have been King. But somehow, he had to stop any TIE enquiries into her. It wouldn't take them long to discover she'd left the country for Corfu and trace the flight payment on a credit card back to him. And how the fuck would he explain that? At least she was safe from Munt, which was the only crumb of comfort he could take from the whole mess.

The information had come from a CHIS which meant it would already be officially recorded in the system, unlike all the information that Tara had given him over the years. There was nothing officially to link Temple to her. But now the word was out Munt was looking for her, he wondered how long it would be before it was also mentioned in conversation in the car being tagged by the Met. It was all starting to unravel. He closed his eyes. He could stop it all by arresting Staunton.

Temple wrapped up the morning briefing. 'I know it's disappointing that we haven't got enough to arrest Harry Staunton, but let's keep going, let's find the evidence. That's all, team, take your actions from Clare.'

The room was broken by a rise in chatter as the officers turned away from him. Any slack they had cut him for yesterday's revelation regarding Newland was at an end.

'Charlie,' Temple called Eaton over to him. 'Ask Kelvin Stubbs to contact his CHIS again.'

'We can find Tara Leyton quicker than any CHIS can.'

'I know we can, that's not what I was going to ask. See if we can find out more about the bounty, I want some context around it. See if he can find out who posted the comments about it online. Sophie Twiner took the comments down, but she never came back to me on who posted them.'

'OK.'

'Then I want you to make some enquiries with the army for me.'

'But what about Tara Leyton? The CHIS has given us a name. We at least have to do a TIE enquiry for her.'

'No, Leyton's a distraction. We're concentrating on Staunton. I'm going to give you a name. I want you to find out about a guy called Dean Caxton. He's ex-army and was in Afghanistan. I want to know regiment, times, dates and places until he left. TIE Caxton.'

Eaton shook his head dismissively. 'How does he come into it?'

'Dean Caxton is an electrician and this card was in Harry Staunton's house.' Temple showed Eaton the card Staunton had given him. 'He called the number when his sink was blocked.'

'But why would Harry Staunton call an electrician when he needed a plumber?'

'That's what I thought, electricians don't unblock sinks and there's no mention of any plumber on that card. He's been told to ring that number and he'll be looked after. Harry had it before his trouble with the sink, that's how he knew who to call. My guess is Matthew Staunton and Dean Caxton knew each other. Caxton was in Afghanistan, so was Matthew Staunton. Matthew gave Harry the card.'

Eaton was impatient. 'Where's this going, boss?'

'Staunton called Caxton to unblock his sink and Caxton's cousin, Ryan Hobbs, a plumber, attended. Staunton says it was this that prompted him to remember he'd left the gun under the sink and that was when he first realised it was gone.'

'So, you think Hobbs took the gun?'

'Staunton is adamant it was gone before Hobbs turned up to fix his sink, but he might be wrong. Caxton has a tattoo on his arm — *CB* . . .'

'CB?'

'CB — Camp Bastion. See if they were there at the same time. And here's Caxton's and Hobbs' mobile numbers, start making enquiries on them.'

'I still don't see—'

'If Dean Caxton and Matthew Staunton knew each other, Caxton might have known about the gun.'

'OK?' Eaton looked unconvinced. 'And do nothing about Tara Leyton?'

Temple pulled his car keys from his jacket pocket. 'No. I don't want us running down rabbit holes. No TIE enquiry on Leyton and tell Kelvin, that's an order. We're not wasting time on it.'

Eaton's expression said that he was convinced Temple had lost it. 'You off somewhere?'

'Back in an hour.'

* * *

'They're getting him ready to take him to Long Lartin. He'll go from there to court for sentence. It's the only chance you'll get to see him before then.'

DC Paul Wright and Temple stood in the stairwell in the back entrance to Swindon police station.

'I just thought it might help, mate.'

'It will. They wouldn't let me near him in custody, but I want to see him.'

'They've parked the prison van further away, so go round there and you'll get a good look. Remember there's cameras everywhere.'

'I won't do anything silly. I just wanted to see the fucker for myself.'

Temple walked to the rear of the building, close to where a white van was parked with its rear doors open, ready to take Newland to Worcestershire. He stood back as the station door opened and Newland appeared, escorted by two officers. Newland stepped forward and stopped, shivering in the cold; he quickly looked around and blinked in the sunlight.

Temple watched as Newland squinted at the bright sun and took his time walking towards the van. A G4 guard gestured to Newland as he looked around, reducing his steps to a shuffle. Before he reached the van, Newland stopped. Suddenly, he turned his head and met Temple's gaze. There was a look of recognition.

Temple looked at the shabby man before him. As seemed to be the way with killers, he was mediocre, nothing special. He looked at his hands, the hands that had been around his mother's neck and squeezed until the life was out of her. The same hands that had grabbed at him that day, shoving him backwards. He lunged forward; he wanted to throttle him, as he'd throttled his mother, he wanted to beat his fists into him. Suddenly, he felt himself pulled back by both arms.

'It's me, mate.' Paul Wright held on until he felt Temple stop resisting.

Temple watched Newland take the few strides into the back of the van. With Newland out of his sight and the van driving away out of the yard towards the security barrier, Temple calmed.

Wright let go of his arms. 'I followed you because I knew the temptation would be too much. Besides, I wanted to see him too.'

Temple shook his arms to straighten his jacket.

'I hadn't intended to do it, but when I saw him, the emotions just got the better of me and I wanted to fucking kill him.'

Wright nodded up to a camera focused on the yard as he lit a cigarette. 'Harker would have loved that.'

'It would have been worth it.'

Wright inhaled. 'Not much of a man, was he?'

'They never are.'

'I suppose he would have looked different back then. Those thirty-odd years have left their mark on him.' They both watched the security barrier rise and the van drive away.

They turned and walked towards the rear of the station.

'I wanted to ask him why he had to kill her, why he hadn't just walked away that day. I wanted to ask him why he hadn't killed me too. He'd already crossed the Rubicon when he killed her, so what difference would it have made to do me too?'

Wright drew on his cigarette. 'Who knows? Perhaps that's what you have to take from this, that he left you alive.'

'Richard said something similar. Do you think he set out to kill that day?'

'Maybe. If it hadn't been your mother, it would have been someone else that day, or the next. Who knows? Maybe he'll talk after sentence.'

258

'Do you think he's only killed once? In all these years, that he's never done it again? It's obviously in him to do it and if he's done it once, what about a second or third time?'

'I don't suppose they'll look any further. It does beg the question though. For you it's over. At least as far as wondering who he is, it is. You've just seen him get into the back of that van. He's on his way to prison and by the looks of him, that's where he's going to die.'

CHAPTER 39

Eaton was waiting for Temple when he arrived back at Marlborough.

'Boss, Matthew Staunton and Dean Caxton were in the same Fusilier regiment and in Afghanistan in 2012.'

'So they knew one another and that's why Caxton's card was in Harry's house. This means that Caxton may also know about the Glock 19 and how Matthew Staunton came by it. He may also know that Staunton smuggled it back with him and where it was kept.'

'But that would only confirm what we already know. Harry Staunton said he hid it from Matthew. And what about Harry saying the gun was gone before the sink was mended?'

'What if he got that wrong?'

Eaton frowned. 'What if he got that *right*, boss? The bloke couldn't have taken the gun if it wasn't there.'

Temple ignored his point. 'How long before telephony brings us anything?'

'A few more hours yet, possibly twenty-four hours, depends on the provider.'

'We have something here, Charlie, with Dean Caxton and Ryan Hobbs, but I don't know what.'

Eaton shook his head. 'We've still got nothing on them, boss. Stubbs wants me to ask you again about digging into Tara Leyton.'

'I said leave it.'

'But Kelvin thinks we could be missing a trick . . .'

Temple had to keep calm. He had to draw their attention away from Tara. 'I don't care what Kelvin thinks. We need to focus on Caxton and Hobbs and the gun. Forget Tara Leyton, OK. Leave it.'

'And where does Harry Staunton fit in with all this?'

'I don't know, Charlie. I don't fucking know yet.'

* * *

Temple was standing on the doorstep of Ryan Hobbs's house, waiting for Sam Mason to answer the door. He could hear a radio inside so he knew she was in. He rang again and knocked on the door with his fist. The radio went quiet and he heard someone approaching.

'Hello, Sam. Sorry to bang like that, I couldn't get you to hear over the radio.'

'Oh, that's all right.' She stood in the doorway. There was no smile today and Temple sensed she might be less helpful. 'If you want Ryan, he's gone to work.'

'That's not why I came. I think I left my pen here yesterday. I think I might have lost it down the side of the settee, where I was sitting,' he lied.

'Oh? I don't remember seeing anything. I'll go and have a look for you.'

She disappeared inside, leaving him at the door. It wasn't the answer Temple wanted. He wanted her to invite him in to look for himself, then he could talk to her. She came back.

'I can't see it, but then this is in the way.' She gestured to her bump. 'Do you want to come in and look for yourself?'

'If I could, I'm so sorry to bother you like this, it's just it was a present and it means a lot to me.'

261

Temple followed Sam Mason into the living room. Under her supervision, he made a show of looking for a pen, lifting cushions and putting his hand down the side of the settee. He tried to make small talk, but she seemed less inclined to talk today. His plan had failed. As he repositioned the cushions, he heard her gasp behind him.

'My waters have broken!' Sam Mason was flustered and red-faced as Temple looked down on the laminate floor. 'I've been having contractions for a few days now. I'm so sorry!'

'You need to get to hospital.'

'But Ryan's not home for hours, I think he's working in Salisbury.'

'Well, I could take you if you want, it will save waiting for an ambulance?'

'I've got my bag ready to go. I'll have to go up and change quickly. If you wouldn't mind taking me?'

'No, like I said, it'll be quicker than an ambulance. Don't worry, we'll be there in no time.'

Sam quickly cleaned the floor in the living room and disappeared upstairs. It wasn't quite the scenario that Temple had envisaged, but it would have to do. He could try and talk to her on the way to the hospital. While he waited for her to come down, he looked around.

He went again to the photo of Dean Caxton on the shelving unit. It was similar to the one he'd seen at Harry Staunton's of his grandson Matthew. He then looked at the photo of Jack Bartlett again in his uniform, next to that of his father in his. A Second World War hero. From all that he'd heard yesterday, Bartlett was certainly that.

Sam appeared suddenly at the door, with a jacket on and bag in hand.

'I'm ready if you are.'

'Let's go.'

In the car, she managed to get the seat belt across, but looked uncomfortable. He started off to the hospital, looking across to check on her.

'How are you feeling?'

'Nervous and a little bit scared.'

'I'm sure you'll be fine. Just hang on. We'll be there soon. How come you didn't opt for Bath Hospital, I'd have thought that was nearer?'

'I've got friends who had really good experiences at Swindon Maternity, so I knew I wanted to go there. It's really friendly.'

'OK. Well, I'll try and take your mind off things until we get there. Did you say you were going to call him Jack?'

'That's right.'

'Since we're on the way to deliver another little Jack into the world, if it helps to distract you, tell me more about his namesake, Ryan's great-grandfather.'

Sam looked at the road straight in front of her, shifting in the seat, still trying to get herself comfortable.

He went on. 'I was looking at the display of the First World War medals in the box frame, with the photo of Jack's father, I thought that was really neat.'

'We had Jack's medals from the Second World War as well, but they were stolen in a burglary.'

'Oh? That's a shame. Did you report it?'

'Yes, but it wasn't us, they were stolen from Jack, he was the one who was burgled. You know what it's like. They give you a crime number and that's it. They put Jack in hospital. He was a fighter, even at his age. He wasn't going to just let someone come in and take what wasn't theirs.'

'Did they find who did it?'

'Nope.'

'I suppose you think the police are pretty useless?'

She smiled. 'Not today though.'

'So, what happened to Jack?'

'He never recovered, not properly.' She moved in her seat. 'I mean, he left hospital all right, they patched him up really well. But he'd been hit about really badly, and it affected him, he wasn't the same after. He was withdrawn, depressed. It made him afraid. It was as if they knocked the life out of him. He was burgled in the summer of 2018 and he died in October 2019. He so wanted to make his hundredth birthday. He'd been so fit and active until then, he was fantastic for his age. This was a man who at ninety-seven still used to mow his own lawn. Dean and Ryan were gutted.'

'I expect they were.'

She fidgeted in her seat. 'I'm going to have to take this seat belt off. I need to shift down a bit.'

Temple's mobile rang, but he let it ring out as he put his foot on the accelerator.

'We're going to be there in about fifteen minutes if you can just hold on, Sam.'

'Please hurry up, I can feel stuff happening. There's no way I want my baby born by the side of the road.'

'I'm pushing it as far as I can, Sam. Have you phoned Ryan?' He kept his eyes on the road.

'As soon as I get to the hospital, I will.' She started to blow loudly.

Temple flashed a driver waiting in front of him to move out of his way which allowed him to make speed, as Sam writhed in the seat, trying to get comfortable. Finally, they reached the hospital, pulling into the A & E bay where he dashed out to find a wheelchair. He returned with a chair and a porter and Sam gently eased herself into it. Temple followed with her bag, going with her to the maternity unit.

'Are you her husband?' a nurse asked.

'No, he's not,' said Sam sharply through her pains.

Temple turned to the nurse. 'He'll be here later.' He touched Sam's arm. 'Good luck, I'm sure you'll have little Jack with you really soon by the looks of things.'

Temple left the maternity unit and walking through the hospital foyer he turned his attention to his missed call.

'DS Cartwright? I was a bit busy when you called.'

'I wanted to touch base. Two of our subjects are now out in a car with Paul King. They've driven to somewhere called Avebury, I don't know if that's of any significance?'

'Exactly where are they?' he heard himself say.

'They've passed through the High Street, stopping down by the church gate. It's as if they're looking for an address there, is that something you can help us with? I thought perhaps that might mean something?'

There was only one reason for King to be in Avebury.

CHAPTER 40

If King was now driving around in a car with others, there could have been some talk on the way. What had been said? Had Tara been mentioned? Did Cartwright already know Temple lived there? She might have heard King talk about him having a gun. His mouth dried.

'Have they said why they're there?' His grip was tight on his phone.

'They're not in the car with the lump so we can't pick up any conversation.'

Temple sighed with relief as she continued.

'They're using one of the Fortunes' cars. But from what we can see, King seems to be the one giving the directions. I've got eyes on them now. Hang on, they're going into the pub. They'll probably be out of the car for a couple of hours now.'

'No, Avebury has no significance, can't help you with that, I'm afraid. Thanks for the information, Zoe. Always appreciated.'

With King cruising around Avebury, Temple had been right to move everyone out of the cottage. He didn't know what it would take to get King to back off but his last recall to prison hadn't seemed to make any difference and neither had

266

the deaths of the Fortune brothers. King wanted his pound of flesh and would stop at nothing until he had it. But right there and then Temple was just grateful they hadn't been in the car with the listening device.

Relieved, Temple called Eaton from the hospital foyer.

'Check out an aggravated burglary report for a white male, Jack Bartlett, summer 2018. It went undetected. I'm on my way back.'

Turning to go out of the main entrance, Temple spotted a familiar figure at a vending machine.

'Sharnie?'

Caught by surprise, she turned.

'*You*? What are you doing here?'

'I'm here on another matter. How are you? How's Elijah doing?'

Her face took on an embittered look. 'Elijah's very sick. His heart's broken, literally broken. That's how he's doing.' She fished out a tissue from her sleeve. 'I've left one of the girls with him now. I need to get back to him,' Her voice rose. 'You're not to go near him, do you hear me? I don't want you seeing him like that and I don't want him seeing you, it'll upset him.'

At the sound of her distress, people had turned to look at them.

'Calm down, Sharnie, don't worry, I'm not going to go in.'

'Just leave us alone,' she hissed and scurried away from him.

* * *

Back at Marlborough, Eaton had dropped a couple of bags of ring doughnuts into the main office as a morale booster. Immaculate as ever, Ruby needed a sugar rush for the next task and reached in, taking the last one.

'So why are we looking at Ryan Hobbs and this Dean Caxton?' she asked.

'It's all part of the Harry Staunton line of enquiry.'

'And you want me to look at an historic aggravated burglary involving a Jack Bartlett because? Can I ask why?'

'Something the boss wants checked out.'

Sitting at her screen, Ruby arched her perfectly formed eyebrows. 'The boss?' She scoffed. 'I can't wait for the new DCI to turn up. Ma'am Shaw said she'll be here soon, then we'll sort everything out. Stubbsy's also livid, says the enquiry's going in the wrong direction. He said he's got a perfectly good TIE enquiry that's being ignored. Are you listening to me?'

Eaton buried his head in his screen, so she continued.

'Stubbsy's doing it anyway, says it could be the murderer. Why Temple is still here is what I want to know. How come he's managed to stay in the job when he's got a child with a sex worker? Tell me that. Never mind all the stuff with Simon Sloper. It's a fucking smokescreen. Something's going on. He was seen at HQ talking privately to ACC Harker, did you know that?'

'When was that then?' asked Eaton, suddenly interested.

'The day after the shootings came in.'

'He went to a Gold Group meeting.'

'They were seen on their own. Perhaps he was reporting back.'

'Look, I don't know anything, Rubs, so let's just get on with it.' He didn't know what to think anymore.

'All I know is the atmosphere here's been fucking awful since he turned up.'

He walked out of the room, leaving her talking to his back. Ruby sighed and started the interrogation of the computer system as Temple came through the door.

He swooped into the doughnut bag as Ruby expertly took a bite of hers, careful not to let it touch her lipstick. Temple scrunched up the empty bag and put it in the bin.

'Where is everyone?'

Ruby didn't look up from her screen. 'Charlie's about, must be down the corridor.' As she finished speaking, Eaton appeared.

'Where's everyone else, Charlie?'

'Kelvin's following up some illegal dog fighting enquiries, Clare's at the dentist and Tom's collating the army records.'

'Ma'am Shaw been about?'

'No. Word is she's busy hunting down the new DCI.'

Ruby gave a slight smile.

'At least that gives me a rest. I saw Sharnie Fortune earlier at the hospital. Apparently, Elijah's heart's broken.'

'Did you see him?' asked Eaton.

'No, she was adamant that I wasn't to go near him.'

'Did they ask after the enquiry?'

'Not a word.'

Ruby interrupted. 'OK, are you ready.' She spoke over the top of her screen. 'I'm reading the burglary report here from 2018. There were two assailants and whoever they were, they seem to have given the old boy a right kicking. He was ninety-seven years old for God's sake, so there was no need for it.'

Temple sat down ready to listen. 'Sam Mason said despite his age, he was in good shape. It didn't sound as if he was one for sitting in a chair all day.'

Ruby shook her head, eyes glued to the screen. 'This is awful. He was left for dead, having been strangled with his own tie. They punched him in the face breaking his cheekbone, his nose, he had whiplash, took numerous blows to the body and broke his hip when he fell.' She stopped. 'They also prised his wedding ring off his finger and broke his finger in the process. They snapped another of his fingers back to get him to tell them where he kept his money.'

'What did they take?' asked Eaton.

'Approximately two thousand pounds in cash, a lady's gold wedding band, a lady's diamond-and-sapphire ring, the victim's gold wedding band and two gold chain necklaces. It also says a Victory War medal and a British War medal and two First and two Second World War medals. All he had.'

Temple and Eaton were now looking over Ruby's shoulder at the screen. 'Anything to indicate who the attackers were?'

Temple was quiet.

She scrolled down. 'Two males, dark-haired, no identifying features.'

'Any photofit?'

'Nope.'

'Fingerprints?'

'Nothing. Just the crime number and some advice about putting in an alarm when he came out of hospital. He was the only witness. It says he was hospitalised for weeks and when he was eventually seen, he didn't remember much.'

'Sam Mason told me that Jack Bartlett fought at Calais in 1940, up against the German army while the beaches were being evacuated at Dunkirk. He was taken prisoner but escaped and made his way back to England. He then went back for more in Operation Market Garden. Not many of them did that.'

Ruby gave a nod to the screen. 'He lived through all that, only to end up being beaten in his own home. Do we know what happened to him?'

Temple sat down in his seat facing Ruby. 'He died five months or so ago. The might of the German army couldn't get him and even at ninety-seven, it took two lowlife scum to put him down. And we couldn't even give him the courtesy of a decent burglary enquiry. There's no doubt it was the cause of his death. He was murdered.'

CHAPTER 41

'Why don't you stay here tonight?' Callie was doing her best to coax Temple not to return to the cottage. He held her close.

'I'd love to, but with Paul King out on the prowl it's best I go back. I'd rather he found me there than here.'

'Can't you tell the hierarchy about him, get him locked up again?'

'We all know he's out. He can go where he pleases.'

'But you need protecting from him.'

'There's no intelligence that he's going to come after me. Just my instinct and that's not enough.'

'What's the point in being a detective if you're not allowed to employ your instincts?'

'Don't get me started.' He leaned back to look at her. 'I shouldn't have told you about King being out, but then I had to get you all away.' He kissed her.

'I want you to tell me, I'd rather know than not know, but I won't sleep well until I know he can't reach you. How's the enquiry going?'

'I've got some new leads to follow but if they turn to nothing, I don't know where I'm going with it next. I think the whole Newland thing is getting to me. It'll be good to get the sentencing over.'

'Speaking of which, have you seen the local rag and the *Telegraph* today?'

'No.'

'Sophie Twiner's followed up her last article about Op Acre. It's gushing about Harker, here look.'

She turned behind her and picked up the newspaper resting on a chair. Temple saw Newland's photo.

'I don't want to read it.'

'Well, *I* have. It's Clive Harker this and Clive Harker that. He's taking all the credit for finding Newland.'

'It's what they do.'

'Why would she write that?'

'Don't know. It doesn't matter. Besides, perhaps she's right, perhaps the credit should go to him.'

'I'm seeing her in a different light.' She put the paper down. 'Are you sure you won't stay? I've missed you.'

'I've missed you too.'

'I wish you could see Ben and Daisy playing in the garden, going off exploring. She's really good with him. She'll be great with the new baby.' She frowned. 'Leigh will continue with her plans to move once she's had the baby, won't she? If she moves away, she'll take the baby and Daisy with her.'

'I know. I've tried not to think about it. Daisy's been so much more settled lately, especially at school, she's doing well again. She doesn't want to go, she wants to stay with us. I didn't have the heart to tell her she'd have no choice. Leigh would never wear it. I promised her we'd sort it. Let's deal with it when it happens.'

After reassuring Callie that he would be careful, Temple made his way back to Avebury. As he closed the door behind him, the cottage was cold and dark. He stood on some post so bent down to pick it up before going into the kitchen. He flicked the light on and went to the fridge to see what he could salvage from the remnants of a white wine bottle that was kept for cooking. He guessed there was about one small glass left.

Draining the bottle into a glass, he went into the lounge, flicking on the small table lamp before sitting on the settee.

He turned on the TV to the news channel for the sole purpose of having another face in the room, then muted it. He gulped down the wine and rested his head back, looking at the ceiling. What Callie had said was true; once the baby was born Leigh was bound to put her plan to move into action. The new baby wouldn't know any different, but it would be a struggle for Daisy. He knew he had to make up some ground with Leigh before she moved, for all their sakes.

As he lay with his head back, his eyes started to close. Just as he was about to sleep, his phone rang.

It was Eaton. 'Boss, you're needed. It's Dean Caxton. He's dead.'

CHAPTER 42

Temple stood with Eaton, looking down at Caxton's body as it lay on a rough slab of concrete next to a barn. Their car headlights shone out in the darkness, illuminating driving rain drenching the clothes on the corpse. Temple hunched under his jacket, pulling his collar up.

'He's unrecognisable.'

'He's taken quite a savage beating, boss, before being shot. Then it looks like they've set fire to his legs. I've can see two entry wounds to his body, there may be more. CSI are on the way.'

'Who found him?'

'The farmer saw lights coming down the track in the dark. Says he gets his machinery stolen now and then so he thought he'd come up and check on the barn. He saw the body in his headlights as he pulled up.'

'Did he get a look at the vehicle?'

'No, just saw dipped headlights as the vehicle came down the track from his kitchen window. It's pitch black out here, and the farmhouse is across that field so there's no way he can say what vehicle it was. He called 999 as soon as he saw the body. Says he was already dead when he saw him.

Caxton had his wallet in his jacket, money intact. Driver's licence gave us the ID.'

Temple crouched down, looking at Caxton's face. 'Christ, he's a mess. Whoever left him here wanted us to know who he was. He struck me as someone who could take care of himself, so how has he ended up like this?'

'I don't know, boss. But you've had contact with him. You'll have to ring ma'am Shaw.'

'I'll tell her in a minute. You know what I'm thinking? Someone's just pocketed fifty grand. We need to send someone round to Ryan Hobbs. We have to find him fast and take him into protective custody. And have a car go round and make sure Harry Staunton's still alive.'

'Boss?'

'Just do it.'

'I'll send Tom and Kelvin.'

Tina Shaw held her mobile to her ear and listened intently. 'Quoits Farm, you say. Where is that?'

'The outskirts of Trowbridge. Ma'am, Caxton was part of the Mitre enquiry. I saw him yesterday and was going to invite him and his cousin in to answer some questions tomorrow.'

'And now he's dead? *Shit*. And you think they're connected to the enquiry in what way?'

'Caxton was in the same regiment as Harry Staunton's grandson Matthew, who had the Glock. Both served in Afghanistan at the same time. Harry said he noticed the Glock was missing when he went to check before having his sink unblocked; he rang Caxton to fix his blocked sink and Ryan Hobbs attended. I was hoping that Caxton would confirm he knew Matthew Staunton.'

'And therefore knew about the Glock?'

'Yes.'

'And you think Caxton shot the Fortune brothers?'

'It was a theory I was working on.'

'Contact DS Cartwright . . .'

'Already have, ma'am. She said her team are at the Fortunes' home address. She saw a car leave earlier this evening, but she's pretty sure the crew she's looking at and their car haven't left all night.'

Shaw sighed. 'I'm coming over.'

* * *

Temple sat in his office with Tina Shaw and Eaton crammed into the confined space.

'This makes things difficult. With Caxton on the slab in the mortuary and you seeing him earlier . . .'

'I know, ma'am, but—'

'You had contact with Caxton, you know how it goes.'

'Ma'am, I have to stay with this now, I feel we're getting close. If we let go now . . .'

'What's your theory around Caxton's death?'

'Sam Mason told me that Dean Caxton and Ryan Hobbs' great-grandfather was the subject of an aggravated burglary in 2018. He died just over a year later. It's got the Fortunes' MO all over it. Caxton was in the same regiment as Matthew Staunton who brought the Glock back from Afghanistan. My guess is Caxton knew about Matthew having the Glock. Harry Staunton noticed the gun was missing at about the time that Ryan Hobbs attended his address to mend his sink.'

Eaton spoke up. 'We don't actually *know* the Fortunes were involved in Jack Bartlett's burglary, boss. There's no intelligence and there's no evidence.'

'No, there isn't, but what we do know is there's a gun, Caxton's link to Matthew Staunton and now Caxton's dead. None of this is a coincidence. And there's something else.' Temple paused. 'We have a leak in the enquiry team.'

Eaton looked up sharply. 'You can't think Caxton's name has come from someone on the team?'

'Like I said, there's a leak. I asked for some enquiries to be conducted into Caxton and Hobbs and now Caxton's dead. How else do the Fortunes know about him?'

Tina Shaw bit her lip. 'That's a serious allegation, Temple.'

'Let's hope I'm wrong and it's not the case, ma'am.'

She defended the team. 'Someone unconnected to this case might have killed Caxton. And who's this Hobbs?'

'They're cousins, very close, ma'am. More like brothers.'

Tina Shaw continued. 'That's not to say he couldn't have killed him. Where is Hobbs?'

'We're trying to locate him now, ma'am,' Eaton explained.

She continued. 'Caxton and Hobbs might have had a falling out and Hobbs killed Caxton.'

'Ma'am, you didn't see the body. It's the work of more than one person.'

They all looked up at a knock on the door. It was Ruby.

'They haven't been able to locate Ryan Hobbs. He's not at his home address and his van as well as Caxton's van is parked on his drive.' She closed the door.

Temple shook his head. 'Ma'am, I'd like to go and see Hobbs' partner, Sam Mason. She's having a baby and is in the Great Western Hospital. It's inconceivable that Hobbs hasn't been to see her. She knows who I am and if she knows anything about all this, she might talk.'

Tina Shaw leaned across the desk. 'Your contact with Caxton means you'll have to step back. In fact, you've put me in a difficult position. Until I can find someone else, I'll have to assume SIO for the Fortunes' and Caxton's murder and Op Mitre. It's late now, come back in the morning and we'll make an entry in the policy book.'

'And Sam Mason?'

'No, stay away. Besides, I shouldn't think you'd be too welcome in the maternity unit at two thirty in the morning.'

CHAPTER 43

Temple explained his presence to the night shift sister. The nurse directed him to a side room and told him to wait. Ten minutes later, she brought a sleepy Sam Mason in to see him in a wheelchair.

'DI Temple?' She looked at the nurse. 'What's this about?'

'I'm really sorry to disturb you, Sam. How's little Jack?'

'He's fine, seven pounds four ounces. I thought the nurse was waking me for a night feed.'

He hated the message he was about to bring. 'Did Dean and Ryan come and see you earlier this evening?'

'Of course, Dean brought Ryan up. They brought in this great big blue balloon with little Jack's name on it.'

'Did they say what they were going to do afterwards?'

'Dean was taking Ryan for a drink, to wet the baby's head.'

'Did they say where they were going?'

'No, just to the pub, normally the Palmers Arms. Why?'

'We've been trying to find Ryan, do you know where he is?'

'What do you mean, trying to find him? At this time of night, he's at home.' She screwed her face up. 'Why are you looking for him? You're scaring me now.'

'Dean was found earlier, he's . . . been killed.'

Her hand went up to her mouth. 'Dean? *Our Dean*?'

'I'm afraid so.'

'Killed? But how? Oh my God!'

'Dean was injured badly. We don't know the circumstances, that's why we wanted to find Ryan, to see if he could help us.'

'Are you sure it's Dean?'

'I'm sure. I've seen his body.'

'But how has this happened? They were together tonight. So, where's Ryan?'

'We are trying to find him. Is there anywhere you think we could look for him?'

'No, he should be at home. If he's not there he would be at Dean's. I can't take this in.'

'I'm sorry, Sam.'

'Dean was only here earlier. Who would want to kill him?' As realisation suddenly hit, tears streamed down her face.

'We don't know. Anything you can tell us will help.'

'Who would do that?' she sniffed. 'And where's Ryan?'

'Did Ryan and Dean leave you in good spirits tonight?'

'Of course they did, they'd just seen little Jack. Ryan was over the moon and Dean was so pleased for us.' She shook her head. 'I can't believe this.'

'So they seemed all right to you?'

'Yes, why wouldn't they?'

'No arguments or anything between them?'

She cried harder. 'No, they never argued. I told you, they're like brothers.'

'What about girlfriends, did Dean have a girlfriend?'

'They came and went. He was married while he was in the army but they divorced.'

'I am sorry to ask you these questions at this time, Sam, but you're the only one who can help us right now.'

'I'm really worried now. Where's Ryan? You must find him. He wouldn't stand by and see Dean hurt in any way.'

'And visiting time was the last time you saw or heard from Ryan?'

'Yes.'

'No further calls, or texts on your mobile?'

She shook her head. 'No.'

'Thanks, Sam. Can you find a good photo of Ryan on your phone and we'll use that to try and find him? Here's my number to send it to and if you think of anything or if Ryan comes in to see you, please ring me. We want to know that he's safe and well.'

Temple was convinced she knew nothing and as the nurse took her back to the ward, he could see all he had done was bring her grief and worry. Where was Hobbs? Caxton had taken him to the hospital and left his van on Hobbs' drive, blocking his van from moving, so wherever he was, he was on foot. If he was still alive, he had to find him.

CHAPTER 44

The main office was galvanised. More staff had been drafted in and Clare was busy with Eaton allocating actions. Everyone was carrying on around him as if he was invisible. Tina Shaw hadn't wasted any time informing the team he was off the enquiry. Feeling like a spare part, Temple went to his office where Shaw had ensconced herself, leaving him to squeeze into a chair in the corner. She pushed a pen towards him across the desk.

'I've made an entry in the policy book if you can sign there.' She stabbed her finger on the page. 'We're running Caxton's murder as a separate enquiry to the Fortunes — you're to stay away from it, from both enquiries actually, since the reason you went to see Caxton and Hobbs was for Op Mitre.'

'It's a bit over the top, ma'am, especially as we're so short of staff.'

'You know the rules.' She watched him countersign the book. 'I suggest you go on leave and then we'll talk about what happens next.'

Before he could answer, they were interrupted by Eaton knocking on the door.

'Telephony have located Ryan Hobbs' phone to Melksham. They're working on it now.'

Temple ignored Tina Shaw's instruction. 'What about their home addresses, Charlie?'

'We've got teams on Caxton's and Hobbs' home addresses and we've put a notice out to all shifts for Hobbs. We've searched both their vans, there's only tools in them. Scene-of-crime say Caxton wasn't killed where he was found, the body was dumped.'

'What about the pathologist?' asked Tina Shaw.

'Starts in an hour. As soon as he gets the bullets out of Caxton, they'll be couriered to NABIS and fast-tracked.'

Tina Shaw looked back at the policy book for a moment and Eaton took the opportunity to indicate to Temple he wanted to speak to him outside. They both took their leave and walked down the corridor.

'Boss, a DS Cartwright was in here earlier, looking for you.'

'I'll contact her.'

'You're off the enquiry then?'

'She seems to want me off. But it makes no sense for me to leave now. It's a mistake to run the Caxton enquiry separately, I'm sure they're linked. I'll contact Cartwright.'

'Who is this Cartwright, I've never seen or heard of her before?'

'She's looking to relocate, wants some information on the area.'

Alone in his car, Temple tapped his mobile.

'Zoe? You were looking for me?'

'Yes. I might have something of interest for you from our lump.'

'What's that then?'

'There was some talk in the car of our crew going back today.'

'OK.' As Temple listened, he saw Tina Shaw come out of the back door of the station.

'And how they were going to spend fifty grand. You told me about a bounty when we first met.'

'I did.'

'Looks like it's been claimed.'

CHAPTER 45

Temple stopped Tina Shaw before she reached her car.

'Ma'am, DS Cartwright's just given me some information. We need to act fast. Can we go back inside?'

Back in Temple's office, Tina Shaw resumed her seat behind the desk as Temple stood in front of her.

'Right, what is it?'

'Zoe Cartwright has just told me that the subjects from London are claiming the fifty grand bounty. You realise what that means?'

She spoke slowly. 'That the Fortunes have had help from their relatives . . .'

'And that they killed Dean Caxton.'

'Hang on, did Zoe say that?'

'No, *I* did. Ma'am, Caxton's body is in the mortuary, Hobbs is missing, possibly dead too, and we've got people claiming the bounty that Elijah Fortune put out to find his sons' killer, dead or alive, the message said.'

'Can I remind you Elijah Fortune is in a hospital bed. All the talk of a bounty was something that hasn't been firmed up, just something that was mentioned on social media.'

'Zoe Cartwright is sitting on a crew of four in a car who are speculating on how they are going to spend fifty grand

and they are leaving to go back to London later today. We have to move in and arrest them.'

'And when they sit in an interview room and say "no comment" and we haven't got anything on them except a recording about spending fifty grand, what do you think will happen then?'

'Ma'am, it has to be the Fortunes.'

'No, Temple, it doesn't *have* to be. It could very well be that Ryan Hobbs has murdered his cousin and is on the run.'

'And why would he do that?'

Eaton knocked before putting his head around the door. 'Just thought you'd like to know. The path's taken the first bullet out of Caxton. It's on a motorbike going up the M5.'

Tina Shaw gestured towards the door. 'Evidence, Temple. That's what we work on.'

'Ma'am, Cartwright has evidence of men claiming the bounty.' His voice was hard and it didn't come out the way he had intended.

Shaw was riled. 'You're no longer on the enquiry, Temple, so you can leave this to me.'

He had to admit, the only thing connecting Dean Caxton to the Fortune shooting was the feeling in his gut. He needed more. In the absence of Ryan Hobbs, there was only one other person who could help.

* * *

'Have you found him yet?' Sam Mason was holding her baby son and looking at him in sheer desperation.

'No, and I feel bad about coming here again when I have no news and when you need your rest to look after the baby. But I have more questions.'

'I've told you everything I know, I just want you to find Ryan.'

'Has Ryan been in touch with you at all?'

'No, I wish he had. I'm going off my head with worry.'

'If he does, find out where he is and tell him to contact me. Now, if we can go back to Jack Bartlett's burglary. How did it affect Dean and Ryan?'

'What's that got to do with it?'

'Please, Sam?'

'They were angry. Angry at who did it, angry at the police for not finding them and angry with themselves because they thought they should have taken better care of Jack. I remember Ryan coming home, we were in a rented flat and he sat on the bed and cried. He'd come from the hospital, said Jack looked so frail. He took a photo of him lying in the hospital, it was shocking.'

'Did they go public with it?'

'No, Jack wouldn't have wanted people to see him like that. Dean wanted to make a public appeal in the news for the jewellery and medals, but Jack didn't want to draw attention to the fact he'd been burgled. He felt foolish.'

'What happened after the burglary?'

'Dean and Ryan went round to the house and tidied it up. We made it nice for when he came out; Jack insisted on going back, but Ryan and Dean gradually made him see that he was vulnerable and the police mentioned something about sometimes burglars come back a second or third time. That done it for Dean. He stayed there until they eventually managed to find a care home for Jack. It wasn't what Jack wanted, but at least they knew he was safe there.'

'Sam, I've been through the burglary report. It says four medals were stolen, and yet when I was round at yours, I saw there are two medals in the display frame on the wall. Were they part of the ones stolen?'

'Yes.'

'But how did they get back in the display?'

'Dean and Ryan were able to track them down. First World War medals have the recipient's name inscribed around the rim; this helped them to get them back.'

'Do you know how they did that?'

'They found them just after Jack died. They were advertised online by a dealer who mentioned the name inscribed on the medals was Jack Bartlett. They knew they were his instantly from the picture because there was also a stain on the ribbon.'

'Do you remember who the dealer was or where?'

'It's in Melksham, the vintage shop. It's always got a Union Jack flying outside, been there for years.'

'I know the one.' He'd driven past it before without any recognition save for the flag. 'How are you coping?'

'I want Ryan back,' she said tearfully. 'I'm so scared. It's all over social media about Dean, my family are going crazy with it. This should be a happy time.'

'How's the baby?'

'We're checking out tomorrow if they're happy. They thought he had a little heart murmur that they've been monitoring and my blood pressure's up. That's no surprise with all this going on.'

'We've had to search the house, Sam.'

'I know, my mum told me.'

'It's tidy, but perhaps not as much as you'd like.'

'My mum's going to see to it. I just want Ryan back. Since we've known that the baby was a boy, this was all Ryan ever wanted. For months now, he's been talking to little Jack. Telling him what they'll do together.'

'How was Ryan this last week?'

'All right, a bit distracted, I suppose, but I put that down to the birth about to happen any day. Now you ask, he was a bit different.'

'Different how exactly?'

'He was quiet. "Not there" is the only way I can describe it. A bit "not there", "not in the room", as they say.'

'You've been a great help, Sam. I'll do all I can to find him.'

CHAPTER 46

The traffic was heavy in the Market Place in Melksham. Temple found the vintage shop and as he went inside, he heard a voice from a woman he couldn't see.

'Mind the step as you come in,' she trilled. 'There's plenty to see out the back as well.'

The place was jam-packed floor to ceiling with vintage goods, with just enough floor space to step through it all. Military jackets and linen hung high from rails around the walls, old chandeliers dropped down and all manner of trunks, tables and shelves full of ceramics and glass required him to be careful as he stepped around it.

'Is there anything you're after in particular?' the voice said. Looking around, Temple was still unable to find its owner. All he could see was an accumulated mass of things. Unable to locate her, he spoke into the air.

'I wanted to talk to someone about some medals.'

'Go on through, Derek's the man you want and he's out at the back.'

Temple walked on through a narrow corridor into a wider, lighter space, with columns of glass cabinets. At the end, a man was bent across a makeshift glass counter, looking through a jeweller's loop at something he was holding in his hand. He looked up as Temple approached.

'Do you need any help?'

'I'm a police officer.' Temple fished out his warrant card. The man gave it a cursory look.

'Always happy to help where I can. I'm Derek.' He extended his hand. 'It's quiet today, do you want a cup of tea?'

'No thanks. Do you sell war medals?'

'I do a bit of militaria, I've got some in those cabinets over there.' He pointed.

'I just need to know if I'm in the right place. A few months ago, a couple of First World War medals were bought from here. I wondered if you might remember . . .'

'I sell a lot of medals, loads over the years.'

'I don't suppose you keep records, Derek?'

He looked at Temple archly. 'Of course I do.'

'This would have been late 2019? I haven't got a specific date.'

'Why are you asking?'

'They were taken in a burglary and the two great-grandsons of the owner tracked them down to here.'

He nodded slowly. 'I remember.'

'You do?'

'Yes, and I'll tell you why. I don't deal in stolen goods, let me make that clear for a start.'

Temple nodded. 'Why do you remember it?'

'I'll tell you. There were two of them, one had been in the army, am I right?'

'That's right.'

'He had a tattoo on his arm, he'd been in Afghanistan. He was a Fusilier.'

'Did he tell you that?'

'Yes, I was in the army myself, so we had some words about it. Then he told me about the medals and the burglary.'

'How did he know the medals were here?'

'I advertised them online. The name of the shop is on there and the location. Whenever I advertise First World

War medals, I always put the name of the recipient with it as it can attract relatives, or people who want to do some research first, to see if it's gone to someone who's mentioned in battle or dispatches. Makes it more valuable then, see.'

Temple nodded. 'So they came in to buy them?'

'Yes. They told me the story about how they'd been taken and they wanted to buy them back. I couldn't let them do that. They were stolen, I'd rather be out of pocket than take money for stolen goods, specially medals from a war hero. They said they were their great-grandfather's and asked me if I'd been offered his Second World War medals at the same time, but I hadn't. So I gave them back the First World War medals.'

'That was good of you.'

'Not really. It's never happened to me before, that's why I remember it. Some people in this game don't care where stuff comes from. But I don't want your lot on me doorstep every five minutes. To tell you the truth, I was a bit embarrassed by the whole thing and them turning up like that.'

'So, how did you get them in the first place?'

'I got caught out, didn't I. A man comes in here, says he's not interested in the First World War and wants to sell them, so I bought them.'

'When was this?'

He flicked through a hardback notebook. 'I keep everything in these books. There we are, end of October 2019. I advertised them in November. Then, when the ex-Fusilier came in, with another lad, saying they wanted to buy them and how they'd been robbed, I had to let them go.'

'Had you taken stuff off the man who sold them to you before?'

'Nope, I'd never seen him before and didn't see him again until now.'

'Now?'

'I've seen him in the local papers, he's one of those men who was shot.'

'Derek, are you sure?'

'It was him, I know it was. It's another reason why I remember the medals. Because of the burglary they told me about, I was able to help them.'

'In what way?'

'Frances, the owner who spoke to you out the front, keeps CCTV for the place, look.' He pointed into the corners of the room. 'Can't be too careful. We can track them coming in, looking around and going out.'

'So, how did you help them?'

'I felt sorry for them and knowing that she'd have the bloke who sold me the medals on camera, I took them up to view it. I'd had the medals for about three weeks when I put them online. Frances keeps the CCTV for a month, just in case. She's got a camera angled in the front of the shop so that it looks out onto the road, just in case someone puts the front window in.'

'So, they were able to see who brought the medals in?'

'Oh yes. They were over the moon. I paused it and they took pictures of him on their mobiles. Not only that, but there was a truck parked right outside with another man inside. The bloke left the shop and got in the truck. They took pictures of that too.'

CHAPTER 47

'Harry, think back again. Are you sure the gun was missing before your sink was unblocked?' Temple sat at Harry Staunton's kitchen table. The gun disappearing before the visit from Hobbs spoiled his theory.

'I'm sure. That's what made me look in the first place. If it was there, I was going to move it, wasn't I, I didn't want him to see it.'

'Could you be wrong?'

'No, I'm telling you it wasn't there. The lad who unblocked the sink couldn't have taken something that wasn't there. I've told you all this.'

'I know you have, Harry. I just wondered if you'd thought about it since and changed your mind.'

'No. It's not a matter of changing my mind. I remember it. I can only tell you what happened. Look, Mr Temple, would you rather I made something up and told you a lie?'

'No, Harry, I wouldn't.' It meant someone else had taken the gun, but who? It put his whole theory in doubt.

Temple went back to the office at Marlborough. Clearly surprised to see him, Clare greeted him with a nervous smile as he spoke to her.

'Any sign of Ryan Hobbs yet?'

She was hesitant, unsure whether to give him the information. 'Nothing. There's been no use on his debit or credit cards. He seems to have vanished into thin air.'

'Where is everyone, I need a statement taking?'

'Charlie's with the scene-of-crime, Tom's with the pathologist and Kelvin's with telephony.'

'Ruby?'

'Taking a statement from the farmer. She should be back soon.'

'Where's ma'am Shaw?' He'd seen her car in the yard, but she wasn't in his office.

'She's here somewhere.'

Temple's mobile rang, it was Callie.

'Hi darling, just to let you know that we're at the hospital. Leigh's waters broke while she stopped by to drop some things off for Daisy, so I've brought her in.'

'Is she all right?'

'She's absolutely fine.'

'Keep me posted.'

'I will. And don't worry.'

Suddenly he noticed Tina Shaw standing in the door frame, she crooked her finger at him to follow her into his office.

'Ma'am, I've just come from Melksham—'

'You shouldn't be here. I told you—'

He didn't let her finish. 'Caxton and Hobbs knew that Liam and Aaron Fortune sold two of the medals stolen from the burglary of their great-grandfather, Jack Bartlett's house.'

'And how do you know this?'

'The man who bought them has given a positive ID on Aaron Fortune by his photo in the newspapers as the same man he bought the medals from. He's also told me when he bought them in October 2019, after advertising them, Dean Caxton and Ryan Hobbs showed up to buy them back. When they told him the medals had been stolen, he showed them CCTV footage of Aaron in the shop.'

She was listening. 'Well, at the very least, Aaron was handling.'

'I suspect Liam and Aaron were Jack Bartlett's attackers.'

'But we have no evidence of that. This has to be based on evidence and facts. This could just be handling.'

'Ma'am, we have the links between Liam and Aaron and Caxton and Hobbs. This is about revenge.'

CHAPTER 48

Coming out of his office, Temple caught Eaton in the corridor.

'Anything from Tom and the path yet?'

'Yardley's still cataloguing the injuries which he describes as extensive, says it will take a few more hours. He's already identified stamp marks on Caxton's body indicating multiple assailants.'

'Christ. I'll let ma'am Shaw know.'

Tina Shaw was standing in the doorway. 'Let ma'am Shaw know what?'

Eaton took his cue. 'Scene-of-crime have taken photos of foot marks found on the body and are in the process of enhancing them now, ma'am. It's already clear there's more than one, possibly as many as three different foot imprints on Caxton's body which indicates at least three assailants.'

Tina Shaw nodded slowly, going back inside Temple's office. They followed, standing with the desk between them.

'So, just where does Staunton fit into all this?'

Eaton looked at Temple and back to Tina Shaw.

'Ma'am?'

'He's still our main suspect, the man who says he had a Glock pistol, the same type of pistol that was used in the

Fortunes' shooting.' Tina Shaw sat down. She looked at Temple. 'You go and see Dean Caxton and now he's dead. We're still no further forward.' She stopped. 'Give us a minute will you, Charlie?'

'Ma'am.' Eaton left the office and closed the door behind him and Temple braced himself to be told to leave the building.

She spoke quietly. 'I'm reinstating you.' She wouldn't be telling him she'd had second thoughts since she'd removed him as SIO; there was every possibility the enquiry would go tits up and if it did, best it did so under Temple's direction.

'Ma'am?'

'I'll answer any questions regarding your contact with Dean Caxton and I'll put my rationale in the policy book. Over to you.' She paused to gather her handbag by the side of the chair. 'Keep me updated.'

Eaton found Temple sitting on the edge of his desk.

'She gone?'

'Yes. Seems I'm SIO again. Don't ask me what her thinking is. This investigation's moving fast, Charlie, let's get on with it.'

Temple's mobile indicated an incoming text message. He opened his phone and stared down at a photo of a tiny baby wrapped in a white towel.

Meet baby Lily. All doing fine xxx.

* * *

Guy Newland faced his barrister across a small table. Now and then, his nose caught the slight waft of expensive cologne worn by the man sitting opposite him which brought the stench of Long Lartin into sharp relief.

The rotten stink of the body odour and bad breath of hundreds of confined men and those before them was all around, it leeched out of every object. Perhaps after a while, he would begin to smell like it too; maybe he already did. Newland was sure he would never get used to it.

'Sentencing will be the day after next. There's no reason to delay, the reports have been written and are being read by the judge. He's preparing his summation.'

Newland was nervous. 'Any indication how long I'm getting?'

'He'll determine that from an assessment of the psychiatric reports.'

'Pseudo psychobabble bollocks. Will you know before I go to court?'

'No, we'll have to wait, see what he says on the day.'

Newland distrusted him. They'd told him he would get ten years, out in five. That would only work if he was convicted of manslaughter and not murder. They'd said they could fix it, but he hadn't heard anyone since his arrest mention it again. They'd said they would fix it with the judge. They could fix anything, that much was true. But he'd feel a whole lot easier once he knew for sure.

He needed to be able to fix on a date and five years in this or any other stinking hellhole was going to be difficult. So long as it *was* five years, he might just make it.

'And what about my medical tests? Will they continue?'

'I'm sure they will. I don't think you need to worry about that.' The barrister sat stiff in the chair.

Newland looked at him. It was all right for him. As soon as he walked out of there, he was going to a life that was totally divorced from the realities of prison. Newland leaned forward.

'I really, *really* do need a word about my sentence. They charged me with murder, but I only admitted manslaughter.'

He tried not to stress about it, but that was easier said than done. Not even thoughts of the lovely Melanie were helping. If anything, that was adding to his rising sense of unease. She'd started to bother him, taking the pleasure out of how he'd used her. The pressure was making him paranoid. It was fine, they'd never find her. Even if they did, she'd be unrecognisable.

The barrister moved back in his chair. Again, Newland caught the delicate smell as it drifted towards him.

'I have told you, Mr Newland, we shall have to wait upon the judge. I am in no position to discover what that will be before the event. His Honour will be the only one to know his judgement before he delivers it.'

Newland looked down at the table. He felt a strange sense of foreboding.

CHAPTER 49

Ryan Hobbs was a dead man walking. He'd only been in the toilet for two minutes and when he went back out, Dean had gone. The barman said four men had come in. He said he knew two of them were from the Fortune family. When one of them headbutted Dean, he thought he was going to have to call the police, but they all left, taking Dean with them.

There was no point in trying to ring or text him as a message from Sam had told him all he needed to know before he'd switched off his phone: *Police have been here. Dean's dead!!! Where the fuck are you? I'm so worried xxx.*

It was then he'd started to shake and he hadn't been able to stop since. *Dean dead.* He couldn't take it in and he didn't know what to do. He wished none of it had happened, he wanted to turn back time.

He kept seeing Sam holding their new baby, little Jack, in her arms. He was so pure and innocent, so peaceful; Ryan envied him. He'd give anything to be with them both now, be in Sam's arms, seeing her sunny smile. He wanted to feel her soft skin and her hair. He wanted to feel her in his arms, drawn in close to him. If he could reach her, she'd tell him what to do. He couldn't remember a time when he'd been so afraid, so unsure what to do.

He was fighting with himself. He wanted to run and keep running. He wanted to run out of his skin, out of his body, leave himself behind somewhere. He wanted the old Ryan back. The Ryan Sam knew. Because this Ryan was too hard to live with. He couldn't deal with this new version of himself. Everything around him was going on as normal but he wasn't functioning properly anymore. Because he wasn't like everyone else anymore. This should have been the happiest time, but everything had been ruined. His whole life was fucked.

He couldn't control the sickening hunted feeling that had sunk deep in the pit of his stomach. Neither could he stop his mouth from drying. It wasn't supposed to be like this. Dean said they had left no trace behind, there was nothing to connect them to the shooting. But he couldn't help thinking he was the cause of it all going wrong and now he'd lost his best friend, a true hero, and his heart was breaking. He shouldn't have been so long in the toilets, he should have been at the bar where he could have faced them with Dean, they'd have had no chance with the two of them. It had been bad enough with Jack, now they had killed Dean.

But how did they know? They'd been so careful, or so they thought. A plan that had seemed so simple, so just and right, had spiralled out of all control. He should have known he wasn't up to it, he couldn't match Dean, not even with all his encouragement. Dean was in a different league and always had been. And he'd let him down. He held his head in his hands and started to cry in despair. It was all so fucked up.

He had to get back to Sam and the baby. He could text her once he was in the hospital. He could meet her somewhere, talk it through. She was the only one who could help him now. Without her and the baby he was nothing, they were the only things worth staying alive for now. But he had to avoid the Fortunes at all costs. If they caught him, he knew they'd kill him.

* * *

Sitting up in bed, Leigh held her baby in her arms as Callie stood beside her.

'She's absolutely beautiful, Leigh, she really is.'

'She is, isn't she. It was worth all the discomfort.' She smiled down at the baby in her arms. 'Hello Lily, hello.'

'Did you know it was a girl?' Callie asked.

'I knew all along,' Leigh admitted. 'I just wanted to keep it to myself, have something to myself that only I knew. I didn't even tell Daisy. Sorry.'

'Don't apologise, I understand. It doesn't matter, she's here and she's beautiful.'

'Here, have another hold.' Leigh handed the baby to Callie. 'Thanks for being here, I really appreciate it.'

'She caught us a bit off guard in the end. I'm not sorry your friend couldn't make it, I wouldn't have missed it for all the world. You were magnificent and so calm.'

Callie gently took the baby from Leigh and cradled her.

'I always planned for whichever of my friends was present at Lily's birth to ask them to be godmother.' Leigh watched Callie as she held the baby. 'Things didn't quite turn out that way, but as you saw her into the world, would you like to be Lily's godmother?'

'Oh Leigh! That's lovely of you, of course I would.' Tears pricked Callie's eyes as she reached out and touched Leigh's cheek. It was a beautiful gesture. 'That's so sweet of you, darling. That really means so much to me.'

'I know it does. But look, it doesn't mean that I'm not still planning on moving away.'

Callie broke her gaze from the baby to look at Leigh. 'Must you?'

'I have to, I want to make a new start. Now the baby's born, it's time to move on.'

'But we get on well . . .'

'Yes, we do. I wasn't expecting us to, but it's sort of worked out, weirdly. Besides, you had nothing to do with the divorce. None of what happened between us had anything to do with you.'

Callie frowned. 'I don't like the thought of you doing this alone.'

'I'm going to move to where I was brought up and where I have some old school friends. I've been sounding them out over Facebook, so I won't be on my own.'

'Do they live far away?'

'We'll be going to Basingstoke, so not nearly as far as Suffolk as I originally intended. I've got a buyer for the house, so I'll be house hunting in the next few weeks. I wanted to tell you now, so everyone knows what's happening.'

'Of course, but I don't want you to go.'

'I *have* to go, Callie. I want my own life. I don't want to be watching you two all the time, which I would if I stayed. It's great that we get on, I really mean that, but I need distance between us all. You love a man who's caused me nothing but pain and I need to be away from him. I need to have a new life.'

'I know it must be difficult for you. I'm sorry for the way things are between you two.' Callie sighed. 'The thing is, I love him, Leigh, and I want a future with him.'

'And that's why I need to go.'

CHAPTER 50

'OK, everyone, I need your attention.'

The main office was electrified as Temple briefed everyone as to what had occurred in the last twenty-four hours.

'We need to plan and coordinate a number of arrests, all at the same time, across numerous locations. You know what to do. We are looking for evidence: bloodstained clothing; items in washing machines and laundry baskets; under beds and mattresses; look in wardrobes; where children sleep; ovens; fridges. Seize all boots and shoes, identify any areas of recent burning, ashes, any areas of soil disturbance.'

Eaton was fired up. 'We have a warrant to take the Fortunes' compound apart. Make sure you've all got forensics suits and plenty of evidence bags. We've got twelve hours to prepare.'

Ending the briefing, Temple was alerted to an incoming text message.

'Shit. Looks like I'll be at Bristol tomorrow for Newland's sentencing. Seems they're keen to get him behind bars as soon as possible. I have to be there, Charlie, so you'll have to look after things tomorrow. We can't delay it.'

'I can handle it, it'll do you good to see that scum get what he deserves.'

Kelvin Stubbs appeared in the doorway, his hand in the air over the heads of his colleagues.

'What is it, Kelvin?' Temple called out.

He approached them. 'Just had word, Hobbs must have turned his phone on again momentarily. It was picked up by a mast in Trowbridge.'

'Still on?'

'No, he's turned it off again.'

Temple turned to Eaton. 'He's alive.'

'Inform patrols, Kelvin,' Eaton instructed. 'Give them the location coordinates and let's see if we can pick him up. We've got surveillance on his house. He'll know Sam will be due home with the baby and will want to see her.'

Temple checked his phone. 'While we're waiting, I'm going to make a quick visit to the hospital, make sure Leigh's all right and see my new baby girl. I'll be back in an hour.'

Eaton nodded. 'I'll shout you if anything crops up.'

Temple stopped at Waitrose to buy some flowers. Leigh would see right through it for the gesture it was and probably not thank him, but as he saw it, he couldn't turn up empty handed, even if she didn't want anything to do with him.

As he stood in the queue to pay, he felt a tap on his shoulder.

'I thought it was you, my little laddie.' Temple smiled at the recognition of his voice. He turned round to see Terry Stokes, his first sergeant when he'd been a probationer; Stokes called all his charges 'little laddie'.

'Hello, Terry, retirement looks good on you. How's the blood pressure?' He'd put on some weight.

Stokes patted his chest through his heavy tweed coat. 'I'm all right. Few aches and pains but nothing serious. I've been reading about your case, Op Acre, in the news.' He waved the local newspaper in his hand. 'Got him at last, I see.'

'Yes, it's been a long time coming. It wasn't quite the way I thought it would happen, but there you go.'

Stokes pointed to Harker's photo on the front page. 'I see shit still floats to the top. Bloody ACC too. Still, it's

303

good to see the job tidied up. There's nothing worse than an outstanding case. I bet you're pleased?'

'More shocked at the moment, but yes, pleased we know who it is after all these years.'

'Old Filer will be smiling down too. The case vexed old Roy, he put his retirement off for a year to try and solve it.'

'Yes, I remember you saying.' Temple shuffled along in the queue.

'We were having a Narpo lunch just yesterday and some of the old boys were talking about the case.'

'Oh yes?'

'It's what we do when we all get together, us retirees go over old times, discuss old cases and the bastards in the job who used to make our lives a misery.' He chuckled. 'It's surprising what comes out. Things you never knew. Know anything about this Newland character?'

'Not much, in fact, nothing more than what it says in the paper.'

'Interesting. There was an old boy talking about Op Julie, you know Op Julie?'

'Yes, drugs bust in the seventies.' Temple was now at the front of the queue.

'It was more than that, my little laddie, changed policing. Anyway, we were talking about Op Julie and someone . . .' He suddenly stopped talking and looked around. Dropping his voice, he continued. 'Get your flowers and come over here.' Stokes indicated to a café area.

Temple checked his watch. 'I've got five minutes.'

'That's all it'll take.'

Temple paid and walked over to where Stokes was stood. He was happy to reminisce, but Terry Stokes had picked the wrong moment.

Stokes kept his voice low. 'So, we were discussing Op Acre and the fact they've found this character for the murder now, when one of the others said that Roy Filer, who was the SIO on your mother's case, was also involved in Op Julie.'

'I didn't know . . .' Temple shrugged.

'Yes, he was. Old Roy became quite an expert on LSD and drugs. It was massive at the time. LSD was seen as a threat. Communes were springing up everywhere, it was all free love and free living, festivals that lasted for days on end, deaths from overdoses or people jumping off bridges thinking they could fly. There was an intellectual movement behind it, going for general acceptance for it. It took hold in all the festivals, so much so, the establishment were getting twitchy, saying the fabric of society was being challenged, it was looked on as a kind of subversion. It was bloody anarchy. The Battle of the Beanfield was a year after your mother's death. Those cops were there to finally break it, it had gathered too much momentum and had to be stopped. Apparently, old Roy believed that they didn't capture everyone when they were investigating Op Julie. They wanted to investigate further but they were told to stop.'

'So?' Temple was becoming impatient to go. All the similar information he had just heard had had him chasing down druggies for the last twenty years, when it turned out all along that his mother's killer was Newland, an opportunistic and random attacker.

'According to what I heard, there were some shady characters in the background, infiltrators, which is why they stopped old Roy from going any further.'

Temple nodded; he really had to go now. Stokes no doubt meant well, but this had all been made irrelevant by Newland's capture.

'Op Julie was 1977, wasn't it?'

'That's right.'

'Year I was born.' Temple made moves to leave. 'I really have to be going now, Terry.'

They walked to the exit together. 'As I say, I was pleased to read that they got the bastard.'

'Thanks, Terry.'

'Funny thing about the T-shirt you were wearing. The paper said that it was found in old Roy's loft, is that right?'

'Yes, his son brought it in. It was still in the exhibit bag.'

'I wonder why he did that?'

'So do I, Terry.'

'Didn't you ever speak to Roy?'

'Yes, twice. I met him in a pub once, I got the impression he turned up because I was the victim's son. I wasn't long in the job, so I suppose he thought he was talking to some wet-behind-the-ears probationer, which of course I was. I probably didn't ask him the right questions and he certainly didn't feel any obligation to tell me anything. Then, years later, I caught up with him in a care home. It was too late then, he had dementia. Op Acre meant nothing to him. But thanks to him hiding the T-shirt in his loft, we have our man.'

CHAPTER 51

Flowers in hand, Temple made his way to the maternity unit at Great Western Hospital. Once through the intercom system, he was directed to a bed with privacy curtains drawn round. He stood for a second, not sure what to do. Nine months ago, he and Leigh had conceived a baby and in that short space of time so much had changed between them.

'Leigh, it's me. Can I come in?'

There was no answer, so he looked for a gap in the curtain and peeped through.

Leigh lay on her side, staring at the baby in a cot beside her. She looked up and seeing him holding the flowers, gave him a weak smile. She quickly tugged at the top of the slip she was wearing to cover herself.

'You'd better come in and meet Lily.'

He laid the flowers on the bed and peered into the cot at the tiny baby. 'She's beautiful, Leigh.'

'Pick her up. She's sleeping.'

Temple took off his jacket and reached into the cot. The baby was weightless in his arms. He immediately registered the lovely almond smell of her.

'She's so tiny. You forget just how small they are.' He sat on the edge of the bed not taking his eyes off the baby. 'Has Daisy seen her yet?'

'No, Callie's just gone back to get her.'

He looked at her. 'And what about you? How are you?'

They were inches apart now in the confined space. She wanted to deflect his attention. Hours after giving birth, she was feeling sore and tired and in no mood for small talk with him. And yet seeing him holding the baby, she was suddenly overwhelmed. She felt a rush of tears coming and confusingly, for a second, she wanted him to hug her. She shook herself.

'I'm all right,' she replied tightly. 'It was pretty quick in the end and she was worth the wait.'

'She's perfect, Leigh.' With the baby cradled in one arm, he found her hand on the bed and gently held it; before she had a chance to react, he lifted it to his lips. She resisted the urge to snatch it away and let him keep hold. She hadn't felt his touch for so long.

'Clever you,' he said.

Suddenly, in the presence of baby Lily for a miniscule moment, it was as if the divorce and all the troubles between them disappeared. Their eyes locked and they smiled at one another, enjoying the sight of their beautiful new baby.

'She's got your eyes,' he told her.

'I was thinking they were yours.' She smiled at him as he kissed her hand again.

'Definitely yours. Look at her tiny fingernails.'

She watched as the new baby fascinated him, her hand resting naturally in his.

'Would you like me to find you a vase?' A nurse's voice cut into the peace they enjoyed.

Temple looked up and Leigh snatched her hand away.

'If you would, please,' he said.

With the moment between them broken, Leigh sat back and rested her head on the pillows, drawing the bedsheet up.

'She loves you, you know, Callie. She told me today. Here we are, sitting with our newborn daughter only hours old, and I've listened to another woman tell me she loves you. That just about sums it up, don't you think?'

Temple looked at her, unsure what to say; the last thing he wanted now was a fight.

'None of this is about Callie. You know I had to do the right thing where Ben was concerned,' he said quietly. 'You know I wanted us to stay together. I never wanted a divorce. Even before we knew about Ben, I was telling you I didn't want a divorce, if you remember.'

Her eyes welled up. 'I'll be moving away once I've sorted myself out. I've told Callie . . .'

'We don't need to talk about this now, Leigh. Let's save it for another day.'

'I'm just letting you know. We won't all be together. That's not how it's going to be. You're not having the best of all worlds, where you can see us all. I'll be able to move on now the baby's here.'

'I need to make sure you're safe and looked after.'

'We're divorced, you don't have to worry about me anymore.'

'There's Daisy, and now Lily, so I do have to worry.'

'Then you'll have to do that from a distance.'

'And if Callie wasn't on the scene, would you be going?'

'Yes, because of Ben. Now you can play happy families with Callie and Ben.'

He kissed the baby on the forehead and placed her back in the cot. Leigh watched him, waiting for him to speak.

'Can I come back again?' he said, ignoring her comments.

'I'll be out soon, let's leave it until later.'

'I'll see you both then.'

He picked up his jacket. She watched him go back through the curtain as the tears came. Tears for the baby, tears of anger, tears for the divorce and tears of frustration at herself because she knew, despite everything, a tiny part of her still loved him.

He pressed the button for the lift and watched as it arrived and the door opened. He stepped inside, all the time thinking of the new baby and Leigh's intention to move away. Somehow, he had to make sure Lily didn't grow up estranged from him. Daisy needed him around now too; she'd be a teen soon and he had to be there for her. He imagined Leigh living far away with the baby and Daisy, trying to do it all on her own. It would be hard and he didn't want that for her.

The lift door opened. Suddenly, he recognised a man standing in front of him.

'Hobbs!'

At the sound of his name, Hobbs immediately turned and ran.

'Ryan Hobbs,' Temple shouted as he started to run after him. 'Stop, police!'

Hobbs continued to run down the long corridors. Temple was in pursuit, but he already knew he'd be no match for the younger man. It was all he could do to keep him in eyesight. He reached for his mobile.

'Charlie, I'm at the hospital, Swindon, get cars here, I'm running after Hobbs.'

As Hobbs headed for the west entrance, Temple kept running. Hobbs was shouting for people to get out of his way when a security guard stepped out in front of him. The guard, taken by surprise, put his hands out to the side as if he was going to stop a goal. Hobbs flexed his arm as he approached and punched the man in the head. The guard went down but not before reaching out and catching hold of Hobbs' legs.

Hobbs fell to the floor and still trying to scrabble with the guard, Temple caught up. He fell on the floor next to him, taking Hobbs' arms and putting them up behind his back.

'You're under arrest.'

CHAPTER 52

Temple and Eaton sat in an interview room in Swindon police station, opposite Ryan Hobbs and his solicitor.

'So, tell us again, Ryan, and this time, don't leave anything out. How did Dean know Matthew Staunton?'

Hobbs was exhausted, but with it came a sort of relief. He'd sit here all night if they wanted him to.

'Dean and Mattie knew each other from their time in the army. When they left the army they kept in touch. They'd both seen a lot in their time and Mattie found it hard to adjust. Dean tried to help him. He'd go and see him, he tried to offer him bits of work, but Mattie struggled with what he'd seen. He had PTSD.'

'Did Dean know about the gun?'

'Dean knew how Mattie had come by the gun because Mattie told him as soon as he got back to Camp Bastion. He looked on it as a lucky mascot of sorts. Dean said they looked for anything lucky, shrapnel, bullets, even dogs, anything that they thought had helped get them safely back to camp after they'd been on a sortie. The gun had saved Mattie's life. Dean knew that Mattie had smuggled the gun back to the UK because he showed it to him once.

'When our great-grandfather was attacked . . .' Hobbs paused and let out a deep breath. 'Dean was choked. We both were, the whole family was. We were so fucking angry. They left him in such a state, he was an old man for God's sake and they beat him. He was worth ten of them. Mattie said to Dean that if he ever found the scum who did it, he would help him and lend him his gun. That's what planted the idea in Dean's head. Mattie died not long after.'

'And when Matthew died, how did Dean know where to find the gun?'

'Mattie told Dean his grandfather, Harry Staunton, had hidden the gun under the sink to keep it away from him. Mattie knew it was there. He watched the old man move it one day.'

'So, did Harry know Dean?'

'No, he never met him.'

'Really?'

'Dean said their paths never crossed.'

'What about Mattie's funeral?'

'Dean went to Mattie's funeral, but he said he didn't hang around to meet any of Mattie's family. Given the way he went, it wasn't that sort of do.'

'And he told you that?'

'Yes.'

'What about the card left in the kitchen?'

'Mattie would have picked it up when doing work for Dean, Mattie must have left it in the kitchen and told Harry to ring it if he ever had any problems about the house.'

Eaton only let him pause for a moment. 'How did you get the medals back?'

'The First World War medals had Jack Bartlett's dad, so our great-great-grandfather's, name on them. Dean knew it would mean a lot to Jack if he could get his dad's medals back to him. It became an obsession. We looked online for months after the burglary at various sites where they might turn up, wanting to return them to Jack to cheer him up, but we never found them.

'A few weeks after Jack died, it was weird, almost like a sign, they turned up on eBay. The shop was local and when we went to pick them up and told the guy they were stolen, he told us he'd only had them a few weeks and showed us his CCTV. We saw Aaron Fortune in the shop and his brother Liam outside in their car. We took pictures from the stills. We didn't know who they were, so we showed them around, asked in the pubs and found out who they were. We had to do your job for you.'

'Why not tell the police about the Fortunes once you identified them?'

'And what would have happened? By then, Jack was dead so couldn't identify them as the burglars. All that time after the burglary, all they would have said was they sold some stolen medals. You wouldn't even have got them to court for that and even if you had, what would have happened, fuck all, that's what.'

'But how do you know they were responsible for the burglary? I mean, they could have been handling for whoever did steal the medals?'

'After the burglary, we'd watched Jack deteriorate, he just wasn't the same again. He lived the last months of his life a timid and frightened man. Even the Nazis hadn't managed that. The Fortunes broke him. Dean would ask him to try and remember what they looked like. He kept on, asking for any detail. One day, Jack came out with it. One of the guys had a chipped front tooth. He said that as one of them was trying to wrench the wedding ring from his finger, he laughed in his face as his finger broke. The tooth was almost in half.

'When we found the medals and the guy showed us the CCTV, we could see Aaron Fortune's face and his half tooth. It was as clear as day on the CCTV. That's how we knew it was him. From then on, Dean wouldn't let it go. It was something he had to do. He asked about and tracked them down to a pub.'

Temple pressed Hobbs. 'So on the night of the shooting, you're saying the Fortune brothers had come to meet you to buy the gun? How did that come about?'

'Because while we were at the shop looking at the CCTV, we could see Fortune looking in a cabinet as the guy was inspecting the medals. The guy in the shop said Aaron Fortune had shown a lot of interest in some old antique deactivated guns.'

Hobbs continued. 'That's what gave Dean the idea. He figured they'd be interested in a modern fully working Glock.'

Temple blinked back at him. His instinct about the Fortunes and the gun had been right. 'So how did he make the initial contact?'

'He approached them in the pub, the Swan, Semington. He gave them some old rubbish about wanting to offload it; they were really interested, especially when Dean told them they could have it for £300. Dean made all the arrangements to meet in the woods. They knew the spot apparently, so were comfortable meeting there. Two days before the shooting, Dean told me about meeting the Fortunes in the pub and asked me if I wanted to help him. How could I say no? I had to do it for Jack.'

'And three months before the shooting, you go and clear the blocked sink?'

'Yes, Dean sent me after having a call from the old man.'

'And where was the gun then?'

'Dean told me that once Mattie died, he wanted to make sure it didn't suddenly disappear if Harry moved it again, so he went to get it.'

'How did he do that?'

'The old man didn't lock his back door. Dean said he just went in and took it one night.'

'And this was before you found the medals on eBay, before you identified Aaron Fortune from the CCTV?'

'Yes.'

'And if you hadn't found the medals or viewed the CCTV, what would Dean have done with the gun?'

'Only he can tell you that and he's not here.'

Eaton and Temple exchanged glances.

'So, Dean arranges for the Fortunes to meet him in the woods on the pretext of selling them the gun and you go with him?'

Ryan nodded.

'What happened?'

'They turned up, we were waiting inside the wall.'

'What time was this?'

'One a.m.'

'How did you get there?'

'On a motorbike, through the woods.'

'Whose motorbike?'

'Dean's.'

'And?'

'They parked up and we waited. I approached the passenger side as the window was already down. I started talking while Dean went round to the driver's side . . .' Hobbs was looking down as he relived it again. 'It was so quick. Dean didn't mess about. He took the gun out of his jacket, raised his arm and shot Liam through the window. Then, before we could really register what had happened, he walked around the front of the car to the passenger side. Me standing there was a deterrent to Aaron getting out of the car and legging it. Then he gave the gun to me.' He stopped to take a deep breath. 'It all happened so fast, Aaron Fortune just froze, he was sitting in front of me, just looking ahead. He didn't fucking move. But I froze too. I went to shoot but I couldn't do it. I kept thinking of Jack lying in hospital, of what those dirty bastards had done to him, but it was no good. My hands were shaking. I fired it but I missed, deliberately. Dean took the gun and fired it straight into his head. The bloke was dead, they both were. It was all over so fast.'

Hobbs shook his head.

'I shouldn't have gone, I was useless. Dean reached inside the car and took their phones which were in their laps and by this time, I'd lost it.' Hobbs put his head in his hands. 'I thought I could shoot him, but when it came to it, I couldn't do it. Dean was a trained killer, he'd seen it all before, but I fell to pieces.

'He had to get me away so he got me back on the bike and we drove off. We had to stop because I kept wanting to be sick. He dropped me at the end of the road, told me to shower, put all my clothes in the washing machine and go to bed so that Sam would think I'd never been out. Before dawn, he went back. He wanted to retrieve the cartridge cases and make sure I hadn't left anything behind, things he would have done if I hadn't freaked out. He said he hid in the woods as a woman was up there calling out for her dog. The dog had run up to Dean and he had to kill it to stop her following it. He said he couldn't risk her seeing him.'

'Where's the gun now?' asked Eaton.

'It was always Dean's plan to return the gun to Staunton's and put it back under the sink straight after the shooting. That's why he chose that location to meet the Fortunes. It was going to be quick and easy to put it back as if it had never moved. If it hadn't been for me, that's what he would have done that night.'

Temple and Eaton looked at one another.

'So, if Harry Staunton had gone to look for it, he'd have found it and it would look like it had never left the house.'

'That's if he'd have remembered where it was. Mattie told Dean he was getting forgetful.'

'So, what did Dean do with it when he couldn't return it that night?'

'He told me he hid it in his van among his tools. There was too much of a police presence in the village for him to go there and put it back under the sink the next evening. When you visited him, he knew he had to get rid of it. He told me on the way to the pub that he'd gone to Harry Staunton's the night before to get it back under the sink, but the kitchen door was locked. So he buried it in the garden.'

'Whereabouts in the garden?'

'He didn't say, just said the garden.'

'And that's where it is now?'

'As far as I know.'

'If Dean had managed to get it back under the sink, did either of you think about the police finding it and matching it to the scene?'

'If Dean had got the gun back under the sink on the night of the shooting, Harry would have been none the wiser that it had ever left. Why would the police have known about it?'

Temple held his gaze. 'House-to-house identified Harry as someone to look at, someone who went shooting in the woods. He's not as forgetful as everyone thinks he is. He actually told us the gun was missing from where he'd left it.'

'Harry Staunton told you he'd lost the gun? Silly bastard.'

'He told us it was missing. When his sink blocked, he remembered it was there, so he went to move it, worried maybe anyone who went to fix the sink might have to go rooting around and see it. It was then he discovered it was gone. The fact it wasn't where he'd last put it played on his mind. Something he shared with us.'

Ryan shook his head. 'Dean never thought the old man would notice the gun was gone.'

'He wouldn't have if his sink hadn't blocked. He hadn't given it any thought since Matthew died. Harry told us and that put him in the frame. We've been searching for it. Tell us again about what happened when you went to wet the baby's head.'

'Dean was on at me to try and behave as normal, when inside I'm freaking out. I can't think straight. It's been really difficult around Sam because I can't stop thinking about what happened. He insisted we do everything expected of us, including going to work and going to the pub after the baby was born. I thought he was mad, I was just about holding it together, but he said we had to function as normal. But I can't eat and I can't sleep. When you came to see me at work, I don't know how I got through it. Part of me wanted to tell you then, to stop the madness going on in my head.

'We left the hospital and Dean parked the van on my drive and we walked to the Palmers Arms. He got the drinks. I haven't been able to stop going to the toilet since it happened . . .'

'We had noticed,' Eaton quipped.

'One sip of beer and it went straight through me, so I went to the gents. When I came out, Dean was gone. The barman told me two of the Fortune family had come in with some others, headbutted Dean and dragged him out.'

'How did the Fortunes make the connection to Dean with the shooting?'

Ryan shook his head. 'I don't know. If only I hadn't been in the gents when they came in.'

'Believe me, Ryan, if you had, you'd have ended up like Dean. You wouldn't have stood a chance.'

Again, Hobbs shook his head. 'Those fucking animals got him. I wish I *had* shot Aaron now.'

'What did you do when you left the pub?'

'I went home. I was going to take the van and look for Dean, but it was blocked in by his van. I couldn't sit indoors, so I walked about.'

'All night?'

'Yes, I just didn't know what to do.'

'And what about Sam? Did she know about this?'

'God no. There have been times when I've wanted to tell her everything, but she knows nothing.' He started to cry.

'Why did you take them on, Ryan?'

'We did it for Jack.' Ryan wiped his face with his hands. 'We couldn't bear the thought of them just getting away with it. Do you know how that *feels*? Dean carried the photo of Jack's injuries on his phone. He told me he tried to let it go but he couldn't forget what they did to him. He let it eat away at him. He tried, he really tried. Jack fought for his country, *really* fought for it. He was fucking heroic. And he went through all that only to come across the Fortunes.' He stopped. 'How could we just leave it? When they burgled Jack, they as good as murdered him, he was never the same again, he died a very frightened, broken man. What would you do if someone did that to someone in your family?'

CHAPTER 53

Temple and Eaton booked Hobbs back into his cell.

'I've never known someone to take so many comfort breaks. He's literally shitting himself. Do you believe him?' Eaton asked.

'That he didn't shoot Aaron? I don't know. He can say what he likes now Caxton's dead.'

'Even if he didn't put the bullet in him, he's still looking at an attempted murder charge and conspiracy.'

'He'll walk from court if he gets a good enough brief and a sympathetic jury.'

'If the online comments about the Fortunes are anything to go by, he might.'

Temple couldn't help but harbour some sympathy with Caxton and Hobbs, after all, he'd been prepared to shoot King if necessary for threatening Leigh and Daisy. He would have done the same as Caxton if King had harmed them. He'd once read somewhere that given the right circumstances, everyone was capable of murder. There wasn't a lot that separated him from Dean Caxton and Ryan Hobbs.

'We've got Stubbs taking a statement from the barman at the Palmers Arms and sweeping up any CCTV. But what that won't tell us is how the Fortunes knew it was Caxton.'

Temple still needed to know whether it was because of a leak in the team.

'It's a good question, boss. What time are you at Bristol in the morning?'

'We've got to be there for ten a.m. I'm going to miss all the action. I'll come in as soon as I'm back.'

Eaton was thoughtful. 'If Harry hadn't told us the gun was missing, they'd have got away with it. Poor old bugger put himself right in the middle of it.'

'We need to find the gun in Staunton's garden. I still want to know what led the Fortunes to Caxton.'

* * *

Temple rang DS Cartwright.

'How's it going, Zoe?'

'No movement.' He could sense the tension in her voice.

'Look, I appreciate this isn't going to go down well, but just to give you the heads-up, we're going to arrest your subjects.'

'Hang on a minute. I've helped you out. You can't do that. They're part of a much larger operation, you can't take them out. Not now.'

'They've implicated themselves by mentioning how they'll split the fifty grand and we all know what that's for. I've got a dead body and they know all about it. I can't let them walk away.'

'You haven't got any evidence . . .'

'I've got your taped evidence about spending the fifty grand which amounts to conspiracy for starters. I want the names of the people in the car.'

'You can't trash four years of investigation. I'll have to ring my boss and I'm not doing anything until he says. I'll get him to call you.'

'I'll talk to whoever I have to. I'm sorry, Zoe, but they're ours.'

Temple spoke with the team and made sure everything was in place for the early-morning arrests. After updating

Tina Shaw on Hobbs' arrest and the arrangements for the morning, he was unsurprised that she insisted on overseeing the operation in his absence. He left for home.

* * *

Back at the cottage, his thoughts strayed back to his meeting with Leigh at the hospital and baby Lily. She had been so perfect, and it stung him now to think she was only hours old and Leigh had already told him she would separate them. If he was in any doubt of the strength of feeling Leigh had against him, she'd made it plain then. She'd make sure it would cost him dearly for hurting her.

His mobile started to ring and he saw it was Callie.

'Hello, darling, I just wanted to make sure you were all right ahead of tomorrow.'

'Your timing's good, I needed to hear your voice. I was just thinking of Lily. I went up to see her this afternoon. Leigh said you were taking Daisy to see her.'

'Yes, she has met her baby sister. Obviously, she loves her already.'

'Leigh's still going to leave, she made that clear earlier.'

'I wish I was there with you. Let's talk about it later. It's a really emotional time for Leigh, for you, everyone right now . . .'

'She meant it. We'll have to face it sooner or later.'

'I know.' Callie could sense he was tired and events were taking their toll. 'I want us all back together.'

'So do I. It won't be long now, I promise. Let's get tomorrow out of the way. Richard will be here shortly. He's staying over tonight so we can all travel to court together in the morning.'

'I'll help Ana first thing, then I'll be straight over. Hopefully, they'll throw away the key—'

They were interrupted by Temple's mobile sounding.

'I'll have to go, I think Charlie's trying to get hold of me.'

They said their goodbyes and Temple looked at his missed calls. He rang Eaton.

'Boss, I've been going through the CCTV from the Palmers Arms and it shows four men approaching Dean Caxton.'

'Can you get a clear look at them?'

'Oh yes. The camera looks out from behind the bar. Get this, the footage shows Georgie Munt, Paul King and two unidentified men. I'm looking at Munt just landing a head-butt to Caxton before they take him away. We've got them.'

CHAPTER 54

The small wood-panelled court room was cold and sombre. Callie shivered as she sat in between Temple and Richard on the hard wooden bench. Across the court to the side, a glass wall separated them from Guy Newland, looking straight ahead, flanked by two prison guards. Temple found it hard to take his gaze from him. Newland looked edgy. If that was the effect prison had on him, Temple was glad.

A little way to their left sat Detective Superintendent Mark Stubbs, alongside Clive Harker and members of the Op Acre enquiry team. In front of them they could see the black-gowned barristers in a huddle. People had also gathered in the public gallery. They straightened as the judge arrived.

'All stand,' the usher directed. Everyone obliged as the judge took his seat. After some preliminary questions from the judge to the barristers, he was ready. He briefly looked over to where Temple was sitting, before looking at Newland behind the glass. With all eyes on him, the judge began to read as he looked down at the papers in front of him.

The judge's voice boomed out across the court room. Reading from the script in front of him, he slowly and methodically transported everyone back to the events of a summer's day in June 1984. Temple listened, the words shaping his own recall of that day.

'. . . and then you put your hands around her throat and throttled her until she was dead . . .'

Callie gently stroked Temple's arm as the details came out. The judge went on.

'I am not convinced from the reports that I have read, that your attack on Gabriella Temple was not in some way sexually motivated. Nor am I convinced that you intended no harm to the child who found you at the scene. On the contrary, you did harm him. You pushed him with force, sending him backwards where he fell. Without any regard to how he was, you then left the scene not to return . . .'

Temple listened, watching Newland. It felt as if the judge was talking about someone else. By now, the air had almost been sucked out of the room, such was the anticipation. Temple looked at the front bench, packed with journalists tapping on their phones, and briefly caught Sophie Twiner staring back at him. He looked back to Newland. The judge continued.

'In fact, you left him in the presence of his dead mother where he stayed, no doubt terrified, keeping a vigil by her side for two days before he was rescued. During that time he must have suffered unimaginable distress . . .' The judge paused. 'Guy Newland, I sentence you to twenty-two years for the wilful murder of Gabriella Temple . . .'

Suddenly, Temple heard a collective gasp as Newland leaped up from his seat, shouting and banging on the glass before the guards restrained him. Temple's eyes hadn't left Newland's, his face was contorted as he shouted. The judge reminded him where he was and ordered him to be quiet.

Richard turned to him, bewildered. Temple saw tears in his eyes. 'Twenty-two years. I hope he dies before it expires. We've waited so long and now it's finally over. It really is over.'

Sitting between them, Callie gently squeezed both their hands. Richard was right. It was over. Temple continued to watch Newland as prison guards guided him out of the confined space of the dock. He wanted his last image of him being led down to the cells. Twenty-two years; it wasn't much. He'd probably serve half, two thirds if they were lucky. They'd spent longer trying to find him. The endless not knowing, the gnawing and exhausting quest for justice. Now the bastard could rot.

Somewhere in the distance the court usher was saying, 'All rise.' The judge stood to leave. The journalists stirred and looked across at Temple. He looked away, taking hold of Callie's arm.

'Come on, we need to get out of here.' They made their way outside into the large foyer where Clive Harker approached Richard Temple and put his hand out. Richard shook it.

'Good result, I think,' Richard mumbled, still reeling from the verdict. 'I'm still not quite sure I believe it's all happened. After all these years . . .'

'Believe it,' replied Harker. 'He won't see the light of day again. It took some time, but we never gave up. In the final analysis, it's the end result that counts.'

Standing away from Harker, from the tail of his eye, Temple saw Sophie Twiner approaching.

'Let's make a move. I don't want to talk to her right now,' Temple muttered. He steered Callie away, but Richard was still with Harker.

'I'm not too keen either, not after the piece with Clive Harker and how bloody marvellous he is.'

He was secretly pleased to hear her say that. Now it was all over, there was no need for Sophie Twiner to continue to inveigle her way into their lives. Callie looked over her shoulder to glance at Harker. 'I wasn't expecting him to turn up today.'

'You must be joking, he's here to take the glory. He can have it. I'll get Richard out of Twiner's way, we can go for a coffee before we head back.'

Richard had walked away from Harker, but Sophie Twiner had moved in and already had him by the arm. As Temple approached them, Sophie greeted him with a smile.

'I was hoping to catch you both . . .' She swung her hair across her shoulders.

'Not now, Sophie.' Temple nodded at Richard. 'Ready to go?'

Sophie broke away from Richard to face Temple.

'Can I have a quick word?' Looking around her, she isolated Temple. Her smile disappeared and she spoke quietly. 'Look, I can imagine you're pretty pissed off about the Harker article, but Rob Carroll asked me to write it. It was . . . payback.'

Temple was dismissive. 'I didn't read it.'

'Then maybe you ought to. I sat with Harker for an hour as he went through it. What was clear to me was that it was personal. I didn't put it in the final piece, but he actually said that he wanted to set the record straight for his granddaughter for when she read it in future.'

Temple felt his anger rise; it was typical of Harker, but equally, he didn't know if he was being played by Twiner.

'I didn't want another article going out with my name all over it. I've got a job to do and that's the last thing I want right now.' He went to walk away. She touched his arm.

'I don't want there to be any bad feeling between us. As I said the other night, Harker was really fucked off about the article we did. It put him under pressure to reignite the enquiry and he didn't like that. His article was written to settle that score.' She stopped for a moment, checking who was close. She lowered her voice further and leaned into him. 'You came to me because you wanted to know who was leaking information about your enquiry.'

'And?' He was impatient to get away from her.

'It was Harker.'

'What? *Harker*?'

She nodded. 'His information came from briefings from Tina Shaw apparently. He's been talking to Rob, building their "relationship", you might say. Well, that only works when both sides have something to offer. Rob passed me more detail to put in about the shooting, saying it came from Harker.'

He'd been so sure it was one of the team. 'Did he know that what he was saying would end up in the paper?'

'Of course.'

'And Harker got a bullshit article in return.'

'With a further one to come for the weekend, syndicated, of course.'

'Why didn't you tell me this the other night?'

'I would have, over some pillow talk, but you weren't up for it. You can't say I didn't try.'

By now, Callie had joined them.

'Tell you what the other night?' Callie looked at them both.

Sophie deliberately looked at the floor before looking back at Temple. 'This is awkward.' She saw an opportunity and couldn't help herself. 'I was round at the cottage the other night.'

Temple took Callie's elbow. 'Come on, let's go.'

* * *

They sat in a café down the street at a small round table. Richard raised his cup of coffee.

'Here's to the judge and the British justice system. We got there in the end.'

'I think I'll be having something a bit stronger this evening,' said Temple, raising his cup.

Callie set her cup in the saucer. 'So, what was Sophie Twiner on about?'

'It was nothing. She came by the house the other night.'

'You didn't say?'

'I forgot, it was no big deal.'

Callie frowned. 'What did she mean when she said, "this is awkward"?'

'I've no idea. But I'm glad it's all over now and we don't have to think about interviews anymore.' He looked across at Richard.

'Yes, the campaign is over. Attractive girl, Sophie. I'll miss her.'

'I'm not sure I will,' Callie muttered, avoiding Temple's gaze.

'We'll have to make a move in a minute. I've left Charlie Eaton with all the work this morning.'

Temple scrolled through a series of texts that Eaton had been sending him while he was in court. The arrests had been made; Munt and King were in custody, along with two of the men DS Cartwright had under surveillance who had been identified from the CCTV at the Palmer's Arms. But they couldn't locate Caleb Fortune.

They walked back to the car park in silence. Temple slipped his hand into Callie's, squeezing it gently. She closed her fingers around his to hold him tighter. The whole morning had felt surreal; finally seeing Newland bought to justice, the whole theatre of his sentencing and at last seeing him taken away. It was a watershed moment and it would take some getting used to, but he already felt lighter than he could remember.

His mobile rang. It was Eaton.

'I don't want to alarm you, boss, but we've just had word. The Great Western Hospital is in lockdown. Someone's taken a baby from the maternity ward.'

CHAPTER 55

'I can't understand how it could happen.' Callie's hand went to her seat belt as Temple sped down the M4.

'Neither can I. The babies are electronically tagged. How the fuck can they lose a baby in this day and age, for Christ's sake?'

Callie looked at Temple. 'Couldn't Charlie give any indication whose baby it might be?'

'No, he heard it second-hand so had no more information, only that a baby was missing and the place was in lockdown.' His guts were twisting. If Lily was the missing baby, Leigh would be hysterical.

Arriving at the hospital, he swung the car into a parking space.

'Both of you stay here, I'll ring you as soon as I can.'

Temple approached a police officer standing outside the main entrance. A flash of his warrant card and he was let through. Once inside, he could sense the tension as people milled around the coffee shop, unable to leave the building. He made his way to the maternity unit where he met another police officer standing guard at the entrance. Temple identified himself again.

'Is there any news on whose baby is missing?' he asked.

'I don't know, sir, I've just been asked to stay here and not let anyone through.'

Temple rushed past her and headed for the ward where he had visited Leigh. The bed was screened by a privacy curtain. He pulled it wide. The bed was empty, so was the cot beside it. His heart leaped.

'Who are you?' demanded a nurse.

'Police. Look where—'

'Do you have ID?' she snapped.

'Where was the woman who was here, Leigh Temple, where is she?'

'Your ID, please . . .'

'Ashleigh Temple was in this bed, where is she?' Temple pulled out his warrant card.

The nurse looked alarmed. 'Your name is Temple . . .'

'Yes, she was my wife, the baby is our daughter, where are they?'

'We can't locate her.'

'What? She was here, yesterday, with the baby, what do you mean you can't locate her?'

'There's some confusion, we have a baby missing . . .'

'For God's sake tell me whose baby's missing.'

'The missing baby's name is Jack Bartlett Dean Hobbs, the mother is Samantha Mason. She's in a room over there.'

Relief flooded through him, but it was short-lived. 'When did it happen?'

'Some time before midday. We're trying to locate everyone who left this morning, who might have taken the Hobbs baby. Mrs Temple discharged herself this morning and she's not answering her phone . . .'

'You can't think she's taken the baby?'

'We're having to explore every avenue.'

Suddenly, Temple thought of the arrests that had occurred that morning.

'She hasn't taken the baby . . .'

He turned and ran out of the unit, stopping at a large noticeboard where he looked at the directions to the various wards. He ran to the lift and punched the button. He got in and took it to the next floor down. Running through the corridor, he turned into the Acute Cardiac Unit and stopped a nurse.

'I need to see Elijah Fortune,' he demanded, taking out his warrant card again. 'Take me to him.'

'This way.' She guided him through a wardroom to a bed with a privacy curtain around it. Temple pulled it back. A teenaged girl sitting on the edge of the bed looked round. Temple looked at the man in the bed.

'That's not Elijah Fortune,' he said to the nurse beside him. 'His name is Caleb Fortune.' The girl and Caleb Fortune looked to each other, saying nothing.

Temple turned to the girl. 'Where's Sharnie? Where is she?'

'Fuck off,' she spat.

He walked round to the side of the bed and looked down on Caleb Fortune and the various tubes hanging from his body. The nurse had come to the monitor by the side of his bed. Caleb kept his eyes on the girl in front of him.

'Sharnie's got the baby, hasn't she, Caleb?'

The nurse intervened. 'You have to go.'

'Caleb? Where is she?'

Fortune remained silent and closed his eyes, shutting Temple out.

'You're coming with me.' Temple grabbed the young girl's arm and pulled her off the bed. He took her outside the ward.

'If you don't tell me where she's gone with the baby, you will be an accessory to murder. You will go to prison for a long time. Now, you tell me where she is, or I'm going to arrest you.'

Through the sullen look on her face, at last she spoke. 'I'll take you.'

'*Fast.*'

She walked at first, then started to run towards the ladies' toilets. With Temple following, she burst in through the door.

'Sharnie, Sharnie Fortune,' he shouted as the girl pushed at the doors of the cubicles. Finding one that didn't open, she stood aside as Temple launched into it, the door clanging hard as it opened. Inside, Sharnie Fortune stood up against the wall of the cubicle, looking down into the bowl of the toilet with a smirk on her face. Following her eyes, Temple saw a naked baby, upside down, the security tag missing.

Sharnie Fortune suddenly turned and went to push him back out, but he swung his fist into her jaw, sending the side of her head bouncing into the back wall of the cubicle. He snatched the baby out of the toilet and took him out of the cubicle. The baby was tiny and unresponsive in his hands.

Temple swiftly wrapped him in his jacket and ran.

CHAPTER 56

Eaton joined Temple over a coffee in the canteen at Swindon police station.

'I've got some updates for you, boss. NABIS have confirmed the bullets taken from Caxton's body match those taken from Liam and Aaron.'

'They used the same gun? How?'

'A couple of the Fortune offspring were hanging around Erlestoke in the small crowd at the bottom of the track at Erlestoke Woods. They clocked Staunton leaving in a car with Tom Caine to go to Trowbridge nick and back home again. Then they saw you visit Staunton and decided to watch his house.'

'Shit. I didn't see them.'

'They saw him leave again with Tom Caine. Just as they were going to make a move on Staunton, they see Caxton turn up one night. They watched him bury something in the garden and when he leaves, they dig up the Glock. That's how the Fortunes got onto Caxton, boss, not because someone on the team leaked his name.'

'How do we know this?'

'You asked us to put CCTV on Staunton's house and that confirmed what Ryan Hobbs told us about Caxton burying the gun in the garden. It showed Caxton's arrival and departure, and then the Fortunes going in after. It was at night, so Staunton was totally unaware. The Fortunes must have then followed Caxton back home and watched him. When Caxton took Hobbs to the hospital the next day, they leaped on Caxton while they were in the pub later that night wetting the baby's head. After they killed Caxton, they wanted Hobbs.'

'How did they know Hobbs was involved, they'd only seen Caxton bury the gun?'

'You saw Caxton's body, boss.'

'Caxton doesn't strike me as someone who would give up Ryan's name, no matter what they did.'

'We both know how persuasive the Fortunes can be. The path's list of injuries included the fact, to quote his report, "the victim had sustained lacerated injuries to the testicles".'

'Fuck.'

'Forensics will see if the footprints found on Caxton's body match with footwear from King and Munt. Found some boots in one of their cars, along with multiple cans of petrol. They were obviously going to torch them.'

Temple wondered if one of the cans had been destined for the cottage. Cartwright had seen King out there. Without doubt he'd been on a recce.

'Elijah was arranging to get King and Munt out of the country. Caleb gave his name as Elijah to the paramedics when they picked him up and that's who they told us they had. Caleb would then have discharged himself, and with us all under the impression Elijah was in hospital at the time of Caxton's murder, they would have all got away with it. With of course, the exception of the London crew, who none of them knew were under surveillance.'

'They didn't bloody follow them on the night Caxton was picked up and murdered though, did they?'

'No, boss, the car with the lump didn't move and two of the London crew weren't spotted when they left with Elijah, King and Munt in the Fortunes' car, so the Met surveillance team sat tight, thinking their subjects were all accounted for indoors.'

Eaton took a sip of coffee before continuing. 'When we showed King photos of Dean Caxton's body, he grinned before he spat on them. You saved Hobbs' life when you arrested him; they were waiting outside to pick him up. He was destined to end up just like his cousin.'

'What about Elijah?'

'We've picked him up. He's bragging about killing Caxton, as he would because now he's been caught, he wants all and sundry to know he's taken revenge for his boys. All the time we thought he was in hospital left him to go about the business of finding and killing Caxton. Sharnie Fortune played her part by keeping up the pretence of sitting by his bed.'

'That's why Sharnie insisted I didn't go and see him. They were ahead of us all the time, the bastards.'

'I wouldn't say that, boss. How did you know Sharnie Fortune had the baby?'

'When the nurse told me which baby was missing, I knew it had to be her.'

'They've already done one interview with her. When they realised they couldn't get Hobbs, Sharnie Fortune suggested they take the baby. They'd watched Caxton and Hobbs go into the hospital with a blue baby balloon with his name on. They're still looking through the hospital CCTV to see how one of them managed to get inside the maternity unit. They managed to get the tag off him, which in fairness wouldn't have been that difficult. Luckily, they didn't take him out of the building, if they had . . .'

'She was intent on killing that baby.'

'They'd killed her son, so Sharnie needed to kill theirs. An eye for an eye, Sharnie said in interview. She said she couldn't do it at first, seeing the baby in her arms, but then she remembered Liam and Aaron. There was no remorse whatsoever.'

'I saw the look on her face. She's pure evil, they're all evil. Thank God they didn't succeed.' Temple recalled the sight of the baby in the toilet and thought of Lily. Had they known his own baby was there, it would have been her. His guts turned at the thought.

'You're the hero of the hour, boss. Bloody lucky, though, a minute longer and she would have drowned him. The baby's doing well now.'

'Yes, Sam Mason texted me. It was good teamwork, Charlie. Make sure we do a Proceeds of Crime Act on the Fortunes, go after their money, everything, take them apart. Seize the lot.'

'We're already on it. It's a great result, boss. Fair play to you. You didn't cave under pressure to nick Staunton. If you had, we wouldn't have gone after Caxton and Hobbs.'

'How is Harry?'

'He's good.'

'All the interviews going OK?'

'Yes, although Munt said something about you, but it didn't make a lot of sense . . . something about you sleeping with a gun under your pillow.'

Temple feigned disinterest. 'Oh?' He took a long drink of lukewarm coffee, masking his face with his coffee cup.

'. . . yes and something about wearing pink flamingo pyjamas, which is not something I'd associate with you, boss, so it was all some made-up shit. Then the usual bollocks about seeing you when he got out.'

'No change there then.' Temple's jaw clenched.

'Don't worry about it. The way they treated Caxton, they're all looking at substantial custodial sentences. Joint enterprise murder for Caxton, conspiracy to murder and attempted murder for baby Jack, not to mention kidnap. You won't see Munt, King or any of them for that matter for a very long time.'

Eaton was right; what's more, Caxton's brutal murder and the attempt on the baby's life now meant that any weight to anything Munt or King said about the gun he'd had, had lost impact. They no longer had any hold over him. But evidently it had been Munt who Daisy had seen at the kitchen door trying to get in that night. The sick bastard had watched

Daisy in her pyjamas and for some reason, he wanted Temple to know he'd been that close to her. Even though they'd be imprisoned, he knew they had a long reach.

'We'll celebrate when we've actually got the convictions. And for the record, I can assure you, Charlie, there's definitely no gun under my pillow and I don't sleep in pink flamingo pyjamas.'

Eaton laughed. 'You in pink flamingo PJs isn't an image I want to think about. But if that's what floats your boat . . .'

'And where's the Glock, Charlie?'

'In an evidence bag.'

'And the London contingent?'

'I spoke to your DS Cartwright,' Eaton said, giving him a knowing look.

'She swore us to confidentiality, I couldn't tell you about her and her surveillance unit.'

'That's all right, boss. I thought she was going to cry when she came into Marlborough earlier. We've got all four of her crew in custody now, they're all implicated, especially the two at the Palmer's Arms.' Eaton paused for a moment. 'Do you want to hear something funny? Ma'am Shaw thought Cartwright was all part of a "covert op" with you and that the men in the car were really Met officers.'

Temple wasn't laughing. 'That's nearly as funny as me letting Sloper go and Harker being my bestie.'

'Point taken. On that note, I've spoken to the team again. They've come round to the fact there's no covert op running on them.'

'Do they also understand how much I detest Simon Sloper and would never have let him go?'

'They do. I spoke to DC Wright and put them straight on a few things. And after saving the life of little baby Jack and potting just about all the Fortune family, I don't think you'll have any further issues with the team, boss. Your stock's riding pretty high. Even Stubbsy had to admit you were right about not TIE-ing Tara Leyton. He was just about to make a passport enquiry when you arrested Hobbs.'

Temple gulped on his coffee. 'I told him to leave it.'

'He knows now it was a waste of time, just as you told him it would be. The team's looking forward to taking you for a drink, boss.'

'We'll see about that.' Relieved, Temple set his coffee mug down. 'There's something else I want you to do, Charlie.'

'Boss?'

'Dig out Jack Bartlett's aggravated burglary file. With what Caxton and Hobbs discovered, let's go in and see if we can get a murder conviction.'

'OK.'

'And what about ma'am Shaw?'

'She came into the office first thing, parading the new DCI.'

* * *

'I hear you've had a good result, Tina.'

Clive Harker's Glaswegian brogue put Tina Shaw instantly on guard. 'All in a day's work, sir,' she answered tightly into her mobile.

'You came across well in the news item. It'll do wonders for community confidence. It's not often we get to score so well over a crime family like the Fortunes.'

She was quick to respond. 'It was a good team effort, all the skills of the team were required for this one. DS Eaton coordinated the arrests and interviews.'

'I hear DI Temple saved the baby's life?'

'Yes, but we don't do heroes on the MCU, he was just doing what he's paid to do.'

'Well said, Tina. A good result all round and I'm sure it was down to some good leadership on your part, too. I just wanted to say well done.'

She ended the call. If he'd rang expecting her to enthuse about Temple, she was glad to disappoint him. Yes, Op Mitre had been a resounding success; they'd solved three murders, prevented the murder of a baby and taken out a whole OCG in the process. Along with Grant Lindford, she was benefiting from congratulatory emails and texts from senior officers from around the region. And in an about-turn, Lindford was now crowing how Temple was a welcome asset at the MCU.

Temple had also won the team round; Tom Caine had even withdrawn his transfer. But she remained sceptical; there was no smoke without fire and despite establishing there was no covert operation, there was still plenty of smoke around both Temple and Harker and Sloper, as far as she was concerned.

CHAPTER 57

Callie pushed down on the cafetiere, releasing the strong aroma of Brazilian coffee beans into the kitchen at the cottage.

'You do believe me about Sophie Twiner?'

'Yes, I believe you.' She smiled. 'There's no more Op Acre, therefore there's no more Sophie Twiner. She's out of our lives now.'

There seemed no point mentioning the drunken night they'd had together before he knew Callie, as she said, Twiner was out of their lives now. There would be no need for professional contact with her either now the DCI was in place.

'Have some of this. It'll do you good,' she said, as she sat down opposite Temple at the table.

'*You* do me good.' He smiled at her before looking around. 'Unlike this bloody place. I've got to get us out of here, Callie. I wouldn't care if I never saw another bloody wooden beam and thatched roof for the rest of my life. The times I bang my head on the beam in the bathroom . . .'

'I'm just grateful that Paul King's back in jail. I can sleep at night now knowing we're safe here.' She smiled at him and poured the coffee into a cup in front of him.

'We both can. Talking about being able to sleep at night, how's Tara?'

'She says she's having a lovely time, it was just what she needed.'

'With everyone remanded in jail and looking at long sentences, it's also safe for her to come back. It was a lovely thing you did letting her go there, you probably saved her life.'

'I was only too glad to be able to help. I said I'd pick her up from the airport when she's ready, see what her plans are. See if I can help her find somewhere better to live.'

He leaned across and kissed her. 'That's a really sweet thing to do.'

'I like helping people.' She looked downcast for a second. 'Seems I can't persuade Leigh to change her mind though.'

'That's got more to do with her feelings towards me than you. You've done more than enough. I get that she wants to punish me, but she's punishing Daisy too. She wants to cut my access to the children and the easiest way to do that is to move away.' He sipped his coffee.

She smiled sadly, nodding towards a letter he was holding. 'Well, what will you do?'

He leaned back in his chair. 'I have to go. I have to see what he wants to say. I'd have jumped at the chance to talk to him when he was in custody and I couldn't, they wouldn't let me near him. When we were in court, I thought I was looking at him for the last time. How could I know Newland would send me a visiting order? It might be the only chance I'll ever have of finding out exactly what happened that day. I can't pass that up.'

'Are you going to tell Tina Shaw you're going to see him?'

'No. I'm not going to give her the chance to order me not to go.' He leaned his elbows on the table. 'I've been thinking about the job too. Maybe it's time for a change.'

'It doesn't surprise me, you've been through so much.'

'I keep thinking about Sharnie Fortune's face when I found her with the baby. It could so easily have been little Lily. If they had had the slightest inkling that my baby was there, they'd have snatched her too. I know they would. There's always been a threat to them, to you, just for me doing the job. But now Newland's in jail, it changes everything. The whole reason for being a police officer was to find him. I don't need to do this anymore. Maybe now it's time to get out.'

Callie was sympathetic. 'If you left the police, what would you do?'

'I've no idea. But the thought of doing something new, something different, feels liberating.'

They were quiet. Callie refilled their cups.

'I was thinking of booking us a foreign holiday for later in the year. We'll take Ana, Ben and Daisy, if Leigh will let us. A good holiday, somewhere warm, will give you a chance to chill out, make some plans. You deserve it after all that's happened.'

He shook his head. 'It's a lovely idea, but I need to get us out of here instead, I know I sound like a stuck record, but I really can't afford it . . .'

'Darling, you need a break. You have to look after yourself too, you know.' She wasn't going to give up. 'I understand about the money and having to find another place. And while you do that, I'll take care of a bit of R and R which you badly need. Imagine us all on a white sandy beach . . .'

'It already sounds expensive.'

'Leave it to me. It'll be our first holiday together and it will only cost us our flights.'

Seeing how insistent she was, he gave in. 'Where?'

'I have an idea.' She beamed. 'Somewhere warm, exotic and far away. I have friends with a place in Thailand, we often do a swap. I promise you, you'll love it.'

EPILOGUE

A pungent smell of disinfectant hung in the air which penetrated through the paper face mask he'd been asked to wear. The prison officer walked Temple into the visitor's centre at Long Lartin Prison. The room was laid out in a grid pattern with two chairs placed either side of a low table. Temple went to a table and sat on a chair with his back against the wall and waited, glancing briefly at the other people who had filed in and were waiting to see their visitors.

Reality suddenly kicked in and his head started to pound with a dull persistent throb. Oddly, as he sat there, his desire to hear what Newland had to say was beginning to fade. There was still time to get up and walk out. The only thing stopping him was the thought of regretting it if he did. He might never get this opportunity again. No one had been more surprised than he to receive a visiting order out of the blue. Now was his chance to get the answers to the questions he'd carried with him for so long.

A door opened in the corner of the room and the inmates appeared. Temple focused on the empty chair opposite him and waited. Before long, the seat was pulled back and Guy Newland sat opposite him.

Newland was wearing a pair of round glasses. He was bearded, scruffy and had lost weight. They both eyeballed each other as silence settled.

Eventually Newland spoke through his mask. 'I didn't think you'd come.'

Temple felt his heart rate quicken along with the throb in his head. He wasn't sure about sitting so close and instinctively inched his chair back. He was suddenly grateful for the mask as he didn't want to breathe in anything related to Newland. What was he doing? This was madness. And yet at the same time, he felt compelled to be there. He'd spent most of his life hunting the bastard and now he was here, once again, it felt like an anti-climax.

'I wouldn't have missed this for the world.'

Again, there was a silence as the two of them stared at each other.

Newland looked around before speaking. Masked volunteers had begun to walk around the room, ensuring visiting rules were adhered to. Newland was suspicious; he'd have to keep his voice low, speak only when they were out of earshot. All bets were off now they'd reneged on the deal. Ten years they said he'd get, out in five. He knew he couldn't trust them; he knew that right from the start, which is why he'd left himself a little insurance policy all those years ago, just in case he'd need it one day. And, as he had foreseen, that day had come. As he saw it, he had nothing left to lose. He had one hand left to play and if there was to be any chance of him getting out of there, he had to set things in train fast.

'There's something you should know.'

Temple didn't respond.

Newland continued. 'You've waited a long time for justice. And now you think you have it, don't you?' Newland leaned into the table between them. 'Only, you don't.'

The pounding got louder in Temple's head. 'Is that right?'

'Yes. You see, I didn't do it.'

'You didn't what? Kill my mother?'

'That's right.'

'And that's why you asked me here, is it? To listen to this shit. So, tell me, why confess to a murder you now say you didn't commit?'

Newland looked around, checking if any of the volunteers were close by. 'It closed the case.'

'I'll tell you what's happening here.' Temple sat back, his head pounding. 'Now you've had a taste of prison life and you know how long you're going to be here, that you'll never come out, you want to change your story.'

Newland quietly repeated. 'It wasn't me; I didn't kill her.'

'So, what were you doing there?'

Again, Newland hesitated, looking around. 'Look, I didn't kill her. I . . . was there. I grabbed your T-shirt. But that's all.'

'You went to grab me by the throat, you were going to kill me too that day. Why didn't you?'

'You're wrong. If I was going to kill you, I'd have done it. In fact, I should have. It would have made my life a whole lot easier. If I had, I certainly wouldn't be here. I was only there to clean up.'

'What do you mean?'

Newland sighed. 'I went to set fire to the caravan. Then you showed up. I couldn't shut you in, knowing you were alive, and set fire to it. Neither could I bring myself to kill you, as I should have. I panicked when you came back. I wasn't expecting it and I panicked and ran.'

'You killed her, you bastard, and now you want to play games.'

'I didn't kill her. I swear. But I *was* supposed to clean up.'

'Who for?'

'The man who did kill your mother.'

'So, there were two of you? You had an accomplice?'

'No, listen to what I'm saying. Your mother was murdered, not by me, but by another. My job was to go in afterwards and set fire to the caravan, destroy the evidence.'

'Why?'

'I was tasked.'

'Who by?'

Newland looked down at his lap in silence. Then he looked at Temple.

'Look, you were lucky it was me. Anyone else would have killed you there and then or left you to die screaming in a fire.'

Temple resisted the urge to reach across and grab Newland by the throat. 'So, what? You want me to be grateful to you or something? Do you want me to thank you, is that it?'

'No, just listen and know I didn't kill your mother.'

'And you know who the killer is, I suppose?'

'Yes.'

Temple forced himself back in his seat. 'I've heard enough. You're pathetic and your mind games won't work on me, you sick bastard.'

'I'm not playing mind games. It's a fact that I didn't kill your mother. You want truth and facts. The killer is still out there, still living. You haven't got justice. You think you have and you haven't.'

'And this is what you wanted to tell me?'

'You need to keep looking. Your mother's killer is still out there.'

'So, who is it then? Give me a name.'

'It's not that simple. But I can help you find him.'

'You *know* him?'

'Yes.' Newland's voice was barely a whisper.

'So why confess to her murder if you didn't do it?'

'I had to.'

Temple was having difficulty suppressing his anger. 'You were caught by your own DNA, that's why you confessed, because you were trapped and now you're never coming out. Save your lies for someone else.'

'I'm not lying. I got twenty-two years for something I didn't do. I did *not* kill your mother.'

'And the small matter of you confessing that you did?'

Again, Newland looked around before speaking. 'To keep the man who killed your mother out of prison.'

'And why would you do that?'

'Because I was told to.'

Temple stood up. 'None of what you're saying makes any sense. You confessed but now say you didn't commit the murder, you know who did it, but you won't say who it is and now you're doing someone else's sentence. Can you hear yourself? You're a fucking murdering liar who now wants to play games.'

Newland bowed his head, before looking back at Temple. 'I know how it sounds, but that doesn't make it a lie. You want justice. You deserve justice. Right now, you don't have it, believe me. I *know* who killed your mother. I'll help you. We can help each other.' Newland stopped. 'You're the only man who can get me out of here.'

'And there we have it. That's what this is about. You're fucking mad if you think I'm going to help *you*. I've carried this shit around with me all my life, trying to remember every little piece of it, reliving and trying to hold onto every second just in case any tiny piece of evidence would make the difference. Over and over again. Now, thanks to the patrol officer who pulled you over, I don't have to do that anymore. You killed her and you're here where you can fucking rot.'

Newland went on. 'Did you not wonder why your blue T-shirt was in Roy Filer's loft? Perhaps he had an inkling of what he was dealing with.'

Temple stood up to leave, scraping the chair on the floor. 'I'm not interested.'

Staying seated and looking up at him, Newland made his last plea.

'You need to be interested. I'm dying. And I don't want to die in here. I want to die with the sun on my face. I don't deserve to be in here. Want to know why I'm here? I saved your life, that's why I'm here. And when I die, what I know dies with me. You'll never know who killed your mother. But you'll need to do what I tell you. It's up to you.'

* * *

Sitting in his car, Temple went over the exchange. He'd been a fool to accept the visiting order. He shouldn't have gone looking for answers, he should have left things as they were. The only revelation had been Newland saying he had intended to set the caravan on fire. Newland even wanted him to think he owed his life to him.

He cursed himself for going. He should have known better; Newland was doing what was standard for many 'lifers' once they see their predicament. They start to say it was someone else, that there'd been a miscarriage of justice. He was annoyed he'd fallen for it; he should have seen it coming with the VO. He should have torn it up. By going, he'd fallen right into Newland's trap to control him, get into his head from his prison cell. How could he have been so stupid?

He'd had a notion that he was going to sit in front of Newland and be able to interrogate him, that Newland would give him all the answers to the questions he'd carried around for years. Instead, Newland had set the agenda, Newland had called the shots, manipulated him and he'd walked right into it.

Temple turned on the ignition. It was time to go home. He could take satisfaction that Newland was sitting in his prison cell. After all these years, it was finally over.

THE END

Thank you for reading this book.

If you enjoyed it please leave feedback on Amazon or Goodreads, and if there is anything we missed or you have a question about, then please get in touch. We appreciate you choosing our book.

Founded in 2014 in Shoreditch, London, we at Joffe Books pride ourselves on our history of innovative publishing. We were thrilled to be shortlisted for Independent Publisher of the Year at the British Book Awards.

www.joffebooks.com

We're very grateful to eagle-eyed readers who take the time to contact us. Please send any errors you find to corrections@joffebooks.com. We'll get them fixed ASAP.

www.ingramcontent.com/pod-product-compliance
Lightning Source LLC
Chambersburg PA
CBHW051327250626
47155CB00007B/2479